QUEEN

OF

CIN

AND

WHISPERS

HELEN CORCORAN grew up in Cork, Ireland, dreaming of scheming queens and dashing lady knights. After graduating from Trinity College, Dublin, she worked as a bookseller for over a decade. She lives in Dublin, writing fantasy novels and haunting coffee shops in search of the perfect latte.

QUEEN
OF
COIN
AND
WHISPERS
HELEN
CORCORAN

A kingdom of secrets and
a game of lies

THE O'BRIEN PRESS
DUBLIN

First published 2020 by
The O'Brien Press Ltd,
12 Terenure Road East, Rathgar,
Dublin 6, D06 HD27 Ireland.

Tel: +353 1 4923333; Fax: +353 1 4922777
E-mail: books@obrien.ie.
Website: www.obrien.ie
The O'Brien Press is a member of Publishing Ireland.

ISBN: 978-178849-118-1
Text © copyright Helen Corcoran 2020
Copyright for typesetting, layout, editing, design
© The O'Brien Press Ltd
Design and layout by Emma Byrne
Cover design by Emma Byrne

1 3 5 7 8 6 4 2
21 22 20

Printed and bound by CPI Group (UK) Ltd, Croydon, CR0 4YY.
The paper in this book is produced using pulp from managed forests.

Queen of Coin and Whispers received financial assistance from the Arts Council.

Published in

DUBLIN
UNESCO
City of Literature

For Tess –

she supported the writing

first.

CHAPTER ONE

LIA

The sheep were undeniably dead. As I examined what the wolves had left behind, and tried not to panic, new footsteps stamped through the frozen grass. I rose, stiff with cold, as a servant hurried a rider towards me. The royal sigil was stitched onto his coat, but I focused on his sleeve: no purple armband for mourning.

A rider would race here in late winter for only one reason.

The King wasn't dead, but he *was* dying.

Uncle had been clinging to life for months. The reports had varied – bleeding, vomiting, recovery, bleeding, vomiting – but still he had lived, complained, and made life unbearable for everyone.

And now –

My aunt had given me enough warning, at least. I'd worried that she wouldn't.

'Your Highness.' The servant bowed and the rider sank to his knees, sweating, and held out a letter. I cracked the seal, tucked the smaller hidden note into my glove, and scanned the expected words.

...no longer eating, can't keep water down, preparations are underway...

I'd waited years for this. I'd expected to feel delight, maybe even relief. My uncle was dying. The throne would finally be mine.

Panic bristled in my throat again. I lowered the note.

Father, please give me the courage to do this well.

'You've made a difficult journey,' I told the rider. 'Please take the time to regain your strength here.'

'The pleasure is mine, Your Highness.' The rider trembled, as if the shadow of my uncle's impending death had hounded him north. He'd probably expected to meet me in a drawing room, not in a field examining slaughtered sheep.

They left me, and I staggered towards a tree and leaned against the trunk. The bark pressed against my coat, reassuringly familiar. The air scraped my nose and throat as I took deep, shaky breaths. I fished the second note out of my glove. Matthias had written two words in a version of our childhood code:

No delays.

No delays. Our phrase for when Uncle's death was imminent and I was to *get down here now*.

Matthias hated that I went north every winter when Uncle could no longer stand the sight of me. I was one of the few nobles who did. 'It's ridiculous,' he'd fume. 'You're up there, freezing and alone, while the Court gets drunk and eats too much.'

'I'm with my people,' I always replied.

'You're the heir. Your people are the entire country, not just your estate tenants.'

We'd argued before I'd left Court in late summer. Matthias had suspected – correctly – that Uncle's health was beyond help and I should stay, while I didn't want to resemble a princess hovering over the crown like a scavenger bird. The throne would be mine whether or not I stayed in Arkaala.

I broke into a run, swearing under my breath, and hurried back towards the manor. We'd have to travel quickly. Uncle must have declined suddenly, or Matthias would have sent more warning to prepare for the trip.

I should have listened to him.

As I approached, the doors leading to the gardens burst open. Mother rushed down the steps. 'Lia!'

The house staff were probably huddled at every window facing us. They'd all heard her improper glee.

I stopped. Stayed silent. Everyone at the windows would slink away; only the bravest would eavesdrop. The sun was still pale, the gardens still bright with winter roses. Everything looked the same as when I'd woken up. But nothing would be the same after this.

'Lia, you will be *Queen*.'

If only Mother's joy was entirely for me. She'd locked horns with Uncle long before marrying my father, their disagreements blooming into steady loathing. At least social propriety would get her into mourning dress. Uncle's death would give her back a decade, where Father's had threaded silver in her brown hair, deepened the wrinkles around her mouth.

I slipped by her and up the steps.

'We need to discuss –'

'We leave for Arkaala as soon as possible,' I said. 'There is little to discuss until we see Uncle.' There was, in fact, plenty to discuss before I saw him. There was much to do and decide. But Uncle wasn't dead yet. He still deserved my respect, even if he'd done little to earn it, and I couldn't act otherwise if I wanted to win over his allies as Queen.

I was being unfair to Mother, to both of us – we'd dreamed of this moment for so long. I'd spent years frustrated by Uncle's inept rule, knowing I could do better but powerless until I inherited.

We were so close.

But I could never publicly rejoice at his demise, and I wouldn't allow Mother to relish hers.

She sputtered as I went through the doors.

I strode down the hall, already imagining the Court bowing and curtseying. A hard bud slowly unfurled inside me, releasing not just relief but anticipation. I'd waited years, biding my time, treading the stormy waves of family hatred to reach the other side mostly unscathed.

Now, I was Queen, a wolf in my own right. I held the chess pieces.

It was time to use them.

Q Q Q

In a moment of decency, Uncle was dying as winter finally lost its grip. Travel would be as swift as the time of year would allow.

As the carriage thundered along the road, the grief finally hit. My chest ached as if someone had dumped cold water over me. I'd spent ten years in my family's estate – too cold in winter, too warm in summer – learning how to be Queen. I'd grown up commanding imaginary armies against Matthias, my oldest friend. We'd wandered through every stream, climbed every tree, and planned our futures lying on summer grass.

Father had died there.

Now the estate would continue without me.

The poor autumn and winter had made food prices soar. About a third of my tenants couldn't afford enough to last them through winter. We'd raided the estate's food stores to keep them alive. Everyone we saw on the road was too thin, and too resigned about it. I'd known Uncle had ignored his duties in favour of the next meal, the next drink, the next entertainment, but it wasn't the same as seeing it.

I worried, even though I tried not to. If I couldn't keep sheep alive, how could I rule Edar?

Bad roads delayed us after several days of rain, so we arrived at Arkaala, the capital, in early afternoon, instead of late at night as planned. My heart still lifted at the crumbling remnants of Empire architecture, surrounded by layers of winding streets sprawling towards the docks.

Then the bells started.

We were too late.

Uncle was dead.

And I was Queen.

'If dying wasn't unavoidable,' Mother said, 'I'd swear he planned this.'

There would be no handover. No last-moment change of feelings from Uncle, no scraps of advice, no blessing. Just a Court flung into grief.

People turned our way as the carriage wound through the streets towards the palace. There were no cheers, no shouting. The mourning bells drowned everything out, except the panic in my head.

As the carriage stopped, Mother said, 'Perhaps Jienne will be indisposed.'

'Her husband is dead,' I said. 'She knows we must pay our respects.'

Mother rolled her eyes. 'Grief won't make her kind. You'll see.'

'*Act sad*,' I hissed, before a footman opened the carriage door.

My aunt, now the Dowager Queen Jienne, hadn't liked me after I was named heir, but was clever enough to stay cautiously civil. Secretly, I knew Mother was right – Jienne had now lost her power, why would she welcome us? As we followed servants to Uncle's rooms, I was absurdly grateful for Mother's black-edged purple armbands – 'The one item that never goes out of fashion,' she'd muttered in the carriage, her eyes sad – so whatever our private feelings, at least our grief *looked* respectable.

I didn't feel respectful. I felt out of my depth: quick steps trying to be measured, sweat, and deep breaths through the nose.

Uncle's chambers reeked of sickness, and stale air, and old blood. It stuck to my tongue, seemed to cling to my skin and clothes. Only long practice kept me from gagging or scratching at my hair. Mother swallowed compulsively, her eyes darting towards the thick window drapes.

Only three people attended my dead uncle. If there had been more – a reasonable possibility, given Aunt Jienne's love, and my hatred, of an audience – they had been swiftly kicked out.

The doors closed behind us.

The physician dropped to his knees. 'Long live the Queen.'

Aunt Jienne rose from the bedside, her skirts rustling. Her dress was the latest fashion – heavily embroidered, tucked at the waist and billowing at the back – but the black-edged purple reminded us that she was the *grieving* Dowager Queen. She kept her expression neutral as she curtseyed.

'Dearest Aunt,' I said and squeezed her hands, 'we grieve for your husband. We will do our utmost to honour his memory and continue his legacy.'

I will make this country prosperous again and gouge out my uncle's rot. I will fight all those loyal to him.

Aunt Jienne's smile didn't reach her eyes. 'I appreciate your grief, and know you will continue his work and bring further honour to our family.'

Empty words; fulfilled duty. Everyone was happy –

'*Such* a pity you didn't make it in time for his blessing,' she added, and stepped back.

– or perhaps not.

The third person strolled forward. I'd changed at our last stop, but my best dress hardly compared to his embroidered red velvet. I matched his charming smile and held out my hands. 'Lord Vigrante.' The Head of Government: my uncle's greatest supporter and greatest manipulator. He radiated charisma and confidence; no wonder Uncle had given him so much freedom.

Lord Vigrante kissed my knuckles. His purple armband didn't match his red velvet, or golden hair, and his charisma didn't match the grief in the stifling room. 'Your Majesty. So unfortunate you've returned under such sad, yet glorious circumstances.'

Aunt Jienne stiffened. It took gall to inform a Dowager Queen, paces away from her dead husband, that she was no longer in favour.

After a too-long pause, I said, 'Your feelings are noted, Lord Vigrante. We will speak later. For now, I wish to mourn my uncle.' I'd wanted to take a few moments to accept the finality of his death, but Jienne would want to mourn, likely alone now that Vigrante had shifted his potential allegiance to me.

Back in the hall, I sucked in deep breaths and shivered. Mother patted my arm, though she looked sadder, more sympathetic, than I'd expected from her behaviour in the carriage. A servant led us first to her rooms and then to the suites that had been reopened for my new status as Queen. It was a relief for another set of doors to close behind me.

In the receiving area, Matthias dozed in a chair. He immediately opened his eyes, gestured at the waiting tea service, and stood with a smile. His maroon clothing only highlighted the sickly tint to his thin, pale face; he likely hadn't eaten or slept much in the last few days. But his demeanour held steady. He was my oldest friend, and would do everything I wanted and more.

He bowed with a flourish. 'Welcome back, Your Majesty.'

I hugged him.

For a moment we were children again, sprawled under a tree. Sunlight dappled our skin. We'd picked out shapes in the clouds and decided how we'd fix everything when I was Queen.

Now we were here. It was time to begin.

CHAPTER TWO

XANIA

I love my sister, but this was one of the days I wanted to throttle her.

'You can't be serious!' Zola said.

'Ernest is unsuitable.' I tried to stay calm, knowing I'd lose her the moment I lost patience. 'You can do better.' His older brother was also up to his eyeballs in debt and, as of last week, no longer had access to his inheritance. But Zola wouldn't care, and technically I shouldn't have seen those papers in the Treasury.

'Ernest is charming.'

'Ernest is *smug*.' I couldn't stop an edge creeping into my voice. Zola clenched her hands against her dress, barely a flounce away from the door. 'People say –'

'I don't care what they say!'

'*He mocks you.*'

My starry-eyed sister deflated into an unsure sixteen-year-old girl. It made me want to break Ernest Blackwood's nose. The punch would be satisfying, and worth the pain and social backlash.

Zola twisted her mouth. 'Of course he does.'

We both knew what he'd said. What everyone said, when they thought we couldn't hear, or our presence went unnoticed. *Clinging onto power. Foolish dead father. Grasping mother. Hopeless daughters.*

Who do they think they are?

'The Blackwoods are Sixth Step.' The edge was gone from my voice – I didn't have the energy for it. 'We are Fifth.' It wasn't unheard of for Sixth and Seventh families to consider the lower Steps for marriages, but –

'We're Fifth *now*,' Zola said.

Mama had done her best. I'd never fault her for remarrying up. But I wasn't sure it had been the right thing to do.

I opened my mouth –

The sound of bells filled the air. We clapped our hands over our ears, but it boomed through the windows and walls, each set of peals rolling into the next. The echoes made my teeth hurt. After the initial flurry, they settled into a dreary three-tone pattern.

Death bells.

The King was finally dead.

The Princess was Queen.

Zola and I locked eyes, then we rushed towards the door. The Court had been rattled for the last few weeks, as it became clear the King's health wouldn't improve. Matthias had informed me that the Queen – the *Dowager* Queen – had held out longer than advised before sending for the Princess up north, and the Court was scrambling to sort out their new allegiances.

These last few weeks, I'd heard far more about Princess Aurelia – 'Lia' to those closest to her, apparently – from Matthias than I'd wanted. For someone who only spent spring and summer at Court, straddling a fragile line between outcast and successor, he knew a staggering amount about her.

'The Court is never careful when they gossip,' he'd said. 'They always say too much.' He'd never said if that was a good or bad thing.

While our stepfather maintained the family line of keeping out of drama and politics, he and Mama were still pulled into the seemingly endless discussions – fretting – about the future Queen's intended changes. So they weren't here to stop us from venturing into the halls and barely-contained chaos. In the uneasy hush, servants hurried while trying to pretend they were calm. Most had a snowflake over the royal crest stitched onto their upper sleeves: they were in the service of the Princess and her mother.

She was due to arrive, just too late for a smooth transition.

A flash of embroidered maroon caught my eye: Matthias rushed through a hallway junction ahead of us, his expression set and intent. I tapped Zola's arm before she called out, and shook my head, trying not to frown. It wasn't that he was rushing like the servants; Matthias hurried everywhere. But his expression had also been hopeful and worried, a strange mix.

Matthias never showed his true feelings. He adapted and discarded emotions and sincerity with dizzying speed. Even knowing how close he'd been to Papa, I still wasn't sure if Matthias presented his real self, or a facade that was easier to interact with. For him to let his emotional guard down like this...

He'd been almost unbearably excited about the Princess's arrival. 'You have no idea how Court will change,' he'd remarked one evening. 'Lia will cut into the rotten core and yank it out. Vigrante's allies have no idea what's awaiting them.' And he'd been acting oddly as the King's health worsened: distracted and distant, as if juggling too much in his head. Thanks to Papa's training, Matthias slid easily through the Step ranks, collecting acquaintances and debts in ways I couldn't. But his cheerful mask didn't usually slip –

Lia.

He'd called her Lia. And I hadn't noticed.

Matthias was Third Step, like Papa had been. Too low-ranked to know the Queen personally.

But only those closet to Princess Aurelia used her family nickname.

A seed of suspicion dropped into my stomach, threatening to sprout tendrils.

Perhaps Matthias did know her.

Like he knew my secrets.

As he whirled around a corner, I turned to face Zola. 'I just remembered, I have to finish an assignment for Coin. I'll be done before dinner.'

She tilted her face. 'The King's just *died*. Taxes can wait.'

I snorted. 'Not according to Coin. I bet he's in the Treasury, insisting on work as usual, while the rest of the Court panics.'

'I'm not taking that bet.' Zola sighed. 'You work too hard for him.'

'I want that promotion.'

Zola squeezed my hand. 'Try and have fun?'

'Oh, absolutely. I'll have so much fun, I won't be able to remember my name.' I blew Zola a kiss and hurried off towards the Treasury, then cut back towards the direction Matthias had gone until I stopped before an unremarkable wall.

I could be wrong about Matthias. I desperately wanted to be. But something was odd about him today, and I couldn't ignore it.

No one else knew what Matthias tried to help me with behind closed doors, and I intended to keep it that way. He was sometimes a friend, but mostly a co-conspirator.

But people didn't know what I was capable of, either, or what I wanted to do to those I hated.

I ran my fingertips down the wall, carefully applying pressure in a sequence until part of it sprung back. I took a deep breath, slid into the gap and, after adjusting to the gloom, started walking.

If my suspicions about Matthias were correct, and he secretly knew the Queen, he wouldn't use the public halls to go to her.

According to him, the passages went back to the palace's foundations. While the network was occasionally expanded by a paranoid ruler, the effort mostly went into maintaining the elaborate sprawl, the full extent of which was only known by the ruling monarch, their heir, and the Master of Whispers. No part of the palace was untouched, and the royal wing had several direct escape routes outside.

Matthias had given me some of the basic codes and patterns to start off with. I'd spent months mapping the routes, pretending it was another of Papa's lessons. He had loved puzzles and ciphers and codes. Every one he'd taught me was a sign of his love. Matthias had said nothing about the royal wing, whose passage sequences worked from different roots, but I'd included it anyway. It was slow, painstaking work, despite everything Papa had taught me, but I'd cracked the sequences.

Most of the passages required an exact pattern to enter and leave, but some of the internal ones only needed the flick of a hidden catch. Each new monarch reset the sequences and patterns, but – as I'd hoped – nothing had changed yet. It was an extraordinary sign of royal trust to know about the passages. When I'd asked Matthias which unfortunate noble he'd wheedled the information from, he'd smiled and changed the subject.

But if the *Queen* had told him...

What had he told *her*? Every time we'd discussed Vigrante's involvement in Papa's murder, had he been helping me or waiting to use it against me?

My throat tightened with fear. I swallowed, and kept on walking, hoping I'd be right about his most likely route.

I finally reached an exit near the royal wing, counting three hundred heartbeats before I stepped out into the hall. I'd never been so close to the royal wing before, which was guarded night and day.

I peered around the corner, just as Matthias stopped before the guards. He held something out for inspection before they waved him through into the wing.

Spikes of terror exploded from the suspicious seed in my stomach.

Hurried footsteps grew louder from the other end of the hall. The Queen and her mother approached, travel-rumpled and – like the servants – trying to pretend they weren't hurrying. I caught a flash of brown hair, pale skin, and purple before I bolted back into the passages. I leaned against the wall. Panic twisted under my skin.

After several deep breaths, I followed a route into the royal wing, avoiding the royal family *and* their guards. The codes and failsafes fell before me, pitifully easy after all my work.

I'd expected the royal wing to be ostentatious. The gilded wallpaper was beautiful, but the design was twenty years old.

Everything reeked of old money, long accumulated wealth. I stepped lightly on the carpet. Portraits speckled the wall, not only of the royal family but their in-laws and extended relatives. They watched me as if they knew I didn't belong.

Around another corner, I faced double doors stamped with the royal seal: the monarch's public study. I glanced over my shoulder, but I was alone. Still, I could hardly march up and knock. No one entered the royal wing without permission. If I was discovered, the Queen would be justifiably furious.

It was easier to focus on that, instead of Matthias lying to me for years. He'd let me rage and plot and scheme, while all along he worked for the Queen. And if he'd told her I wanted to avenge Papa's death...

Plotting murder wasn't a problem – until the Queen discovered it. Then it usually ended in a meeting with an executioner's axe.

The doors opened. I ducked back around the corner. Matthias stepped into the hall.

Betrayal and fury washed over me in a sweat. My hands tingled. He *had* lied – to me, my family, perhaps even Papa. He'd never once hinted that he knew the Queen. How long had he been working for her? Years? Had I risked myself, my family, with secrets that could be used against us?

I should control my anger, douse it with rationality and calculation. Instead, I stepped towards Matthias and reached into my skirts. I curled my fingers around the comforting weight of my dagger hilt.

CHAPTER THREE

LIA

I inhaled the scent of spiced tea, then let out a long breath. 'Who supported Alexandris becoming the Opposition Leader?' A political problem was always easier to deal with than my family.

Matthias passed me a list of names in code. I'd kept the northern nobles on side for years, but Opposition support was my best weapon against Vigrante. Alexandris's political career was stable and mediocre – not the makings of a strong leader.

I tapped the list of names. 'Any proof they're in Vigrante's pocket?'

He passed me a sheet of numbers. 'With the old King's coin.'

My uncle had been an over-generous ruler. As his health had declined again this year, the Master of Coin started giving me copies of the financial reports. I wouldn't know how bad the debt was until our first meeting, but I didn't hold out much hope for the Royal Treasury's prospects.

Matthias glanced around the study. 'Needs a change,' he said.

'I was considering redecorating in red. The dark green will be depressing in winter. Speaking of green' – I tried and failed for casualness – 'what happened to the gentleman with the green velvet waistcoats? I thought it was going well.'

'The green velvet gentleman decided I was too boring. Or I thought he was. We were too boring for each other,' Matthias said. 'This isn't the time to discuss my love life.'

Taking a moment for him, even three sentences, would hardly bring the country to a standstill. 'I need a meeting with Alexandris,' I said, instead of asking, *When did this happen? Why didn't you tell me?* 'He has to stick his neck out more.'

'Easily done.' Matthias hesitated. 'And my recommendation for dealing with Vigrante?'

I clenched my jaw. 'My opinion hasn't changed.'

'My concern hasn't changed, Your Majesty.'

'My opinion outranks your concern.' When I'd returned north, Matthias had stayed in Arkaala as my eyes and ears. I'd known he would be eager when I was Queen. But his eagerness often turned into overconfidence. I didn't enjoy reminding him of his place, but I wouldn't let him control me as Vigrante had controlled Uncle.

'I presume the money Uncle promised would have come from taxes?' I asked.

Matthias nodded.

'The Court won't support reforms if I disregard Uncle's promises.'

Matthias's nostrils flared. 'Your uncle unclipped Vigrante's leash and let him run wild with promises. He didn't care, once he had his wine, and food, and his entertainment. Your aunt didn't care, once she had her wine, new clothes, and her entertainment.'

'Killing Vigrante won't win me the Court's favour,' I said flatly.

I rose and went around the desk towards the bookshelves. Most of these books were usually found in Step libraries, nothing that truly indicated Uncle's tastes. I trailed my fingers across the spines and paused at a volume of war poetry. The poet had risen to prominence during Great-Grandfather's reign. My grandfather had later quoted his best-known poems to justify his aggressive rule.

I didn't enjoy war poetry.

Matthias and I had spent years debating how Vigrante would fight my legislation and turn the Government against me. And since he'd entered politics, there had been deaths. All apparently natural, of course. Nothing led back to him. Nothing could be proven. Vigrante's hands looked clean.

Killing him wouldn't help me. I had to secure my own power base first. But I was royalty, born from a noble house. Vigrante had no bloodline to fall back upon, only a political title and a rise to power through allegiances built on Uncle's coffers. Such allegiances always turned fragile, eventually. I wanted Vigrante gone. If I cut him from the Treasury purse-strings, his own allies could destroy him for me. I just had to survive the fallout.

Surviving a political fallout brought me to another matter. 'Have you made progress on my Whispers?'

Matthias could juggle being my secretary and temporary Whispers for only so long. He'd kept my position at Court secure up until now, but a proper Whispers would keep me alive.

'I have someone in mind,' he said. 'Xania Bayonn. Lady Harynne's daughter.'

'And the late Baron Bayonn's daughter.'

Most people wouldn't have interpreted Matthias's face spasm as old grief, but most hadn't known him since childhood. Bayonn had practically been a father to Matthias, teaching him the necessary skills to navigate Court and serve my interests. His death had hit Matthias harder than losing his own parents. The guilt of being convinced of Bayonn's murder, but unable to prove it, made him uncomfortable around the Bayonn family.

But they weren't influential. Whispers usually came from a high Step; it made it easier to navigate social circles.

'An unusual choice,' I said. Xania Bayonn wasn't just from a lower Step – she was young. But then, so was I. And if she was suitable for Whispers, her social rank aside, then Matthias trusted her. He wouldn't be reckless about such an important position.

'She has potential,' he said. 'I'll arrange a meeting.'

'Very well. You may leave.'

I returned to the desk after he left, but pushed my cup away. The tea now looked like blood. The room felt stifled by the ghosts of my ancestors. The grief swelled inside me again, tinged with spite. As I grew up, Uncle and I had loved each other less and less; yet the throne was mine now, and I would be a better ruler.

Raised voices outside propelled me up and towards the doors. I flung them open and froze.

CHAPTER FOUR

XANIA

The carpet muffled my footsteps, giving me a few more moments of stealth. 'How long?'

Matthias whirled. His face tumbled through shock, surprise, guilt, then settled on anger. 'Xania.'

'*Miss Bayonn.*' He'd lost the privilege of my name. 'How long have you been working for her?' *What secrets have you told her?*

'It's not –'

I whipped the dagger up.

He went still.

'How long?'

He flicked his gaze from the dagger to me. 'I've known her since childhood.' He hesitated. 'However you're imagining I betrayed you, I didn't.'

Careful phrasing. Typical Matthias.

The doors burst open, and the new Queen stood in the doorway.

Fear rolled in my gut.

'Drop the dagger.' This close, layers of powder couldn't quite hide the grief or exhaustion on her pale skin. But her gaze still pinned me. *'Drop it now.'*

She spoke as if she'd never been disobeyed in her life, which was probably true. Refusing her meant courting death.

I let the dagger slip from my fingers.

Matthias nudged it towards the Queen with his boot. She scooped it up and held it at her side.

'Your Majesty,' he said through gritted teeth, 'may I present Miss Xania Bayonn, daughter of the late Baron Bayonn and Lady Harynne.'

'If this is a joke,' the Queen told him, 'it's in poor taste.'

'It isn't. I don't appreciate having the business end of daggers pointed at me.'

My legs tensed, though running was futile. The Queen knew my name now.

She narrowed her eyes. 'How did you convince the guards to let you through?' She looked between Matthias and me, then at the walls. So she *had* told him about the passages – and he shouldn't have told me.

Matthias grimaced.

At the sound of an approaching patrol, the Queen gestured at him and stepped back into the room. He pulled me inside before I could protest. The Queen shut the doors. The guards' footsteps faded around a corner.

'Release her,' the Queen said, and nodded towards the chairs at her desk.

I sat, keeping my head down. Mama had drilled etiquette into me for years as my most effective shield.

The Queen placed my dagger on the windowsill behind her. I waited for her to speak first. Only the ticking clock broke the silence, until Matthias took an incensed breath through his nose.

'I'm aware this isn't the meeting you intended, but here we are,' the Queen snapped. 'So instead of acting like a spoiled child, Baron Farhallow, I suggest you *salvage it*.'

Meeting?

I looked up. 'I... I beg your pardon, Your Majesty...'

'It's a bit late for politeness now.'

Matthias snorted.

'Would you prefer I leave you both alone with the dagger?'

'No, Your Majesty,' he said. 'I would not.'

'Good. Start explaining.'

'May I rise?'

She flicked her fingers. Matthias surged to his feet and paced. He finally took a deep breath and locked his hands behind his back. 'Your Majesty, this is Miss Xania Bayonn, daughter of Baron Bayonn and Lady Harynne, step-daughter of Lord Martain of Kierth.'

It felt ludicrous, but I stood to curtsey. At least my skirts hid my shaking knees.

'Her father died four years ago,' Matthias said. 'Her mother remarried a year and a half later. We believe her father didn't die of natural illness.'

'I know we need proof.' I flinched at my loud tone, but added, 'I've been trying to find it for years.'

The Queen broke a Farezi sugar biscuit in half and studied it with more care than it deserved. 'You're Fifth Step, Third Stepborn, with limited prospects. You don't have the social mobility nor means for revenge.'

'Blackmail isn't always secrets and gossip,' I said. 'I know the Sixth and Seventh Step families who've been living beyond their means for years –'

'Unsurprising.'

'– but don't have the credit trail they should. I know whose dowries are comprised of loans. I know who ruined their spouses' fortunes. Money talks, even when people try to hide it.'

'You work in the Treasury.'

'And I know exactly how empty it is.'

The Queen stiffened. 'That is classified information known only to the Master of Coin.'

'Don't worry, he's trustworthy,' I said. 'But I'm good at numbers. And figuring things out.'

'Apparently.' Her face hardened. 'While Matthias may have granted you access to the passages' – he squirmed – 'he wouldn't dare give you the codes to the royal wing. And the guards would never let you through without my permission. Yet here you are.'

'It took a long time to break the codes,' I said. 'If it helps.'

'Not really.' The Queen dropped the biscuit pieces onto the plate. 'This is your choice for my Whispers?' she asked Matthias. 'A woman driven by vengeance who goes where she pleases?'

My stomach dropped.

Whispers?

I was nearly eighteen, only a year younger than the Queen; if I'd been born into a higher Step, I might have been one of her ladies. But her *Whispers?*

'I– I– *no.*' I surged to my feet.

The Queen lunged forward and slapped her hands over my wrists. Her grip was surprisingly strong. It didn't matter that I knew Matthias, or we both thought Papa had been murdered, or that Matthias had kept his connection to the Queen from me. If I didn't do what the Queen wished, there would be no mercy for me.

If I was in her position, wielding her power, I'd do the same.

I sat back down, her hands still on my wrists. 'I can't be your Whispers.'

'Who do you believe murdered your father?'

If I said his name, I couldn't take it back. But Papa deserved justice, and this was only way I could do it. 'Lord Vigrante.'

My gut twisted even at the sound of his name. In public, he was always polite, respectful. Everything about him indicated an unflappable, upstanding man. He'd probably already tried to insert himself into the Queen's confidence.

But he wasn't trustworthy.

He'd killed Papa.

Only Matthias believed me. No one else would even consider going up against one of the most powerful people at Court.

Papa had been a good man. Court had no use for good men.

'Why do you believe this?' the Queen asked.

'My father died from illness. Six months after his death, the physician who attended him was trampled by a horse in the city. But his family were rewarded with promotions, and his children suddenly married well.'

It was a reasonable suspicion, but difficult to prove. Matthias agreed it fitted Vigrante's pattern of indirectly rewarding those who did his dirty work.

The Queen frowned. 'Then it's in our interests to work together.'

'I'm Fifth Step through my mother's remarriage –'

She released my wrists. 'Don't repeat what I already know. It doesn't make you better qualified to bring Vigrante down instead of being my Whispers.'

My cheeks burned, though she was right. I could get all the blackmail, all the evidence possible, and it would still be my word against Vigrante's.

'But,' the Queen said, 'with royal power backing you...'

'I serve you in exchange for...?'

'You already have merchant contacts through your family's business affairs. I'll give you the funds and contacts to gather informants from the Steps and rebuild Edar's spy network.'

'I still won't have the social mobility you need for a Whispers.' Historically, domestic threats had usually involved the Sixth and Seventh Steps, and Parliament – all areas I would be unwelcome.

'I'll handle that,' the Queen said. 'You work in the Treasury. It won't be difficult to involve you in certain affairs.'

I had a vision of all the bankruptcy files in my future.

But Coin would be suspicious if the Queen suddenly insisted on my promotion. He'd keep an eye on me. But her uncle had surely demanded more outrageous things.

'And if I refuse your offer?' The Court didn't publicly acknowledge Whispers, but everyone knew the position didn't come with a long lifespan.

'If you had proof of Vigrante's involvement in your father's death before now,' the Queen said, 'and could have killed him without implicating yourself, would you have done it?'

At this point, I gained nothing by lying. 'Yes.'

Silence.

I broke it. 'So it's blackmail, then? I become your Whispers, and you conveniently forget I want to murder Vigrante?'

Matthias sucked in a breath. Bluntness probably wasn't *done* in the higher Steps.

People died all the time. Step nobles usually paid others to poison on their behalf, so murder never led back to them. If the Queen wanted to make an example, she could reveal me to Vigrante. He'd have me before an executioner in days. And she would have him in her debt.

The Queen smiled. Warmth blossomed over her stern expression.

I swallowed.

'No,' she said. 'Not blackmail. I'm not Vigrante. There is no trust in blackmail.'

There was no trust between us anyway.

'You have a choice, small as it is. Matthias feels you're suited to being Whispers, and I trust his opinion. And,' she added, 'no one else could offer you such a chance at vengeance.'

It's in our interests to work together, she'd said. The Queen and her uncle had felt differently about duty and responsibility, and she'd avoided Lord Vigrante during her last few Court visits. Rumour had it she'd disliked his influence over her uncle.

Matthias wanted her to be a certain kind of Queen. But I doubted that someone who dismissed blackmail could win against Vigrante.

'May I consider your offer?' I asked.

She was right: no one else, not even Matthias, could give me this opportunity. But I wouldn't become Whispers on a whim. It meant controlling information and misdirection, intercepting threats to the monarch's life. It was risk after danger after risk, and if I wasn't careful that could extend to my family.

'Of course.' After a moment, she said, painful and soft, 'My father also died from illness. I will never know if it was deliberate.'

Maybe this was my chance for answers that she'd never get.

'But you must prove yourself first.' The Queen smiled at my raised eyebrows. 'Did you really expect me to trust you with my life without hesitation?' She picked up my dagger from the windowsill and held it out to me.

'Prove yourself, and the position is yours,' she said. 'I'll help you take Vigrante down. No blackmail. No traps.'

My heart leaped with hope, yet my common sense insisted on caution. 'How will I know when to prove myself?'

'You managed to break into the royal passages and stay alive after threatening Matthias. You'll recognise the appropriate situation.'

I hadn't kept myself alive so much as she'd decided I wouldn't die. But I was, as she'd pointed out, still alive, so I kept my mouth shut.

I took my dagger from her.

CHAPTER FIVE

LIA

Two days after we closed the family crypt on Uncle, I met with the Master of Coin.

'Your Majesty, sympathies on your uncle's passing,' Coin said. 'You have no money.'

I reached across the desk for the stack of paper.

My slim hopes for this conversation now seemed optimistic. We were drastically in the red – had been in debt since Grandfather's final year on the throne. Thanks to my uncle's frivolity, we'd never recovered.

I drummed my fingers. 'Please explain how we can afford Uncle's funeral and my coronation?'

'I begged,' Coin said. 'Essentially.'

'Shouldn't we put the money to better use?'

Coin ran a hand through his greying hair. 'The people want pomp, no matter how much they claim to hate it. No pomp? Rumours will spread about Edar's finances. Then they panic. You don't want that.'

'You want pomp, yet act like these pages personally offend you.'

'They *do* offend me,' he said. 'I hardly enjoy scrimping and stretching our credit.'

'If you no longer want this position –'

'I'm the best you have. I kept your uncle in his lifestyle, Parliament relatively happy, and everyone else from rioting.' Spots of colour blazed in Coin's cheeks.

'If I had the money,' I said, 'I'd give you a raise.'

Coin's blush deepened.

'But sadly we don't. Show me the Steps' expenditure lists.'

A shuffle of paper, and he passed me another sheaf.

Rage burned in my throat. 'I was unaware the *Dowager* Queen would still receive such... large amounts.' The paper trembled in my hand.

'It's reasonable enough.' From the way *reasonable enough* stuck in Coin's throat, my uncle and aunt had pelted him with the phrase until he agreed. 'The Dowager Queen is expected to maintain a certain lifestyle.'

'Our monthly incomes are now the same. I doubt she will be entertaining more than me.' I'd hoped Aunt Jienne would avoid this sort of indirect attack. I couldn't let it stand.

'Are you certain you want to wage this battle, Your Majesty?'

'Quite certain.' I smiled grimly. 'I want a full expenditure review. Quietly, to avoid tarnishing Uncle's memory. You're abundantly capable, Master Coin, but it's time a monarch paid attention to our finances.'

The Master of Coin waited, as if for a punchline. When it didn't come, he smiled. 'I'll do my best for your coronation, Your Majesty.' The coronation wouldn't be until after a month of official grieving, and though preparations had quietly started once it was understood Uncle wouldn't recover, there was a lot still to do. I was trying to immerse myself in ruling to avoid thinking about it, but everyone kept mentioning it.

'Before you get too excited' – his smile faded – 'I have two requests.'

'Whatever Your Majesty wishes.' Coin was probably reevaluating our entire conversation, deciding that for all my grand talk I was the same as Uncle: only concerned with getting my own way.

'I require funding.'

'For what purpose?'

'For the Master of Whispers.'

'Ah,' Coin said. Few spoke of the position, or the duties involved. The Whispers didn't just protect me, but also Edar and its people. The identities of active Whispers were never publicly disclosed for their safety, but they had financial resources like all the other Masters and Mistresses, including accounts.

'Will this be a problem?'

'Of course not, Your Majesty,' Coin said. 'The money will be found.' For all his complaints about our finances, he would never refuse money to my spymaster. 'Will that be all?'

'No.' This was a gamble. Coin wasn't a fool. He'd kept the strained Treasury functioning despite my uncle and aunt's demands. There was no logical reason for my request, except that I wanted it, and I couldn't plant the smallest link in Coin's mind between Miss Bayonn and Whispers. 'I propose a weekly meeting where I'm kept informed of our financial affairs.'

'I highly approve,' Coin said. 'I will make the time.'

'I want Xania Bayonn promoted to the position.'

Instead of blankly staring, as I expected, Coin narrowed his eyes. I couldn't overstep in his domain, but I needed regular contact with Miss Bayonn. She would also join my ladies, but a promotion would give her additional Treasury access.

'She hasn't the necessary experience,' Coin finally said. 'Not that I'd trust anyone other than myself to report to you.'

'Your concern has been noted, but Baron Farhallow speaks highly of her.' Or he would have, if our introduction had gone as planned.

Coin's jaw flexed. He didn't speak for several moments, as if trying to calculate how badly this could reflect on him if Miss Bayonn offended me.

'If she's unsatisfactory, you can take over.' I paused, then threw out my last gambit. 'Surely you agree it's time for a new generation to prove themselves?'

Coin relaxed. A new young monarch, eager to promote those

her own age, was someone he recognised and could handle. And if I was proven wrong – well, it was more leverage for him that I needed his guidance. 'Very well. Her father was satisfactory' – high praise from Coin – 'but her mother *does* come from a distinguished banking background. What about a trial run, Your Majesty? A month, then we'll review her performance?'

'Agreed. That will be all.' He rose and bowed. When he reached the door, I added, 'And Master Coin?'

He froze.

I tapped the paper with my aunt's outrageous budgets. 'After my aunt and I have discussed her lifestyle expectations, I believe we have the necessary money for your raise.'

Coin opened and closed his mouth, then: 'Your Majesty...'

'You may leave.'

It wasn't bribery when the Queen ordered it. Or so I assured myself.

Everyone, no matter their noble intentions, had a price.

CHAPTER SIX

XANIA

Coin's temper had been short today, his instructions clipped and incomplete. Everyone had given him a wide berth. Now we were the last ones in the Treasury.

'Up here, Bayonn,' he said. 'Now.'

The Queen had warned me to prepare for this. It hadn't made it easier. I'd worked hard to prove myself since joining the Treasury, determined to get promoted on my own merits. She'd ruined my efforts with barely a raised eyebrow.

From the tight set of Coin's mouth, he was either proud or furious with me. Maybe both. With him, they were often two sides of the same... well, coin.

He tapped his pen against his blotter. Not a good sign.

'Bayonn, how did you attract Her Majesty's notice?'

'I impressed her.' Not the smartest thing I'd ever done.

Coin jabbed the pen nib into the blotter. 'Never impress a Queen.'

'I'll take that into consideration for the next one.'

He graced me with a raised eyebrow and a faint smile, then stood. 'Follow me. Her Majesty requested that I trust you with new duties, and I am her servant.'

I followed him up the spiralling steps behind his desk.

The Treasury grew every few years: the paperwork and records constantly demanded more space. When the rooms strained at the seams, they'd looked up instead, carving mezzanines between the higher floors, looping stairs into the gaps to connect them.

Coin liked to tell visitors the groaning shelves would probably collapse, eventually, and kill us.

Two floors up, he unlocked a door I hadn't been allowed through before. The smell of old paper and older parchment hung in the air. A large table took up most of the room, surrounded by walls of locked drawers. Splashes of colour and engraved symbols beside the keyholes denoted the shelving systems. Only Coin fully knew how it all cross-referenced. It wasn't enough to become Master of Coin through bribery or outside influence; without knowledge and experience, the Treasury would devour itself within days.

'Sit,' Coin said.

I faced a stack of paper, pens, and ink.

He sat opposite me. 'I will speak. You will take notes.'

I'd had sessions like this with my supervisors. They examined my Treasury knowledge, drilled me on how to respond to unusual paperwork, or nobles digging their heels in against the reality of their finances: everything I needed to know to rise up the ranks. Being examined by Coin would be harder, but not impossible.

When he finally paused for breath, ink splattered my papers and trembling fingers. A steady ache throbbed behind my right eye.

'Take a moment, Bayonn.'

I cleaned my fingers. 'If this is what the Queen's weekly meetings are like, why would anyone want to rule?'

'Excellent question,' Coin said. 'Welcome to duty's pretty chain. Why are we concerned about the potential southern drought?'

'It could threaten the harvests.' Coin had recommended increased port trading to soften the blow, but – 'If they're affected, the Queen will have to buy grain. If Farezi realises our harvests are failing, they'll raise their grain prices.' And Coin would have to find the money somewhere, regardless, so people could still eat bread.

The long, curt lesson of droughts, and harvests, and upset nobles – everything feeding into everything – made my head spin. My usual grumbling about paperwork and budgets felt puny. The Queen was the heart of Edar, but when the Treasury felt pain it affected everything else.

The Treasury's funds depended not only on taxes, but on nobles approaching Coin for loans instead of the banks. I'd never truly realised how much Coin had to be aware of so everything ran smoothly. No part of the precarious balance under his control could fail.

Not even the groaning shelves.

Coin frowned, and reached for one of the many sets of keys on his belt. He eased a key off and held it out. 'Do *not* make me regret this, Bayonn.'

It was reassuringly solid in my palm. The symbols carved into the head corresponded to the drawers it opened. Coin guarded access to his kingdom jealously. Those directly under him who'd worked here the longest had keys to specific rooms or records, but still had only a combined fraction of access. No one could loan a key to someone else. It meant the rest of us had to run around to get any necessary extra files. It made for frustrated, long days, but you adapted to Coin's methods or didn't work for him.

I was years away from getting any key. Or I had been. 'You honour me, sir.'

'No. I honour our Queen.'

Someone knocked on the main doors below. We stared at each other. No one visited the Treasury this late at night.

'Stay here.' Coin hurried downstairs as the knocking turned into pounding.

I crept towards the railings and crouched to peer down at the main floor. Coin's cat – a mass of silky black and white fur, known only as *Coin's cat* despite all the names people had tried over the years, and just as grumpy as him – crept out from wherever she'd been hiding, and butted her head against my legs until I scratched behind her ears.

He flung open the doors. '*What*?'

'Master Coin.'

I stiffened at Lady Brenna's voice. She and Lord Hazell were influential Government members – and Vigrante's closest allies. To reach him, you went through them first.

'Lady Brenna.' Coin's voice held a note of surprise. 'This is unexpected.' He stepped back to let her into the room.

Her pale brown curls tumbled around her shoulders. She flicked at imaginary creases on her green dress. 'A word in your office, please,' she said. 'I'm not on Vigrante's business.' Her tone didn't quite ring true.

'Of course.' Coin sounded wary. He led her to his office, which he only used for meetings, preferring to supervise us while he worked. The door shut, almost decisively, as if warning me not to eavesdrop.

I sighed and returned to the room, the cat chirping as she raced ahead.

Brenna was hardly ten years older than me. When she was my age, her family had hoped for a match in Farezi's higher circles, who disliked their noble ladies considering careers. A long-term Treasury rumour insisted that Coin had offered her a position that completely bypassed the lower ranks, which her family had refused on her behalf. But Vigrante had seen the ghost of her potential. No wonder she'd allied with him.

I hefted the key in my palm, eyeing the drawers around me. My key had been engraved with a barbed rose, a peacock feather, and a quarter moon, splashed with red. I opened drawers with those symbols, trying to figure out what Coin had granted me access to – or what the Queen had demanded I have access to.

I now had information on people and families I wasn't normally privy to. But Coin's punch of a lecture, and each drawer I opened, hinted that it extended to other areas in the Treasury connected to the Queen.

And Coin surely expected me to keep up with my current work.

And if I became the new Whispers...

I'd just have to learn to survive on less sleep.

I pulled open another rose drawer. I'd expected more papers on Sixth or Seventh Step families, including delicate information like ill-advised loans they'd bargained Coin for, but this one was full of Government members' financial information.

'*You're a Treasury employee,*' the Queen had said. '*It won't be difficult to involve you in certain affairs.*'

It must have infuriated Coin to give me this kind of access.

I rubbed the engraved symbols on my key. No one beyond myself and Coin would access these drawers for a while. Not only had the Queen insisted on giving me increased access, but it looked like she'd also forced Coin to rearrange his system around it. She'd promised me royal power to fuel my vengeance, and played the first card of her promise.

I pulled out two files and spread them on the table.

Lady Brenna.

Lord Hazell.

I had no proof they'd helped Vigrante orchestrate Papa's death. But they kept Vigrante in power, vocal in their support in return for his favours and reach. If I wanted to expose Vigrante's weaknesses, destroying his power base was a good place to begin.

I glanced towards Coin's office. He and Brenna had been briskly familiar, as if they'd kept in contact despite her alliance with Vigrante.

Papa. I had to think of Papa.

Going after Brenna and Hazell wouldn't bring him back, or be true vengeance for his death.

But ruining them would be a start.

☿ ☿ ☿

A week later, I smoothed my sleeves and officially gave up on my appearance.

Mama turned me to face her. Zola and I had inherited lighter shades of her brown skin, but I shared her tight curls that she'd scraped into a bun. She nodded. 'Good. You won't embarrass us, or yourself, before the Queen.'

'Thank you, Mama.' I managed not to roll my eyes, but smiled as she hugged me.

She let me go to answer the knock on my door. Zola rushed in, followed by Lord Martain. He beamed and rocked on his heels, as we settled into our usual routine of awkward but sincere affection. I didn't doubt his love for Mama, but I still wasn't sure if he'd wanted two almost-grown children to follow her into the marriage.

Zola grinned and held out a small box. 'This is for you.'

'A promotion should always be celebrated,' Lord Martain added.

Weekly financial meetings with the Queen was a promotion far beyond my current responsibilities, but my family pretended otherwise. Now that Matthias was officially the Queen's new secretary, Mama assumed he was behind my new role. She'd hopefully never find out about the actual job I'd inadvertently put myself up for.

'Lord Martain, this is unnecess–'

He held up a hand. 'Please, open it.'

I lifted the lid. A brooch nestled in silk and velvet: a little bird, its wings suspended in flight, painted in sky-blue and yellow enamel – Lord Martain's family colours – and edged in gold. Its eye was a tiny sapphire.

Lord Martain was proud of me.

The bird blurred. If I succumbed to tears, I wouldn't stop crying. 'Thank you,' I whispered.

He rescued the brooch from my shaking hands to pin it. He

would never replace Papa, but he made Mama happy. That was enough.

Zola flung her arms around me. 'Show her how wonderful you are.'

I tried to muster a confident smile. Before I lost my nerve, I grabbed my folder and hurried out.

This would never work.

But if I didn't prove myself, the only path left was to the executioner.

Papa deserved justice.

And I deserved to live.

Matthias's advice raced around my mind: 'She's less formal than her uncle and grandfather, but there are still rules. Three steps forward, curtsey, and wait for her acknowledgment. You sit when she allows it. If she offers refreshment, she'll serve. She'll dismiss you, and *don't* stand before she does.'

Our meeting yesterday had been awkward – I was still angry that he'd kept his friendship with the Queen secret, even though no one in Court had known except for the Queen's mother – and Matthias had hid behind brisk professionalism. But while my trust in him was shaky, he'd still recommended me to the Queen; my success would also be his.

I entered the royal wing by showing my mark to the guards. Safe and boring. All too soon, I stood at the doors to the Queen's private study.

Papa wouldn't have been afraid. And neither will I.

I knocked.

'Enter!'

The Queen was scribbling on paper when I walked in, but beckoned me forward without looking up. I took three steps and sank into a curtsey: skirts held out, back straight. My breath went in and out with the ticking clock.

Her pen didn't stop.

As the seconds trickled by, my legs ached. If she didn't acknowledge me soon, I'd start trembling. Falling over wouldn't be the best start.

Finally, just as I considered abandoning etiquette and falling, the scratching nib stopped.

'Oh, damn it, rise.'

I straightened, keeping my head down.

'We're in private,' she said. 'I'm not going to behead you for looking at me.'

That was easy for her to say. Protocol worked itself around her. Protocol *existed* for her.

'*Look at me.*'

I raised my face. 'Your Majesty.'

'Sit.' She jabbed a finger at a chair.

I sat.

The Queen's private study was smaller than the public one, yet the turquoise walls and golden wood made it more inviting. It suited her, but right now she didn't suit it. She was sickly pale, with dark circles under her eyes: understandable, considering she'd recently entombed her uncle. I thought she'd reschedule our meeting, but Lord Martain had said, 'She doesn't have time. Monarchs never have enough time.'

She was too pale for her mourning purple. The colour was royal, a symbol of their authority and old divine power. A period of royal mourning was the only time the rest of us could wear it. The monarchy edged theirs in black, adding another layer to their grief.

'Some rules,' she said. 'Those who work with me don't show fear. Even if you're terrified, learn to hide it or we'll accomplish nothing.'

'Yes, Your Majesty.'

Tired or not, she fitted into rooms with gilded wallpaper and heavy curtains spilling to the floor. The small crystal chandelier over our heads was cut in an older style, but worth more than my parents could ever have afforded.

'If I make an incorrect statement or assessment,' she continued, 'you're expected to speak up. Coin argues with me when he feels it necessary. Matthias tries to see how quickly he can prick my temper, but don't follow his example. Public protocol is different, but I don't have time for elaborate ceremony in private. Understood?'

'Yes, Your Majesty.' There was no point in admitting I didn't know how to navigate a less royal protocol.

'Good.' She pushed her papers aside. 'Coin said he prepared with you?'

I'd spent time with Coin every evening since our first meeting, drilled until my head hurt and his nerves frayed. Nothing had been said about Brenna's visit.

The Queen rose. 'Follow me. Don't bring your papers.'

We went through a side door, then two empty rooms, until she stopped before a double door and grasped the handles.

She glanced at me. 'You wanted to prove yourself, yes?'

I nodded, though it was less *want* and more *had no choice in the matter*.

'I don't like surprises.' Her smile held little warmth. 'But I like surprising others.' She flung open the doors and stepped into the room.

A wall of noise hit me: laughter and chatter, brittle-bright, a packed room of nobles on display. Vivid satins and silks with intricate embroidery, smooth velvets, jewels flashing in the candlelight.

As I followed the Queen, a crystalline moment of silence spread. A servant should have announced her first, giving them all precious seconds to prepare.

They curtseyed and bowed in unison, chorusing, 'Your Majesty!' They surged apart, creating space for her to glide towards an elevated chair – the only seat in the room. She sat.

Another pause, like a bated breath. Unsure what else to do, I stood beside her. Voices suddenly broke the silence, crashing against each other.

I like surprising others, she'd said.

Despite their surprise, I was the unsettled one. I was the one who didn't belong.

The room was large for entertaining, dark blue with dove-grey wood and silver accents. It felt cold. Servants held trays of glasses and small, delicate foods. Now facing the crowd, I recognised them as Sixth and Seventh Step, all Opposition politicians. The Queen had arranged a gathering to win their support.

Matthias wasn't here.

The Opposition was a balance to the Government, usually with differing opinions on legislation. Collectively, Parliament was supposed to keep the monarch in check. The current Opposition had united around their mutual loathing of Vigrante, but was hindered by Alexandris's weak leadership. The Queen would need their support when Vigrante and his Government inevitably opposed her reforms.

'Your Majesty.' An elderly gentleman approached and swept an efficient bow.

Lord Ealkenor, my memory informed me. *Low Seventh Step, astute businessman, frugal to the point of miserly*. Papa had admired his business sense, and despised everything else about him. Lord Ealkenor's family had put him in charge of their financial interests, though they, too, despised everything else about him.

The Queen held out her hand out for him to kiss. 'Lord Ealkenor. We're so pleased you accepted our invitation.'

He brushed his lips over her knuckles. His eyes flickered towards me. My shoulders tightened.

She gestured to me. 'This is Miss Xania Bayonn, daughter of Lady Harynne and the late Baron Bayonn: the newest of my ladies.'

He raised his eyebrows. My pronounced lack of title and Papa's lowly one hung between us. Theoretically, a Queen chose whoever she wanted to join her ladies. Realistically, they were from Sixth and Seventh Step families who'd always supported the Crown.

A baron's daughter did not make a royal lady.

I curtseyed.

He bowed. 'Isn't it a royal lady's duty to *mingle*?'

It sadly wasn't her duty to commit violence on the Queen's behalf.

The Queen's smile turned wintry. She pressed her fingers against my sleeve in a silent command.

'Ask Lord Ealkenor what the Pastry Master thinks of him,' I whispered. Lord Ealkenor was notorious for entertaining with thin fillings and sparse batches to make his money stretch. No one enjoyed his gatherings.

Only the barest quirk of her mouth betrayed her. I curtseyed and stepped off the dais, aware of the eyes upon me. I didn't know where to go. I only knew these people as glimpses in the halls, names in whispered gossip. Our families were not friends. Being announced as one of the Queen's ladies didn't give me the right to simply join their conversation –

Well. Actually, it did. Being one of the Queen's ladies surpassed my rank.

'*I'll handle that*,' the Queen had said, at my concerns about my lack of social mobility.

I had to prove how I responded to unfamiliar situations.

'Miss Bayonn!' A woman, two years older than me with pale skin and ash-blonde hair, stopped before me.

I smiled. 'Lady Terize.' We worked together in the Treasury. She was lower Sixth Step, but lacked airs and was generally pleasant to be around. But her lack of self-confidence led to mistakes, so we often fixed her work together before it reached Coin.

She clasped my hands. 'It's a relief to see a familiar face!' She was too polite to say I shouldn't have been here at all. 'Is your family here?'

I shook my head.

'A pity.' She led me back to her group. 'Let me introduce you.'

I might have been Third Step-born, but Mama had taught me etiquette as thoroughly as any Sixth or Seventh Step child. I could make small talk in my sleep. When they asked how I'd joined the Queen's ladies, I said, 'I made her laugh.' It didn't satisfy them.

I followed Terize, smiling, laughing, complimenting people,

and silently tallying the prominent politicians. Terize's mother, Lady Patrinne, was deep in conversation at the opposite side of the room.

Terize avoided her. Everyone knew Lady Patrinne's hand lay heavy over Terize's self-doubt, and she publicly criticised her after too much wine. Someone so indiscreet about family couldn't be trusted, but she could still be useful.

When Lady Patrinne had tried to get one of her elder daughters accepted into the Dowager Queen's ladies, she'd been politely, pointedly rebuked. But the new Queen was a fresh start. If I 'influenced' her into accepting Terize, who was kind when her mother wasn't pulling her strings, it was a step towards gaining a Parliamentary informant.

A smattering of whispers tugged me out of my thoughts. A gentleman approached the dais with a full glass in one hand and a wine bottle in the other. The whispers died into silence.

'Lord Naruum,' the Queen said calmly.

He held the glass towards her. 'I propose a toast, Your Majesty, to stronger ties between the monarchy and Opposition.' He bowed, as much as the glass and bottle would allow. 'With my compliments.'

The Queen didn't reply, her gaze fixed on the glass.

The unspoken rule in Court, for all, was: don't drink from a glass that didn't come from a servant or wasn't poured by the host. It didn't prevent all poisoning attempts, but it was a signal of trust. A monarch's every drink and meal had to pass a poison-taster.

The Queen couldn't drink it, of course. But she risked offence if she refused, which Lord Naruum was surely trying to provoke. Why else would he offer her untested wine in a room full of politicians?

No one moved, poised for whichever ill-fated decision the Queen would make. They were all wealthy, most from old bloodlines, and all bound by tightly knotted webs of etiquette and manners. They wouldn't come to the Queen's rescue. Though it would privately come with great favour, it would also involve public embarrassment.

Logic implied Naruum's wine wasn't poisoned, but what if logic was wrong?

If I became the Queen's Whispers, my greatest responsibility was to keep her alive.

And I had to prove myself.

As the guards at the walls moved towards Naruum, I darted forward, as if I'd caught my shoe on the rug. I unbalanced myself enough that when I slapped a hand on Naruum's shoulder, as if to catch myself, it wasn't entirely a farce. I slammed my heel, hidden by my skirts, onto his foot.

He yelped. The glass and bottle went flying, and those in the wine's path dived out of the way.

The rug was thick enough to save the bottle from shattering. It didn't, however, keep the wine in it.

I had already moved back, as if in horror, so it didn't splatter against my hem or shoes. Silence fell again, brittle with horrified amusement. I kept my head down. Better to pretend embarrassment against their pitying smiles. I'd prevented a situation where the Queen would have to give offence, but had publicly humiliated myself in the process. I was Third Step-born, now Fifth. I didn't belong, Queen's lady or not. This only proved it.

If Mama heard about this, not even being chosen by the Queen would save me.

The sapphire in Lord Martain's bird glimmered at the edge of my vision, almost mockingly. The thought of his pride made my chest hurt.

But the wine was gone.

Lord Naruum seemed frozen to the spot. He should have been outraged, should have berated me for my clumsiness, anything that stressed this was my fault and he'd acted with the best of intentions.

He stayed silent.

'Miss Bayonn.' The Queen's voice dropped into the quiet.

I risked a glance. 'Your Majesty.' She seemed calm, her royal training hiding her true emotions.

She raised a hand for the guards to pause, then gestured me forward, subtly putting me between her and Naruum. She held out a folded, sealed square of paper. 'I have a message for Master

Coin, if you would kindly deliver it.' The request was mere formality.

'Of course, Your Majesty.' I took the paper, curtseyed, and backed away. The nobles parted for me. I didn't look at anyone. Servants opened the doors as I drew near, so I didn't have to fumble for the handles.

The doors closed, leaving me in abrupt quietness.

My shoulders slumped. Relief and delayed fear thrummed inside me. I glanced at the paper.

It was addressed to me.

I broke the seal and unfolded it.

Well done, Miss Bayonn, the note said in neat, curling letters.

Something warm swelled in my chest, a pleasant sort of tightening. She'd written this before our meeting. She couldn't have predicted what would happen in that room. But if something had, she'd expected – hoped for? – me to succeed. If I hadn't, I never would have seen this.

I hoped whoever had to clean the carpet was careful, just in case.

φ φ φ

When I joined the Treasury, Mama gave me a new room in our suite so I had somewhere private, doors that I could close on everyone and everything. I stared into the flickering candles, unable to stop thinking about Naruum, and his wine, and the

Queen. Shadows danced along the walls and ceiling, pooled in the corners.

The world outside my door had intruded and wouldn't go away.

I kept wondering if I should go to the Queen, before common sense reasserted itself. Even if I used the passages, I could hardly knock on the wall of her apartments to be let in. As if I had any right to be there.

Papa had been poisoned, a slow-acting one that feigned a long illness. I knew this, yet had no proof. But I couldn't shake the image of Naruum smiling as he held out the glass. I'd assumed that by forcing the Queen to refuse the wine, he'd wanted to sow distrust between her and the Opposition. But his reaction after didn't make sense. Had the wine been poisoned? Why would he try to harm the Queen in a room of politicians, an attempt so public it could only fail?

Are you all right? I wanted to ask her, though assassination attempts surely didn't unnerve her. *Are you worried? Do you know what to do with him?*

Did I do the right thing? Did I prove myself?

Do you trust me a little more now?

I blinked. I was at my door that opened onto the hall, had wrapped my fingers around the handle. I let go, stepped back. I couldn't ask her any of those questions. I wasn't her Whispers yet. Much had been promised, but nothing confirmed.

I extinguished the candles and climbed into bed. I stared at the ceiling, but couldn't quieten my whirling mind.

CHAPTER SEVEN

LIA

The household had been up before dawn, submerging me in hot water to wash the princess from me. They'd brushed and twisted and pinned my hair.

For all of my financial fretting, I'd allowed no compromise on the dress. I'd parade through Arkaala before returning to the palace to be crowned. Clothing made no difference to my ability to rule, but people would remember what I wore. The dress was deep blue, the bodice and skirt heavy with gold and silver embroidery. My cloak was gold, edged in pale fur – too hot for an early spring coronation, but tradition demanded it.

My necklace, a large sapphire set in silver, had been my great-grandmother's. I wore little face-paint, to limit the damage from nerves and the heat of too many people in one room.

I still looked a princess playing at being Queen.

A knock.

'Enter.'

Mother held a large box stamped in gold leaves and vines. She bowed, her eyes wide in the mirror. 'I– you–'

'I know,' I said, surprised at how sad I sounded.

Her mouth twisted in a half-smile. 'Not what you expected?'

'I'm not sure what I expected.' I hadn't anticipated political manipulation being so exhausting. I'd never used silence so much before to unnerve nobles and politicians into assumptions. They wanted so much, because they could. It was enough to make me scream, because *I* could.

And I hadn't anticipated someone trying to kill me so soon.

Two days after the Opposition gathering, my physician had confirmed what I'd suspected: Naruum's wine had been poisoned, strong enough to kill me. When Matthias had confronted him, Naruum insisted the dose would have only *temporarily indisposed* me.

When the information leaked, the Court and Parliament had infected themselves with panic. My parents had employed poison-tasters before my birth, had been almost matter-of-fact about the unavoidable consequences of being royal. Privately, no matter how I'd been taught, the attempt made me want to never leave the royal wing again. Publicly, I couldn't let it affect me. The Court didn't know how to react when I calmly continued with my daily routines.

Behind closed doors, Matthias tried to pry answers from Naruum and had also won our argument. He insisted on more guards for the coronation, while I wanted the original number to keep up the pretence of normality.

Mother eyed me, then put the box down. It was only when she reached forward that I realised she intended to hug me.

I flinched.

She froze.

A flush crept up Mother's neck; my own face was already aflame. *Well. We haven't even left yet, and the day is already ripping at the seams.*

I hadn't wanted Mother to know about Naruum's poisoned wine, but it was better she heard the truth from me. She'd cried. Even if she was matter-of-fact about risks during my childhood, that was before we'd lost Father.

'If you hug me,' I said, 'I'll cry, and I'm not sure I could stop.'

'Ah.'

'I hope Father would be proud today,' I said: a tentative apology.

'Of course he would be.' Mother squeezed my shoulder. 'Kneel, please. The shoes make you too tall for me.'

I knelt. She placed the heir's circlet, silver and steel-wrought, on my head. I'd worn it only a handful of times. It was heavier than it appeared. Father had looked elegant and dashing wearing it in his portrait. I felt like I was wearing part of a costume.

Mother adjusted the circlet against my forehead, then stepped back, satisfied.

I stood. Took a deep breath. Let it out. Squared my shoulders.

Mother curtseyed, proper and deep. She smiled – all forgiven now? Possibly? 'Long live the Queen.'

Please, Father, I thought, as I walked to the door, Mother behind me. *Grant me the strength to get through today. Help me make you proud.*

Since the Opposition gathering, I sometimes jerked awake in the deepest part of night with the taste of wine in my mouth, sweet poison on my tongue.

All I had to do, as Matthias kept saying, was show up, be crowned, and still be alive by tonight. Not difficult.

Please, Father, let me survive.

CHAPTER EIGHT

XANIA

Anticipation filled the throne room, as strong as the scent of roses around us. Blue and silver banners hung around the room. The largest, emblazoned with the royal crest, hung above the throne.

We'd arrived early enough to get a prized vantage spot on a Fifth Step gallery. We weren't as close to the throne as the royal family or Seventh Step nobles, but still had a good view. Zola and I spent the time people-watching and whispering about the fashion.

'What will her dress look like?' Zola mused.

'Blue.'

She thumped my arm.

'*Must* you act like children?' Mama asked, but couldn't hide her smile.

'Here's Duchess Sionbourne,' Lord Martain said, as the Queen's mother entered the royal gallery.

The Dowager Queen arrived soon after. She wore navy blue

with white embroidery, a subtle hint of her prior status that wouldn't upstage the Queen. She and the Duchess exchanged small talk, only a slight stiffness betraying their mutual dislike.

There was a momentary hush when the Arch-Bishop and two bishops stepped onto the dais. Edar didn't hold much with religion anymore, but the Order still performed ceremonial state duties. One bishop carried a black bell, a finely-wrought knife, and a bowl filled with fire on a small table. The other held the royal sceptre.

The Arch-Bishop balanced the crown on a cushion. Over two centuries old, burnished silver and set with sapphires, it was forged when Edar was tearing itself apart. The Queen's great-grandfather had kept it instead of designing a new one.

Trumpets blasted in the distance; the Queen had returned to the palace.

I'd forgotten about the blindfold until she entered amid a flurry of bows and curtseys. She walked slowly, her hand light upon the steward's arm. I'd still bet my pitiful inheritance she was shaking inside.

It was Sannaa, one of the oldest historians whose written work still survived, who'd first mentioned monarchs wearing blindfolds during their coronations. They would travel blindfolded amongst their people, trusting in their divine surety.

The divine right to rule was long gone, but the tradition remained. Sannaa had also claimed no monarch was protected during their coronation, but no one believed that. Judging by the guards lining the walls, neither did the Queen.

Her gown swept around her. Her circlet gleamed. The ends of the silk blindfold fluttered behind her.

Zola drew in a harsh breath.

'I know,' I murmured, over the pounding heartbeat in my throat. 'Blue dress.'

Zola choked out a laugh, then ducked her head at Mama's glare.

The cries started from the doors, gaining in strength as the Queen travelled up the room: 'Long live the Queen! Long live the Queen! *Long live the Queen!*'

When she reached the dais and knelt, everyone cheered.

Coronations, it turned out, were boring. A lot of back and forth about honour and duty and upholding the law. Justice and Mercy. Maintaining order. Working with Parliament, while standing firm against them when necessary – politicians had been trying for years to get that part removed.

Papa's death had turned me cynical. But something close to hope swelled inside me as the Queen answered each question with steady conviction, luring me into thinking: *She'll be different to her uncle and grandfather. She won't fling money away and demand more extravagance in return. She won't drain our country and beggar us.*

She will be just. She will be merciful.

With the vows almost finished, I leaned forward. Papa had told me about this part when I was little, and we were just close enough for me to catch glimpses of it.

One of the bishops lifted the bell, holding the clapper until the right moment. The other set the bowl of fire before the Queen. She tilted her face towards the rising heat.

'By the air I breathe –' she said.

The bishop turned left and rang the bell.

'– the counsel I listen to –'

The bishop turned again and rang the bell at the throne.

'– the blood I spill –'

The bishop rang the bell to his right. The second bishop picked up the dagger and pressed her fingertips against the Queen's hands. She turned her palms up and held them high over the fire.

'– I swear to uphold the law and govern my people wisely until my death.'

The bishop rang the bell above the Queen's head. The second bishop drew the knife over her palms in a blur. The Queen didn't flinch. I squinted, and could just make out the blood pooling in the Queen's cupped hands, before she let it fall.

The flames devoured the blood.

This part was older than the First Empire, older than most religions. If a ruler accepted the crown and its power, they also accepted its hardship by shedding their blood. The Queen's blood had fallen upon the flames and purified her.

The bishops were already removing her blindfold, cutting it to wrap around her palms. Finished, they stepped back as the Arch-Bishop approached with the crown.

She lowered her head.

'By fire and vow and blood, you swear to uphold Edar's laws as did those before you.' The coronation vows never had a back-up sentence for the previous monarch being selfish and useless. 'I crown you Queen Aurelia, Fourth of Her Name, Fourth of Her Line, First Protector of Edar and Servant Most High.'

He placed the crown upon her head. It felt like everyone took a breath together.

'Rise.'

She stood, steady despite the pain she was surely feeling. The bishops passed her the sceptre; she held it as if her palms weren't bloodied. She turned for our adoration.

'Long live the Queen! Long live the Queen! *Long live the Queen!*'

For a moment, amid the roars and cheers, she looked ready to weep.

ⵚ ⵚ ⵚ

As Fifth Step, we were invited to the private celebration after the ceremony. Well, as private a gathering as a banquet can be. While the Queen went to the balcony to greet the crowds, we headed into the banquet hall attached to the ballroom.

I followed Zola's gaze to Ernest Blackwood, the centre of his group as always. 'No. We talked about this.'

'We need to show ourselves. We can't be rude.'

'Why is nothing *he* does ever rude?' I muttered.

When Ernest saw Zola, his expression went cold. I could hardly believe he'd ever liked her.

Etiquette demanded that Ernest acknowledge us first. He stayed silent until his companions shifted uncomfortably. Zola trembled at the slight. I silently counted to ten. Again, the urge to break Ernest's nose overwhelmed me.

Then I nearly toppled to the floor, courtesy of Matthias.

'Miss Bayonn! I'm so sorry, please forgive me!'

I gritted my teeth as he pulled me up. His cologne stung my nostrils. 'Please, Baron Farhallow, no apologies necessary.' I plastered a smile on my face. He grinned, then glanced at my sister.

'Miss Zola, lovely to see you again!'

My sister, to her credit, answered him with admirable smoothness.

Matthias turned to Ernest. 'Marquess Ashfall. Are you quite well? I hope your bout of inexplicable silence isn't contagious.'

Ernest and his group stared.

Don't laugh, don't laugh.

Matthias bowed. 'Miss Bayonn, Miss Zola, please follow me. There's someone who wishes to make your acquaintance.' He swept off. It was a lie, but a way for us to leave with dignity. As the Queen's personal secretary, Matthias now had more power than his Third Step rank warranted.

'*Lovely* to see you, Marquess Ashfall.' I beamed and hauled Zola away before she could protest, or I laughed.

'– an upstart,' Ernest snapped behind us. 'He considers himself *much* too highly. Her Majesty will immediately replace him once a better candidate presents himself –'

Zola turned quiet as we wandered through the crowds, but brightened when we sat for the meal. At the final course, she looked at her dessert in despair. 'I don't think I can eat it.'

'I will gallantly eat yours and mine,' I said. 'It has custard. I'm not leaving it behind.'

As Zola picked up her spoon with renewed determination, I returned to watching the Queen and Matthias.

At her arrival, we'd paid our respects along with everyone else. She'd smiled and talked with her mother and aunt throughout the courses, but now she looked ready to sleep for a century. Matthias stood at the wall behind her chair, occasionally conferring with the staff. He'd stopped Zola from suffering more embarrassment than Ernest had already thrown at her, but he was wrong if he thought this improved things between us.

Despite his position, he and the Queen had hardly spoken today. No wonder they'd managed to hide their friendship for years. He looked poised, cheerful, and competent. But I knew – or thought I knew – him better. Despite his smile, his face gleamed with sweat. His laughter was slightly too loud. All this could be explained away by stress – organising a seven-course meal with copious alcohol for too many nobles wasn't easy. But Matthias thrived on stress. And there were too many guards against the walls. The Queen might pretend nothing had changed since Naruum's assassination attempt, but I'd bet Matthias didn't agree with her.

The extra guards were a precaution, but...

If Matthias was unusually stressed, it wasn't a good sign.

When he slipped out through a side door, I pretended a trip to the privy. I caught up as he entered the passages and crept in after him.

The passages' dim lighting still unnerved me: a wavering gleam that shimmered from the walls. I couldn't figure out if it was natural, a remnant from the First Empire's myths, or something created to intimidate people who stumbled upon them, unaware.

A shout exploded in the distance, abruptly cut off. Sweat burst under my arms, and I hurtled towards the noise. My arms scraped against the walls. The sounds of grunts and scuffling footsteps grew louder.

I whirled around a corner. Matthias was struggling to get a masked man against the wall. I rushed forward, dodging Matthias when he reeled back from a punch. The man lunged towards me. Silver flashed in his hand. Of course he'd have a weapon when I had none. They were banned from coronations and funerals; we'd been searched before entering the throne room and again at the banquet hall.

Our parents had taught Zola and me basic skills to disarm knife opponents and defend ourselves, even without weapons. Lord Martain had insisted our skills be kept sharp. Panic shrieked in my brain, but my body reacted from years of practice. I crossed my hands around his wrist to stop the knife. His eyes widened as I forced his hand up and twisted. I couldn't remember which joint to hurt, so I slammed my heel into his foot instead. His cry turned into a wheeze, as I forced him to his knees and yanked the knife away.

Matthias pinned him against the wall.

I braced my palms against my knees and panted. The man's jaw twitched, like he was about to grind his teeth.

'His mouth!' I said.

Matthias shoved his fingers between the man's lips, but he'd already bit down and swallowed. It was too late. Matthias released him and stepped back.

The poison was quick. The man slid down the wall. Spit bubbled down his chin. When he reached the ground, he went still.

For a moment, we stared in silence. Matthias finally swore at the dead assassin with quiet, harsh efficiency.

Revulsion shot through my veins, turned sour on my tongue. A dead assassin was worthless. It was easier to focus on that than the horror of a man killing himself before me.

Matthias closed his eyes. The rage fled from his face with terrifying speed. 'I was going to knock him out.'

'You're welcome.' No matter what he said, he hadn't been in control of the fight.

He had the grace to look sheepish, but asked, 'Do you still want to do this? Face-to-face death is ugly.'

Fine words considering Matthias had dumped me on this path. 'Who does – *did* – he work for?'

'I have my suspicions,' he said. 'A handful of assassin groups use suicide-by-poison when things go wrong.'

'Would Vigrante have hired him?'

Matthias shook his head. 'He wouldn't try this so soon after Naruum. This was probably orchestrated from abroad. If Lia dies, the Crown passes to Farezi.' He worked his jaw. 'But who hired him? The timing is suspicious so the Farezi royalty would deny it, though they benefit from Lia's death. Whoever is behind this, they didn't think it through.'

'They still tried to kill the Queen.'

Matthias rubbed his forehead. 'Indeed.'

'Was her uncle targeted like this?'

'From what I've heard, no,' Matthias said. 'But Vigrante probably helped to prevent these situations.' He crossed his arms. 'Everything would be easier if Lia didn't despise Vigrante, and he didn't want her to rely on him like her Uncle had.' He gestured at the dead assassin. 'I'll find out who hired him. It'll take some careful tugging to reach the source, but I'll manage.'

'Like you managed me?' I hated the bitterness in my voice. Even if I'd thought he was on my side, and we were something like friends, he'd used everything Papa had taught him – everything Papa didn't teach me because it wouldn't help my marriage prospects – for the Queen's benefit. When Matthias had offered to help me avenge Papa's murder, his loyalty was still ultimately to her.

'I wasn't setting you up for Lia's benefit.' Matthias leaned against the wall. 'I had you in mind as her Whispers for a while. But I didn't intend to introduce you like that.'

'You still offered to help me for *your* longterm goal.'

'She needs a Whispers.' Matthias smiled. 'Besides, she enjoyed your first meeting. And, of course, you stopped Naruum.'

I wanted to say *Anyone would have done that*, but no one else had. It unnerved me how quickly I'd slipped into the Whispers mindset. And the Queen had manipulated me so easily by having me prove myself. She'd sized me up within minutes and guessed I relished a challenge.

'You should go back. You'll be missed.'

'I'll think of something,' I said. 'Will you be able to easily... dispose of him?'

'I'll think of something.' Now Matthias looked ready to sleep for a century.

'You don't need to tell me death is ugly,' I said. 'I'm already well aware.'

Papa's memory stretched between us.

'I know,' Matthias said softly. 'I shouldn't have said that.'

'And if I have to embrace ugliness to prove Vigrante killed Papa, I'll do it.'

As I turned to leave, he said, 'Well done. This will please the Queen, and she was already impressed with you.'

I paused. 'How is Lord Naruum?'

'Temporarily indisposed by questions he's unable to answer.'

I ignored Zola and Mama's frowns when I returned. Now the Queen's exhaustion and brittle expression painted a much different picture: someone worried about assassins when she should have been celebrating.

I thought of Naruum's wine, and the questions I'd wanted to ask her later that night. And she'd wanted me to succeed, written a note of encouragement in the hopes she'd get to give it to me.

Perhaps for all her promises, her authority, she wanted me to tell her *my* decision.

CHAPTER NINE

LIA

The morning after my coronation, Miss Bayonn strode into my study.

I lowered my pen. 'Good morning.' Everyone else was still in bed, but the paperwork didn't care that I'd just been crowned.

Her appearance was carefully neat: she'd taken her time and hadn't rushed here. 'I'll do it. I'll be your Whispers.' Another pause, before a belated, 'Your Majesty.'

I hadn't expected relief, but it cascaded over my tight shoulders all the same. 'I don't believe it was *your* decision.'

Miss Bayonn raised an eyebrow. 'No one forces a Whispers into the job. It's the quickest way to be assassinated.'

I gestured at the empty chair. 'Sit. There are conditions.'

She sat. 'Of course.'

'We will have weekly meetings,' I said. 'I won't manage you, any more than I would Coin or the others. But as you're Fifth Step, I'm willing to use all influence to help you.'

'I'm not in a position to make requests, but I'd appreciate prior warning before being dragged into a room of politicians.'

I smiled. 'Would *you* expect a Queen to openly favour her Whispers before Court or Parliament?'

'No.'

'With Naruum's poison,' I said, 'and the assassin last night, I'm now twice in your debt.'

We fell into an uneasy silence.

'Why are you so calm?' Miss Bayonn finally asked. 'They surely didn't teach you to treat assassination like this.'

'Not quite,' I said. 'But I was raised with poison-tasters. There are prices to pay for royal privilege. It's our responsibility to accept them.'

'That's ridiculous,' Miss Bayonn said. 'At least there were more guards yesterday.'

'Matthias insisted.'

'Good. Prepare yourself for more if I'm your Whispers.' She held my gaze. 'Keeping you alive will be *my* responsibility. I'll use everything that helps me – including more guards.'

'Very well.' I wanted to smile, but feared she might think I was belittling her. Her green dress, embroidered in yellow and white, suited her. Something flared in my chest – determination? stubbornness? – at her firm tone. I noted the sensation, then put it aside to examine later.

Miss Bayonn cleared her throat. 'I want to go after Vigrante's inner circle.'

Neither Lady Brenna nor Lord Hazell liked me, though they'd certainly liked the benefits of Uncle's money through Vigrante. 'Do you suspect they're connected to your father's murder?'

'Not entirely. But attacking his power base will weaken him.' She hesitated. 'And the situation with Lord Naruum?'

'He is currently my guest.' A guest behind locked doors, with the weight of execution over his head. 'When he's not succumbing to hysterics, he's not saying much, and none of it useful. It wasn't a particularly *good* attempt. Even if I refused the wine and offended the Opposition, I would have eventually mended things.'

'An assassination doomed to fail?'

'Possibly.' I frowned, rubbing my thumbnail over my lower lip. 'Lord Naruum and Lady Brenna knew each other as children. There may be a link there.' I glanced up, just as Miss Bayonn's gaze slid away.

'Emotions make people do foolish things,' she said.

'Like brandishing daggers?'

She smiled ruefully. 'Perhaps. By becoming your Whispers, I can avenge my father. You gain little if I become your spymaster.'

A sensible observation. 'Matthias is loyal, and we're practically family. Now that our friendship is known, he's too obvious a choice for Whispers.'

Miss Bayonn nodded.

'You're the youngest Treasury employee in decades. And Coin

wouldn't have accepted you unless he considered you an asset.'

She stayed silent.

'Matthias loved your father more than his own. Not a day goes by that he doesn't feel the loss.' He'd never tell Miss Bayonn, reluctant to encroach on her grief, but she needed to know so they could work together.

'So I'm good with budgets and need to feel sorry for Matthias more,' Miss Bayonn said. 'Hardly the qualities of a spymaster.'

Apart from Matthias, no one had spoken so frankly to me in years. I'd forgotten what it felt like, a spark against the stifling duty, etiquette, and pomp that had surrounded me since childhood.

'You watch and listen,' I said. 'You broke into my wing through the passages. You want to avenge your father and you're willing to be ruthless. My Whispers must be ruthless.' Matthias called me too idealistic, but I'd grown up in a part of Edar where it was easy to die from freezing cold and starving predators. I'd always known I'd have to make brutal decisions, and so would my Whispers. 'Matthias believes in you,' I continued, 'and when dangerous situations arose, you didn't hesitate to help. That gives me faith in you.'

I couldn't decipher her expression.

'I want to approach Lady Patrinne,' she said. 'Her daughter, Terize, works with me in the Treasury. If I convince you to accept her into your ladies, I think Patrinne will offer her support. She could be a Parliament informant.'

I leaned back, considering. I'd invited Lady Patrinne to the Opposition gathering because it would have been worse not to. After my aunt's insult, I hadn't thought I could easily gain her support.

'Yes, it's worth it a try.' I stood and went to fill two small glasses of rosé. In the north, we drank it to celebrate and mourn. In winter, we mulled it. It tasted like home. Our fingers brushed as I passed a glass to her.

'To your new position, Miss Bayonn.'

'To new partnerships, Your Majesty.'

We drank.

When she turned to leave, I lingered on her waist and the hinted flare of her hip.

I drank the last of my wine too quickly. Unlike the spark, this tightness in my chest wouldn't be examined later.

Ψ Ψ Ψ

Mother eyed my barely touched plate. 'Queen or not, I can still scold you for not eating.'

I sighed.

Now that I was crowned, everyone wanted everything done at once. Meetings after meetings; endless paperwork needing my signature and seal, much of it neglected by Uncle. Adding insult to injury, Vigrante rejected my legislative proposals and returned them with 'suggestions'. Almost a week after my coronation, all I felt was exhausted and worried. I hadn't once seen Uncle look how I felt; he'd passed control of Edar to others for an easier life.

His route was sometimes tempting. But Mother would never forgive me. She'd raised me as Father would have wanted. Taking the easy way out was unacceptable.

Mother's annoyance turned to concern. 'My dear, are you sleeping? You don't look well.'

'I'm fine.'

The concern changed to parental outrage. 'How do you expect to rule well if you're not eating or sleeping properly?'

'I manage.' I poured the wine. 'Here. We might as well have it out while drinking.'

Her face crumpled back into hurt. 'That's how you consider spending time with me?'

'No, of course not!' Mother opened her mouth. I gripped my wine glass. 'But that's what it feels like. I'm already dealing with enough people who think they know better than me. Forgive me for thinking you were the one person who'd leave me be!'

I hadn't realised my voice had risen until the last words rang out. I put the wine glass down before I accidentally shattered it.

Mother laid her hand over mine. 'Eat,' she said gently. 'You'll feel better.'

The food was delicately flavoured and exactly the same as the

Court's. My aunt and uncle had dined privately and requested different meals. I'd stopped this within days of returning to Arkaala. Jienne still dined separately out of spite, but now she ate the same food as everyone else. I tried to eat with the Court, but some days I couldn't face it.

'I wish you'd talk to me more,' Mother said after a while.

My mouthful turned sour. Matthias would appreciate me complaining to someone else. But Mother couldn't listen without offering her own opinions, especially when I didn't want them.

'You have enough to worry about,' I said.

'You think I don't worry about nobles trying to poison you?'

'It's being dealt with,' I said flatly, before we could get into the same argument again. She wanted me to punish Lord Naruum's family, which I'd refused: they'd already disowned him. Matthias had filtered rumours into the Court about Naruum's supposed confessions, rendering the gossip useless. The Steps had turned to fresher news as Matthias continued his interrogation.

'Instead of needlessly worrying you,' I said, 'perhaps we could have another arrangement?'

Mother narrowed her eyes.

'You know things others won't tell me now.' Now that I was Queen, people only spoke of banal matters. It was lonely.

'Indeed,' she said.

'If there's anything you hear that would benefit me, I'd appreciate being told.'

Mother laughed and patted my hand. 'Lia, such formality! You want me to spy for you. I already do, as I spied for your grandfather and your father.'

My face grew warm. Lord Vigrante and the Court underestimated me. I had to remember not to do it to others.

We settled to finish the wine. Mother leaned her cheek against her fist and frowned.

'What?' I'd slipped from Queen to the easier role of daughter.

'Be careful of Lord Vigrante,' she said.

'Oh, believe me, Vigrante and I understand each other perfectly. Our dislike is so sincere, it doesn't even need acknowledgement.'

'Have you had much luck gaining allies from the Opposition?'

'I'm getting there.'

'Yes, when Third Step girls aren't tripping into nobles,' Mother said.

'Nobles with poisoned bottles of wine! And Miss Bayonn is Fifth Step now, *born* Third.'

'But really, my dear, having her join your ladies?'

'No one else reacted so quickly,' I said quietly. 'Matthias trusts her, and I trust him. I need the nobles to forget the wine and Lord Naruum.' I had to pretend the poisoning meant nothing, or I would crack in public and never recover.

'Oh. That's simple,' Mother said. 'Pick carefully from the Opposition, and increase their standing in Court. Offer improved marriage prospects for their children. If one of your ladies wears something interesting, make it a fashion statement but credit them – something your uncle and aunt never learned. Do all this, and *suggest* they steer gossip in new directions.'

I poured her the last of the wine. 'Keep talking.'

CHAPTER TEN

XANIA

The windows and glass doors took up a wall facing a courtyard, filling the room with sunlight. Everyone's jewels glittered and their silks gleamed. The small dining room was for the Sixth and Seventh Steps, admittance controlled by servants. Only the Queen's mark, stamped with the briar and sword, had got me through the doors, and an abrupt silence had descended upon my entrance.

Above the Fifth Step, the noble ranks thinned. The families could trace their bloodlines back centuries. Many claimed an ancestor who'd married into royalty at some point. They never sold their estates to pay debts. It was possible to marry up into the Fifth. Marrying into the Sixth was difficult; reaching the Seventh was a generations-long aspiration.

Edarans boasted about our flexible nobility. Just not that it took generations to reach the highest ranks.

They all grew up in the same little world, so they knew I didn't belong.

I was, however, Mama's daughter, so I held my head up as I was led to an empty table. Gossip hissed around me. By the time I was seated, everyone likely knew I was the one who had careened into Lord Naruum.

Lady Brenna and Lord Hazell sat nearby. While they were at a table of Hazell's friends, Brenna was in control. Her peach dress warmed her bare shoulders. If she wasn't loyal to Vigrante, it would have been distracting.

She glanced at me, then returned her attention to her table.

After nearly an hour, Lady Patrinne finally swept in. Her yellow silk dress must have cost a fortune, though she showed her pride in the cream overdress, neatly embroidered in gold and studded with yellow topaz shards. Her table was at an angle so she could watch everyone else.

I swigged the last of my tea, arranged my napkin to signal I'd return for my belongings, and stood.

Recognition sparked on Patrinne's face as I approached. She sipped lemon-water. 'Miss Bayonn. Has the Queen's favour propelled Lord Martain up to the Sixth?'

'Not quite, Lady Patrinne.' I forced a smile. 'I'm here at Her Majesty's behest. May I sit?'

'No. I find my appetite suddenly insufficient. Come, walk with me.' She stood, linked her arm through mine, and politely dragged me though the glass doors and into the courtyard.

Lady Patrinne's blonde hair had silvered at her temples. Her mouth naturally turned downward. We walked through the courtyard to a gravel path running parallel to the walled gardens. 'I understand your family doesn't move in *certain circles*, but you should know the Queen values subtlety above all else.'

I remembered the Queen smiling before she threw open the doors to fling me at the politicians' mercy. 'So I've heard.' Patrinne flicked an irritated glance towards me, and I added, 'My lady.'

She sniffed. 'Why did you choose that dining room to approach me?'

'It's loud. We wouldn't be easily overheard.'

'Never underestimate the Court's ability to eavesdrop,' she said. 'No one can hide on this path. If someone approaches, we can easily see or hear them and change topics. So: Her Majesty needs me as an ally.'

'I'm sure she can be convinced to accept Terize into her ladies.'

'If Her Majesty holds me in such regard, why send *you* with the overture?'

The air was cool. A pleasant fragrance still lingered from the morning rain. It should have been peaceful.

'Because the other ladies find Terize ridiculous,' I said. 'The Queen needs to hear about her from me.'

Lady Patrinne pursed her mouth. 'Unsurprising. Terize has never made particularly good impressions.'

It would help if Patrinne didn't always rip Terize to shreds. 'Others don't give her the chance to shine,' I remarked.

'One works with what is at one's disposal.'

We lapsed into tense silence. Our heels crunched against the gravel.

There was no easy way to segue into this. 'I'm not solely here on the Queen's business.'

Patrinne smiled. 'And we come to the crux of the matter.'

I put my hand into a pocket, withdrew a white mark stamped with an embellished *W*, and held it out. 'I'm also here on the spider's business.'

Lady Patrinne stopped, watching me uneasily. 'What have you entangled yourself in, child?'

My stomach dropped. I'd been so focused on proving myself to the Queen, and what becoming Whispers would mean for avenging Papa, that I'd forgotten the Master of Whispers was feared and rarely spoken of.

'This is not like attracting the Queen's notice,' she said. 'Those tangled in such schemes don't escape them.'

'Too late.' The Queen had agreed it would be easier for me to pretend that I was a spoke in the Whispers' wheel, caught in his schemes, instead of the actual spymaster. Now I questioned our wisdom.

'And what is the spider's incentive for my co-operation?'

'Alexandris will fall, eventually,' I said. 'He isn't strong enough to lead the Opposition.'

Lady Patrinne smiled mirthlessly. 'Does the spider plan to put me in his place as an obedient puppet?'

'In return for your co-operation, and *information* that will benefit the Queen, the spider will aid you when the Opposition seeks new leadership.'

Her expression turned calculating. She had her own sources for dirt on her political colleagues, but to have a spymaster help ruin her opponents... 'And if I reject the offer?'

'The Master of Whispers wonders if your eldest daughter knows *precisely* why her beloved abandoned his suit?'

Lady Patrinne's shoulders stiffened.

'And does your eldest son know you threatened to destroy a lady's family because she had the misfortune to love him?'

She seemed calm, though unaware that she was rubbing her thumb and forefinger together. Her expression shifted, revealing the tiniest spark of approval, possibly even grudging respect. 'Well played, Miss Bayonn. Well played.'

'Have you reconsidered your position?'

'Yes. I must regretfully decline.'

I ground to a halt. 'I beg your pardon?'

'Even if I responded well to threats,' Lady Patrinne said, 'you're playing a dangerous game. You won't survive.'

'And if Terize were to join the Queen's ladies?'

'I might reconsider. But that depends on how close you are to Her Majesty, doesn't it? Good afternoon, Miss Bayonn.' She walked on ahead, until she turned and disappeared from view.

I'd been so confident, so assured in the power of Whispers, that it had never occurred to me that someone would refuse. A spymaster without informants was useless.

I returned to the dining room and ordered a carafe of pear cordial. A bad taste, suspiciously like failure, lingered in my mouth.

CHAPTER ELEVEN

LIA

Miss Bayonn seemed convinced she could waltz into a position she'd never held and effortlessly juggle it with her Treasury work. As Queen, I admired her determination. As myself, I wanted to point out she was useless to me if she collapsed from exhaustion.

When she wasn't buried under her Treasury work, she pored over files, especially those of Vigrante's oldest allies, trying to find a financial error, strange or deliberate, or any link to Naruum.

While I worried about Vigrante, and the fragile trust between the Court and myself, my future marriage loomed. It made sense to choose a husband from abroad, as I'd invite internal fighting by choosing an Edaran one. Through my contacts, Miss Bayonn was also setting up new agents in the foreign Courts, especially in my potential suitors' retinues.

Some days it felt like snails could make faster progress than me. The politicians from the lower Steps and middle classes wanted progressive change, and the oldest Step families were equally determined to dig their heels in. I was left dealing with the ill will.

I resisted the urge to rub my eyes. I'd called this meeting; I had to stay awake during it. Miss Bayonn drummed her fingers against her armrest. My gaze fell on her slim hands; my own fingers twitched, and I pressed them against my lap.

'For people so close to Vigrante,' she said, 'Brenna and Hazell's records are spotless. Their families are successful; they pay their debts reasonably on time; they don't hold grudges for generations. My stepfather annoys more people on a daily basis.'

'Spotless records are probably one of Vigrante's conditions.'

'They're all hiding *something*,' Miss Bayonn muttered.

I thought of my twitching fingers, and stayed silent. *You're the Queen. Control yourself.*

'I've been thinking–'

'Oh dear.'

'I want to try and build a relationship with Lord Naruum,' Miss Bayonn said, politely ignoring my attempt at humour. 'Gain his trust. Matthias can only threaten him for so long.' She grimaced. 'I know Lady Brenna must have something to do with this, but the family has closed ranks–'

'Unsurprising.'

'–and everyone has apparently forgotten they knew each other.'

'If there's something they don't want anyone else knowing,' I said, 'the Sixth and Seventh Steps will ensure it's kept quiet. It's how we uphold our mystique.' I smiled at her unimpressed look.

'If Lady Brenna is behind the wine, she had to be nervous that Naruum will eventually confess.' She paused. 'How *is* he?'

'Perfectly well,' I said. He was still alive, which was more than he deserved.

'I still want to speak with him.'

'Of course. I must cut this short – I'm due at Parliament for the final arguments before the vote.'

Matthias and I had argued for weeks about my first legislation proposal, which would give merchants more control over their side of noble contracts – including breaking the contracts themselves, something only nobles could do up until now. He insisted I shouldn't alienate the higher Steps so soon. I felt it was better to gain the merchants' support.

I knew exactly how beneficial good relationships with merchants could be. While my family's estate was mostly known for sheep and wool, my income also involved herds of cattle and horses, and forest lumber. My ancestors had been shrewd business people long before they were royal; most of our merchant contracts went back generations.

Parliament, ideally, had equal numbers of merchants and the middle classes in their lower benches. Most had drifted to the Opposition because of Vigrante's broken promises, though Alexandris's good intentions rarely succeeded. I wanted the merchants and middle classes to help push my legislation through: a formidable voting bloc that Vigrante would have to take seriously.

If this proposal didn't pass, Matthias could crow all he liked.

Miss Bayonn nodded. 'Have you used my suggestions, Your Majesty?'

'Yes,' I said. 'You were right to clarify the selling clause.'

It wasn't uncommon for Step nobles to supplement their income through merchant trade. But contracts usually favoured the nobles, including profit percentages and the ability to dissolve the contract. Merchant families were often trapped in bad contracts, sometimes for generations, if the nobles wouldn't break them, with limited choice of routes and goods.

The new legislation would give merchants more choice and power, helped by opportunities to increase fleets and trade. They could depend less on nobles for additional income, eventually leading to increased competition, more variety, and hopefully lower prices.

Miss Bayonn had expressed reservations as the majority of her family's income came from trade. I'd said, repeatedly, that merchants wouldn't end profitable, beneficial relationships, but she'd taken it as a challenge to find gaps and loopholes in my proposal.

And she had. In my initial draft, I hadn't restricted nobles from selling their contracts out of embarrassed pride before merchants could break them. I hadn't considered it, precisely because it wasn't done. If nobles didn't break the contracts, they were inherited by their children. I wanted to give merchants a chance to free themselves of unfavourable contracts, if they wished. But nobles didn't sell them. It was an insult, and merchants passed down grave insults like heirlooms.

Miss Bayonn and I had rephrased the wording. As compensation for being one monarch against many politicians, I could see the legislation one final time before it was sealed and read out before the debates. I'd quietly slipped the restricted selling clause in this morning.

Lord Vigrante still underestimated me.

But I'd win.

Miss Bayonn's posture relaxed. 'It was a logical addition.'

'Well, your logic is an asset.'

'Vigrante won't settle for this.'

'Of course not.'

'He'll humiliate you, somehow.'

'Then we must anticipate his response.'

She nodded, then rose after me.

'Good afternoon, Miss Bayonn.'

She curtseyed. 'Good afternoon, Your Majesty. May the vote go in your favour.'

Her skirts swirled. I dropped back into my chair after the door closed. I didn't have time for this. I was *not* like Uncle, distracted by foolishness and – and – *swirling skirts*.

I had an argument to win.

Uncle had only sat with Parliament to open it, so in that respect, I was already an improvement.

The legislation was now out of my hands, but I still had control over my appearance. I'd changed into a blue tunic-style jacket, split at the sides and back for easier movement, with trousers and heeled boots. My hair was braided and coiled so the crown would sit easier. As heavy as the damn thing was, I had to wear it before the politicians.

I stood in the antechamber, trying not to pluck at my clothing. If the vote went my way today, it would set the standard for all my future political involvement.

A servant knocked and entered at my call. 'Lord Vigrante wishes for an audience, Your Majesty.'

There was nothing left to discuss.

The servant admitted him.

Vigrante smiled and bowed. 'Your Majesty.' His red jacket was embroidered in golden roses as bright as his hair.

'Lord Vigrante.' I remained standing.

'I wanted to wish you luck, Your Majesty. One's first Parliament is always the most difficult.'

Vigrante probably had his merchant contracts ready to sell if my legislation passed. He hadn't mentioned the loophole, and I also intended to stay quiet.

'You're most kind, Lord Vigrante.' It was easier to use politeness to hide the rage and indignation bubbling in my chest. He wouldn't have tried to undermine Uncle, but then, he wouldn't have had to.

'Your uncle had faith in Parliament,' Vigrante said. 'No one would judge you for sharing that same faith.'

Of course you would.

'Then I must beg you to have faith in me, Lord Vigrante. And it wouldn't do to open Parliament late, would it?'

He went still, then said, 'No, Your Majesty,' before leaving.

I stood by the door. Shouting and the creak of wood filtered through, as the ministers took their seats amid last-minute discussion.

The servant approached and bowed. 'Your Majesty, they're ready.'

The doors creaked open. As my titles were bellowed out, I fixed my gaze on the royal banner over the throne and started towards it.

I sat and swept my gaze across Vigrante and the rows of nobles, middle classes, and merchants. 'Members of Parliament' – my voice rang against the walls – 'I bid you welcome. Who has the opening arguments?'

Everything went as expected, all centred on the nobility's concerns. They didn't care if merchants were trapped by poor contracts or unrealistic demands, or feared a vindictive noble would ruin their reputations, once nothing changed for them.

The politicians retorted at each other, while I kept my attention on Vigrante. He was cool, unruffled.

I only spoke when tempers frayed, or the Steps tried to drown out the merchants. While people found it amusing when Parliament debates turned into shouting matches, it wasn't enjoyable being in the middle of one.

'How can changing trade agreements benefit Edar at all, never mind the Steps?' a noble demanded from Vigrante's upper benches. 'The merchants already have enough power.'

Gasps and hisses rang from the merchant benches. There was rarely much love between the Steps and merchants, but nobles generally tried not to openly show their scorn.

'The merchants are the wheels that keep our trade moving,' I said. 'More competition means lower prices, which means more employment and money spent, which eventually benefits us all.'

The Government attempted to rile the Opposition, coaxing them towards a shouting match that would only benefit them. I stayed quiet, too aware of Vigrante watching me, waiting for my strike as I waited for his.

I straightened; the arguments fractured into silence. 'We're doing no one any favours by twisting ourselves into knots.' I kept my tone pleasant, my hands relaxed against the armrests. 'May the legislation be read out?'

Nobles fidgeted during the reading. Vigrante remained calm, almost bored – until the inability to sell existing contracts was announced.

For one wonderful moment, his calm faltered.

Silence spread through the chamber. The nobles' expressions ranged from shocked to calculated, while the merchants and middle classes looked astonished.

'Why the shock?' I asked. 'I wouldn't expect anyone in Court or Parliament to fear these clauses.' And if they *did* have something to fear, now they were warned: the days of my uncle's Court were over.

Vigrante recovered first. 'Of course not, Your Majesty. No one has anything to fear.'

The mood had turned: the merchants and middle classes were almost gleeful. I'd cornered the Steps neatly: if they didn't vote it through, it would seem they wanted unfair contracts to continue. The ones who built friendly terms with their merchants, like the Bayonns, would be elaborate and showy in their vote, keen to embrace change that would eventually 'benefit us all'.

Lord Ealkenor called for a vote, backed by Lady Patrinne, whose daughter had joined my ladies two days before. I silently counted each raised hand and 'Aye'.

When the vote tipped in my favour, Vigrante's clenched jaw betrayed him.

CHAPTER TWELVE

XANIA

The Parliament arguments went deep into the evening. Once again, I was the last one in the Treasury. Even Coin had retired, probably waiting for whatever headaches the new legislation would bring.

My head throbbed as I stared at numbers. When the clock chimed, I finally locked my work away and left. The halls were mostly deserted – I'd missed the evening meal, and everyone had returned to their rooms or joined small gatherings. I ducked down a small corridor and into the passages. As I trailed my fingers along the shimmering walls, rage boiled in my veins.

I stepped out into a corridor on the opposite side of the palace, shut up for years as the old King had preferred his courtiers close by. My heels thumped against thin carpet as I approached a plain dark door. Two guards stood on either side. I held out a note embossed with the royal seal.

One of the guards entered with me and shut the door behind

us. Dim candlelight flickered, high on the walls so Naruum couldn't use it as a weapon against himself or anyone else. The room smelled of dust.

The light couldn't soften the circles under his eyes, the deep lines around his mouth, or how his skull strained against his skin. His hair was still dark brown and curly, his nose and cheekbones still strong. But a good nose didn't make up for poor judgment. I'd never like him, but I still internally recoiled at the hopelessness in his sunken eyes.

'Lord Naruum.' I sat at the opposite side of the table. 'How are you?' Chains were looped and secured through holes gouged into the wood, keeping him manacled to the table and chair. He ate and slept in an adjoining room, one arm still chained.

'I'm perfectly well. Comfortable beyond all expectations.' His words began sarcastic, then trailed into resigned despair; this *was* better than anything he could have hoped for. He rocked back and forth for a few moments, the chains grating against the table, before he added, 'I know I'm at the Queen's mercy.'

I sighed. 'Lord Naruum, you know damn well no monarch would drink from an untested glass.'

A strange expression, a mix of shame and relief, flickered across his face.

My eyebrows jutted together. 'You panicked' – he jerked – 'or you wanted to fail. Or both. I'd panic if I were to assassinate the Queen in public.'

He eyed me loftily. 'You forget yourself, *Miss* Bayonn.'

'Yes, yes, I should be ashamed, with my Third Step roots and Fifth Step notions.' I didn't need a mirror to know my smile wasn't friendly. 'Try a different song, Lord Naruum. If I believed it, I wouldn't be able to get out of bed in the morning.' It was almost a relief to finally say what I so often thought. Lord Naruum could no longer depend on rank and etiquette as a shield. Here in this dusty room, he may have been Sixth Step, but I held the power. I was in control.

'Did you think slamming into me would win you royal favour?'

'I had the least to lose by stopping you,' I said.

'You had no way of knowing the wine was poisoned.'

'I couldn't know it *wasn't.*'

Had he been duped? An attempt to bring about his downfall through the Queen? It might explain his embarrassing sloppiness. But whoever he'd allied with, whoever he was trying to protect, he must have trusted them to offer the Queen untested wine.

The Queen had said Lord Naruum and Lady Brenna had been childhood friends.

Naruum was already teetering towards brittle fear. I could work with this.

'Lady Brenna,' I said. 'Her new wardrobe is lovely, isn't it?'

His expression slackened, before his cheeks reddened. 'I have no idea what you mean. We haven't spoken in years.'

I practically tasted his lie on the air. I imagined it like a sharp briar between us that would draw blood if he made another mistake.

My smile was as cruel as any twist of thorns. 'Of course, Lord Naruum.' I stood. 'The Queen believes someone else is hiding behind your actions. No one has confessed. No one has begged for your life. Only Her Majesty and myself believe in you, Lord Naruum, and you won't help us.'

His face twisted. The chains clicked together as he sagged. 'I'm afraid you're mistaken, Miss Bayonn. I acted alone.'

I drew out my silence until I held out my closed fist between us. I opened my fingers to reveal the Whispers' mark.

'The Queen's mercy doesn't last forever, nor does the Whispers',' I said gently, surprised at the pity pricking my chest. But then, he *was* pitiful.

Lord Naruum swallowed.

I left. As I made my way back through the passages, I turned over the conversation in my head, trying to find a crack I could coax wider.

A Pastry apprentice with a crush on Zola had introduced me to a maid assigned to Lady Brenna's rooms. I wasn't entirely certain of the maid's loyalty, but I paid her to inform me of Brenna's comings and goings, and any overheard snippets about meetings or conversations. Nothing useful yet, but Brenna could still slip up.

Naruum's family. He hadn't mentioned them, and I hadn't

supplied any information, waiting to see if he'd ask. But he seemed too afraid to know if they'd been punished for his actions, or if they'd rejected him to save themselves from royal fury.

His sister, who loved him the most, still wanted to see him, even though their parents had disowned him. But if anyone could bend the rules, it was the Queen – and me.

CHAPTER THIRTEEN

LIA

I held up my glass. 'To success!'

'To further success,' Matthias retorted.

Miss Bayonn smiled and clinked her glass with ours.

The whiskey burned pleasantly.

'If you keep this up, Your Majesty,' Matthias said, 'the Master of Coin might offer to bed you in a fit of joy.'

The whiskey tore through my throat as I choked.

I scowled at Matthias, trying to suck in air without coughing. 'He's more likely to sleep with you!'

'Not my type, Your Majesty, thank you,' Matthias said.

I changed the subject to safer ground than bedrooms, too conscious of the morning sunlight against Miss Bayonn's skin. 'Have your family's merchant partners cancelled your contracts, as you feared, Miss Bayonn?'

'No, Your Majesty,' she admitted. 'But it's only been twelve hours.'

I kept smiling. 'Unscrupulous nobles will be fretting today.'

I'd almost sent a servant to find her last night, after the vote had gone through. Matthias had reminded me she was visiting Lord Naruum and probably wouldn't want to deal with us afterwards. So I'd left her alone, but sent a summons this morning.

Matthias drained his glass and grimaced. 'It's too early for whiskey.'

'It's my first legislative victory,' I said. 'We'll drink if I want to.'

'How *royally authoritative* of you, Your Majesty,' Matthias said. 'Now you've actually accomplished something, the nobles will be clambering to offer their support. I need to rearrange your schedule.'

'You may leave, Matthias.' I pointed to the folders on her lap. 'Miss Bayonn and I must discuss Lord Naruum.'

Matthias paused, then bowed and wished us a good morning.

After he shut the doors, I asked, 'How did Naruum seem last night?'

If I focused on him, then I wouldn't notice her mouth when she smiled.

I could not look at her mouth.

I'd spent years avoiding the Court's romantic games, too conscious of the power my favour held. While everyone else had flirted, and kissed, and fondled in the shadows, I'd nursed Matthias through his heartbreaks. But when a girl smiled at me, her gaze lingering a moment too long...

And now Miss Bayonn had rushed headlong into my path.

And somehow, over the last few weeks, my mind and body had inexplicably decided: *Yes, you. There's something about you that makes it difficult for me to concentrate on ruling a country.* A lady who enjoyed balancing accounts and daydreamed about ruining everyone she hated.

If Father could see me now, he'd disinherit me on the spot.

'Naruum is nervous and resigned to his fate,' she said. 'When I mentioned Lady Brenna, he claimed they hadn't spoken in years, but his reaction hinted otherwise.'

I tilted my hand so the whiskey slapped against the glass. 'If Brenna's behind this, it's reasonable to assume she's carrying out Vigrante's orders.'

'He wouldn't approve of anything so sloppy.'

'He probably didn't intend on sloppiness.'

I rubbed the groove between my eyes. 'Vigrante can't be allowed get away with this. If he's not behind it, we can't let him think no one will be punished for attempting to kill me.'

Miss Bayonn nodded. 'Lord Naruum doesn't know his family has disowned him.'

'You believe him so easily swayed?'

'You didn't see his panic. If he's working with Lady Brenna, he believes wholeheartedly in whatever she convinced him.'

'You have an idea?'

'Lord Naruum is close to his sister. If I let her see him...'

'And knowing Brenna has abandoned him—'

'He'll have no one to turn to, except me,' Miss Bayonn finished.

'Clever,' I said.

To many, especially those who didn't spend time at Court, this would seem heartless. But the Court devoured itself with gossip, speculation, and backstabbing – only to be expected when many nobles stayed in Arkaala and employed others to run their estates. Manipulating and destroying others was always appealing when one didn't have anything else to do.

Lord Naruum had to confess.

I handed her a sheet of thick, smooth paper. 'And to add to your problems.'

Miss Bayonn frowned, brushing a finger across the signature and wax seal. 'Your Farezi cousin certainly condescends to you.'

'Rassa's unbearable.' My great-granduncle had married into Farezi after Great-Grandfather had become King. This also meant that Rassa, the Farezi prince and a general pain in the neck, was also my heir until I had a child. 'If you've anything else to report, please tell me it's better news.'

'Not really,' she admitted. 'The west is getting too much rain, but it's not going south. An improved harvest is unlikely. We need to buy more grain from Farezi.'

I sighed. 'Before they get wind of this and we have to negotiate against their grain's sudden, astonishing price hike. Has bad is the flooding?'

'It's affected the usual estates,' Miss Bayonn said, 'but the rivers have coped so far.'

'Put it out that we're monitoring the situation.' If the worst happened, and the west was hit by chronic flooding, I'd have to pull the money from somewhere – upsetting *someone* – and the south would immediately demand help with their drought.

I drummed my fingers. 'We could offer a financial incentive for the western nobles to collect rain water and send it south. Or the southern nobles could compensate with trade... I'll speak to Coin. I insist things will be different to Uncle's reign, and yet still ask him to pull money from thin air.'

'Everything costs, Your Majesty. Even good deeds,' Miss Bayonn said. 'I have nothing further to report. If that's all...?'

'Of course.' I made to stand, then blurted, 'The ladies are kind to you and your sister, yes?' I didn't expect the truth – one didn't tattle, and the ladies would be clever enough to make their snobbery difficult to prove. But though the official meeting was over, I didn't want her to leave.

Miss Bayonn paused her paper shuffling and slowly met my gaze. 'They're perfectly cordial, Your Majesty. Lady Astrii often enquires about my work in the Treasury.'

I brightened. 'Lady Astrii is interesting. You should encourage that friendship.' I regretted the words immediately. Astrii's family were high Sixth Step and friendship overtures could only come from her.

Miss Bayonn smiled wryly. 'And Lady Terize and I are friends, of course. She's always pleased to see me. Sometimes it's a relief. Sometimes not.' She hesitated, then added, 'I'm seeing one of my family's merchants later this evening. I'll gauge the mood on your new legislation.'

I smiled. 'Has your mother promoted you?'

She scowled. 'If I can do extra work for Coin *and* you, Mama feels there's no reason I can't do the same for her.'

My smile threatened to turn into a grin.

Something flickered across her face, too quick for me to catch. 'I'm expected at the Treasury soon – with your permission?'

I took the hint and stood. 'Thank you, Miss Bayonn.'

'I'm at your service, Your Majesty.' Her formal words only strengthened my embarrassment. After the door closed behind her, I dropped my face into my hands and groaned. This is what attraction turned me into?

Matthias would howl with laughter if I even hinted about this, no matter that I'd nursed him through his many heartbreaks. It would pass soon enough, especially when the suitors came. I'd grit my teeth and bear it.

Somehow.

CHAPTER FOURTEEN

XANIA

After dinner, I hurried back to my rooms to prepare for my meeting with Lariux, one of my family's merchant contacts. At one of the large intersections, I slowed in the crush of people feeding from several halls and a large staircase.

Lady Patrinne appeared beside me, her deceptively light grip iron-strong around my arm. 'Walk with me, Miss Bayonn.' She steered me through the crowd.

'The hall furthest to the left,' I said.

'Rushing somewhere?' she asked as we entered it. The crowd gradually thinned around us.

'A merchant meeting in the city.'

Patrinne raised an eyebrow. 'Worried about your family's contracts? Your mother would hardly treat merchants unfairly, especially considering her previous *career*.'

We weren't ashamed of Mama's old banking career; it was how she and Papa had met. My great-grandmother had come from Rijaan, promoted until she'd helped stabilise Edar's banks in the aftermath of the Queen's ancestor usurping the crown. Mama's gift for numbers far surpassed mine, and her budgeting ability had saved us after Papa's death. She'd kept up his merchant contracts for the income, though it mostly bulked up our dowries; as a Fifth Step lady and wife, it would be unseemly for her to return to banking.

'I'm getting new contracts signed, if you must know,' I said.

Her nails dug into my sleeve, forcing me to keep step with her. 'I wish to apologise.'

'Are you ill, Lady Patrinne?'

Her glittering smile could have cut glass. 'Don't *try* me, Miss Bayonn. Or I will abruptly recover from this bout of reconsideration.'

'Reconsideration?'

'I have been thinking.'

I swallowed the urge to retort: *A dangerous pastime*. 'Oh?'

'Perhaps I was too hasty when we last met,' she said. 'Information is power, after all, and we both need it.'

'And...?' There was also the matter of Terize now being one of the Queen's ladies, despite Patrinne's skepticism that I could make it happen.

'There are conditions.'

Of course there were. Patrinne's love for her children probably came with conditions. 'Yes?'

'In exchange for information I feel is pertinent to your

employer's interests, I want safety and advance notice if there are manoeuverings that could affect my family and me.'

'Your talent for escaping a room before it goes up in flames is well-known.'

She laughed.

My brain flicked through conflicting thoughts, trying to decipher everything Patrinne wasn't saying: *We are not public allies, I will not help you if your ties to Whispers are discovered.* 'What else?'

'Foreign royalty will soon descend upon us.'

I'd already waved goodbye to more of my precious time.

'I want you to save Terize from herself.'

I ground to a halt, forcing Patrinne to stop with me. 'So she can marry well?'

'I'd be obliged if she managed it.'

I glared at her. 'Terize doesn't need my help.'

'You're Fifth Step,' Patrinne said. 'You have no idea of the headache involved in marrying off Sixth Step children.'

I did, actually. Matthias had quizzed me until I knew the family trees by heart. The convoluted bloodlines and marriages would make anyone's head hurt.

'Fine. If there's a chance of a good match, I'll help Terize.' Unless Zola caught someone's eye, in which case Terize would have to help herself.

Patrinne eyed me, as if guessing my thoughts, then nodded. 'Very well.' As we resumed walking, she added, 'I've heard...

interesting rumours about Lord Naruum's current living arrangements.'

I sighed. 'Enlighten me, Lady Patrinne. I know you're desperate to rub my ignorance in my face.'

'Tell your employer,' she said, 'that when he next speaks with Lord Naruum, perhaps he should ask why Lady Brenna broke off their engagement.'

I opened my mouth, but nothing came out. We were outside by now, crunching in gravel that led to a tiered terrace garden. Patrinne released me and headed towards the terrace.

'Wait!'

She turned, her head politely tilted to the side.

'You warned me last time about playing my hand in public,' I said. 'But we were in the corridors for this entire conversation. Anyone could have heard us.'

She smiled, satisfied, like I'd proven myself. 'Courtiers gossip and plot and scheme, Miss Bayonn. Even Her Majesty would worry if we stopped. If things were overheard, consider this: both of us were careful not to mention any words that would be the most damning of all.' She sank into a mocking curtesy. 'Perhaps there are things even I can teach you in your current *situation*.'

As she walked away, I wasn't sure whether to admire her cunning, scream, or do both.

Arkaala had built itself on and around hills. The higher you went, the more room there was to build in peaceful quiet.

After the Second Empire's fall, the merchant families had flourished, free of the trade stranglehold. The most successful families had slowly encroached upon a hill and bought homes as noble lines ended or floundered in financial difficulty.

Ten years ago, soon after Papa started negotiated trading contracts with him, Lariux finally moved his family further up a hill.

We sat in Lariux's office on a mezzanine overlooking his training pen. Two apprentices sat at their desks, pretending not to be curious about our conversation. I'd known Lariux for years. Papa had brought me along to his meetings, where I'd quietly read with a glass of cordial.

I'd somehow become an equal to Lariux, of sorts. As Whispers, I now had my own office. It was worlds away from sitting elbow-to-cheek in the Treasury pit. I didn't want Coin's position – too much stress – but trying to concentrate while surrounded by the yelling, swearing, and tears associated with Edar's finances, I often wanted his office.

After Matthias and I had fought the assassin, and from my daydreams about avenging Papa, I'd expected drama and tension to always accompany the Whispers position. The situation with Naruum *was* tense, but being Whispers also involved a *lot* of paperwork.

Along with building new relationships with palace servants, I'd put out feelers for likely informants in the Steps. I'd also sent my first batch of letters to potential agents abroad. I'd written, and burnt, and rewritten them, worried that my words sounded too young and the foreign agents would refuse me.

I hadn't realised so much of being Whispers involved sitting still, waiting for my webs to vibrate. But the webs wouldn't vibrate unless I did something, so I kept a firm grip on my worry, sent the enquiries, and cajoled people into giving me information.

When I mentioned the waiting, the Queen said, 'And what happens if you die while chasing after information? My uncle never divulged the identity of his Whispers to me, and I'll have none as your network crumbles. If you are caught, my secrets aren't safe. The Master of Whispers has always kept the webs strong for others to run along. That will not change.'

But if I couldn't run on the webs, how would I discover the truth about Papa's murder?

'Miss Bayonn?'

I wrenched my attention back to Lariux. 'My apologies, Mr Bisset.' I handed him papers. 'These are the changes Mama proposes for some of the contracts. Nothing unusual, but she acknowledges things have... changed.'

Lariux took a swig of cider. 'That's one way of putting it.'

As we haggled, he didn't treat me differently to Mama. He tested me, mostly for stubbornness and confidence, not lack of experience. I occasionally chanced beyond Mama's suggestions, mostly to see how he'd react, and received the verbal equivalent of a gentle smack on the head.

When we were finished, Lariux leaned back in his chair and held up the cider jug. 'Another?'

I smiled. 'No, thank you. I should get back.' By now, Lord Martain's carriage driver should have scoffed a meal and gossiped with the staff. If I sweet-talked her, she might tell me something interesting. 'How do people feel about the Queen's new legislation?'

Lariux eyed me. 'There was some immediate concern, of course. Most expected a hidden sting.' He sighed. 'I never intended to cut ties with your mother – why would I throw away good business? But the long-term benefits will be considerable.'

We jumped at a clanging bell from outside, followed by a shrill whistling. The city guard's request for back-up, rarely heard on the hills. I bolted from my chair and hurried downstairs.

'Miss Bayonn!'

I ignored him. Outside, people rushed past Lariux's gate. Dread squeezed my throat and chest.

Lariux caught up with me and grabbed my arm. I whirled, barely stopping myself from lashing out.

He glared, panting. 'Your mother would have my guts if something happened to you.' I'd nicknamed him *the Fox*, after his thin face, red hair, and profit-inducing cunning, but he sometimes treated me more like a daughter than a business contact.

I glared back just as fiercely. 'You're not my parent, *Mr Bisset*. Let me go.'

His mouth thinned, but he released my arm and we rushed towards the crowd growing by a canal. The city guard was hauling something from the water.

Not something. *Someone.*

'A body,' a man muttered. The word hissed and rolled through the crowd: *body body body*.

People always ended up in the canals, and the river and the sea, despite royal and parliamentary disapproval; tainted water wasn't good for anyone. But the Steps fought with poison, and merchants battled each other with trade and besmirched reputations. Dumping someone into a canal was too crass for them.

'It's a boy!' the same man said, and all thoughts of crassness and reputations fled.

Lariux worked his jaw for a moment, then squeezed into the crowd. I followed right behind him.

I caught a glimpse of a pale face before the guards closed around the body, bellowing for us all to step back. Lariux moved towards the man who'd seen the body. 'Garjian, did you recognise him?'

Garjian nodded. 'Riavaan's eldest son.'

Lariux cursed.

Riavaan. I knew that name. They were one of the oldest, most distinguished merchant families. Vigrante had coerced them into contracts years ago, probably so he'd seem more legitimate as he rose to power. Marius Riavaan, the current patriarch, had supported the Queen's legislation, surprising everyone by going against Vigrante.

And now his eldest son was dead.

The Steps still peered down at merchants from the heights of their titles and bloodlines, but no one threatened their children. It wasn't good business. It wasn't *right*.

Garjian focused on me, wary rather than assessing. 'Who's your shadow, Lariux?'

'This is Miss Bayonn–'

Garjian's expression sharpened. 'The baron's daughter.'

'Yes,' I said.

Garjian looked from me to Lariux, his mouth downturned, as if he regretted saying anything around a noble, even one my age.

Lariux pressed his hand against my shoulder. 'We'll take our leave. Safe home, Garjian.'

We walked back in silence. As Lariux's gate loomed towards us, I asked, 'How old was he?'

'Fifteen, I believe.'

Only a little younger than Zola.

I wanted to stab something. Preferably Vigrante's heart.

'The family had contracts with our common friend.' I took great pleasure in alluding to Vigrante as such, as did Lariux. 'And when they broke them, he killed their son.'

I'd convinced the Queen to use the selling clause against Vigrante. In my own way, I'd caused this boy's murder. If I hadn't pushed, maybe this family would be furious at Vigrante for selling their contract, not in mourning.

'Surely someone witnessed him being thrown into the canal?' I asked.

'Possibly. If they're willing to admit it.'

There were rumours about a man who'd done Vigrante's dirty work for years. There was, of course, no direct link between them. But...

'This was sloppy,' I said.

'Yes,' Lariux said. 'Whoever did this won't be around for long.'

Once the connection between Vigrante and the Riavaan family became common knowledge, everyone would realise this was a message to the Queen. Many nobles were convinced she would 'see sense' and reverse the new laws, but more merchants than I'd expected planned to terminate contracts with difficult nobles. Vigrante hadn't waited for the Queen to reconsider.

I'd expected him to be angry.

I hadn't expected him to murder a boy.

I had to stop underestimating him. All of Vigrante's subtle manipulation eventually resulted in genuine repercussions. Papa's death had made that clear.

The Queen was going to burst a blood vessel when I told her. *Several* blood vessels.

I had to spin this to our benefit, somehow.

I stopped at Lariux's gate. 'I need a favour, Mr Bisset. Not for my family.'

He folded his arms.

'I need you to find out as much as possible about the murder, its investigation, and how the Riavaan family – and our common friend – respond. What they do and *don't* say. How soon the man we suspect ends up dead. Anything – I would greatly appreciate it.' This was about as subtle as a battering ram. But the boy's death meant there was no more time for niceties.

'Who else would greatly appreciate my information?' Lariux asked.

I swallowed. 'I have unintentionally found myself in the... the spider's services.'

'You foolish child.'

If only he really knew how involved I was. 'Mama doesn't know.'

'Of course not,' he said. 'She'd lock you away and deal with the spider herself.'

Or face the Queen.

'I won't reveal your name. I'm just a link on the chain. I don't even know who the Whispers is.'

'I'll see what I can find out,' Lariux said. 'But I'm not drawing attention to myself. The ranks will close after this.' He rubbed his face. 'We can hammer out the details of this *arrangement* at our next meeting.' He frowned, his disappointment clear, though he had no right to judge me. He wasn't my father. I was in this position precisely because of Papa's murder.

'Your ships will be in next week,' he added.

'I'll tell Mama. Goodnight, Mr Bisset.' I paused. 'Thank you for keeping our contracts. It was good of you.'

'I don't throw away good business.'

I stood there, awkward in my silence, then curtseyed.

'A servant will bring out your things. Until next month.' Lariux bowed and went back inside.

I stood in his driveway, waiting for my cloak and papers, and wondered how to explain a boy's murder to the Queen.

ⴲ ⴲ ⴲ

The Queen went still during my report.

'Again,' she ordered.

I hesitated, then repeated it all.

The Queen lowered her head. Her hair was pulled back into a twisted braid, a few wisps floating around her face, so she couldn't use it as a shield. She dragged her nails against the blotter.

I flinched. 'Your Majesty–'

'Quiet.'

I swallowed my words.

'Damn him!'

'Your Majesty—'

'Don't! *Don't.* He's a lying, scheming coward. *How dare he?* And don't bother saying *I did my best*—'

'You didn't! We let a boy *die.*'

She clamped her mouth shut, then tilted her head, as if I'd done something unexpected and interesting.

I didn't feel interesting. I'd shouted at the Queen. I'd been encouraged to act like I wasn't afraid of her, but this went beyond any acceptable tolerance. 'My apologies, Your Majesty, I didn't mean … that is …' I bypassed a curtsey and dropped to my knees, staring at the carpet. My thundering heartbeat overwhelmed my harsh breathing.

No response. No laughter. Nothing.

A gown rustled. The Queen's perfume – a floral scent built from roses – curled around me. She knelt. Heat radiated from her skin. I forced my shivering to slow.

Cool fingers reached under my chin and raised my head. The lamplight cast parts of her face into shadow, turned her grey eyes darker. The light caught her rouged lips.

Her thumb hovered near my mouth. My breath caught, before I swallowed, fighting not to lick my lips.

She released my chin and stood.

Breathe! Breathe. You need to breathe. I sucked in air. She held out a hand to help me stand, but I gasped out, 'No, thank you, Your Majesty,' and staggered up.

She went to a cabinet near her desk. A clink of glass, a trickle of liquid, then she continued to the seating area near her desk. She nodded at a chair. I collapsed into it, and accepted the glass with shaking hands.

'Calm yourself,' the Queen said. 'I won't punish you for shouting at me.'

She thought I was shaking because of *that*.

'Your uncle would have, Your Majesty. So would your grandfather. Even your father wouldn't have allowed such disrespect.'

'I didn't give you the brandy to look at.'

I took a gulp. It was smooth, with a warm burn. I glanced around the room, refusing to linger on her eyes, her lips, the splash of shadow across her collarbone. The thick curtains were drawn, the hems sprawled against the carpet. It felt like the room was closing in around me, oppressive instead of safe.

'I have it on good authority people shouted at Father when it was necessary,' the Queen said. 'He usually overstepped as a diplomat.'

I sipped the brandy.

She tilted her glass between her hands, then sighed. 'Vigrante killed a boy. It shouldn't surprise me, and yet…'

Because you're an idealist, I thought. *You were born into wealth, and privilege, and you've never had to truly fight for anything until now.*

I'd never been an idealist, even before Papa's death.

The Queen had built up political support and passed laws to benefit the merchants and middle classes, yet still believed people would do as she said because she expected them to.

'The boy was only a little younger than my sister,' I said. '*I saw him.*'

Her bleak expression tightened. 'Are you reconsidering our agreement?'

When I closed my eyes, I saw Zola fished out of the canal instead of the merchant boy. It had been easier when this felt like a chess game. Vigrante had made it real.

'No. But ...' I hesitated, yet had to say this. 'You must anticipate how far people like Vigrante will go – and who they'll kill – to get what they want. This could only get worse because Vigrante lacks your support, but isn't afraid of you.'

She didn't speak.

'We need him to make a mistake that you can openly punish, so the Court knows your laws can't be flouted by anyone, noble or not.'

I took a deep breath. 'I must be ruthless for you. I need your permission to do what is necessary.'

The Queen remained silent. Heat spread across my face and down my neck.

'Your Majesty,' I added.

'Lia,' she said. 'Those closest to me call me Lia. In private, so may you.'

'I couldn't–'

'You've earned the right.' She quirked her mouth. 'I can order you to, if you prefer.'

I lingered again on her collarbone. 'That's unnecessary.' I squared my shoulders. 'I'm inviting Lord Naruum's sister to visit him.'

'His family disowned him.'

'But his sister loves him most,' I said. 'She'll tell him because she'll want his forgiveness, and he needs to hear it from her to confess. We need an admission of guilt involving Lady Brenna.'

She frowned, considering, then nodded. 'Have Matthias escort Naruum's sister. I'd prefer she didn't see you.'

I nodded. 'May I leave to prepare, Your Maj – Lia?'

She smiled faintly. 'Of course. Goodnight... Xania.'

She murmured my name, almost drawing out the syllables, then rose.

I closed the panel after me, then leaned against it, trembling. Her damn collarbone. And I'd liked how she said my name. Very much.

Nothing good could come from this. I was Fifth Step; she was the Queen. The power imbalance was ludicrous. Logically – as if logic mattered – I knew why things had changed, even if I couldn't pinpoint when it had happened.

She was confident and decisive, a natural result of privilege and comfort. It had drawn Matthias to her years ago, and I wasn't the only one who noticed it now. She no longer tolerated the Court's prevailing attitudes. Ladies who'd never met the Dowager Queen's standards of beauty and attitude now found the new Queen considering their opinions.

Perhaps Matthias was right. Maybe she really could change everything.

Sometimes she watched me like I was a puzzle she couldn't solve. Sometimes she held my gaze longer than our conversation warranted. Once or twice she opened her mouth, as if to admit something, but never did.

It didn't matter. I could never let any hint slip that she intrigued me. If she ever acknowledged anything, or pursued me, I wouldn't be in a position to refuse, even if I wanted it. And while she'd never shown any inclination towards her uncle's pettiness, I didn't want to test her. The easiest way to keep myself and my family safe was to never be in a position where I could reject her.

I rubbed my face. I'd wake tomorrow and mock myself for letting my thoughts get this far. In the harsh light of day, even contemplating she could be attracted to me was ridiculous.

Her collarbone was still distracting.

It didn't matter. I had a job to do.

ૐ ૐ ૐ

When Naruum saw his sister in the doorway, he blinked, as

if fearing a hallucination. He was bathed and shaven, freshly dressed, his hair combed; as presentable as possible, under the circumstances. But there was no way to hide his terror, his regret, or the chains.

I watched through the spyholes in the passages. As Vianne hugged him and choked back a sob, I tried to ignore my pricking conscience. Naruum had offered Lia poisoned wine.

He hadn't been beaten. He hadn't been tortured: I didn't need his lies to make the pain stop. We'd asked him the same questions over and over – *who gave you the wine, why did you do it, who are you protecting?* – and each time he wouldn't answer. We'd worn him down with fear, but I needed him to break.

And his family abandoning him – *Brenna* abandoning him – would do it.

Vianne straightened her shoulders, sniffed, and wiped her tears. 'Naruum, how could you do this?'

He shook his head. 'It... it wasn't poisoned...'

'The royal physicians say otherwise. If the Queen had drunk even a little, she'd be dead.'

'The royal physicians lie–'

'Why would the Queen lie about something that makes her look weak?'

I was starting to like Vianne.

Naruum slumped.

'*Why* would you do this?'

'Vianne–' Naruum reached towards her, but the chains pulled him up short. 'It's not important, not now.'

So foolish. I circled back to the question that had no good answer: Why had Brenna chosen Naruum? Surely she had known he wouldn't succeed?

'*Not important?*' Vianne's eyebrows jutted together; her voice rose an octave. 'Our family is in disgrace. Our friends have abandoned us. Mother and Father *disowned you*–' Her eyes widened.

Naruum swayed in his seat. 'No...'

Vianne's eyes gleamed with tears, but her jaw hardened. 'What did you expect? You shamed us.'

If I'd injured Matthias with my knife and Lia had been less forgiving, I could have been in chains with Zola demanding answers.

'Then why did you come?' Naruum asked. His hands shook, and the chains knocked against the wood.

Vianne started crying again. 'You're my brother. I love you. But you can't blame us for your mistakes.' She stood. 'I've tried to change their minds. But they won't. They hope the Queen will eventually allow us to leave Court.'

His face drained of hope. 'You're leaving me.'

'The Queen won't pardon you. She'll keep you alive until you give her answers, or she runs out of patience.'

I waited.

'I love you,' Vianne whispered, 'and I'm sorry.' She tried to kiss his forehead; he turned away. She left, weeping softly.

I counted sixty heartbeats, then released the panel and stepped into the room. After delivering Vianne, Matthias had gone to take my place in the passages.

Naruum had pressed his face into the table, but it couldn't stifle his wretched sounds. Pity pricked my chest again, but I steeled myself against it. I was Lia's Whispers. I was her justice.

'Lord Naruum,' I finally said, more gently than he deserved.

He raised his tear-streaked face. Straightening in his seat, he swiped his fingers across his red-rimmed eyes. 'Miss Bayonn.'

I'd contemplated drawing it out, but now I simply wanted this over with. 'You and Lady Brenna were previously engaged. She broke it. Did you do this for her? What did she promise you?'

He frowned, then jumped when I slammed my hands on the table.

I leaned in. 'You have no one left. Your family has abandoned you. Lady Brenna hasn't begged the Queen for clemency. She doesn't even publicly speak your name. The only mercy left to you is the Queen's, and she is running out of patience.'

Tears slid down Naruum's face.

I waited.

'Lady Brenna and I were engaged' – his voice cracked – 'until two years ago, when she reconsidered her decision.'

'When she began to support Vigrante.'

'She said her feelings had changed,' he said. 'In reality, I no longer suited her rise in status.'

From Vigrante's point of view, it made sense. The fewer ties Brenna had to her past, the more loyal she would be to him.

'How did Brenna explain the wine to you?'

Naruum traced the whorls on the table. His mouth trembled. 'If... if I did a favour for her, this once, s-she would reconsider our engagement. She assured me it wasn't poisoned. The Queen would merely feel ill for a day or two.'

I didn't scream. I didn't dig my nails into his eyes. I didn't wrap the chains around his neck and squeeze until he was silent. I took a breath, another, and then another, until the fire within me changed from a killing rage to disdain.

'You're a fool to believe someone would make the Queen ill instead of killing her,' I said. 'No one survives after attempting either.'

'I wanted to believe her,' he said. 'I loved her. I still do.'

'Then I pity you.' Now I knew why Brenna had convinced Naruum, an unlikely assassin, to attempt this, when she knew he would fail. This had been Vigrante's test. It was possible she still loved Naruum, but she valued Vigrante as an ally more. By doing this, she'd proven her loyalty to him and rid herself of Naruum, an uncomfortable reminder of her past.

If she'd left Naruum alone, perhaps he eventually might have found someone who truly cared for him. He would have been happily married in the country, safely away from Court.

Now, he was imprisoned and powerless, with no hope of survival.

'Brenna knew you wouldn't succeed,' I said, 'and she convinced you to do it anyway.'

He wept again, whether for himself, or for Brenna and the love he still felt for her.

'I need proof,' I said. Hopefully his foolish love had led him to equally foolish actions.

'There are letters,' he whispered, 'hidden in one of my bed-chamber walls. I was... I was supposed to burn them.'

I didn't glance towards the passages. Matthias was probably already gone to retrieve the letters. I wanted to feel victorious, but instead I only felt tired.

'On behalf of Her Majesty, thank you for your co-operation, Lord Naruum.' I hesitated, ready to turn and leave the room. But there was little else to say: I couldn't promise him salvation or safety. Now that he'd admitted the truth, he would die.

'Will there be mercy?' Naruum asked. There was no hope in his voice, but if he hadn't asked, he might have tortured himself to his final moments that there could have been another outcome.

'Only the Queen can give you mercy now,' I said. 'And she has little to spare.'

The guards closed the doors on his cries for forgiveness. I headed towards the royal wing, where Lia waited for me.

CHAPTER FIFTEEN

LIA

The row of letters sat neatly on my desk, arranged by date: Brenna's sloped, elegant words coaxing Naruum to offer me the wine.

She'd suggested he sneak into the Opposition gathering – an ideal opportunity, since there would already be tension between the politicians and myself.

The Master of Ceremonies decided on my set of glasses right before an event. He assigned my servers carefully, who knew they would die if my food or wine was tainted after a poison-taster had sampled it. They didn't let their trays out of sight. There was no easy way to poison the glasses, so Brenna had surely known Naruum wouldn't succeed.

'There's no hope of mercy.' It was a statement, not a question, as if Xania knew it was futile, but had to say it anyway.

Whatever Naruum had wanted to believe about the wine, no courtier was oblivious to the consequences of trying to harm me.

'No,' I said.

Brenna had grown up with Naruum. She knew he was gentle, idealistic, and in love with her. She surely knew that he'd keep any letters from her instead of burning them. If Xania had suspected that Naruum would break under his family's betrayal, Brenna had already known.

Someone knocked on the doors. Matthias went to answer. After a few moments, he returned with a sealed letter. 'A servant delivered this from Lord Hazell. You were to receive it immediately.'

I broke the wax and a smaller note, with Lady Brenna's seal, fell into my palm.

I skimmed the first few lines of Hazell's note. My hands went numb. I was suddenly on my feet.

'Lady Brenna is dead,' I said. 'Lord Hazell found her. My presence has been requested.'

Matthias grabbed my arm. I had somehow moved halfway across the room without realising it. 'Why would he summon you?' he demanded. 'Why not alert the palace guard? Why not *Vigrante*–' His eyes widened.

'Not if he suspects Vigrante is behind her death,' Xania said.

I stared at Matthias's hand on my arm until he released me, then folded up Hazell's letter and handed it to Xania. 'This can't be on my person.' When Matthias opened his mouth, I added, 'Nor yours.' Xania was only known as the newest of my ladies. No one would assume she kept dangerous letters for me.

She considered me for a moment, then nodded and tucked the letter up her sleeve. I kept Brenna's one in my palm.

'Naruum,' Xania blurted out. Horror bloomed on her face.

She was right to be afraid. It couldn't be a coincidence that this had happened on the night Naruum had finally confessed.

'Matthias and I will go to Hazell,' I said. 'Xania, go to Naruum. Hurry.'

She rushed into the passages. Matthias and I walked towards Brenna's rooms, our pace steady to avoid undue curiosity. I broke the seal and unfolded her note:

Your Majesty, I apologise for my misdeeds.

I am the reason Naruum offered you the wine. I cajoled him into a gamble that could only fail. He did it for a love I do not deserve.

I swore this would not be my confession, but what else can it be, now?

Vigrante's favours always come with a price. Mine was distancing myself from my family and breaking my engagement. But while the distance from my family proved invigorating, I soon regretted abandoning Naruum.

Eventually, I asked Vigrante to let me regain Naruum's affections. Vigrante does not compromise well, but I realised that too late.

He did not lie, so much as allow me to believe things that would never happen. I convinced myself that Naruum would succeed and poison you, though I assured him it would merely indispose you as he otherwise wouldn't attempt it. Then we could reforge our engagement, and our feelings for each other would remain unchanged. Vigrante let me believe, even as I encouraged Naruum, who believed my lies in turn.

When you arrested him, I kept silent, but my rage grew towards Vigrante. I knew Naruum would eventually confess: he is not strong. I would no longer be useful to Vigrante, and he is cruel when someone has outlived their usefulness. I will be dead, but if Naruum dies, it wasn't by my hand. I am already the cause of his death; I still love him enough that I won't be the instrument of it.

We know the depths of Vigrante's cruelty; better I choose my own fate and prevent his attention from turning to my family.

I am the reason Naruum offered you the wine, but Vigrante is behind it all. I wish for Naruum to be pardoned of a traitor's death, and for my family to remain unaware of Vigrante's involvement. They will mourn me, but I want Vigrante to get the punishment from you that he deserves.

I apologise for my misdeeds, but know better than to beg forgiveness. Even the Queen's mercy has limits.

Brenna

☥ ☥ ☥

When we turned onto the hall leading to Brenna's apartment, our footsteps broke the silence. We'd met a pair of patrolling guards several halls back, but limited them to polite nods and a soft greeting. I didn't want to alert anyone until I knew what I was dealing with.

It no longer seemed a sensible decision.

Matthias and I stopped before Brenna's doors. Her words spun in my mind, presenting a more fragile, vicious side to her alliance with Vigrante.

As Brenna rose in power, she'd taken her own rooms, despite unmarried children remaining close or attached to their family suites. Now it no longer seemed an assertion of growing status, but Vigrante gently separating her from familial influence. My stomach, already uneasy, rolled harder.

I opened the doors.

Hazell froze, mid-pace, and attempted a shaky bow. 'Your Majesty.'

He was tall, slender apart from his wide shoulders. His dark hair was twisted in long, unfashionable curls, but he'd always been more concerned with what suited him than Court fashion.

'Lord Hazell,' I said.

'Your Majesty, thank you for coming so swiftly.' His gaze flickered between Matthias and me.

'Where is she?' I asked.

He glanced over his shoulder, and I strode by him.

It must have been poison. Brenna lay as if asleep. Her pale brown hair gleamed, but a cold finality clung to her, wrapped in unnatural stillness. There was nothing peaceful in the silent room.

Something constricted my chest. More death, all of it foolish; pettiness wrapped in power-plays. I had to remember Brenna knew precisely what she'd encouraged Naruum to do. She didn't deserve pity – and yet, the sight of her clung to my skin, a horror that couldn't be scoured away.

I walked back out. 'What happened?'

Hazell looked shocked at my sharp tone, then ashamed. 'I don't know. I didn't know anything... until this arrived.' He held out a note, as small as the one hidden up my sleeve. Brenna had ordered him to come here, and then to summon me.

'Would she have sent anyone else such a note?' I asked him.

'Me.'

We all whirled.

Vigrante stood in the doorway. For once, he wasn't neat nor impeccably dressed. His wrinkled shirt and trousers had been hastily thrown on, a waistcoat or necktie nowhere in sight. His hair was sleep-tangled. His expression worried me: no hint of his polished smile, and his eyes were smudged in shadow.

'She's dead,' he said flatly.

I gestured at the bedroom and followed him inside.

Vigrante took a ragged breath at the sight of her. 'Shall we be frank, Your Majesty?'

You have no idea what that word truly means. 'I've only ever wanted frankness between us, Lord Vigrante.'

His distress could be part of an elaborate ploy. He could be upset, reeling, and still have orchestrated Brenna's death. Vigrante wore emotions, true and false, like layers of clothing: easily put on and easily discarded.

His expression returned to calmness, but his eyes betrayed his exhaustion. This was the real Vigrante, brittle and furious when his plans careened out of control.

'You took all her choices away,' I said.

His pretence at calmness shattered into disbelief. 'You think I'd toss allies aside so frivolously?'

'The Riavaan boy in the canal.'

Anyone else would have looked chagrined or resigned. Instead, he met my gaze and shrugged. 'Accidents happen. Such a loss.'

'I've heard interesting things about the man who fled the scene.'

Vigrante didn't speak.

'Perhaps frankness isn't to your taste,' I said. 'There's also an interesting connection between Lady Brenna and Lord Naruum.'

'I warned her about him.'

Everyone knew how Vigrante treated his allies when they disappointed him or their usefulness ran out. Ruined reputations were the least of their worries; several had succumbed to sudden illnesses. With the rift Vigrante had orchestrated between Brenna and her family, and Naruum confessing to her conspiracy, no wonder Brenna had concluded this was the last choice left to her.

Despite her death, Vigrante still underestimated her. Her notes to him and Hazell were likely different. Hazell had looked terrified at Vigrante's appearance, and had followed Brenna's instructions and sent for me. Vigrante would resolve this the moment he and Hazell were alone, but if he didn't know that Brenna had written to me, I could still use it to my advantage.

'It would be unfortunate,' I said, 'if the consequences of Brenna and Naruum's connection were discovered. And her allegiance to you is already well-known. How terrible if her death reflected upon you, Lord Vigrante.'

He narrowed his eyes. 'I'm listening, Your Majesty.'

A better Queen would have revealed Brenna's confession to the Court and let the pandemonium run its course. But she was dead: it no longer mattered if her confession was true, or one last deception. It was a weapon Vigrante didn't know I had, and I would guard it with the care and respect it deserved until I could use it.

'If the Court learns that Brenna and Naruum concocted the wine scheme together, suspicion would *publicly* deflect from you.' Vigrante wasn't naive enough to think the Court wouldn't gossip behind closed doors. 'They would know some of the truth, and your reputation would be mostly salvaged.'

'And if I disagree?'

'Your reputation would not be salvaged.' Vigrante had discarded Brenna, his supposed ally, as cruelly as the merchant boy, but I'd orchestrate Brenna's revenge through my own vengeance.

'And what are your terms for my salvaged reputation?'

'You will pay the Riavaan family a death price for their son,' I said, 'and express your deepest condolences for their loss.' It was the closest Vigrante would come to admitting his part in the death.

His nostrils flared.

'If you do not,' I added, 'consider the depths of your unsalvage-able reputation.' *I'm not my uncle, Lord Vigrante. My displeasure runs long and deep.*

Vigrante's face tightened. Then he raised his chin. 'As you wish, Your Majesty.'

It was a pitiful victory, but it was mine. And humiliation was still a punishment to Vigrante, who traded on intimidation and secrets. Xania, Matthias, and I could build on this.

'And it would be in our mutual interests to work together on further legislation, Lord Vigrante, would it not?'

He took longer to answer this time, as if he could see the trap I'd set around him, helped by Brenna's desperate final act.

'Yes, Your Majesty,' he finally said, 'I believe it would.'

CHAPTER SIXTEEN

XANIA

The guard was not only a traitor to the Crown for killing Naruum, but he'd tried to be clever. The Palace Guard had stationed themselves at the most obvious exit from the castle, the least obvious, and three others of varying importance. The traitor had bolted towards the least obvious exit, then doubled back towards one of the lesser three, and finally sprinted to the most obvious. He'd rushed right into the waiting arms of his fellow soldiers.

I stood by Naruum's bed, and tried to breathe through my mouth. The scent of blood lingered. The guards had covered him with a heavy blanket.

The Commander of the Palace Guard had looked furious when I'd hurried towards Naruum's room, then resigned when I'd held up the spider's mark.

I'd injected my voice with every possible ounce of authority and confidence. 'I'm here on the Whispers's orders. I'm to see the body.'

After informing me of the situation, the Commander had gone to supervise the traitor being taken to the dungeons. I remained with the two guards who'd discovered Naruum when they'd entered to remove the food tray. They'd given him some dignity in his death with the blanket, then waited outside for the Commander to return.

I glanced up as the Commander returned. 'The guard is imprisoned and chained,' she said. 'Everything is ready for Whispers.'

I stood. 'I will inform him.' The Commander would have to report to Lia, which gave me time to see the guard. I was slowly building a team of agents to work with the guards, and while I wanted information without using physical torture, I'd recruited Kartek and Curjan as exceptions of last resort. They would join me.

This once, for this guard, I wanted to break him through violence, as if it could bring Naruum back.

φ φ φ

I rubbed my eyes hard enough for spots to appear. The guard had been easy to crack; I was convinced he'd agreed to Vigrante's bargain on impulse. He'd coughed up names that Curjan was now tracking down. They were hopefully real people linked to Vigrante, but he'd have kept his hands publicly clean, as always.

As I was sending a message to Matthias, informing him of

Naruum's death, one arrived from him: *Her Majesty has been detained. She will summon you when ready. Try and get some sleep.* Relief, sadness, and disappointment twisted in my stomach. But I told Kartek and Curjan to alert me to any new developments and left, detouring to my office to pick up dispatches before retreating to my rooms.

I took deep breaths until my shoulders relaxed. Then I went to my desk, unfolded two dispatches from Farezi and Othayria that I'd put aside to handle Naruum's escalating situation –

I shoved the thought away and focused on the letters. The Farezi dispatch – a decoded letter, accompanied by a theatre booklet – was mostly about Farezi's harvest hopes and price speculation.

The theatre booklet held more sensitive information; tiny dots pricked above certain letters. I went back and forth through the sentences with different codes until I had it all. The agent had discovered Rassa's true date of departure for Edar, two weeks earlier than originally planned; the high-ranked members of the retinue; and potential diplomatic replacements. Nothing certain about any spies in the mix.

The letter from Othayria was shorter, less detailed. That agent was still finding her feet. Most of it concerned Prince Aubrey, another of Lia's future suitors. I wanted to know everything: his likes and dislikes, strengths and weaknesses.

Decoding helped for a while, but Naruum and Brenna kept

intruding. While I sat, blanketed in soothing quietness, Lia faced their grieving families. I kept wondering if I should be there with her, but it was no place for me. I'd sought information on them, desired their secrets, threatened Naruum. I was never meant to face the consequences of my duty beside Lia, only wrestle with – and resent – my conscience.

It was easier to be Whispers when decoding correspondence and creating new codes, building up knowledge to use later. When everything was set in motion, it all turned murkier, more distasteful.

No matter. It would help me take down Vigrante. This was the price I had to pay. Naruum had perished because he'd allowed himself to believe things that could never be real. I wouldn't make the same mistake.

A brisk knock from the wall almost made me drop my pen. I froze. It was Lia's signal.

Why would she come here?

Another knock: I stood and went to the wall. I flicked the catch to open the panel, then backed away. My heart pounded.

Lia stepped into my room. 'Apologies. This seemed the safest way.' Her face was haggard pale. But the candlelight gleamed against her hair, and her back was still straight, her mouth –

I looked away. Of all times to be distracted, this was not only ridiculous, but shameful, even if I wanted to cling to anything good right now.

'Your Majesty,' I said, 'would you like to sit?'

My family's apartment was technically hers: the monarch owned the palace, and the majority of the Court rented their rooms from the Crown – I'd once looked up the long, elaborate contract to settle a bet between Terize and myself – but Lia responded as if visiting a noble's estate. We spoke in whispers. My family had retired hours earlier, but if they suddenly woke, heard voices from my room, and discovered the Queen –

They couldn't order her out... but you could never tell with Mama.

Lia slid a folded square of paper from her sleeve. Our fingers brushed as I took it, but her expression betrayed nothing. I gently smoothed the paper and frowned at the first line.

When I reached the signature at the end, I had no words in me at all.

'Every time I feel a shred of goodwill towards Vigrante,' Lia said, 'something like this happens, and I remember precisely how much I want him dead.'

How trapped Brenna must have felt by her family's decisions for her, all paths cut off so the only choice left was Vigrante, until she couldn't ignore the shadows around him anymore.

'Such a waste,' I said.

Lia pinched the bridge of her nose. 'She likely used a poison that failed her heart. Something that could be explained away.'

'What did you tell her family?'

'Enough of the truth: Naruum's confession, and how Brenna's matched his.' Her mouth twisted. 'At least Naruum's family know his murderer has been captured, even if I implied Brenna bribed the guard.'

Naruum's face flashed in my mind. He had bled from his ears, and eyes, nose and mouth. He'd choked on the blood.

I swallowed. 'So you're obeying Brenna and keeping quiet about Vigrante's involvement?'

'The Court will speculate anyway,' Lia said. 'I'll keep quiet for as long as it's useful.'

Something soured at the back of my throat. Once again Vigrante had been behind someone's death and he'd escaped unscathed. But this time Lia was deliberately allowing it. 'So he wins again.'

When I glanced at Lia, she looked worse than ever. 'From a distance, Brenna looked like she was sleeping. But the illusion failed when you came closer.' Her voice was faint, pained. 'She... she made me think of Father – *after*.'

Papa's deathbed rose in my memory, bright and sharp. I instinctively, viciously, shoved it away. Now wasn't the right time, not when Naruum's bloody blanket was trying to imprint itself in my mind.

'If we keep letting Vigrante escape the consequences,' I said, 'we'll never prove anything.'

'Every time one of his plans fails, we're closer to him making a bigger mistake. He didn't expect Brenna to do it, I think, not really.' Lia hesitated. 'He'll pay the Riavaan family a death price for their son with his condolences. He's not escaping all the consequences. It's only a small victory, but it's a start.'

'Curjan is investigating some names,' I said, after another few moments of silence. 'I suspect they're all linked to Vigrante, but the usual safeguards will be in place.'

Lia rubbed the space between her eyebrows. 'If the guard can't give anything else useful, he must die.'

'I keep trying to untangle it,' I said, 'as if I can find the right thread, and pull it, and pinpoint how we could have stopped it all.'

'Try not to. It won't end well.'

We stared at each other. Something warm lingered. It usually flickered between us at night, after too many hours talking, wading through reports and hypothetical discussions. The heat turned us drowsy, softened rank and status. I tried not to think about it in harsh daylight.

She glanced at the papers on my desk. 'News?'

'Reports on Farezi and Othayria.'

Lia frowned. 'The marriage market seemed much farther away last year.' Back when being Queen was a potential future, until the King complained of shortness of breath and stomach pains. 'It's horrible to admit, but the suitors may distract the Court from... this.' She let out a frustrated sigh. 'All this from poor family decisions and a broken engagement. You want to know where we could have stopped it. I want to pinpoint where Brenna felt her final choice was to die alone, from her own hand, and stop it happening again.'

'Then we stop Vigrante. He puts people into these situations.' His methods were simple, clever, and despicable, manipulating people's loyalty until they failed him. And they *all* failed him, eventually.

'I don't think I'll ever forget the sight of Naruum's body.' I immediately regretted the words. 'I hardly know why.'

Lia squeezed my arm. 'That means you'd make different decisions to Vigrante. Don't be ashamed of it.'

I didn't speak, hardly breathed, and didn't acknowledge the action. The warm flickering slowly died, buried under layers of rank and privilege reasserting themselves between us.

I'd seen what love had driven Brenna and Naruum to, and how far the consequences had spread.

Lia ruled Edar and would eventually marry for an heir. I was her Whispers and would avenge Papa's death.

Love had ruined Brenna and Naruum.

Love would not ruin us.

CHAPTER SEVENTEEN

LIA

I stopped on the terrace and lifted my face to the sun. Spring had given way to summer, but so far the sticky heat that I hated had stayed away.

'I can't wait for proper summer,' Xania said wistfully.

'You *can't* consider this cold.'

She mock-shivered and laughed. 'Never visit Rijaan, Your Majesty. You'll melt.' She hoped to eventually visit her maternal family's homeland, past Eshvon to the south-east. A republic, it had scorching summers and a worrying amount of coastal erosion from storms.

Xania and I wandered through the gardens, our idle discussion turning to the grain situation. Transporting excess water to the south had initially helped the drought, but the spring storms weren't reaching the south. If this continued, the harvests would fail.

I couldn't hedge my bets anymore and we'd started purchasing grain. I'd used smaller sellers for the last few weeks, but now Farezi had caught on.

Xania passed me a price sheet.

'They've *never* charged us this much!'

She nodded, already looking weary. She'd likely been in earshot during Coin's reaction. 'Coin thinks this is the King's doing.'

I'd never liked the Farezi King. He'd stomped on his Court's attempt to start a government, and everyone knew – including him – that his wife held the true power. From everything I'd heard about Rassa lately, he'd chosen to emulate his father instead of his mother.

'The King thinks he's being clever.' I handed the paper back so I wouldn't rip it apart. 'He's as subtle as a battering ram.' I'd expected Farezi to take advantage, but this was ridiculous. I narrowed my eyes at Xania. 'Does Coin know you have this?'

'He may not know I copied it while he shouted at people.'

'You have that face on you – *Don't worry, I have an idea.*'

'How have relations been with Eshvon since you took the throne?'

'Better...'

When the Second Empire had crumbled, and we became our own countries again, Othayria and Eshvon had risen under matriarchal rule. Relations between our countries had been poor for decades. Eshvon also produced grain, but exported it east because of Farezi's stranglehold. When I became Queen, I'd immediately sent reconciliation greetings to Othayria and Eshvon. Now it looked like that might be useful, even if it involved grovelling.

'You suggest approaching Eshvon?'

'At worst,' Xania said, 'they rebuff us and we pay through the nose to Farezi.'

The thought of Rassa's smugness made my skin crawl. 'We have little to offer Eshvon for selling us grain behind Farezi's back.'

Xania slipped her hands into her dress pockets. 'Eshvon has too many daughters. Queen Juliaane wants to marry several of them abroad.'

I tried to follow her train of thought.

'Othayria is sending their first-born son,' I said.

'And Prince Aubrey and Princess Isra have always been close. They'd surely enjoy a reunion free from their families.'

'I should encourage Eshvon to send their youngest daughter in exchange for grain?'

'There have been worse compromises,' Xania said.

'If Coin hasn't already considered it, I'll suggest it. I imagine he'll find me soon enough.'

We sank into a comfortable silence, matching each other's stride.

Almost a month had passed since Brenna and Naruum's deaths. Vigrante, who'd kept his head down for a while, had publicly sympathised with the southern crisis, then tried to encourage the western nobles not to send water. His tactics had unexpectedly backfired, fuelled by rumours dogging him since Brenna's demise and his death price to the Riavaan family.

Around my ladies, I'd inflamed some of the worst rumours. When I left the room, those who thought Xania couldn't over-hear protested my opinions. The loudest were discreetly relieved of their positions. We didn't want to remove all of Vigrante's spies, or someone else would fill the vacuum.

'Rassa will be arriving soon,' Xania said.

'Yes.' I turned into the nearest walled garden, then froze when I realised it was Baron Bayonn's garden. While his family still visited, the royal gardeners now oversaw the daily upkeep.

The winter roses, true to their name, hadn't survived spring's arrival, but others had been planted so that something bloomed every season. The soft spring roses were giving way to bold summer flowers.

'I apologise,' I said. 'If you wish to leave—'

'I still visit.' Xania's face had turned into a courtier's mask, care-fully hiding any trace of sadness. 'Papa loved this place.'

'Mother still likes the winter roses.' It was poor solace, but awkward silence felt worse.

'The Duchess is kind.'

Mother rarely did anything out of kindness, but I accepted the politeness. 'Matthias often comes here to be alone.' Their friend-ship had somewhat recovered, but I kept trying to smooth things between them. Considering how I'd reacted to Matthias reveal-ing the passages to Xania, my attempts weren't just misguided, but hypocritical.

'That's good of him.'

'Rassa's letter was remarkably cordial.' I'd never considered him a safe topic before.

'No unexpected food or wine deliveries,' she said.

'He probably considered it,' I said, 'and had common sense knocked into him.'

'I marvel at the sincere concern you royals muster for each other,' Xania muttered.

'If you think it's bad now, wait until they're all here and the marriage wheels start properly turning. After choosing a husband, I think I'll go up north for a month to be alone.' I attempted a wry smile. 'And they say love is dead.'

'It is when it involves a crown,' Xania said.

'Perhaps a foreign courtier will fall in love with you.' It was like I had to drag a rusted nail across my hopeful infatuation.

I felt her drawing away from me, as always when I mentioned marriage or romance. 'No, Your Majesty, I hope not. I don't wish to leave Edar.' We went quiet again, until she added, 'I fear you're the romantic here.'

'My mother would be shocked.'

Xania smiled crookedly.

My heart swelled, then squeezed painfully. *A romantic, indeed, nursing foolish, futile hopes.*

Coin appeared at the garden's entrance, scanning until he

found us. Xania, tensely conscious of the sensitive information she'd 'borrowed', slipped away. Even as I wanted her to stay, I felt relieved as Coin stomped towards me. Nursing futile hopes was dangerous.

Ω Ω Ω

'You need to eat something,' Xania said. 'Coffee is useless if you pass out.'

A few weeks ago, I'd invited her to join Matthias and me at breakfast. Her discomfort had made me glad he was with us. But I demanded nothing more than her company, and what little conversation we managed – neither of us was morning people, which made it ludicrous in hindsight – and she'd slowly relaxed.

Matthias wasn't here this morning, dealing with last-minute preparations for Rassa's arrival. Xania was also focused on it, which seemed to explain her lack of awkwardness around me today.

I drained my cup and refilled it. 'Rassa will expect me to breakfast with him. He lingers over his food. I need to be hungry.'

Xania nudged a plate towards me. 'One pastry, Lia. It won't kill your appetite.' She paused, then looked away, as if she didn't trust her expression.

Sometimes, it felt like she considered returning my tentative attempts at signalling interest. Other times, it felt like flinging hope at someone determined to be oblivious.

I ate the pastry.

'What's Prince Rassa like in person?' she asked, as I overloaded another one with butter.

'The last time I saw him was before we returned to Edar after my aunt's final miscarriage,' I said. 'He liked swords and horses. He liked me, except when I ran faster or dented his head with a practice sword.'

'Sounds like a perfect match,' Xania said.

'Perhaps,' I said, hoping my expression matched my breezy tone.

'Do you want me around much in public?'

'Please. And if you should find someone you like, pursue them with all intent.'

'I don't plan on husband-scouting, Your Majesty. Or wife-scouting.'

A knock saved us from ourselves.

Matthias poked his head in. 'The Farezi party is about an hour away, Lia.'

'I have to find Zola,' Xania said. 'I promised her we'd watch the Farezi arrive together.'

I crushed my flicker of disappointment. 'Of course.'

She curtseyed and left.

'Perhaps Your Majesty wishes to follow her like a puppy?' Matthias asked.

I almost threw a pastry at him, but didn't want to waste it.

Φ Φ Φ

'I hardly recognised you, dear cousin.' The corners of Rassa's hazel eyes crinkled. It was difficult not to resent his laughter lines, while servants used powder to hide the shadows under my eyes.

'Your eyelashes still put mine to shame.'

Rassa's smile dimmed. 'My one failing, according to my father.'

'Your father is old-fashioned.'

Rassa had asked to speak privately after breakfast. I'd suggested a walk through the gardens. We were close to the Bayonn rose garden, though I didn't want him to see it after being there with Xania. It felt like a secret between us and Matthias.

Naturally, Rassa stopped at the entrance. 'Are these your mother's gardens?'

'No, hers are on the other side. But she's officially taken over all of them from Aune Jienne.' Mother and Aunt Jienne's battle over the gardens pricked something in my memory, but it faded before I could focus on it.

'Why your mother?'

'She enjoys overseeing the gardens. Jienne only felt it was expected of her as Queen.' As we stepped inside, I added, 'It's a winter rose garden, so the flowers are off-season.'

'Ah, I remember your craze a few years back,' Rassa said. 'A few showed up at home. Mother wishes to expand her winter gardens. Edaran rose cuttings would be a fitting contribution.' He flashed me a grin. 'Could I speak to the gardener?'

'A baron created them with the gardeners,' I said. 'He died a few years back, but I'm certain his widow will speak with you. Her eldest daughter is one of my ladies.'

'You must introduce me, then.'

'I expect you not to break my ladies' hearts.'

Rassa held up his hands, laughing. Sometimes it was too easy to forget he wanted to take Edar from me. Perhaps this was all a facade to make me doubt his true intentions.

He'd inherited his mother's clear, pale skin and her thick-lashed eyes, trying to offset both with a neat beard. His dark brown hair fell to his shoulders in waves, and he'd perfected displaying his arm muscles and chest when he ran his fingers through it. He reeked of charisma, but I had what others didn't: immunity.

I sighed. 'Enough. Why did you want to speak privately?'

Rassa glanced at the nearest bench. 'May we sit?'

'No. Start talking.'

'Father is concerned.'

'Ah.'

'I wish you'd let us sit. You know he's never liked your mother. She kept you from Court because of her petty feuds—'

'Your father is concerned about my ability to rule?' I was glad we hadn't sat; it made it easier to stop and face him. 'Careful how you answer, cousin: this could greatly affect how Edar regards Farezi.'

'I disagree with him.'

'I'm sure you do,' I said.

'Every ruler has a learning curve when they take the throne. I'm dreading mine.'

I started walking again, making sure to stay ahead. 'Your father must be eager for a marriage match.' Of course he would be: a puppet King through which he could influence Edar.

'There are many advantages to a marriage link with Farezi.'

'I'm always in dire need of a man's advice.'

'You think most highly of your secretary's advice!'

'My secretary does not rule.'

'Edar hasn't had a Queen in over a century. Your uncle was weak–'

'And you assume I'll be the same? I've been locking horns with politicians since I took the throne!'

'No one expects you to battle them alone forever,' Rassa said. 'My father only has to contend with his nobles. You have an entire *Parliament* to handle–'

'I won't be manipulated instead of protecting my people.'

Rassa's face crumpled. 'Oh. Oh no.' He collapsed onto the nearest bench. 'You're an idealist. This is dreadful.'

'So this is what you think of me.' I folded my arms. 'A foolish idealist living on borrowed time, who needs a man to oversee her rule.'

'Lia, you must marry for an heir, regardless of–'

'Regardless of *what*?'

'Nothing,' he said, looking mortified.

My anger meant he'd never suspect my stomach was rolling with panic. I'd always been so careful, once I'd realised where my preferences lay. I'd never flirted with a lady, never showed a hint of attraction, until–

When I opened my mouth to argue further, he snapped, 'Cousin, enough!'

This was my crossroads. I could push Rassa from annoyance to anger, and ruin everything before it properly began. Or I could swallow my fury and be cautious instead. I'd do everything to prove his father wrong, and find out what Rassa hoped to achieve by coming here.

I'd also use enough of his rashness to leverage our negotiations, not only for grain. The less I had to depend on Farezi or Eshvon, the better.

'At least you can feel *some* shame.' I kept my voice light, if not entirely cordial.

Rassa attempted a smile, sunny again. 'I can feel many things. Shame, happiness, sadness... desire.'

'I don't wish to hear of your conquests!'

He coaxed me into taking his arm when we left the gardens. We probably looked like an ideal pair of royal cousins. No one would know there should have been invisible briars curling between us, the thorns sharp and poisoned.

CHAPTER EIGHTEEN

XANIA

I woke to hammering on my door.

I shot upright. Sunlight pierced the edges of my curtains, brighter than when I normally woke. My throat swelled with panic.

I hurtled out of bed and opened the door so fast, Zola almost hit me with the fist she'd held up for another knock.

'You overslept! You *never* oversleep.'

'What's wrong?' I was normally early, so hopefully Coin would forgive me this once. My stomach grumbled. I peered hopefully at the wrapped napkins balanced on her palm.

'The Othayrian delegation's already arrived,' she said.

All thoughts of food fled from my mind. We hadn't expected them until this evening. They must have travelled through the night. Why was everyone obsessed with arriving *early*?

I grabbed the napkins, and hauled Zola inside with my other hand. 'Help me get dressed.'

When I was mostly presentable, we ran towards the throne

room. 'What's the prince like?' I asked.

'I don't know,' Zola said. 'The entourage met Her Majesty in private. But she's introducing him to the Court now.'

We reached the throne room and plunged into the crowd, squeezing by people until we found Mama and Lord Martain near a pillar.

Mama frowned. Zola and I had done an acceptable job, considering our speed, but I probably radiated hints of a frazzled morning. Mama, naturally, looked impeccable.

'I overslept,' I said, before she could say anything.

'You work too hard for Coin,' she said.

'I'll always be grateful he took a chance on me.' Coin had been quieter since Brenna's death. I kept thinking about their private meeting, and whether he knew more than I'd realised.

'There's a point when gratitude is no longer required,' Mama said, 'and when he should no longer expect it. We're in a lower Step, not destitute.'

Zola stopped the foundations of an argument by clutching my arm. '*Look at him.*'

The morning sun took great pleasure in shining upon Prince Aubrey's black hair and light brown skin. His nose was long and straight; no fist fights in his youth. He stood at least a foot taller than Lia, and there were hints of muscle under his layers of linen and silk.

Every courtier would be swooning after him by noon.

Lia would have to fall for him. It would be ludicrous not to.

I felt the phantom touch of her fingertips under my chin, remembered how I could hardly breathe while she'd stared at me – all the times she'd teased and flattered, weighing certain words and sentences –

'He's handsome,' I said, when I realised Zola was waiting for my verdict.

'*Only* handsome? If Her Majesty won't marry him, I will.'

'He's not saying much.'

'They rode through the night,' Mama said. 'You wouldn't be saying much, either.'

Lia sat on the throne, carrying most of the conversation with Aubrey. Small talk apparently didn't come easy for him – unusual in a prince. But, as Mama had said, he'd ridden through the night. Remarks about the weather and first impressions of Edar would be a struggle for anyone right now.

Lia knew what was expected of her. She kept eye contact, her body angled towards him, though she didn't flirt or try anything untoward. She murmured something, making Aubrey suddenly laugh. It was impossible not to look at them, side by side, and see the powerful couple they could become.

A muscle twinged in my neck.

Lia rose from the throne. As Aubrey hovered behind her, she stepped to the edge of the dais, ready to formally introduce him. Pressure tightened in my chest. As if I had any right to resent him.

He'd probably make her laugh, eventually.

CHAPTER NINETEEN

LIA

Princess Isra, the youngest Eshvon royal – and the reason we'd bargained grain at a better price – arrived two days after Aubrey. She stepped from the carriage, entirely focused on me, while no one else could take their eyes off her.

My pulse raced.

If Isra had been the second or third daughter, she'd have more marriage offers than she knew what to do with. But she was the youngest, and even beauty only mattered so much at the bottom rung of the inheritance ladder.

Isra lived in southern Eshvon, close to Rijaan, where Xania's great-grandmother had come from. (I couldn't think of Xania right now. Not now, not like this.) Isra's brown skin, with warm bronze undertones, had deepened from the summer heat. She wore linen and trousers, and Eshvon's famed burnished gold jewellery. My hopeful suitor waited behind her.

Isra paused at the top of the steps, then bowed.

Someone in the crowd sighed.

'Your Majesty,' Isra said, 'I bring congratulations from their Royal Majesties, my honoured parents, upon your ascension.'

'Thank you, Your Highness,' I said, relieved my voice was steady. 'Long may their reign continue.'

During Uncle's reign, Queen Juliaane had kept her existing trade agreements but openly disliked our Parliament's rising power. Now I was Queen, Juliaane had regained interest. Her eagerness didn't sit well with me, but I couldn't show my displeasure until after the Eshvon caravans arrived.

Isra flicked her fingers at the waiting suitor. 'My brother, Prince Hasan.' He stepped forward, nervous, but executed a perfect bow. The eldest son, but in matriarchal Eshvon, Isra was in control.

'Your Majesty,' Hasan said. I held out my hand. He brushed his lips over it, then smiled hesitantly.

I returned his smile. Harmless. Utterly harmless. It was his sister I had to worry about.

'Prince Hasan,' I said, 'we bid you welcome.'

Rassa stood in the crowd, thin-lipped with annoyance. Farezi and Eshvon had a long tradition of misunderstanding each other. Matthias caught my gaze and raised his eyebrows. Xania, standing beside him, kept her attention on Isra. I'd seen Xania once since Aubrey's arrival, when she'd stiffly apologised for not anticipating Othayria's unexpected entrance.

Matthias sauntered over at my gesture, but Xania slipped away.

⊕ ⊕ ⊕

A week later, I arrived for breakfast and found Xania and Matthias talking quietly. He'd finally coaxed her to rejoin us – since Isra's arrival, Xania had pulled back from me. She was my Whispers, a member of the Treasury, one of my ladies – but we didn't feel like friends right now. Maybe I'd only imagined we could have been.

'Good morning, Lia,' Matthias said, and poured my coffee.

'Morning.' I took a gulp, welcoming the burn, and ripped a roll to pieces.

He eyed my plate. 'You slept wonderfully, then.'

'No one else is awake?' Xania asked.

'Of course not.' I poured a bowl of chocolate, which Aubrey was fond of and the younger courtiers had embraced, and dipped my bread into it. 'They don't have countries to run, so they can drink and sleep as much as they like.'

The morning was cool and overcast, with rain threatened later. The Court would remain inside and entertain the Othayrian and Eshvon guests, while those from Farezi slept off their hangovers. Except for Rassa, who drank less so he could remember everything that was said. He'd probably try to annoy me later while I worked through paperwork. Xania would be in the Treasury, while Matthias helped me catch up and kept Rassa at bay.

Apart from a morning hour and time spent with public

appeals, my life had turned into days of walking, gossiping, and riding. I drank rivers of coffee and tea during lunches, dinners, and private entertainments. And everyone smiled, and laughed, and flattered, flattered, flattered. I was ready to scream, and Matthias had grown anxious about the piles of paperwork.

Edar couldn't grind to a halt while I chose a suitor, and I wouldn't evoke my uncle's memory by delegating in favour of entertaining. I hoped today would mark a subtle shift in expectations. The royals would wake and discover I'd spent the morning working and, because I had a Court ready to entertain them, that more of my future time would be spent doing the same.

'Has Vigrante tried anything?' I asked.

'Not yet, Your Majesty,' Xania said, as if I wouldn't notice her reversion to my title.

Matthias, who'd watched my bread dipping in horrified fascination, grimaced.

'He goes out of his way to speak with Princess Isra,' Xania said. 'They're cordial in public. It's too soon for them to have private meetings, but I'll station agents in the passages around his rooms and the Eshvon suites.'

'And the Othayrian suites,' I said. 'Vigrante might try to befriend her through Aubrey. Be careful around Vigrante's part of the passages. We should assume Uncle told him about them.'

'Do you think Vigrante knows about our deal with Eshvon?' Matthias asked.

'Juliaane and I were careful, but all it takes is one loose tongue.'

He glanced at Xania. 'Isn't Zola playing for Princess Isra tonight?'

She nodded. When Isra had learned that Zola practised with the royal orchestra, she'd insisted on a performance.

'How does Zola feel about Isra's interest in her music?' I asked.

Xania raised an eyebrow. 'She knows better than to question it.'

'Oh, before I forget,' I said, attempting nonchalance. 'Aubrey recommended a writer to me. I read one of her books and I think you'd enjoy it. Perhaps you could join me one evening, and I'll give it to you.' Every time I convinced myself to follow through with this, I also remembered what had happened to Brenna and Naruum because of their feelings.

And yet...

Matthias examined my bowl of chocolate as if to give us a poor illusion of privacy.

Hopeless, I thought. *Hopeless, hopeless, hopeful.*

'I ...' Xania stopped, as if hoping she could politely refuse without causing offence, when others would practically commit murder for the invitation. 'I... I'd be delighted, Your Majesty.'

Matthias whipped his head up, his surprise mirroring my own. Xania shifted in her seat, but otherwise stayed calm. Did she actually *want* to spend time with me, or did she feel she couldn't refuse?

'Wonderful. I'm looking forward to your sister's performance.'

I drained my coffee and stood. 'Matthias, I expect you in my office in ten minutes. Paperwork awaits.'

He saluted me. I swiped him playfully across the head; he laughed and ducked. After saying goodbye to Xania, I hurried towards my office. With any luck, I'd be safely behind my desk before anyone came looking for me.

CHAPTER TWENTY

XANIA

Prince Aubrey of Othayria was pleasant, kind, and didn't gossip. He was patient with courtiers who became emotionally undone in his presence, but didn't overly favour anyone. He probably worked through a list in revolving order for walks, discussions, and literary and musical recitations.

But I couldn't resent him for enjoying Zola's music. 'The Eshvon Court appreciates musical ability almost above all else. Isra's excited to hear your sister play.'

His kindness seemed genuine. He found something to compliment in everyone.

'You're both very kind, Prince Aubrey.'

I still didn't like him.

'He could be nice,' Matthias had said earlier, after Lia left. 'Nice people *do* exist.'

'He's a prince,' I'd replied. 'Princes aren't nice.'

I liked being with them for breakfast again. I'd missed Lia, usually at night when I normally reported to her. This still surprised me. I'd become comfortable with our formality turning into a royal version of friendship. Too comfortable.

I'd no choice but to stack formality between us again. The foreign nobility had reminded me, sharply, of the gulf between us. I was her Whispers. She could like my company, but I'd never be anything more to her. I had to remember that, especially when wishful thinking tried to convince me otherwise.

She'd marry – probably Aubrey – and have children and rule Edar until she died. Maybe one day she'd feel obliged to elevate me to a higher Step, and I would despise her pity.

But I couldn't imagine Aubrey as her husband.

'Do you play, Miss Bayonn?' he asked, jerking me out of my grim reverie.

I fixed a smile to my face. 'The viola, like my sister. Papa had no musical ability, so he lived through us.'

'You're not playing tonight?'

'My sister has the talent, Your Highness. I'm merely proficient.'

I'd been perfectly fine before I met Lia. Spending time with Zola had been enough, as had learning the necessary skills to avenge Papa. Matthias had filled the need for an occasional friend. But Lia offered something beyond friendship, fragile and possibly wonderful. It excited and frightened me.

The doors opened. Everyone sank into curtseys and bows as Lia entered, wearing a deep blue dress with a silver netting overskirt. Aubrey stepped forward to greet her. I moved towards

Terize and the other ladies.

Lia stopped me, gesturing to the chair on her left. 'Here, if you please, Miss Bayonn.' My stomach clenched. It wasn't the seat of highest honour – that was Aubrey's on her right – but she was still ignoring protocol. Thin as their blood link was, Rassa was still entitled to her favour. She had put me in his seat.

She pressed her fingers against my arm. 'Rassa will survive. Compliment his eyelashes.'

I raised an eyebrow, and her smile sharpened.

Every time I tried to stay unnoticed, she dragged me into full view. Maybe she wanted to keep me a secret in plain sight.

Footsteps stopped before us. I glanced up at Rassa; he did little to hide his surprise.

'Cousin?' He spoke politely, but with a hint of condescension, as if reminding Lia of his place. Like any of us could forget.

'Since Miss Bayonn's sister is playing tonight, *Cousin*,' Lia said, 'I've given her a place of honour.'

'Of course.' Rassa beamed insincerely. 'And Prince Aubrey?'

'Prince Aubrey and I have a conversation to resume.' Lia's politeness sprouted thorns.

In other words: she was seriously considering Aubrey as a suitor, and favouring him accordingly.

I should have been happy. Aubrey was the ideal suitor. Instead, I wanted to punch his symmetrically handsome face.

Everything kept betraying me: my body, my feelings, my

common sense.

Rassa's gaze locked with Lia's, though his body language stayed calm. Aubrey stiffened. I slowed my breathing.

Then Rassa dropped into the seat beside me with a flourish. 'Miss Bayonn.'

'Your Highness.' I reluctantly held out my hand, then gently tugged it out of Rassa's grip after he kissed it.

Rassa watched people as if gauging their potential usefulness, calculating how long he'd have to humour them. People whispered he'd left a trail of discarded allies and broken hearts back home. I'd managed to secure more agents into place before he'd left Farezi, and their information confirmed some of the rumours. His sincere lack of responsibility set Lia's teeth on edge.

He had a dashing smile when it was genuine. I didn't want it directed at me.

'Miss Bayonn.' The corners of his eyes crinkled. 'I've done my research on you.'

The back of my throat prickled. 'There's little to know about me, Your Highness.'

He laughed too loud, deliberately drawing gazes towards us.

Lia stiffened, but kept her attention on Aubrey.

'Everyone has secrets,' Rassa said.

If he was going to play this game, I'd humour him with as much decorum as my rank allowed. 'Even you?'

'Especially me.'

'Then what do you know about me, Your Highness?'

'Miss Xania Bayonn, elder daughter of Lady Harynne and the late Baron Bayonn,' he said, 'born Third Step, now Fifth thanks to your stepfather, Lord Martain. Through your father, you have little fortune of your own.'

I kept my smile steady. When Papa became besotted with Mama, he'd exaggerated the health of his finances. While Mama had been flattered by Papa's interest, marrying him was also a way onto the Steps. When he'd admitted his genteel poverty, she still married him, but never lost her hard practicality. Since it had saved us after Papa's death, I could only hope I'd inherited it.

'It's curious,' Rassa continued. 'I know enough about Edar's Steps that Fifth isn't usually high enough to warrant royal attention. What does Lia see in you?'

I want to kill our common enemy. 'I make her laugh.'

'That's all it takes to join Lia's ladies? Amuse her?'

'Stranger things have happened.'

A line appeared between Rassa's eyebrows. He really was ludicrously handsome. As Lia wore Edar's colours, he sported Farezi's: a golden silk shirt, with dark green embroidery at the collar and cuffs, and a fitted waistcoat in the same green. He sprawled in his chair, his ankles crossed. A calculated facade on display.

'You must certainly be... amusing,' he said.

I'd assumed Lia liked whom she pleased. She certainly hinted her attraction to me. But Rassa implied something delicate and secret. Lia had never flirted or become involved in romance. I'd assumed she took her future duty seriously and wanted to avoid unnecessary complications, but maybe she wasn't attracted to men.

If Lia had been bumped down the succession line, as everyone had assumed would happen, she could have married any noble lady she wanted. But she was Queen and needed her own heir.

Had she unintentionally revealed something around Rassa, given her preferences away? My stomach plummeted. He thought I was Lia's dalliance, her amusement before she chose a husband.

It took all my self-control not to recoil from him. With a single sentence, he'd turned this fragile thing between us – glances and half-finished sentences, punctuated by discussions and silence and hesitant smiles – into a farce consumed by baser instincts.

Not that I didn't feel those. When it was late and I was half-asleep, it was too easy to wonder what kissing her would feel like. And more.

I'd taken too long to answer. A smirk ghosted over Rassa's mouth. I smiled at him like an ideal courtier. Mama would have been proud.

'Prince Rassa, I must say, your eyelashes are *extraordinary*.'

Mama would not be proud of this.

But Lia would be.

Rassa's eyes lit up with rage. His first genuine reaction. I almost admired it.

I don't like you, I realised, surprised at the accompanying relief.

His smile resembled bared teeth. 'Thank you for the compliment, Miss Bayonn.'

Be careful, Rassa. Keep all your threads neat and tidy, so I don't pull one and see where it leads.

Zola walked to the front of the room with her viola. Silence fell. Her opening notes released the tension Rassa had built inside me. While she played, he couldn't speak.

Lia brushed her fingertips across the back of my hand.

Her layers of lace cuffs hid the gesture, but my body reacted like she'd trailed a hand down my back. I tightened my fingers against my seat, somehow suppressing a shudder, as my thoughts splintered. All I wanted was for her to do it again.

I let out a breath, cringing at the slight tremor I couldn't hide. Lia moved her hand to the small space between us. She otherwise didn't move, didn't look at me, gave no inclination that she'd done anything. She watched Zola, as if only the music mattered.

I inched my hand over and pressed it against Lia's.

She still didn't move, didn't even flicker her eyes towards me.

But she smiled.

And so did I.

CHAPTER TWENTY-ONE

LIA

The next morning, Xania walked in and stopped when she realised we were alone. Her eyes narrowed. Perhaps this hadn't been such a good idea, after all.

'The others won't rise for a while yet.' Dawn had broken almost an hour ago. I'd deliberately chosen the east-facing breakfast room for the morning light. Which also happened to catch the embroidery on Xania's bodice.

She didn't move. 'Have I displeased Your Majesty?'

'What? No.' How could she think that after last night? 'I want to apologise. I haven't spent much time with you recently. And...'
I want to know where we stand with each other, whether you're playing along because you feel you must, or –

'Your Majesty isn't obliged to. I thank you, however, for acknowledging my sister's talents.'

This hadn't been the conversation I'd hoped for. Whatever she'd felt last night, when I touched her hand, was now hidden behind etiquette and formality.

Xania's expression turned uneasy. 'I didn't mean–'

'I missed you.' I didn't mean to say it, but it was impossible to ignore, especially when I caught glimpses of her in the halls. It was worse at night, when I was too tired to even summon her for a report. I wanted our routine back.

As the marriage circus took up more of my time and attention, the Court's undercurrents were slipping through my fingers. Too much noise, too much bluster; both effective smokescreens. The foreign nobles also weren't shy about voicing their opinions about politicians. If I weren't careful, they'd start a rift between the Court and Parliament.

As Xania finally sat opposite me, I gestured the servant away. She nodded or shook her head as I lifted each dish lid. When her plate was full and I'd poured tea, she murmured, 'Thank you.'

The rising sun brightened the room. We ate in silence, until she smiled over the rim of her teacup. 'You missed me.'

A weight eased in my chest. 'You'll be unbearable from now on.'

'I'm not Matthias, Your Majesty.' But she used my title without her earlier stiffness.

I didn't know how to explain last night. I wasn't tactile like Uncle, who'd kissed fingers, slapped his courtiers on the shoulders, even hugged them after drinking. It wasn't the same as offering her comfort after Brenna and Naruum.

Maybe it was easier to explain without words. I took a breath, then brushed the back of her hand.

She trembled.

'May I summon you tonight, Miss Bayonn?' I immediately regretted the words, especially when dismay flickered across her face. 'Not for...'

'I understand.'

The memory of her face in firelight and shadow engulfed me, the feel of her skin, how close I'd come to tilting her face back and –

She turned her hand underneath my fingertips so our palms faced each other, then pressed them together. My hand tingled. The sensation raced up my arm.

I swallowed.

'If Your Majesty wills it,' she said. 'I have much to report.'

I coughed and gently pulled my hand back. My cheeks burned. Perhaps this was my saving grace, for Xania looked amused rather than furious or embarrassed.

I wanted to ask about her discussion with Rassa. Aubrey had been thrilled I'd actually read the author he'd suggested and hadn't stopped talking until Zola played, making it difficult to eavesdrop. Judging from Xania's tense posture, she hadn't enjoyed the conversation.

'Good morning, Your Majesty!'

We jumped as Isra walked in. She wore wide-legged Eshvon trousers, and a long tunic embroidered in red. While Edar and

Farezi favoured delicate embroidery, Othayria and Eshvon preferred large, elaborate patterns on their clothes. She'd pulled her gleaming hair back so it fell in curls.

She hesitated before us. There was no telling how long she'd been watching.

I gestured at the chair beside Xania. 'Good morning, Princess Isra. I believe you already know Miss Bayonn, one of my ladies?'

Xania nodded politely. 'Your Highness.'

'Miss Bayonn!' Isra brightened as she sat. 'Miss Zola's sister?'

Whatever had happened between us, the true triumph had been Zola's. Isra, delighted with her music, had engaged Zola in deep discussion for the rest of the evening.

As Isra enthused about Zola's talent, Xania added to the conversation as best she could, while I let my thoughts drift.

Isra hadn't pursued a marriage like I'd expected, instead carefully building up a social circle in Court, mostly of women. She and Matthias had also struck up a tentative friendship, adding fuel to Vigrante's irritation.

I wasn't sure whether to be impressed because Isra had ignored the role expected of her, frustrated since word would eventually reach Juliaane, or suspicious of Isra's true intentions.

Prince Hasan arrived. In an orange robe and brown trousers, accented by a cream shirt with gold thread, he resembled a sunset glimpsed through autumn trees.

Hasan bowed. 'Good morning, Your Majesty; sister, dearest –

and Miss Bayonn!'

If Xania felt mortified at his undignified surprise, she hid it well. 'Good morning, Your Highness.'

Isra's eyelashes fluttered in what I suspected was horror.

Rassa and Prince Aubrey swept into the room. Matthias followed, and barely suppressed his amusement at Hasan's clothes.

Hasan greeted Rassa and Aubrey with cheerful deference. Aubrey replied kindly. Rassa was barely polite. If I'd been a dog, my hackles would have been up at how Rassa's gaze lingered on Xania. She didn't react, but I couldn't tell if she hadn't noticed or refused to acknowledge it.

I only had to get through today, while trying to decide what to say to Xania tonight. If there were any right words at all.

ღ ღ ღ

I was curled up by the fire – it had turned unexpectedly cold – when a knock sounded from the wall. I lowered my book and waited for the second pattern, and stood as the panel slid back. Xania stepped into the room.

'You were invited as one of my ladies,' I said, 'not as Whispers. You could have come through the door.' I was impressed by her caution, but kept my tone amused for a lighter mood.

'Better to be cautious, Your Majesty,' she said, faintly reproachful, 'since anyone could have overheard you this morning.'

'I apologise,' I said, since I couldn't argue against my foolishness. 'And no titles.'

She sighed. 'Lia.'

For all my insistence, I usually avoided saying her name. I'd seen her reaction when I'd said it before, and wanted to savour it the next time. I gestured at the covered plates and silverware on the table. 'Are you hungry?'

'I will never refuse food,' she said firmly.

I served a pale fruit wine, and picked at my plate while she ate. My words had fled.

'How are you enjoying your time with your guests?' she finally asked.

I dropped my fork onto my plate. 'My paperwork is a mountain that could kill if it leans the wrong way. I only have time to myself before I sleep. I spend my days surrounded by people waiting to trip me with smiles and words. And my choices for a husband are a bore, an intolerance, and someone too charming to trust.'

Xania looked torn between laughter and regret that she'd spoken.

'And you ask if I'm *enjoying my time* with them?'

'Princess Isra enjoys her time with you.' There was no trace of Xania's smile now.

I sipped my wine and chose my words carefully. 'No one can deny Princess Isra's beauty and charisma.'

Xania's mouth twisted. 'Of course.'

'But every conversation with her is a potential trap. She's the scholar in the family.'

'Beautiful *and* intelligent?'

'Yes.' I refilled our glasses, and gestured towards the couch. 'The delightful Prince Hasan is her distraction. I'm not expected to marry him – they'd probably stop me if I tried. *She's* the one meant to be here, regardless of the grain agreement.'

'Shall I investigate her entourage again?'

'I'd prefer you investigate with Matthias, but since she befriended him, Isra probably suspects he arranges more than my schedule. I'm afraid you must do most of the work.'

Xania nodded. 'If that's all Your Majesty requires...'

'What?'

'I... now I have my orders...'

'I invited you here as one of my ladies,' I repeated, a harder edge to my voice, 'not as Whispers.' And yet we'd slipped into a Whispers discussion anyway.

Her gaze fell on my discarded book.

'It's one of Aella's novels,' I said, heading the inevitable off at the pass.

'You don't strike me as the type.'

'*You* don't strike me as the type to judge.' I smiled, and ran my hand over the battered leather cover. Aella had made her name in popular romances. Many inferior imitations had followed her success. 'I spend most of my day reading correspondence and appeals,' I said, 'or the legislation drafts Vigrante and I fling back and forth. What do you think I want at the end of the day: history tomes or novels?'

'They're not well written–'

'Aella's *imitators* aren't well written. Have you actually read one of her novels?'

'No,' Xania admitted.

I hesitated, then held out the book.

'No, I couldn't possibly–'

'Take it. Then come back next week and we'll talk about it.'

Xania tilted her head. The fire retained enough strength to splash shadow and light over her face. She wrapped her hands around the book. Her fingers brushed mine. After a moment, I let it go.

I wanted to kiss her. I wanted her to kiss me.

I wanted.

She left. We must have made our goodbyes and curtseys. I was on the couch again, alone, though I didn't remember returning to it.

I shouldn't have given her the book.

I didn't regret it.

CHAPTER TWENTY-TWO

XANIA

I was ten pages into Lia's book when someone knocked on my connecting door. I flopped against my pillow, groaning, then shoved the book into the blankets and climbed out of bed.

I opened the door. 'Zola?'

She held up a tea-tray. 'You're in bed early.'

'I'm tired.'

She used the tray as a shield to get by me. 'Well, I can't drink this all by myself.' She went to my side table and busied herself with the cups. I stared as if I could make her leave through sheer force of will. Then I sighed and pulled out a half-empty box of Farezi chocolates.

She peered inside. 'Oh, good, you haven't eaten all the nice ones.'

'Next time I will,' I muttered, and she stuck out her tongue. 'To what do I owe this pleasure?'

'Lord Martain is reciting sonnets at Mama.' She splashed tea into her cup to check the strength. 'And you've been acting strange lately, even for you. Is everything all right?'

I froze with a chocolate near my mouth. It wasn't impossible to hide things from my family – they knew nothing about Whispers, or why Matthias and I had grown closer after Papa's death – but I'd spent the last few weeks juggling too much work and too many cunning people to keep up the facade.

I ate the chocolate. 'Everything's fine. Work is busy and I'm tired.'

Zola drank her tea. Her silence and steady expression meant she didn't believe me, but would play along. Until she got Mama involved, who would believe nothing.

Her gaze drifted over my shoulder; she lowered her cup. I turned. A corner of Lia's book poked out from under the blankets.

'What are you reading?' she asked, already half-out of the seat to take a look.

'Just a romance novel.' It was the wrong thing to say. I didn't read romances. I was surrounded by people obsessed with feelings and pleasure, so I didn't bother. But Zola did. She'd insist on reading one I'd willingly picked up. I darted towards her, and slapped my hand over the book when she tried to pick it up.

'It's... a book,' Zola said.

'It's...' I didn't have time to concoct a suitable lie; perhaps using Lia would be enough. 'It's the Queen's book. I don't want it ruined.'

'Her Majesty gave you a *romance novel?*'

Wrong.

'We were arguing about them. It's one of Aella's,' I said.

'You hate them!'

'Exactly. I said they were badly written. She claimed otherwise and forced me to read one to prove her point.'

Zola stared at the book. 'The Queen reads romance novels.'

'Everyone needs a hobby.' It had only been ten pages, but I already suspected what kind of romance it was. I couldn't let Zola see, though she'd be excited to read it. The Queen reading romances was one thing. The Queen reading romances between two women was another.

Zola raised her eyebrows. 'Should I leave you alone with the tea and your *romance*?'

If only she knew. 'Yes, please.'

Zola rolled her eyes, but accepted the box of chocolates, then let me push her back out the door.

I glared at the book, begrudgingly finished my tea, and brought a fresh cup back to bed.

When I reached the point where the two women met, I knew what would happen. I kept reading, trying to ignore my screaming instincts. By their first almost-kiss, my tea was cold.

I'd never allowed myself to fall for anyone. As the eldest, my marriage would better our family prospects, so it was easier to avoid Courtly romances.

It felt like Lia had, by giving me this book, revealed a part of herself. Showing it to anyone else felt like betraying her. Ludi-crous, considering what Lia knew about me, but still.

The plot was ridiculous and comforting – an entanglement between a pirate and a lady – and I couldn't stop reading. When I closed the book, my candle was guttering. I'd only manage a few hours of sleep. I ran my fingers across the cover. It was worn from age and rereading, but still carefully preserved: well-loved.

The pirate and lady had worked together to destroy their ene-mies. The pirate continued her course until she'd tired of plunder and blood and returned to her lady. They'd lived their remaining years together, happy, with the implication the pirate had occa-sionally returned to her old ways.

It was too neat an ending. I couldn't believe a pirate would willingly give up the sea, or that the lady would patiently wait for her. But Aella's novels had never accurately reflected life: one of the biggest reasons for her success.

I lay in bed, turning the novel's ending around in my head, wondering if I dared admit what Lia was hinting.

CHAPTER TWENTY-THREE

LIA

Although a member of Government, Admiral Diana of Casa High, commander of my naval forces, didn't bother with politics unless someone – usually Vigrante – tried to interfere in her domain. She was medal-ranked, competent, and ruthless. We weren't at war, so I'd left the Navy alone when I became Queen. I hadn't known what to expect when Diana requested a meeting.

She didn't flinch from my gaze. 'The Master of Whispers didn't work with me last year,' she said, 'but involving their network would make it easier, should they be amenable.'

Hopefully, my reeling thoughts weren't completely obvious. In hindsight, considering last year's poor harvests, and Uncle's expensive tastes and poor diplomatic relations, grain must have come from *somewhere* so people wouldn't starve. Up north, focused on my own estate, I'd assumed Uncle had ordered someone to handle it.

And someone had. Just not through Uncle because he hadn't cared enough.

At least Diana felt confident enough to inform me that she wished to resume stealing grain. But I didn't appreciate the implication that I would automatically give my consent.

I understood her reasoning for last year: Edar had needed grain, and Uncle had done nothing. The problem wasn't even piracy, familiar to every country with a coastline. But having foreign royalty in Edar, with the expectation that I'd marry one of them, made stealing their grain a delicate matter.

And I'd done what Uncle wouldn't: reached out to Eshvon and wrangled grain without depending on Farezi.

'We appreciate your foresight and will consider your suggestion,' I finally said. 'We negotiated with Farezi' – painfully – 'and Eshvon is sending a portion of their harvests.' In return for their youngest princess running around my palace. 'For now, this is enough.' In other words: I wouldn't *currently* condone Diana's piracy, and there would be consequences if she ignored me.

Something flickered in her blue eyes, quickly hidden. Her hair, so dark it reflected a blue sheen, bore the marks of sun and salt. Her hands were well-cared for, if not entirely smooth from her chosen life. She needed little to support her commanding presence, and I'd likely not met her expectations.

'Very well, Your Majesty,' she said. 'The Navy will do whatever necessary to help Edar. We simply await your orders.'

I rose, forcing her up with me. 'We thank you for your continued service, Admiral.' We eyed each other, before she bowed and left. I sat, picking at the conversation, then decided I needed fresh air.

A walk should have helped, but I felt no relief. I rounded a corner in the gardens and found Vigrante walking with Isra. As if my morning needed more complications.

She smiled, as bright as her long turquoise tunic and trousers, but Vigrante looked resigned.

'Good morning, Your Majesty,' Isra said.

'Good morning, Princess. Lord Vigrante.'

He mustered a smile. 'Good morning, Your Majesty.'

Vigrante had been quiet since Rassa and the other royals had arrived, almost six weeks ago. We still lobbied legislation back and forth, comments scrawled in the margins, but without any real energy. He'd actively involved himself in Isra's conversation and much of her entertainment. Either he knew about my grain deal with Eshvon, or he suspected something and hoped it would be useful.

'Lord Vigrante was telling me about your new merchant laws,' Isra said. 'You should have seen Mother's reaction to them!'

I'd never forgive him for killing the merchant boy. At least Vigrante looked uncomfortable, even if Isra didn't know why. For the first time in his career, he probably wanted Matthias to appear and summon me away.

Our conversation was cut short when a woman appeared on the terrace: Vigrante's second-in-command. He was summoned away instead.

'He's a snake,' Isra said after he was gone. 'I presume you've no way of easily removing him?'

I hid my surprise. 'His Government must hold a vote of no confidence. I can remove him if he's a threat to Edar or myself, but I practically need to catch him committing treason.'

'Your grandfather was a fool to let the nobles form a Parliament.'

'There would have been civil war if he hadn't. I may not have been born, and we wouldn't be here talking.' I smiled.

Isra went silent, working her mouth in thought. My skin itched.

I enjoyed our conversations, and hoped she found me tolerable company. But the longer she was here, watching her navigate Court, I was more and more convinced she was here for her own interests, and not her mother's.

We were embroiled in a political game, of sorts, one that I didn't know the rules for.

Footsteps approached: Matthias. Keeping my gaze on him, I said, 'I'm sure your brother and cousin are anxious for your company., Your Highness.'

She bowed and nodded at Matthias. 'With Your Majesty's leave.'

He folded his arms and didn't speak until she was out of earshot. 'Dare I ask?'

'It would appear Vigrante's efforts to befriend Princess Isra are in vain,' I said. 'Or she simply enjoys stringing him along.'

'As she also enjoys stringing you along?'

I sighed. 'For someone who prides himself on observation, you seem oblivious that she flirts with everyone *except* me.' And Xania, I realised, as cold sank into my bones.

'I require your opinion,' he said.

I'd never refused Matthias, no matter my exhaustion or never ending list of duties. But I could sense the unfair lecture brewing.

'I'll come to you this afternoon.' I went back inside before he could respond.

I stalked through the halls. Anyone who tried to catch my attention backed away at my expression. I finally ended up in the gallery, before Father's portrait.

I had his grey eyes and slightly-too-big nose. Mother said my exasperated smile was the same: tight, with the left corner of my mouth jutting up.

Father would never have allowed so many to control him.

I wish I could ask you what to do. Even though he'd probably say no one else could make decisions for me.

He'd been a romantic, somehow, Mother said. Their marriage had been arranged, but he'd known her at Court. When my grandparents sent him off as a diplomat with his new wife, their affection had deepened from living in an unfamiliar country. He'd loved Mother, despite signs she wouldn't be an ideal Queen.

Maybe she'd been exactly the kind of Queen he wanted. While my uncle and aunt's marriage had cracked as the years passed without an heir, my parents had remained devoted. Mother held tight to his memory.

I needed a husband I wouldn't despise, someone I could be comfortable around even in the absence of passion, and eventually I'd need to have a child.

But I couldn't convince myself to want what I needed.

CHAPTER TWENTY-FOUR

XANIA

As Vigrante tried to impress Isra, Hazell, his closest ally after Brenna's death, spent little time around the foreign parties. Instead, he spent more time with Alexandris and lower Step nobles not invited to Lia's gatherings. I suspected a pre-arranged divide and conquer approach.

Most of the Steps didn't notice the staff. The royal family were exceptions: many of their servants had been with them for years. Hazell, thankfully, didn't care once his assigned servants did their work with little fuss. Within a few days of his first discussion with Alexandris, I'd bribed one of Hazell's servants with a better position elsewhere and installed an agent in their place.

Yet whenever I felt capable as Whispers, my Treasury work was happy to prove me wrong.

I was frowning at a set of figures that weren't balancing – and trying to ignore Coin's cat thumping her tail as she sprawled on my desk, dozing – when Terize stopped before me with a folder. 'Please look at this,' she said softly.

I stared at rows of new figures and almost missed the discrepancy. Almost.

I frowned. Tugged a piece of paper from under Coin's cat and re-calculated. Got a different number. Frowned some more.

Terize leaned down. 'Lord Frijian' – her supervisor, who was above mine – 'said it was a calculated error and to ignore it. It didn't make sense, but he was... firm.' Which meant he'd yelled at her. Coin didn't like Frijian (and nor did his cat), but he produced results, and one of the required qualities for Treasury work *wasn't* a pleasant demeanour. Terize's face turned anxious. 'I'm sorry for bothering you – but, well, this isn't the first I've found, yet Frijian says...'

I wanted to shake her. She'd been brave enough to quietly defy Frijian – he'd yelled at me once, right in my face, and my heart had been in my throat even as I'd yelled back because it was the only way to make him *stop* – but was still dumping the problem on me. I didn't need more work. But it was my own fault. I'd fixed so much for her, now she assumed I'd automatically do it.

Instead, I said, 'I'll see what I can do.'

As if sensing my frustration, she reached for the paper, then jerked back as the cat hissed at her. 'No, no, you already do enough for me – oh, *why* doesn't that cat like me? It was just – it's such a *large* discrepancy.'

Large was an understatement. If Mama had received this loan, the discrepancy would be the difference between Zola and I getting new dresses this year and adding enough to our dowries to easily marry into the Sixth Step.

'Ignore the cat. No, I'll do it. Frijian is horrible to you.' I ignored her protests until she returned to her desk. I scowled at Coin's cat, reluctantly scratched her chin, then glared at the papers. I could do this. I'd done it before.

It was a ridiculous mistake. Heads would roll when Coin found out – including Frijian's, for refusing to take it seriously.

I was so focused, I didn't notice something was wrong until silence fell. I looked up. A servant in Farezi livery was talking to Coin, who whirled and glared into the Treasury pit. His gaze landed on me.

'Miss Bayonn.' His words dropped into the hush like pebbles into a pond. 'Up here, now.'

I locked my work away and stood, aware of everyone's stares. What did Farezi – what did *Rassa* – want with me? Nothing good, surely, considering our last conversation, but I could hardly refuse to see him.

The servant bowed. 'Miss Bayonn. His Royal Highness, Prince Rassa, requests your presence.'

'The honour is mine.'

As the servant turned, Coin leaned in close and murmured, 'Keep your head, girl.'

As I followed the servant, I kept coming back to my most experienced Farezi spy. I hadn't heard from her in weeks. She'd infiltrated Rassa's circle, so I'd assumed she'd need time to gather new Court sources after he left for Edar. Now her silence worried me.

All too soon we were at his suite. As the doors closed behind me, I broke out in a sweat everywhere possible.

'Miss Bayonn.' Rassa strolled in, his hands held out in welcome. 'I hope you weren't *too* shocked by my impulsiveness!'

I curtseyed. 'Your Highness. How may I be of service?' The words felt wrong.

'I feel we started off badly the other night,' he said. 'I wish to make amends.'

From anyone else, it would seem genuine. From Rassa, it felt like a trap. I wanted to laugh, turn on my heel, and stalk away, but he was the Farezi Crown Prince. It wouldn't be worth it.

'Of course, Your Highness. Amend away.'

The corner of his mouth quirked. 'I see how you amuse Lia.'

I followed him into an intimate room for a small gathering. A table strained under gleaming china and bright desserts.

I'd never, ever tell Lia, but now I realised why Rassa had brought his own Pastry Chef. Each cake had a flourish boasting of the long, intense training required of a Farezi *pâtissier* or *pâtissière*. Our kitchens simply couldn't replicate it.

The cakes ranged from creamy to sharp: dark chocolate and cinnamon; vanilla; a particularly lovely coffee cake that Lia would enjoy. There were rows of macarons and flavoured spun sugar. We ate pomegranate sorbet, an Eshvon specialty, as palate cleansers between courses. For the Farezi heir, only the best would do.

My stomach agreed.

As we sucked on spun sugar (I resisted stirring my tea with it to see his reaction), Rassa snapped his fingers. A servant nodded at his rapid-fire Farezinne, too quick for me to decipher, and returned with a silver platter.

'*La Religieuse*,' Rassa announced. The pastries, shaped like the old Farezi female clergy, were eaten for ceremonial purposes – birthdays, engagements, occasionally weddings – and nostalgia. They symbolised Farezi's old Empire and religious power. They were understandably less popular in countries conquered under the Second Empire.

They were also traditionally eaten when parents first met their new daughter- or son-in-law.

Was he hinting about my feelings for Lia? Or was it a subtle jab that I'd never marry as high as the company I kept?

'My mother always said important matters must be decided over *La Religieuse*.'

'Your mother is wise, Your Highness.'

He impaled his pastry nun with a fork and dragged cream across the plate.

I stared sadly at my own nun. Perhaps they looked so delicious because no one ate them, only destroyed them while flinging steel-sharp words at each other.

'No matter how much you amuse her,' Rassa said, 'why does Lia *care* so much for you? She shouldn't allow you to mix above your rank.'

Maybe he wasn't suspicious, merely socially oblivious. He seemed to consider Lia a lesser royal cousin to be indulged. He wouldn't spend more time than necessary with someone like me, so why should she? And he didn't want to understand, so he never would.

I carefully beheaded my nun. The vanilla filling had a hint of strawberry. 'The Queen doesn't need to explain her actions to anyone, Your Highness.'

He waved his fork dismissively, an action that would have disgusted Lia's mother. 'She must, because of your Parliament. Farezi does not need to justify itself. Our people know better.'

As one of *those who should know better*, I stayed silent. If he was trying for a better impression, he'd failed. He was treating me like an Upper Step lady, while reminding me of my actual rank.

I fantasised about throwing my *Religieuse* in his face and walking out. But it would be a waste of excellent pastry.

'I've offended you,' he said.

I was rubbing my fork between my thumb and forefinger. I dropped it on my plate and forced a smile. 'You want to make amends, Your Highness, yet insult my Queen and country. I am... discombobulated.'

Nobles from the Upper Steps would have navigated this with

more finesse. Lia wouldn't have hesitated in putting him in his place. I didn't care.

Rassa smiled. 'Have you ever considered your prospects abroad, Miss Bayonn?'

Was he offering me a *job*?

It could have been worse. He could have proposed marriage.

'Not especially, Your Highness. My family is in Edar. I have no desire to leave.'

The irrational part of me insisted *Lia Lia Lia*.

'You should. Lia finds you amusing now, but her favour won't last. You'll annoy her, eventually, and one's star in Court always falls faster than it rises.'

As a good courtier and Whispers, I should keep my mouth shut and note anything Lia could use against Rassa.

'I do not respond well to insults.'

Or I could succumb to pettiness.

Rassa dropped his fork onto his pastry and cream battlefield.

After a long moment, grudging respect sparked on his face. Or perhaps admiration for my potential death wish.

He stood, which allowed me to get up. At least my dress hid my trembling legs. 'We'll talk again, Miss Bayonn.' His smile was more warning than reassurance. 'You're extremely interesting.'

I wanted to be the dullest person alive.

I curtseyed. 'I look forward to it, Your Highness.' We held eye contact for a long moment. He looked away first, and I escaped before anything else could go wrong.

I couldn't figure out what he'd meant to achieve by this. It was more than disliking me, or disapproving of my friendship with Lia. And Rassa didn't seem suspicious about whether she had an ulterior motive for favouring me, so perhaps he simply thought I was trying to rise above my rank.

My mind flashed back to Lia's book, hidden in my room. It was time to return it to her.

And the next time something like this happened, I'd finish my *Religieuse* before sparring with steel-sharp words.

CHAPTER TWENTY-FIVE

LIA

The Little Church was one of the palace's religious relics. No one could bear gutting the small room, with its stained glass and serene calm, so it stayed forgotten through indulgent neglect. I'd spent hours there when I was younger, reading and thinking and hiding from the Court. Someone would find me, eventually, in the portrait gallery. But no one would think of looking here, and I wanted more time alone.

I pushed open the dark doors. The plain outside was deceptive: the room was large and bright. Pale walls reflected sunlight through stained glass windows. Figures stood in the panes, intricate and tall, the Edaran gods who had slowly turned into myths, twisted into symbols of nature and seasons, their lives perhaps as invented as their legends.

Lady Winter stood in the tallest window, surrounded by snow and dark branches, flanked by her companions, Twilight and Night. We celebrated her during Midwinter, when the Queen danced in a pale, fragile dress, joined by the King and a favourite as Twilight and Night.

I sat in a pew and stared up at Lady Winter. I would be her this year, as my aunt, grandmother, and great-grandmother had before me. And I'd most likely dance with Aubrey to show my favour.

The church door opened; I sighed as familiar footsteps came up the aisle.

Correction: no one would think of looking for me here – except Matthias.

He sat beside me on the pew. The silence grew long and taut between us.

'I'm sorry,' he finally said.

'When I walk away,' I replied, still focused on Lady Winter, 'it isn't a challenge for you to find me.' I could count on one hand the number of times I'd heard Matthias apologise. It didn't come easy to him. That didn't mean I had to hear it.

'I don't trust Isra,' he said.

'None of us trust her,' I said. 'You don't get to be cranky about it. If she's stringing me along, it's nothing to do with a lack of flirting.'

'Possibly because she's realised you want to flirt with Xania more than anyone else,' Matthias said, soft and tense.

I closed my eyes. Took a deep breath. Matthias had known me the longest of all. Of course he would notice this.

'Nothing has happened,' I said. *Nothing probably will, even if I want it to.* 'I don't even know if she feels the same.'

'Xania can't keep her eyes off you.'

'That means nothing.'

Matthias scoffed. 'That means everything, for both of you.'

'Since when are you a master of relationships?'

He laughed, and sprawled more comfortably in the pew, his hair and skin stained blue, red, and green from the glass.

I rubbed my mouth, staring at Lady Winter, who had loved and been loved. 'I gave Xania one of Aella's novels.'

Matthias slowly turned to face me. 'One of the terrible ones?' he asked, almost hopefully.

'My favourite.'

'You gave her the pirates?' He groaned. 'If you want a pirate, have the Admiral divorce her wife! What are you trying to accomplish?'

'I don't know.'

'What are you *hoping* to accomplish?' His abrupt sternness surprised me.

'*I don't know.*'

'Has Xania spoken to you since?'

'No, but it was only yesterday.' Panic, temporarily banished by Vigrante and Isra, returned in full force.

'Zola's been infatuated with ladies before,' Matthias said slowly. 'She swoons and admires from afar. Xania never seemed interested in anyone. I assume you didn't hint at your *general* attraction when you gave her the book?'

I wanted to hide under the pew.

Matthias dragged a hand down his face. 'I've seen how you look at each other. And the Court gossips. They feel Xania's too low-ranked to deserve so much of your attention.'

'The Court can't function without gossip.'

'There's another way you could use this to your advantage,' Matthias said, pulling me from my gloom.

'Please, enlighten me.'

'Should you marry Aubrey – well, Xania... could... there's precedent, though they never really proved it with your grandfather...'

I stared at him, bewildered. It took several moments to follow his train of thought. 'You mean... for her to be my mistress?'

Matthias flinched at the distaste in my voice, but he should have known not even to suggest it. Even as their marriage had shattered, my uncle and aunt had remained loyal to each other. Great-Grandfather had been besotted with my great-grandmother, who, by all accounts, had been more than a match for him. But Grandfather had surrounded himself with many favourites, though if anything had gone on behind closed doors, it had done so with my grandmother's knowledge.

But I wanted a partnership, not a mistress, and it wasn't Xania's fault I needed an heir.

Maybe it was better to admit nothing. Pretend the book had been a gesture between friends.

I'd probably marry Aubrey, who was the best of my options. He was calm and poised: an ideal prince. Yet despite knowing he'd be an excellent husband, I wouldn't be content in our marriage, never mind happy. We'd have a kind marriage, utterly lacking in passion. I'd grown up knowing – expecting – this, but after meeting Xania and allowing myself to imagine something different –

Foolish. Foolish foolish foolish.

I took a trembling gulp of air and buried my face in my hands. My eyes and throat burned with tears dangerously close to the falling.

'Lia! Lia!' Matthias tugged my arm, forcing my head up. I caught a glimpse of his stricken expression, before a sob cracked from me. I leaned forward, and he closed his arms around me in a hug.

I cried into his shirt. 'I don't know what to do.'

'I... I think you need to talk to her,' he said after a few moments. 'This – this isn't ideal, but I don't think either of you can keep ignoring it.'

'Matthias, what if she feels the same? What if I'm not imagining it? What about Aubrey?' He was comforting and familiar. For a moment, it felt like we were children again, unconcerned by our distant future. Papa wasn't dead yet, nor were Matthias's parents and Baron Bayonn. We hadn't hardened from so much loss.

He hugged me tighter. 'We'll deal with that later. Be happy. Kiss her. It's a *good* thing.'

I let out a shaky laugh. 'This must make you long for romance again.'

He pulled away. 'No, Lia. In this, I wouldn't want to be you for all the riches in the world.'

CHAPTER TWENTY-SIX

XANIA

I shook my head at the neat columns of figures and symbols. 'I understand your calculations to here, my lady' – I pointed a third of the way down the paper – 'but then it's gibberish.'

Lady Astrii frowned. 'Surely we're past the point of titles?'

'Forgive me, Astrii. Habits die hard.' Between her and Lia, all palace conversation would be informal within a year.

Astrii was a friend of sorts, more than I'd expected from any of Lia's ladies. I liked having someone to talk to when Zola wasn't here and Lia was occupied with the royals. Astrii had caught me peering at her mathematical theories one day, and started enthusiastically explaining before I could apologise. Where I used numbers to balance budgets and handle bankruptcy, Astrii used them to invent and construct.

Her father, Lord Rathun, oversaw Zeffari, Edar's largest southern port city. Her love of mathematics ran in neither side of her family. She cared about dresses, manners, and witty conversation because her father insisted on it for potential suitors. It reminded me too much of Brenna and her family, but Astrii didn't seem in danger of a similar fate.

Astrii put her papers away. 'Your heart's not in it today, Xania.'

So much for hiding my distraction. 'I'm sorry, Astrii. It's nothing to do with you.'

Lia sat near the window, brooding at the rain. Everyone stayed away from her. Hasan was losing badly to Rassa at cards. Lia had noticed me when I arrived, but I'd curtseyed and hurried over to Astrii. The book, and what it hinted, loomed between us.

I dragged my attention back to Astrii. 'Have you heard from Eraxiun?'

Her eyes lit up. For all Astrii's supposedly unladylike activities, her marriage prospects were undoubtedly helped by her beauty. Her skin was darker than mine, like Lord Martain's. But we had the same tight curls, which she wore as thin braids twisted and pinned together. We'd cemented our budding friendship by sharing combing tricks.

'His reply arrived two days ago,' she said. 'He's still sceptical, of course, but he admitted a working engine is possible with further adjustments. It's not so farfetched, considering what they used to achieve during the First Empire.'

'I'll believe it when I see it.' A metal invention for travelling across the country, fuelled by slow-burning wood and coal. It seemed absurd, but Astrii claimed it would take people from the north to Arkaala in less than a day – if proper funding could be secured and the necessary infrastructure maintained through taxation.

We stood as Aubrey and Isra entered the room. After they greeted Lia, Isra joined Rassa and Hasan, while Lia motioned for Aubrey to sit beside her. They spoke quietly.

Something large and oppressive squeezed against my ribs. As if I had any right to jealousy.

'Xania, your head's still in the clouds!'

While Astrii's voice held a teasing note, the edge in it made me tense. The ladies never truly forgot I was Fifth Step. At times they couldn't help showing their superiority. To her credit, Astrii looked momentarily ashamed before suggesting a card game poorly suited to two players.

'You're just jealous,' she said, dealing out the cards and pieces as if nothing had happened.

I laughed. 'Of your esteemed correspondence with Eraxiun? Please, don't make me hurt your feelings.'

'Pardon me, ladies, but are you talking about Eraxiun?'

We stared up at Aubrey.

I recovered first and stood to acknowledge him. 'Prince Aubrey.'

He smiled. 'Such formality.'

Because I'm jealous of you, and it sickens me, for you've been nothing but kind.

'You know Eraxiun?' Astrii asked, excited.

'I know *of* him.' Aubrey sat at our insistence. 'He refuses to correspond with a "royal rat", as he calls me.'

I tried not to laugh.

Eraxium lived in Rijaan, my great-grandmother's homeland. As a republic, they scorned royalty and noble titles. The social structure seemed bewildering, but the Riija probably thought similar of Edar's Steps.

'Your parents don't fund schools as much as Eraxium thinks they should,' Astrii said, unfazed.

'I'm trying to convince them otherwise, believe me,' Aubrey said, delighted. 'You correspond with him? Please, tell me everything!'

Unable to help myself, I looked over at Lia – and froze.

Rassa and Isra stood before her chair. She looked calm, almost bored, by whatever Rassa was saying. But her knuckles were white as she gripped the armrests. She and Isra glanced at me, and my stomach dropped.

What was Rassa saying?

Isra looked uncomfortable and worried, which made me worry in turn. I didn't realise I was halfway out of my seat until she shook her head ever so slightly.

'Miss Bayonn?' Aubrey followed my gaze. His expression hardened, and he gestured for me to follow him across the room. His smile didn't reach his eyes. 'Are we missing a fascinating discussion, dear cousins?'

'I was telling Her Majesty and Princess Isra of the *fascinating* discourse Miss Bayonn and I had yesterday,' Rassa said.

It shouldn't have sounded remarkable. There were dozens of public places we could have met and spoken: the halls, the libraries, the dining rooms, even outside the Treasury.

But his tone slithered down my spine. He made *fascinating* sound insidious.

Edarans didn't publicly insinuate what Rassa hinted about me.

'Cousin,' Lia said, barely civil, 'you forget—'

'*I beg your pardon, Rassa?*' Aubrey snapped.

Silence rippled through the room, before everyone awkwardly resumed their conversations.

Aubrey glared at Rassa. The calm, kind gentleman was gone, revealing a furious man with clenched teeth. Perhaps the muscles underneath his shirts weren't for show.

'You heard me, Cousin,' Rassa said.

'No, I heard bile.'

Aubrey's outburst gave Lia time to recollect herself, though not before she cast an incensed look towards him. Isra also didn't hide her exasperation. This probably wasn't the first time she'd witnessed Aubrey storming to someone's defence.

They could all make their displeasure known to Rassa, with little consequences. I was in no such position. None of them, naturally, considered this for a moment.

I had to be subtle. I'd allow no one, not even a royal, to treat me like this.

I dragged my lips into a smile. 'Prince Rassa exaggerates, I'm afraid. We did indeed speak, but it was hardly *stimulating*.'

Isra pretended to cough, but not before I caught her grin.

'How unfortunate, Miss Bayonn.' The ghost of a smile flickered over Lia's mouth. 'Rassa, I expected better of you.'

Aubrey looked like we'd started speaking backwards.

I couldn't decipher Rassa's expression; part of me didn't want to.

'My mother would also have expected better of me,' he finally said, 'since she taught me the art of conversation.'

It wasn't an apology. But it was surely more than other women in my situation had received from him.

Lia wore a serene smile like a mask.

Aubrey deflated.

Isra slipped her arm through mine. 'Walk with me, Miss Bayonn.'

As she drew me away, Terize rose from another table, as if to excuse me from Isra's clutches. Isra flung a scathing look towards her, and Terize dropped back into her seat.

'If I were you, I'd reconsider that friendship,' Isra said. 'Lady Terize lacks power, so she clings to whoever she feels has it. Eventually, you'll be insufficient for her needs.'

I gritted my teeth. 'Terize would be far more successful if everyone stopped underestimating her.'

'Perhaps. I apologise for Aubrey,' Isra said. 'He sometimes lets chivalry get the better of him. It's still no excuse.'

If I'd been Sixth or Seventh Step, I could have said exactly what I thought of Aubrey's old-fashioned chivalry. Instead, I said, 'The prince is kind.'

Isra smiled. 'He's an idiot. As for Prince Rassa, there *is* no excuse.'

Was this a potential hand of friendship? She admired Zola's music. She and Matthias had built a friendship on sarcasm and vicious philosophical debate. But she was royalty. Her generosity and friendship only went so far.

When I remained silent, Isra turned to lighter matters. My anger towards all of them hardened into resolve.

I'd go to Lia about the book tonight. Whatever was building between us, she wasn't the only one in control of it.

CHAPTER TWENTY-SEVEN

LIA

Despite the roaring fire, I couldn't shake the chill in my bones.

Xania's expression at Rassa's insinuations: mortified and resentful. The gall of us royals, smothering her with our privileged indignation when she could counter Rassa's hideousness herself. I had no idea how to apologise. She had every reason to be furious and embarrassed.

'I'm going to bed,' I announced to the room. 'I'll know what to do in the morning.'

The sound of a tapped sequence came from the wall, loud in the silence. My heartbeat sped up.

It was hers.

I crept to the wall as the sequence finished.

Another few heartbeats. Then Xania whispered, 'Your Majesty?'

'Xania?' I flicked the catch on the wall. We'd arranged no

meeting tonight.

She held out a book. My Aella novel. 'I... I thought I should return this.'

My heart hammered for another reason. 'You didn't read it.' Maybe this was her polite answer.

'Oh, I did!'

I'd given it to her two days ago. 'I – I didn't realise you read so quickly.'

She flashed a smile, a hint we might be on more stable ground than I thought. 'It was engrossing, Your Majesty. And... enlightening. The plot is ridiculous, but entertaining.' I couldn't stop staring at her mouth. 'I... I'm not sure what you expect from me.'

'I expect you to sit, please, and we'll discuss the book.' As she sat, I tapped my fingers against my hip. I'd had a plan for this. I'd intended on being better dressed for a start, with wine and food ready. I'd wanted to serve Sekran food from the north-east, Father's first diplomatic post. I'd thought it would impress her. Now, it seemed ridiculous.

'Do you need refreshment?' I asked, falling back on dependable etiquette.

'No, thank you.'

'Well, I do. Feel free to change your mind.' I settled for a red wine and placed a glass before her, a suggestion not a demand, and sat with a sensible gap between us.

'I want to apologise– I began, as she said, 'Your Majesty–'

We stopped, gesturing at each other.

When she didn't speak, I said, 'I want to apologise for earlier. You're fully capable of defending yourself.'

'Queens don't apologise.'

I threw etiquette to the ground. 'For all you claim I can't be or can't do, at least accept what I am.'

She focused on her untouched glass. 'My apologies, Lia.'

I swallowed, then nudged my hand against hers.

After a moment, she smiled. 'Chivalry isn't dead with Aubrey around, then?'

I laughed. 'No, definitely not!'

'Isra says he'll apologise.'

'If he didn't realise his mistake, she'll tell him.' I took a large swallow of wine, as if it held my courage. 'I still want to hurt Rassa for what he said, though I have no right.'

'I want to hurt Aubrey every time he's pleasant to you, and I have no right.' Xania's face turned slack with horror.

Joy swelled in my chest, pleasantly straining, before it was engulfed by terror. It was one thing to daydream and want her. It was another to come face-to-face with her feelings.

'Your Majesty, I apologise–'

'Enough.' For once, I wanted this to go as I hoped. 'What did you think of the book?'

Xania stared at me, incredulous. 'The plot was ridiculous. But I don't think you read it for that.'

'No.' Warmth rolled in my stomach. 'I still wouldn't turn down a dashing pirate.' The words were soft and deliberate.

'Oh, I don't know.' Xania took a gulp of wine. 'I've always preferred dashing princesses.'

I smiled. Swirled the dregs in my glass, then put it aside.

Xania's gaze flickered between my eyes and my mouth. She bit her bottom lip, and I hissed in a breath.

Discussing the book was dangerous.

Being here was dangerous. This close, this alone, relaxed with warmth and wine and wanting, the gap between us slowly decreased.

Xania's chest rose and fell; the light struck off the gleaming threads in her teal dress. I couldn't look away.

'I think I'm about to do something inadvisable,' I murmured, tantalisingly close to her mouth. My pulse pounded in my throat, my ears, my head: *yes yes yes*.

'Please,' Xania breathed.

I wrapped my arms around her, her mouth met mine, and all I could taste was wine. Her perfume teased the air around us.

My hands slid down her arms and around to dig into her back. She made a small sound. All I could feel taste think was the pressure taste warmth of her mouth against mine.

We pulled apart, gasping. Her eyes were glazed. My hair had tumbled from its pins. Had she done that? She must have.

She smiled. I shivered at the heat in her heavy-lidded eyes.

I wanted.

I wanted.

She wanted.

'I think I'm about to do something inadvisable,' she said.

'Please,' I said. 'Please.'

She slid her fingers into my hair. I opened my mouth to hers.

She trembled against me and I was undone and I didn't care.

CHAPTER TWENTY-EIGHT

XANIA

Lia kept making this soft sound, between a gasp and a whimper. My hands wanted more, my mouth wanted more. Her soft sound turned into a yelp when I trailed my lips down her throat.

Her fingers scrabbled against my back. My head reeled, and the world tilted.

We landed on the floor in a tangled heap.

'*Are you all right?*' I asked, horrified.

Lia closed her eyes and laughed.

I eyed her, before a giggle escaped me. She leaned against my shoulder, still laughing. Her breath ghosted against my neck, before she kissed the spot where my collarbone and shoulder met. My breath caught. She brought her fingertips to her mouth, then pressed them against my lips.

I kissed her fingers gently.

She made the sound again.

I wanted.

We kissed, and everything blurred until we had to pull away. My heartbeat drummed in my ears.

Lia struggled for air, her cheeks bright red. 'So... so...'

'Yes.'

She inched her hand towards mine; I wrapped our fingers together. Her laugh turned into a sob, but she wasn't crying. She raised our interlocked fingers and kissed my knuckles.

I'd never come close to swooning or fainting before, but if I passed out now, I completely understood why.

'Well,' I said, 'now I know you feel the same.'

Lia raised an eyebrow. 'I gave you a novel about women falling in love.'

'Anyone could give me that. *Matthias* could give me that book.'

'Matthias would give you a historical account of notable female pirates. No romance.'

I scoffed, but it was easy to return her smile. We kissed slowly this time, the carefulness making my hands tingle and chest hurt. According to Zola's novels, we should have been tearing at each other's clothes, but this was terrifying enough, and Lia didn't strike me as the clothes-ripping type. Even in my daydreams, she'd stayed sensible.

When we broke apart again, I glanced at the clock and groaned. 'I should go.' I couldn't risk being late to work. I could hardly tell Coin I hadn't got enough sleep from kissing the Queen.

Lia trailed her fingers up my arm, and sighed as I shivered.

'I suppose.'

A small knot relaxed inside me; a tiny fear that she'd want me to stay, whether or not I was ready.

She got up, then helped me stand. 'Good night.' She brushed her lips across my knuckles.

I swallowed. 'Good night.' My hand trembled as I opened the panel and stepped into the passages. I leaned against the wall after it closed, waiting for my head to stop spinning. I'd hoped for this, but now I felt terrified. She was the Queen; I was barely Fifth Step. I was her Whispers; I was supposed to keep her safe.

But I'd coaxed *sounds* from her.

I pressed a hand over my mouth. A smile curved against my fingers.

I turned right. After twenty steps, I knew, like a bucket of cold water over my head, that I wasn't alone.

Since the foreign royalty had arrived, Matthias and I inspected the passages every three days, checking the subtle clues and failsafes that kept them secure. The passages were the Whispers' domain, but I'd always been cautious because we'd never discovered my predecessor's identity.

I'd passed several failsafes on my way to Lia; none had been disturbed or tampered with. I turned left. A wire I'd stretched between the walls, thin and fragile enough to cleanly snap, lay on the ground.

Someone was exploring.

I headed towards a large intersection, and pressed my right sleeve against my bodice. I plucked at some loose threads, swiftly unravelling them. My dagger slipped from the sheath sewn into my sleeve, solid and reassuring in my palm. Unlike at Lia's coronation, this time I had a weapon.

It was quiet enough that I easily caught the sound of someone's heel grinding against loose grit behind me. My heart picked up. I embraced the adrenaline. It would keep me alive.

I hid the dagger against my skirts and counted my breaths. I reached the intersection, turned against a wall so I kept the entrances in sight, and waited.

A dozen heartbeats later, I heard footsteps. I could have drawn them further into the passages, but I didn't want to impulsively use a different exit in case someone saw me. Waiting to strike first wasn't much smarter, but it was the best out of my poor options.

The person stepped into the intersection.

I moved before I could doubt myself, and slashed at their face.

A low cry. I'd already moved towards his knife hand, stomping on his foot at the same time. The knife snagged on fabric, before a soft give. The man hissed and aimed his boot at my shin. I yelped, darting away from his knife swipe.

Pain burned across my chest and upper stomach. The blade had cut through my dress and corset. I swallowed my scream and tried for another lunge.

I got him across the face again. I switched my dagger to my

other hand as he flinched, and slammed my palm into his nose. He reeled back towards the wall. I barely caught his knife with my own. The blades scraped against each other, as I curled my other hand into a fist.

His nose crunched.

His head smacked the wall with a similar sound, before he slumped to the ground. I swayed, gasping for breath. Pain roared through me. I pressed my hand against my dress. It was already wet with blood. I needed help.

I also needed to put this man somewhere he couldn't escape.

I attempted deep breaths, light-headed, terrified of passing out. This was what my life had come to: not being knifed to death, yet responsible for the man who'd tried to kill me. Right now, kissing Lia didn't feel like suitable compensation.

'All right,' I told him. 'I suppose I better do something with you.'

I bullied my cloudy mind into logic. I had to keep pressure on the wound. It didn't feel deep enough for panic, but I wasn't sure how much blood I'd lost, so pressure it was.

Well. My dress was already ruined.

I cut at my underskirt, wrapped strips around my chest, cursed as I struggled to tighten them. The pain was now a steady burn, with occasional flares. I'd no illusions about how much it would hurt when a physician got involved. How could I explain this? Fifth Step ladies didn't get themselves into these situations.

Worry about that later.

I pulled the man away from the wall. I'd have to drag him. He wasn't much taller than me, but I could feel muscle in his shoulders and arms. I gripped his upper arms, braced myself, and started pulling him back the way we'd come.

It hadn't taken long to reach the intersection before. Time and distance mocked me on the way back. My arms ached. Sweat pooled under my dress. The bleeding, which I thought had slowed, started again. Fresh warmth spread across the dried, stiff fabric.

Only a little further. You'd feel worse if you were dying.

The light-headedness returned. I'd probably collapse into Lia's arms. Zola would be so proud of me.

When we reached Lia's wall, I didn't care about patterns or finesse, or acting like a swooning damsel. I dumped the man near the edge of the panel, then hammered at the wall, swaying, the dregs of my energy gone.

The panel opened. Lia peered out. Her face brightened, before something gave me away. She stared at my chest, frowning at the underskirt strips, then realised the darker stain was blood.

She yanked the panel open wider, her eyes wide. 'Xania, what happened?'

I stared down at my chest. 'It looks worse than it is.'

'Let a physician decide.'

She gently helped me into the study, then stood, flexing her hands open and closed. She was frightened.

I swayed, leaning against her when she reached for me. 'The man who attacked me is in the passages.'

'If I let go, promise you won't topple?'

I nodded, and she stuck her head in the passage, then turned back to face me with a raised eyebrow.

'He's not dead,' I said. 'I only knocked him out.'

'How did you get him here?'

'I dragged him.'

'While bleeding?'

I nodded.

She cupped my face in her hands. 'You're wonderful. I'll tell you properly when this is over, but just so you know.'

I blushed – it hurt – then looked away, which also hurt. Everything seemed to hurt. 'I... I... need to sit down.'

Lia jerked back, mortified, then helped me to a chair. She rummaged in a drawer for a thin towel and pressed it into my hands. 'Keep it against the wound.' Now she resembled the Lia I knew, brisk and competent. She strode towards a row of bells and yanked two of them.

'Who are you calling?'

'A servant to wake Matthias,' she said, 'and my physician.' She gave me her best queenly stare. 'You're not leaving until you've been treated. Do you know the best thing about the royal physician?'

I shook my head.

'She swore an oath of silence when she took the position.' Lia's expression hardened. 'If anyone finds out about this, it will be from you, me, Matthias – or her.'

Polite knocking on the door.

'I'll help you into the next room,' Lia said. 'If it's the servant for Matthias, I don't want them to see...' She eased the panel back until only a sliver of the passage showed – if the man regained consciousness and tried to flee, she'd hear him – and helped me into the adjoining room. I barely swallowed a wince as I sat. She rubbed my arm, attempted a smile, and returned to the other room.

The pain changed to a steady throbbing. Lia returned, followed by a woman with deep auburn hair and blue eyes. Lia took my hand. 'It's easier if you do what she says.'

The woman laughed. 'The same can be said for you, Your Majesty.'

Lia's physician was about a decade older than us and sternly cheerful. Lia supplied her with hot water and towels. When my dress had to come off, she retreated to wait for Matthias.

I hissed at the bared knife wound, slashed diagonally from the inside of my left breast towards my stomach. The physician carefully washed away the blood. 'You're lucky,' she finally said. 'The brocade and corset protected you from the worst. You need stitches, but it won't scar badly if you're careful.'

She didn't need to say what would have happened if I'd worn a different dress, or moved slower.

Her brisk competence was intimidating: before I knew it, she was ready to stitch me up. I gritted my teeth as she worked, silently counting each stitch.

'Can you take bed rest?' She rubbed balm onto bandages that went over the fresh stitches, then wrapped everything in dry bandages. She spoke without much hope; if I was being treated in the Queen's quarters, I was clearly involved in things best kept secret. I couldn't have bed rest for something I couldn't explain.

'No.'

'Of course not. Then see me every morning. Come before or after breakfast. I'll give you my mark so an apprentice doesn't enthusiastically send you away.'

'I can change the dressings,' I said.

She smiled. 'Her Majesty thinks highly enough of you to wake me in the middle of the night. Your well-being is now my concern. Don't worry. I'll include lectures on the dangers of intimate involvement with knives.'

My laugh turned into wheezing as my wound pulled.

'No laughing, for a start. Knife wounds are not a laughing matter.' She narrowed her eyes. 'And remedy whatever is the cause of your lack of sleep.'

After giving me powders I could dissolve into drinks for pain relief, the physician left. Lia mixed a dose and waited with crossed arms until I drank it all.

She gave me mint tea afterwards. 'I think she deliberately makes them taste foul.'

'How long have you known her?'

'She was my physician at home. When I took the throne, she came south with me.'

I squeezed her hand. 'Thank you.'

'I could hardly do nothing...' She bit her lip.

I kissed the back of her hand.

Lia swallowed. 'You should sleep. You'll be in pain tomorrow. A servant will walk you back.' Now that the passages were compromised, we would have to be careful. I would hardly be attacked in the halls, but Lia probably feared I'd pass out.

'What about the man? And Matthias?'

'We'll tell you in the morning,' Lia said. 'You need to rest.'

She was right, but I was still irritated that she'd automatically taken control.

We stood at another knock. Lia brushed my cheek and kissed me. 'Good night, Xania.' Her eyes gleamed with tears. 'I... I...' She shook her head in frustration.

I'm glad I'm alive, too. I leaned up, ignoring the pinch in my chest, and kissed her back. 'Good night, Lia.'

The servant didn't speak as we walked, likely irritated at being awake but too professional to show it. I strained to hear other footsteps in the silence.

I checked my locks five times before carefully crawling into bed. I lay there for a long time before I tipped over the edge of sleep. Pain pricked at the edges of my consciousness, a warning of what awaited me in the morning.

CHAPTER TWENTY-NINE

LIA

There wasn't enough face powder in the country to help me with the day ahead.

'You look about as good as I feel,' Matthias said.

'You're most kind.'

He collapsed into a seat and scraped his hands over his face. 'Can we claim illness and go back to bed?'

In the entire time I'd known Matthias, he'd never shown weakness. But he'd dragged Xania into this, and now she was hurt. I dumped sugar and cream into his coffee, as he sat miserably with his guilt.

I passed his cup over. 'Have you seen her yet?'

'No answer when I knocked. I presumed she was with your physician.'

We drank and ate despite our lack of appetite, steeped in silence, until Xania walked in. She moved carefully, her face tight, but attempted a smile. 'Good morning.'

'Don't even think of curtseying. You'll faint.' I jabbed a finger at the seat beside me. She meekly lowered herself into it.

Matthias raised his eyebrows. 'Did you manage any sleep?' he asked her.

'A little.' She nodded when I pointed at the teapot. 'I woke before dawn, but didn't try to sit up for a while.'

'Are your stitches all right?' I asked.

'I didn't pull any. The physician is satisfied, though she'd be happier if nothing had happened in the first place. How is our friend this morning?'

'Better than when he regained consciousness last night. What did you hit him with?'

'The wall,' Xania said serenely. 'Has he said anything?'

'Not yet. Kartek and Curjan are enjoying the challenge.' Matthias undermined his calm words by tearing up a slice of bread.

'So you've no idea who employed him?' I asked.

Matthias eyed more of the bread. 'Not yet.'

'It was probably Rassa,' Xania said.

Matthias and I stared at her. She continued eating Matthias's shredded bread.

I recovered first. 'Any particular reason?'

She sipped her tea, then said, 'I did actually meet him, but not for what he implied.'

'What happened?'

'We ate dessert,' Xania said, 'and he threatened me.'

'He *what*?'

'Don't act so surprised, Your Majesty,' Matthias muttered. 'Rassa isn't subtle.'

'I'm going to—'

'What, Your Majesty?' Xania's eyes narrowed. 'What precisely are you going to do?'

Rage thickened in my throat, choking my common sense. 'I don't know! Why didn't you tell me this last night?'

Matthias's eyebrows drew together, likely at my tone, but I was too furious to care.

Hurt flickered across Xania's face, swiftly followed by anger, then embarrassment. Of course she wouldn't have wanted to admit what Rassa had done. I had no right to lash out – even if, when I closed my eyes, I saw her standing before me, bloody and panicked.

'I'm sorry,' I said.

She nodded uncomfortably.

Matthias looked between us, perplexed and suspicious. I'd fussed since Xania had arrived, and not only had she allowed it, she'd addressed me by title only after I'd provoked her. And, as Xania had said last night, monarchs didn't apologise. Uncle never had, and even I tried to avoid it.

Whatever expression was on my face, it made Matthias gulp the last of his coffee. 'I've suddenly remembered something I should do.'

I waved him off. To most people, his speed would have been

unseemly.

Xania frowned. 'You didn't need to make him leave.'

'Yes, I did. I shouldn't have been angry that you didn't tell me about Rassa.'

She shrugged.

I pressed my lips together hard enough to hurt, but my voice was still thick as I said, 'When I saw you bleeding last night, I – you could have *died*, and it would have been my fault. You were in the passages because of me.'

Xania's mouth trembled. 'I didn't choose to be your Whispers lightly. I knew there would be danger.'

We sank into an uncomfortable silence. I turned my cup in circles, searching for the right words. 'I'm not sure how to balance these... these feelings with my duty. Our duty.' Mine as Queen, hers as Whispers.

Xania considered my words, long enough for me to worry, then stretched her hand out. I placed my palm in hers. 'I understand,' she said, soft and serious. 'I... I know it was only a kiss. And you're my Queen, I should hardly expect anything–'

'But there is something.' My hand tingled. I desperately wanted to drag her across the table and kiss her, even though it would hurt her stitches.

She laughed unsteadily, and I wondered how badly she wanted to kiss me, too. 'Yes, yes, there is.'

I would have to marry Aubrey. It would be better if we rejected these feelings, even now that we'd admitted them.

Instead, we sat, our palms together, close enough to kiss.

ⴲ ⴲ ⴲ

Ten minutes into my weekly meeting with Vigrante and Alexandris, I wanted to scream.

'... at least my Government is getting legislation *through*,' Vigrante snapped.

'How dare you!' Alexandris said. 'You blocked the extra funding for the *orphans*–'

'I intervened on that,' I said mildly.

Vigrante hadn't even been *against* the extra orphan funds. He'd blocked Alexandris's legislation because that's simply what he did, as Alexandris spent these meetings being a burr under Vigrante's saddle because that's what he did. I'd had to use one of my precious overrules to push the funding through.

Alexandris flushed. 'Apologies, Your Majesty.'

'My lords, is there anything we actually need to discuss today?'

'Yes,' Vigrante said.

Joy.

'Speak, please.' If we kept to our usual timetable, there was about another fifteen minutes left.

'It's about your marriage, Your Majesty,' he said.

'As far as I'm aware, nothing has been decided. Unless you

know something I don't.'

'Oh, no, Your Majesty! It's just... you don't appear to be giving incentives to anyone.'

'I never intended to imply my choice through incentives.'

'Ah.'

'Say what you mean, Lord Vigrante.'

He made a good impression of worrying over his words. Alexandris chewed a pastry loudly.

'Should you choose Princes Aubrey or Hasan' – he smirked at Hasan's name – 'well... Othayria and Eshvon have never had Edar's best interests at heart.'

Unsurprising, with our close ties to Farezi.

I arched an eyebrow. 'We are well aware of this.'

'My Government shares my concerns, Your Majesty. As does the Opposition, no doubt...'

Alexandris tensed.

I sighed. 'What you mean to say – when we're all turned grey, apparently – is you fear I'll put my husband's interests before Edar's.'

Vigrante squirmed. He'd probably expected me to wait him out. Unfortunately, I'd no patience left today. 'It's a legitimate concern.'

Silence.

'Would either of you have said this to my father?'

'With greatest respect, Your Majesty,' Vigrante said, 'your

father didn't marry a foreigner.'

'You wouldn't be happy if I married from the Court, either. I already know the rumours: my husband will grasp for power through me, or behind my back. Yet I can hardly remain unmarried and childless.'

Vigrante turned red. 'I – Your Majesty–'

'Enough.'

He clamped his mouth shut.

'Is there anything else to discuss?' I asked Alexandris.

'No, Your Majesty,' he said, 'as far as I'm aware.' His enquiring look at Vigrante was mild and insulting.

Vigrante's nostrils flared. He shook his head, then stopped. 'Actually, a moment, if you please, Your Majesty? Alone?'

Finally. 'Of course.'

I wished Alexandris well until the next meeting, ignoring his anxious expression, then faced Vigrante when the doors closed. 'Speak.'

'Half my Government wishes to reconsider your merchant legislation,' he said. 'I'm suppressing them. Somewhat.'

So this was what he'd been doing while I played the marriage game. 'Has the bill given them cause for concern?'

Vigrante raised his palms. 'The foreign nobility dislike Parliament's *distasteful influence*. They seem equally appalled that we passed legislation to help the merchant classes.'

Laws proposed by me, so obviously none of these opinions had been voiced in my company.

'How has the Opposition reacted?'

'Alexandris has kept the Opposition in line,' Vigrante admitted. Unsurprising, since the Opposition had been the bill's strongest supporters. If Alexandris hadn't kept them behind it, he risked facing a power grab. Vigrante wouldn't be under the same pressure.

'And what is your advice?' I asked. Of course he wanted to drip in my ear.

'I can delay a new vote until next week,' Vigrante said, 'but it *will* be put forward. I suggest compromise.'

His compromise, I reminded myself, was getting someone else to kill unwanted allies and enemies. I had to remember Brenna. I had to remember the Riavaan boy.

And I could never back down on something I'd already made law.

'Unacceptable.'

'Then you must make an example of those who want to repeal the merchant laws.'

I raised my eyebrows. His motives most likely stemmed from his pride: a new vote would weaken his position, and reflect poorly on him if Edar rolled back newly passed laws. We were already considered backward and unsophisticated without our politics and law-making appearing unstable.

'I can suffocate the motion for a revote,' he said, 'and give you the associated names.'

'People whose views no longer correspond to yours, perhaps?'

'Perhaps.'

Was this how he'd got what he wanted from Uncle? Influenced him so subtly that it was impossible to consider anything else?

'I'm not my uncle, Lord Vigrante.'

'Believe me, Your Majesty, I'm fully aware.'

Matthias would have advised diplomacy. Xania would have kept Vigrante talking.

I couldn't stomach edging around his webs any longer. It was time to cut through to his heart. The merchant legislation was my first political victory. How better to make me look weak than by overturning it? So why was Vigrante, after months of fighting me, trying to stop it instead of encouraging it?

'What prompted this change of heart?'

He sighed. 'Your uncle was much easier to work with.'

'My uncle was easier to manipulate.'

'You underestimate how many miss him and his Court.'

'My heart bleeds.'

'Think beyond his weaknesses, as you consider them. Rassa and the Farezi Court, for example, remind people what they enjoyed about your uncle's reign: his generosity, his humour, his indulgence. As their nostalgia grows, they'll resent you.'

Mother had always been secretly relieved that she'd never become Queen. Now I realised why. It was impossible to win.

'The people you want expelled from your Government. Do they also fondly remember my uncle's reign?'

'So they say to your foreign guests.'

On Vigrante's encouragement, no doubt. 'What are you not telling me?'

'I have no wish,' he said, 'for our Court to resemble Farezi's – or any other. In this, I will support you, no matter my personal feelings.'

Unsurprising, since the foreign nobility despised the political system that gave Vigrante – with only a political title – his reach and influence. Something had alarmed him, and I was now the best of his bad options.

If I agreed to help him, I was no better than Uncle. I'd be turning my back on the merchants, and the boy murdered for my efforts. I'd be turning my back on Xania and Brenna's vengeance.

Was I any better than Uncle?

This was the closest I'd come to having Vigrante's support. For all I despised him, I couldn't deny his influence. Having this sort of leverage over him could only make me stronger.

Mother had always warned my idealism was too rigid, that I'd have to sacrifice for what I wanted. What had Uncle dreamed of, his hopes and aspirations? Had Vigrante's first compromise been too easy to accept for an easier life?

'We will consider your suggestion, Lord Vigrante,' I said, 'with the care it deserves.' I wouldn't promise him anything for now –

not after murder, and months of stalled legislation.

'Very well, Your Majesty.' He stood and bowed. 'I await your response.' If he was frustrated or resigned, he hid it well.

That was the problem: he manipulated so well, his lies and truth didn't look all that different.

CHAPTER THIRTY

XANIA

When I opened the door to the hall, my hopes for slipping by my family evaporated. Zola, leaning against the opposite wall, pointed at the double doors to the main suite. I sighed, but followed her back inside.

She hugged me. 'Happy birthday!'

Mama had been determined to celebrate our first birthdays after Papa's death. 'He loved you,' she'd said, when Zola burst into the first of many tears during her day. 'It's an insult for us not to celebrate being alive when he is not.' I'd hidden my grief better, but Mama found me weeping the night of my birthday anyway.

If she had wept, she did it far away from us.

Mama's hug enveloped me in her familiar three-rose perfume. 'Happy birthday, my dear.' I hugged her back, then briefly embraced Lord Martain before he turned uncomfortable. The table groaned under all the food. I was eighteen, finally of age. My family had insisted on a fuss.

Zola and I were third-generation Riija through Mama. We

considered ourselves Edaran, but she'd passed down the heritage our family had kept since Great-Grandmama's arrival here. I could swear in Riija, read and write it a little, and had a decent grasp of the culture and history so I wouldn't humiliate myself if I ever travelled there.

I liked having some of the foods Mama grew up with on my birthday, especially the meat dishes, thick with garlic or ginger and shallots, followed by date syrup on thick bread or a cream dish drizzled with violetta honey. If Mama's suppliers had a good trading season, there were candied rose petals, which I planned to introduce to Lia in the hopes she'd make them popular. Zola was less enthusiastic, but tried not to show it as it worried Mama. She'd been one of the first to marry outside of Arkaala's Riija community, and she feared being in the Steps meant her culture would fade from our lives.

We sat around the table, talking and laughing, goading Lord Martain to eat until he sweated. He pressed a box into my hands, pretending offence when I protested. I unwrapped it carefully, pressing the bright paper flat, and stared at the necklace: burnished Eshvon gold. The set opal pulled light into itself, changing from green to red to blue with flashes of gold and purple.

'This is too much,' I said.

Lord Martain smiled. 'You're of age.' He winked. 'Don't expect it every year.'

Zola bounced in her seat, grinning as she shoved a smaller box towards me. My suspicious look turned to outrage when I opened it and found earrings of the same gold, twisted to climb up the edge of my ear – the latest fashion, thanks to Isra. 'You absolutely could *not* afford these!'

'I have sources.'

'I helped her,' Mama said, and handed me her own present, 'because this wasn't purchased.' From the shape and weight, it involved books. Her expression, mingled sadness and regret, made me pause before I opened it.

I couldn't remember why the leather notebooks looked familiar until she said, 'They were your father's. He wanted you to have them when you were old enough. He said they'd amuse you.' When I frowned, she added, 'His words, not mine. You know what he was like.'

I did. I hadn't thought about his writing in a long time. Papa had spent hours meticulously recording his thoughts: how to make his Treasury work faster and easier, new flower-breeding techniques, or simply recording his day.

'Why now?'

'I don't know. He insisted I keep them in the vault until you turned eighteen.'

The vault was the last remnant of Mama's banking career. She owned it, and used it to store our family documents and deeds. It couldn't be searched without her permission.

I opened a notebook and flicked through the pages. At the

sight of Papa's neat cursive, a flowing record of days and weeks and months, I swallowed until the threat of tears passed. 'Thank you, Mama.'

She came around the table to hug me.

Lord Martain coughed, and clapped his hands together. 'Dessert?' he asked, too brightly, his relief stark when I laughed.

ϙ ϙ ϙ

I couldn't resist a small jump from the passage into Lia's study later that evening. She lowered her book and smiled. 'Happy birthday!' There was no fire, no tray, no refreshments. She wore a plain, rose-pink dress. Her hair fell loose around her shoulders.

My breath still caught.

Lia beckoned me to another wall. She tripped it behind a shelf of Othayrian blue and green porcelain figures, and took my hand as we stepped into the passage. Her thumb brushed my wrist. Everything narrowed to that pinpoint of warmth on my skin.

After several turns, she stopped and opened another panel.

Rows of candles filled the room. The room was larger than Lia's private study, with dark furniture and two stuffed bookcases. A table was laid out with crystal, silver, and covered dishes. Drawn curtains kept the night at bay. The elegance hinted at outrageous money.

A Queen, trying to impress me. Papa would never have

believed it.

A thin box, wrapped in blue and silver paper, nestled between dishes. We sat, and Lia nudged it towards me. I ran my fingertips over the smooth paper before peeling it open to reveal an unmarked mahogany box.

A slender pen lay on crumpled blue velvet. It was reassuringly heavy, black and stamped with golden briars. A tiny rose covered the body of the nib, finished with a delicate, thorn-like tip.

'I can't accept this. It's too much.'

Lia's face was a comical mix of disbelief and outrage. 'Are you trying to give my gift back?'

She was a Queen, and before that a princess and heir presumptive; her gifts were carefully chosen. No one refused them.

'These pens can survive anything. I used one as a dart, and the nib survived.' She had the grace to look ashamed when my mouth dropped open. 'I was ten. Not my finest moment.'

And that was the crux of the matter. Lia was frugal as Queens went. She fretted about her estate's savings, and her household, and her tenants. But before they were royal, her family had been wealthy Seventh Step. Her father had never been forced to sell the crumbling family estate and rent a palace suite instead. Her father hadn't learned how to work with merchants, and taken a Treasury job to improve his income. For all their simplicity, Lia's clothes reflected her status. Her frugality was always for someone else, never herself.

She thought nothing of giving me a pen worth a significant portion of my dowry. And she didn't care that I couldn't give her something similar.

But I did care.

I shook my head. 'It's too much. Please.'

Lia sighed and took the box from me. 'You need to accept this.'

'I can't–'

'No, you *need* to.' She carefully held the pen out. 'Hold the nib away from you. Twist the gold band on the spine.'

I frowned, but followed her instructions. A needle shot out from underneath the nib, viciously thin and gleaming. Lia waited for me to figure it out.

'Poison,' I said.

She nodded. 'If you're in a situation without a weapon, buy time with this. Poisons won't corrode the cylinder. Matthias keeps his in pockets sewn into his jacket linings. I have pockets sewn into my clothing. You're important to me. My enemies are yours. It's my duty to keep you safe, as you do for me.'

Cold trickled down my spine. She'd gifted me the means to kill.

The knife attack in the passages must still haunt her. We'd eventually got garbled information from the man who'd attacked me, but it had led to a literal dead end of bodies. He'd also briefly slipped into a Farezi accent, but it wasn't enough proof for anything. It wouldn't be the first time a trained assassin faked an accent to muddy a trail.

Matthias was furious when I resumed using the passages once my stitches healed, even though we now changed the royal wing's codes daily. But the passages were mine as much as his. I wouldn't be frightened from using them.

'Thank you.' I twisted the poisoned needle back into hiding, and returned the pen into the box with trembling fingers. I cupped Lia's face and kissed her until she pulled back, laughing unsteadily.

'I – I need a drink, I think.' She poured wine, a perfect complement, I'm sure, to the meal neither of us touched. Such a waste of food.

My stomach felt full of spinning knives. The wine, sharper than I liked, slowed them a little. I'd take any form of courage right now.

Lia drank too fast, twining our fingers together. This back and forth hinting of *more* had gone on for weeks since our first kiss. It tinted every walk, every conversation, even when we were only reading aloud to each other. Pulling away after kisses was getting harder.

She never pushed, or cajoled, though her eyes made her desire clear. And slowly, slowly, the fear of doing *more* had eroded into *want*.

'So,' Lia said, 'was my present the best?'

'The crown makes you terribly overconfident.'

'The arrogance makes everyone talk faster, so I can take it off quicker. It's heavy.'

'It was a close second.' I smiled at her mock outrage. 'Mama gave me some of Papa's old journals.'

Lia's face lit up. 'Much better than a poison pen.'

'I don't know – with my history, the pen will probably come in useful.' My smile faded when she didn't return it. 'It was a joke.'

'I know, but...'

'No,' I said. 'No more guilt. It's over. I'm the one who got a knife to the chest. If anyone should feel something about this, it's me.'

'My apologies.' I laughed at her grave tone, then kissed her again. It started off careful and slowly deepened. When we pulled back and gazed at each other, something changed.

Heat radiated from her as she slid behind my chair and coaxed me up. Her fingers slid down my neck, her mouth following close behind. I shuddered. She trailed her fingertips up and down my arms, then circled my waist, pulling me closer, still pressing gentle kisses to my neck.

I pressed her hand to my mouth, my kisses soft and fleeting until her breath was as unsteady as mine.

I wanted this. I was ready. This was mine, even if little else about us could be.

As she tugged at my bodice laces, I asked, 'Are you seducing me?'

'Is it working?'

I turned. We kissed until she tightened her fingers in my hair, and I clung to her to stay upright.

$$\oplus \ \oplus \ \oplus$$

I woke to the sound of rain against the windows. The fire had burned down to flickering coals. I shifted, savouring the smooth sheets and warm blankets.

Lia wrapped her arm around my waist. 'What's wrong?' she mumbled, drowsy with sleep.

'Nothing.'

She kissed the nape of my neck.

'Did they teach you seduction before or after the political manipulation and curtseying?'

She laughed, and we sank into a comfortable silence.

'There were girls I liked, of course,' she said after a while, shifting her arm as I turned to face her. 'I eventually told Matthias. He's the only man I ever considered kissing, but all it proved was I didn't want to kiss men and he didn't want to kiss women.'

Now wasn't the time for jealousy, yet I still asked, 'Have there been many?'

'Women?'

I nodded.

'One,' she whispered against my mouth.

My body tightened.

'By then, I knew I'd be Queen, so romance was inadvisable.' She tucked her head against my shoulder. 'If Mother or Uncle found out, or any of the other countries – well, marriage negotiations would be awkward.'

'So you've been alone.'

'I've *admired*. And comforted Matthias over his relationships. But no, I didn't want to act – until you.'

I should have been flattered. Instead, terror scorched my insides.

'And you?'

'No one. It never felt like the right time.' It still didn't, but that hardly mattered now. 'Zola likes men and women. But I'm the elder. I'll marry whoever Mother feels will improve our prospects. But then you returned to Court.'

'Well, why *wouldn't* you be attracted to the Queen?'

'It's not the crown that makes you arrogant!' I trailed my fingertips down her face, and let out a shaky breath as she kissed my palm.

It was easy to imagine the future of my daydreams: sitting with her in the evenings, teasing her taste in novels and attempting to better the intimate scenes; laughing at her in the morning before she'd had coffee. It felt too close, too possible, all lies. None of it addressed the reality of loving a Queen or ruling a country. Falling for her had been inadvisable enough; succumbing to my feelings was worse. As Whispers, I already worried about keeping her safe. This, whatever it was, would make everything more difficult.

Her smile faded. She traced my knife scar. 'Don't think about it now. Everything always seems worse at night.'

We both jumped at the pounding on the door.

Lia caught my wrist before I leaped from the bed to hide. 'Only Matthias has permission to–' She tossed the blankets aside and reached for her robe.

The door burst open when she was still tightening it around her waist. Matthias rushed into the room.

Lia's cheeks turned bright red. 'You know better–'

'Get dressed!' Matthias's eyes were wild, his face sweat-slicked. His shirt gaped open, without a neckband or waistcoat, over rumpled trousers. 'Vigrante is dead.'

CHAPTER THIRTY-ONE

LIA

The Queen storming through the corridors commanded respect – or fear. Nobles scrambled out of my way. No one made eye contact.

People were already swarming at Vigrante's rooms, and scuttled back at the sight of me.

'Your Majesty–'

I ignored Matthias and strode through the doors.

Vigrante's entrance room was undisturbed: elegant in red and gold with black accents. Simple, sturdy furniture and hunting paintings of acceptable standards. A bookcase, its contents well-read rather than decorative.

His bedroom door stood ajar.

I walked in.

My stomach rolled. The scent of blood hung in the air, curdled on my tongue when I swallowed.

I would not vomit. Or faint.

Vigrante had fought back. I followed his bloody path to where he lay sprawled and cold. Someone had closed his eyes.

I didn't want to go any further. I feared disturbing anything that might reveal who'd killed him.

I had to make it clear I hadn't orchestrated this. The animosity between us was well known. Even rumours of my involvement in his death would destroy the fragile balance between monarchy and Parliament. Edar would explode into civil war.

Perhaps both Vigrante and I had been manipulated.

I stepped back into the hall, hoping others would take my trembling for rage instead of fear.

Xania stood at the edge of the crowd, alert and tense. She'd waited before running after me so we didn't arrive together. Now I wished she'd stayed behind. I wanted her separate from this, untainted from the blood and violence in Vigrante's suite, even though she was my Whispers.

'The Commander of the Palace Guard will report to me, as will the guards who last patrolled here.' My voice simmered with anger. Nothing could be gained from politeness at this point. 'We will find who is responsible for this, and there will be no mercy.'

ֆ ֆ ֆ

My eyes burned from lack of sleep. The entire Court would know Vigrante was dead by breakfast. This was the last drop of time left before everything descended into panic.

I paced in my bedroom.

Xania stared at the wall.

Vigrante's death had been denied to us both. I'd never fulfill Brenna's final wish.

'You should return to your family.'

Xania looked as if I'd demanded she sprout wings and capture the sun.

'You must be accounted for.'

'But–'

I glanced at my unmade bed, remembering her warmth, her skin, our laughter as the rain struck the windows. I wouldn't experience something that lovely, that simple again for a long time.

I banished the memory for now. It would help when things were too much to bear. 'If I say I was with you, your family will find out.'

'You're ashamed, Your Majesty.'

My title stung. 'Of course not. But I can handle the gossip. The scandal. You and your family...'

'We're not strangers to gossip,' Xania said. 'Mama would care about my happiness, after the shock – but if I destroy Zola's chances...'

I kissed her cheek. Truthfully, I wanted her to stay. Her reasons for going after Vigrante had been personal – and the loss of vengeance, which had fuelled her for so long, would eventually hit. I wanted her to scream and cry with me, where she could show it freely.

'You should get back.' I hesitated. 'If you want to tell them about us, I'll speak with your family.'

'If you think diplomats are difficult, wait until you deal with my mother.'

She kissed me. Despite my strengthening headache and the fear hammering against my ribs, I sighed when she pulled back. 'We should have given in weeks ago. We could have enjoyed this more.'

'I won't let this ruin being with you,' she said.

'One of us is wise.'

'I'll reread Hazell's file again,' Xania said. 'His discussions with Alexandris could have masked a bid for power. And a guard must follow you everywhere.'

I nodded. 'I'd prefer if you only used the passages with Matthias, but—'

'That's not possible,' she said firmly. 'We can't always wait for each other. I'll be careful.'

I sighed. 'Very well. And start thinking of who should investigate Vigrante's death. I'll summon you and Matthias later.'

She kissed me again before leaving.

The silence pressed against me.

A knock: Matthias entered with a tray of coffee and whiskey.

'We could drink the coffee first, or lace it with whiskey, or—' He broke off when I wrestled the decanter open and sloshed whiskey into the teacups. 'Or we could get drunk.'

'No.' I took a large swallow. 'I only need enough to help the coffee kick in. I won't be sleeping for a while.'

'You and Xania actually slept?'

It was a ludicrous thing to say, under the circumstances, but laughing felt better than I'd expected. 'For a little while.'

'At least one of us has something to look forward to at night.'

I gulped more whiskey. 'Vigrante couldn't have planned this better if he'd actually intended to die.'

'May he rot,' Matthias said, almost fondly.

'Please tell me you didn't orchestrate this. It's a shambles, and I expect better from you.'

'I expect better from myself. Alexandris is an obvious choice, but it's too easy.'

'Doesn't matter if it can't be traced to him.'

'Alexandris is too idealistic for a politician,' Matthias said, 'never mind having the stomach for orchestrated murder.'

'Xania suspects Hazell.'

Matthias tilted his head, considering. 'Potentially. Puts his discussions in a different light.'

Vigrante had kept his head down after Brenna's death to wait out the whispers and criticism. Hazell had been visibly horrified in Brenna's rooms, but I'd assumed his fear wasn't as strong as Vigrante's grip on his obedience. Perhaps I'd underestimated Hazell's resentment of Vigrante, and his ability to lunge for power when it was close.

Matthias finished his whiskey and went to pour another. I moved the bottle away, and he reached for the coffeepot instead.

'Vigrante spoke to me privately yesterday.'

Matthias froze with the coffee in midair. 'And?'

'He offered a compromise.'

'Ah.'

'The Court, especially those in Parliament, has become too influenced by our visitors. Vigrante claimed they planned to overturn the merchant laws. He was suppressing it – and would stop it, if I made examples of certain nobles.'

'Whose support he'd be sorry to lose, I'm sure.'

I toyed with my cup. 'Something spooked him.'

'The influence of the foreign nobles? Rassa? Though he openly scorned Vigrante.'

'Rassa acts on his father's encouragement.'

Much to my relief, Matthias put the coffeepot back on the table. 'Would Farezi want to try and reclaim its empire?'

'If they do, Edar has always been the weakest. It makes sense to follow the old conquering pattern.'

Matthias's eyes flashed. 'Not with you on the throne.'

Pretty, loyal words, but not encouraging when I had to make the decisions.

'What did you tell Vigrante?' he asked.

'I'd think about it.'

Matthias raised an eyebrow.

'It was Vigrante's first decent overture since I became Queen. I could hardly throw it back in his face.' I ignored Matthias's eyeroll. 'What if' – I remembered how Vigrante had referenced Farezi during our conversation – 'what if Vigrante fooled us all? What if he so desperately wanted me gone that he reached out to Rassa, unaware of Farezi's true intentions? And if Rassa realised Vigrante suspected something... would he have had him killed?'

'Possibly,' Matthias said, after a moment, 'though we need proof. Rassa surely knew there was no shortage of people to blame the murder on. Vigrante was a good political spider, planting threads on his allies and enemies. Now he's dead, what happens in the next few days should be interesting.'

Some fortunes would suddenly dry up. Some nobles would find themselves abruptly out of favour. Engagements would crumble. What sticky thread had Vigrante attached to me? It'd be easier to paint a target on myself and let Parliament take aim.

And we'd have to pay close attention to Hazell. The thread of loyalty between him and Vigrante had snapped, but that didn't mean there weren't other threads leading to other secrets.

'Xania should be here,' Matthias said.

'I sent her back to her family.'

'Lady Bayonn's no fool. If she knows Xania was gone last night, she'll get the truth out of her.'

'I told Xania she should tell her family.'

Matthias's eyes widened.

'Not about being Whispers,' I hastily added. 'About being with me.'

More surprise, swiftly hidden, before he asked, 'Are you telling your own mother?'

I grimaced. 'I need to calm the Court and Parliament first.'

'Better your mother hears it from you instead of the gossips.'

'She'll destroy me.' I was throwing away her years of work.

'I'll try not to smile while she does.'

I shook my head. 'Court and Parliament first.' I'd have to act swiftly. If they suspected I was floundering because of Vigrante's murder, they'd turn on me. Words wouldn't be enough. I'd have to make overtures.

'They *will* panic,' Matthias said. 'No one in Court has died so brutally in years. You must reassure them.'

Panic buzzed at my temples. If this had happened to Vigrante, he would have threatened and cajoled to stop his authority from collapsing.

Perhaps it was time to adopt his methods.

This was probably what Vigrante would have done on Uncle's behalf. I'd sworn never to be like Uncle. But I was the last of my line, and I had a legacy to uphold.

'You know what Parliament wants and fears. I need you to make promises. Vigrante's death is a tragedy' – Matthias's eyebrows shot up – 'but we can't discover the truth if we give in to fear and anger. They must stay strong. They must remain calm.'

'Strong and calm with their loyalty bought.'

'Their loyalty bought for long enough so I can think.'

Matthias pressed his lips together. After a few moments, he rose. 'Very well.'

He turned on his heel and left. I understood his anger. This wasn't me. It wasn't the sort of Queen he'd helped bring to power. But if using Vigrante's methods kept everything I'd worked for from crumbling between my fingers, I'd do it.

I couldn't think about Xania.

I couldn't think about Brenna lying cold and still.

I wrapped my hands around the coffeepot.

Breathe in.

Breathe out.

When I threw it against the wall, I only felt shame as murky as the liquid dripping down the wall.

CHAPTER THIRTY-TWO

XANIA

When I turned into the hall leading to our rooms, Mama and Zola were just ahead. I couldn't hear them clearly, but their tight postures were warning enough. Zola saw me first. Relief burst through her worry.

Mama whirled around. '*Where have you been?*' She frowned. 'You're wearing yesterday's dress.'

My stomach twisted.

Lord Martain opened the door and peered out. 'Perhaps you should all come inside?'

Mama rounded on Zola, who attempted a weak smile.

'Move, both of you,' Mama said.

I sat beside Zola. We exchanged resigned looks.

Mama faced us in a chair beside Lord Martain. 'Where were you?'

'With the Queen.' There was no point denying it. Yesterday's clothes would soon explain themselves.

Lord Martain voiced his suspicions first. 'For how long?'

'Since yesterday evening.'

'The Queen so desperately needed entertainment that you couldn't leave?' In other circumstances, I would have laughed at Mama's outrage.

'Not precisely.'

Zola squeezed my hand.

'It wasn't for the Queen's entertainment.'

Mama's eyes widened, as she reassessed my clumsily redone hair and rumpled demeanour.

'It was for Her Majesty's... pleasure, I suppose.'

Mama closed her eyes, as if she couldn't bear to hear more.

'Only hers?' Lord Martain's voice was mild. I wasn't sure if this was good or bad.

'Ours,' I admitted in a small voice. 'Our pleasure.'

Zola's grip threatened to bruise my hand.

'Ah.' Lord Martain ran a hand over his mouth and chin.

Mama pressed her hands over her eyes and took deep breaths.

After several moments, I ventured, 'Mama...'

'I'm despairing,' she snapped. 'Give me a moment.'

Zola's face reflected my misery.

'I thought you valued your chances of a good marriage,' Mama said.

I hadn't thought about that before now. With Lord Martain's help, Mama hoped I might marry into a higher Fifth Step family. Being with Lia complicated that. If I was already involved with the most powerful person in Edar, no Step marriage could compare, and suitors would have to contend with my having the Queen's public and private favour.

'Oh,' I said.

'Throwing away your chance at a good marriage to be the Queen's *amusement—*'

'I'm not her dalliance!' *I'm her Whispers. I'm the person she holds in the dark as she tells her secrets. I'm far more than just someone in her bed.*

'What, she plans to marry you? Don't be ridiculous, Xania. You're her uncomplicated distraction.'

As if an uncomplicated distraction calculated murder for Lia, managed her spy network, discussed how to manipulate Parliament and the Court. An uncomplicated distraction who made the Queen whimper from a kiss, dig her hands into my back to pull me closer. One didn't cede control or emotions to an uncomplicated distraction.

'I...' Zola coughed. 'That's not true.' She quailed under Mama's glare, but said, 'The way Her Majesty looks at Xania...' She thankfully didn't mention how I looked at Lia. Admitting I acted like a lovestruck girl would accomplish nothing.

Lord Martain snorted. 'You think monarchs are beyond desire? Her Majesty can look at Xania all she wants. It doesn't mean she'll give her the respect she deserves. Or protect her.'

Zola and I hadn't expected Lord Martain to like or love us.

But now he leaned forward, his eyes narrowed, his mouth pressed thin. Perhaps his love had developed in time, and we had been unable – or unwilling – to see because it didn't resemble Papa's love.

'This...' I struggled to say words I'd hardly let myself think about. 'This isn't a fancy. I'm not her distraction.'

'Is she willing to present you to the Court?' Mama asked. 'She's trying to find a husband.' I knew Mama's harshness masked worry for me, yet it still hurt.

'No. But she's not happy about it.' I hesitated. 'Matthias and I–'

'*Matthias!*' Mama exploded. 'Of course he'd have something to do with this–' She groped for Lord Martain's hand.

'Being close to the Queen isn't advisable right now,' he said, unknowingly mirroring Rassa's warnings; I shivered. 'She and Lord Vigrante disliked each other. The Court will be hard-pressed to believe she isn't connected to his death.'

'We're Fifth Step,' Zola said. 'The Queen's favour can only bring us fortune.'

'If she contains Vigrante's murder,' Mama said, 'and keeps authority over the Court. Association with a disgraced Queen could destroy us.'

'We could hardly be worse off than we used to be,' I said, more bitterly than intended.

Mama snapped her fingers, forcing me to look at her. 'There is always further to fall.'

I'd foolishly hoped, despite knowing better, that they'd be happy for me, as if only my feelings mattered. Mama and Lord Martain wouldn't simply accept my *association* with Lia. Mama had clawed her way up from Third Step to Fifth, risen from no family holding, no husband, no alliances to the fondness and security provided by Lord Martain. She wouldn't put our family in jeopardy unless Lia proved she could provide more and better.

The ticking clock stopped the silence from turning unbearable. I wanted to run until my chest hurt and I could cry somewhere in peace.

But only a child ran away to cry.

'I want to meet her.' Mama ignored our astonishment. 'You've always been sensible, always cautious when Zola was indiscreet' – Zola yelped – 'Of *course* I knew about your infatuations.'

Mama eyed me, still grim. 'You wouldn't fall for the first person who complimented you, not unless you respected each other. It's... unfortunate it's the Queen, but we should meet before I condemn her.'

Only Mama could act like a Queen should request her approval to love her daughter.

It took hours before Mama left me alone in my rooms, and we argued when she tried to take my keys. I could understand her fear that I'd entangled myself in dangerous things, but couldn't assure her everything was fine because it wasn't.

I waited, furious, then finally slipped out. I needed to see Lia. Protecting her as Whispers had been a matter of professional pride; now it was far more. If she died – *no*. The coppery tang of fear filled my mouth. I wouldn't allow it.

A servant approached from the opposite direction, and pressed a note into my palm as she rushed by. I ducked into a small empty room, tucked myself into a corner so I faced the door, and cracked the seal.

I translated the note as I read. A dispatch had been left in the passages for me. A discreet mark at the corner of the paper meant *urgent*. I was supposed to drop everything to read it immediately.

I hurried to a quieter hall and slipped into the passages.

At the drop spot, I eased out the hunk of rock hiding the dispatch and gritted my teeth at every scrape and crumble of stone. The packet, battered and worn smooth, had passed through many hands, but the seal was unbroken. There were the usual marks for *stealth* and *caution*, written in my network's code, and again: *urgent*.

My hands shook as I unfolded the layers of paper. I leaned against the wall, using its wavering light to read.

My most experienced Farezi agent, the one whose theatre booklet I'd deciphered to stay calm after Brenna and Naruum's deaths, had sent the dispatch two weeks after Rassa left for Edar, then run to ground. Her security had been compromised. I wasn't surprised it had taken so long to arrive; in these situations, extra caution prevented interception.

The agent would get in touch again when it was safe. I'd have to retire her. But the end of the letter made panic race over my skin.

One of Farezi's spymasters – called the Shadows, as I was Whispers – was in Rassa's entourage. My agent didn't know who they were, or what they looked like. When she'd tried to find out, she'd roused the suspicions of the wrong people.

I hoped she was still alive.

I still believed the man in the passages was an assassin, not a spy – his ultimate goal had been to kill me, not gain information – but the Farezi Shadow could have hired him if they suspected I was more than one of Lia's ladies. I'd only been Whispers since spring, now up against an experienced spymaster.

This also further complicated Vigrante's murder, and the attack on me. Were they linked?

And why would a Farezi Shadow accompany Rassa here?

☖ ☖ ☖

My expression went still and hard. 'You're doing exactly as Vigrante would.'

'Yes,' Lia said. 'I must maintain control until we know what to do.'

I tried to curb the feeling of betrayal. 'You don't have the money nor means to fulfil any promises.'

'Of course I don't,' she said, almost wearily. 'But I need to stop them from turning on me. We must investigate Vigrante's death. The Court and Parliament panicking won't help that. I'll deal with the promises later.'

This was completely unlike her. She knew better than to make promises she couldn't keep. I'd planned to tell her about the Farezi spymaster, but her demeanour made the words stick in my throat. She seemed brittle, yet coiled to lash out at the same time.

Instead, I said, 'I've chosen Lariux Bisset to help investigate Vigrante's death.'

'You value Lariux as an agent,' Lia said. 'Are you certain?'

'Yes,' I said. 'Assuming he agrees.'

'Of course,' Lia murmured, but drummed her fingers. I tamped down a spark of irritation. Lariux had been associated with my family long before I'd met her. He was my responsibility. I wouldn't throw him into Court intrigue unawares.

'I'll make him a baron when this is done,' Lia said. 'Third Step. A decent beginning.'

A lovely bait. I almost wanted to refuse on Lariux's behalf, but we needed someone connected to me in place quickly. A bloody image of Vigrante's end flashed in my mind. I shoved it away.

'You should go,' Lia said regretfully. 'Matthias wants to see you.'

About Lia's promises to the Court and Parliament, no doubt. I hoped it wasn't just so he could vent over her mistake.

We kissed before I left. Lia had taken an hour for herself – for us – before returning to her frantic Court. She was trying to continue as normal so they'd remain calm, while Matthias offered bribery on her behalf. Tomorrow, she'd meet Vigrante's successor.

I hurried through the passages towards Matthias's office, but stopped at the voices through his wall. Why was Coin here?

'This doesn't put you in the best of circumstances, Master Coin,' Matthias said coldly.

'How quickly your opinion changes. I'd hardly present my treason in neat rows of figures.'

'If you were bluffing, yes, you would,' Matthias said. 'You're ideal for such deceptions.'

'True,' Coin said, 'except you assume a situation exists where I'd collude with Vigrante.'

I stiffened.

'Oh, you'd never *willingly* collude with him,' Matthias said. 'But you're not immune to blackmail.'

'If you're referring to that wretched clerk who can't decide if his hair is red or blond,' Coin said, 'I knew he was Vigrante's within his first hour.'

'You fed Vigrante false information.'

'Of course. The King gave him too much. I'd hardly allow him to swindle more.' Coin sounded like he still wanted to throttle Vigrante, dead or not. 'I suspected he lied about his personal wealth, but... not this.'

A crackle of paper being flicked through. 'I agree,' Matthias said. 'The discrepancies point toward treason.'

Treason? Proof now, finally?

'With that amount of money, no wonder he kept everyone happy.'

'Can you tell me your source?' Matthias asked. 'You hardly stumbled upon this, or you'd have already fired the entire Treasury.'

Coin had, in fact, fired people before for misplacing papers. His system was chaos, but *organised* chaos.

A long silence.

'I suppose I can tell you now,' Coin finally said, 'since she's dead.'

Brenna? It had to be.

'Brenna,' Matthias said, unknowingly echoing me. 'You never forgave her family for turning down your job offer.'

'She could have been Master, eventually,' Coin said. 'So much wasted talent. She visited the Treasury several times. She wouldn't admit it, but I knew Vigrante had trapped her. If I'd known what she and Naruum planned...'

'You only received these papers recently?' Suspicion tinted Matthias's voice. If Coin had proof of Vigrante's treachery all this time and kept it to himself...

'Brenna's parents emptied her bank vault last week,' Coin said icily. Six months after her death, but they could probably only do it now without publicly succumbing to grief. Mama had opened Papa's only a few weeks after his death, driven by money worries, and cried in her room afterwards. 'They found a Treasury box marked for my attention.'

'And they didn't open it?'

'They couldn't. I gave the box to Brenna, and she returned the key to me before... she died. This pile of discrepancies is only the first I'm certain of.'

Brenna had worked against Vigrante with Coin. Had she come to Coin for help during my lesson in the Treasury? He *had* been surprised to see her. Had she turned against Vigrante because she'd known Naruum and herself were doomed?

'You failed her,' Matthias said.

'She – she hoped I could protect her,' Coin said. 'But the King was dead, and the new Queen untested against Vigrante. I begged her to go to Rijaan – I could recommend her to any bank – but she refused.'

Before now, I would have said Coin occasionally manifested paternal instincts for the younger Treasury staff. I hadn't thought his voice could hold so much pain for one of us.

Perhaps Matthias felt he'd overstepped, for he said, 'I must pass this on to Whispers.'

'I'll finally meet him, then?'

'Aren't you thrilled?'

'Hardly. *You* could be him, for all I know.'

'I'm not Whispers,' Matthias said. 'I don't have enough time.'

As if *I* did.

'You're more than capable, from what I've heard.' A creak as Coin stood, groaning. 'I'm too old for these games.'

'They'll pry the Treasury from your cold, dead hands.'

'It'll take time to properly examine the rest of the tampered records,' Coin said, ignoring the flattery, 'but I'll report back to you – and Whispers, of course, once we've been acquainted.' He left before Matthias could reply.

I counted heartbeats, now reluctant to enter, but knowing my luck, Matthias would hear if I tried to sneak away. I opened the panel and stepped into his office.

'Eavesdropping is rude.'

'Should I have stuck my fingers in my ears? What did he give you?' If Matthias could ignore Coin's display of emotion, so could I, for now.

He held out the papers. 'Brenna hid Vigrante's true financials in her bank vault. Presumably he never knew, or he'd have killed her himself. They don't *quite* match Coin's official records.'

Coin had become a Master from being good at his job, not from powerful connections. Once he found a mistake, he didn't stop until he found them all.

I trailed a finger down the rows of columns, frowning. 'So she knew before she died.'

Matthias's mouth curled in disgust. 'Yes, apparently she didn't *fully* betray Vigrante. A pity she didn't hide them somewhere that relied on her family discovering them earlier.'

'She probably assumed Coin would tell Lia, no matter what he promised,' I said, still focused on the numbers. 'And she wanted to protect her family from Vigrante by putting the records somewhere they wouldn't touch until months after her death.'

'Whatever Brenna felt,' Matthias said, 'Vigrante still stole from Edar, and it was carefully, beautifully done.'

'Discrepancies in Vigrante's personal accounts doesn't mean he did that.' I almost didn't want it to be true – it was the perfect way to destroy Vigrante, and he was already dead. There was little justice for Papa in this.

'Perhaps,' Matthias said. 'But Coin knows numbers and balances as intimately as he knows his husband. He reopened the old King's account records.'

The atmosphere grew jagged edges.

'They were tampered,' Matthias said.

Like the mistake Lord Frijian had bullied Terize about. I'd tried to see how far Frijian's mistakes went, but the files were far above my access rank. Because of Coin, I avoided unnecessary attention to myself at work, and I hadn't sought Treasury informants. Quietly copying Farezi reports was one thing; breaking into secured files I had no business going near was another.

When had these 'mistakes' started? How many people did it

involve? Coin had sniffed out many of Vigrante's spies over the years, but a Sixth or Seven Step noble, like Frijian, would be careful and intimidate others into silence.

If I'd been less cautious – less indebted to Coin for the chance he'd given me – maybe I would have known about this before Vigrante was murdered.

I massaged my temples. 'If the Court finds out–'

'We should be more worried about Parliament. Those who got nothing from Vigrante will scream about this. Now that he's dead, they'll blame Lia and Coin for not stopping him sooner. If they turn against her, Lia will never have true authority again. At best, she'd be a puppet Queen. At worst, they'd end the monarchy.'

'Her promises mean nothing,' I said.

'They know they're worthless,' he said. 'She wanted to look strong, decisive, but now they know she's worried. She's shown her hand. They'll reject her if the right person replaces Vigrante.'

This was what had bothered me about Lia's rashness: how quickly she'd acted like Vigrante without thinking it through. Gambles had worked for him because he'd backed up his bribes with knowledge and secrets.

'Why didn't you stop her?' I asked.

'She'd already succumbed to panic,' he said. 'It doesn't happen often, but the last time it did, years ago, she didn't speak to me for three months. She's Queen now. If I argued like before, she could remove me from her service. Better to minimise the damage instead of losing access to her.'

'And now we've a bigger mess to handle.' As if I could scorn him, while keeping quiet about the Farezi spymaster. I'd find out their identity, actually do what was expected of me, then tell Matthias. Even when we knew, we'd still have to be careful. Lia could hardly publicly rebuke Rassa about it.

Matthias rubbed his eyes. 'Yes, I made a mistake, is that what you want to hear?'

'No.' I wanted to know how to fix this.

'I knew we'd come up against treason sooner or later,' he said, 'but against Lia, not the entire country.'

'Isn't it the same?'

'Not when it involves her uncle's accounts.'

I hesitated. This was a gut feeling, fuelled by my dislike of Rassa and my fear of his spymaster. But I still asked, 'How likely are the discrepancies to lead back to Farezi accounts?'

'Don't bet on those odds,' Matthias said.

CHAPTER THIRTY-THREE

LIA

Mother buried her face in her hands, trembling. When she looked up, I almost recoiled at the fury in her eyes.

'I know this isn't–'

'How dare you do this to me? To your *father*?'

Of course she'd use him against me. As if I didn't already torture myself about his expectations of me. 'Father is no longer with us,' I said gently. 'We'll never know what he would think.'

Her expression flickered with disgust, contempt: things she'd never directed at me before. 'Is it easier, now, to use his death as justification?'

'Remember to whom you speak.'

'My daughter. Queen or not, my dear, I gave birth to you. You have my blood as much as your father's. He sacrificed so much for you. He *loved* you.'

I surged out of my seat. 'He would *not* be horrified that I love a woman!'

'Of course not!' Mother snapped, as I paced. 'Have as many

mistresses as you want. What you do in private with that Third Step girl–'

'*Fifth* Step–'

'Through her mother's remarriage! What you do in private doesn't concern me. But you're a Queen. You *must* marry and conceive an heir.'

'If they know I was with her last night, the Court won't speculate about my involvement in Vigrante's murder.'

Mother waved a hand dismissively. 'If the Court believes you had him killed, they'll fear you, and you can use that against them. And by that logic, if you had him killed, then why are others who oppose you still alive?'

'Killing everyone who disagrees with me isn't subtle.'

Perhaps it was how I spoke, matter-of-fact instead of exasperated, but fear flickered over Mother's face before she controlled it.

She'd never looked at me that way before, either.

⊕ ⊕ ⊕

When I returned from visiting Mother, Matthias and Isra were glaring at each other over his desk.

'Princess Isra,' I said, instead of screaming at another problem showing up, 'how unexpected. Matthias, stop trying to set her on fire with your eyes.'

He clenched his jaw. 'I informed Her Highness you already

have another meeting.'

My next meeting involved facing Xania's family.

'Your Majesty,' Isra said, unusually grave, 'you have no reason to humour me. But we must speak.'

I glanced at the clock. 'Be succinct. '

Matthias didn't bring refreshments, nor did I order any. Isra pulled folders stamped with the Eshvon pomegranate and Juliaane's personal seal from a bag.

'Has Eshvon brought danger to us?' I asked.

'No,' Isra said. 'You've already welcomed it.'

The first folder detailed an Eshvon noblewoman's financials. Her family had Farezi ties, so she'd spent a summer in the Farezi Court, swapped with a cousin. While there, according to bank documents and family statements, she'd grown close to Rassa and loaned him money.

A lot of money.

'He swindled her.'

Isra pursed her lips. I mentally reconsidered every interaction she'd had with Rassa, and could only admire her for not ruining him on the spot.

The noblewoman had eventually returned to Eshvon, penniless and disgraced. Her furious family had appealed to Juliaane and Navid. They wouldn't openly humiliate Rassa's parents, but Juliaanne had allowed Isra to investigate after she showed interest.

'As the youngest, I'm the least of Mother's worries,' Isra said. 'I had a lot of freedom.'

Which had likely changed after the scandal that sent her here.

And when Isra had looked at things closer –

'No.' I almost crumpled the papers. 'That's impossible.'

She'd tracked the 'borrowed' funds to Vigrante.

'I'd normally insist the numbers don't lie,' Isra said, crossing her legs, 'but in this particular matter, I feel they're... bending the truth.'

'Oh?'

While Matthias and I had only speculated that Vigrante had thrown his lot in with Rassa, here was proof, even if it raised more questions than it answered. I tried to fit everything Vigrante had championed during Uncle's reign, and fought against during mine, around this new revelation.

'It's too convenient, Your Majesty, and you know it.'

And too sloppy on Rassa's part.

'Yet you waited until Vigrante's death to give us this information.'

'Would you have done differently?' The golden autumn light warmed Isra's skin. She sat easy in her power and privilege. 'Were our situations reversed, you would have waited before revealing anything to my parents.'

That was why she'd befriended Vigrante. Not to gain delicate information – he was a seasoned politician, for all his faults, and would have known better – but to trace the link between him, Rassa, and the Eshvon money.

Perhaps Rassa felt it was easier to usurp me with a scandal between Vigrante and Eshvon. If so, he was far more intelligent than I'd realised. Or his father was.

This reeked of his father.

'Has Eshvon... heard whispers about Farezi ambition?'

Isra narrowed her eyes. 'Perhaps.'

'If neighbouring countries are annexed, the rest *will* follow.'

'Eshvon and Othayria are not weak.' Her words swelled with false bravado. When the Second Empire fell, we'd disbanded our Empire-controlled armies in response. We'd set aside ambition and conflict to rebuild our national identities, including Farezi now that they no longer controlled an empire. Naval fleets had been carefully negotiated for those economically dependent on the sea. We settled our differences through diplomacy and trade, refusing to let a conflict grow that needed army resolution.

Our ancestors had believed this would help prevent another Empire. Naturally, ambitious nobles had tried every few generations to raise armies in their respective countries. It was how my great-grandfather had taken the throne. But the Farezi royal family had swiftly, brutally, quashed any attempts by their nobles. But if it involved regaining their former Empire?

How long had Rassa's father planned this? How many contingencies had it involved, should plans fail or people die? Matthias would give almost anything to know it all.

'If Edar falls, Othayria and Eshvon are not safe,' I said. 'We were all Empire-ruled once.' Isra should have been worried, not hiding behind her pride. 'What do you want in exchange for this?'

'You'll marry Aubrey,' Isra said. 'Everyone knows this. So I want to stay in Edar.'

I let my silence speak for me.

'I can't go home.' Her tone was breezy, flippant, but she couldn't hint her regret. 'I should secure a future here.'

'Very well. You have the joy of informing your mother.'

'I'll influence your arts culture,' Isra said. 'She'll be *thrilled*.'

I flicked through the pages again. The urge to destroy Rassa boiled in my stomach.

'I presume these are copies?'

Isra nodded. I wouldn't have given away my only proof, either.

'We will keep you informed.'

'Please, allow me to assist however I can.' She smiled. 'And Rassa has ensured this is more than an Edaran matter.'

'That would please us.'

Isra's smile flashed, bright as sunlight. 'I look forward to it, Your Majesty.'

CHAPTER THIRTY-FOUR

XANIA

Less than an hour before Lia met my family, I decided looking through Papa's journals would somehow keep me calm.

When I was a child, Papa had sat at his desk, filling pages with his neat handwriting. I drowned in memories of his voice, his smile, his laughter as he chased me through the gardens before we worked together on puzzles.

I didn't know what to expect. He'd died under suspicious circumstances, but it didn't mean he'd *known* anything suspicious. It didn't make him less dead. Maybe I was a fool for believing Vigrante had murdered him. Did it still matter now that they were both dead? Had I become Lia's Whispers for nothing? Between her work and the Treasury, I only had a sliver of leftover time devoted to Papa's death. I was nowhere close to proving his murder.

I closed the notebooks and wiped my eyes.

Zola poked her head around the door. 'She's here.'

My heart jumped into my throat, but I forced myself to look

calm as I walked into the reception room. Lia sat by the fireplace, near Mama and Lord Martain. I sat beside Zola. I wanted to grip her hand, but couldn't betray my nerves.

'Miss Bayonn.' Lia's voice was calm, almost brisk, but her gaze lingered on me. 'I hope you're well.'

'I'm very well, Your Majesty,' I said.

Lord Martain blotted his face, as Mama remained silent.

Lia tugged at her lace cuffs. 'Shall we dispense with the formalities?'

Mama's eyebrows shot up. 'That's how little you regard my eldest daughter?'

'I assure you, I hold Miss Bayonn in great esteem.' Lia leaned back. 'We both care deeply for her, Lady Harynne.'

'Pretty words,' Mama said. 'Your uncle had the same flair.'

Lia's smile turned wolfish. 'Mine comes from my father.'

They eyed each other. Mama had dressed as befitted a Fifth Step wife: fashionable material, quality without being gauche. Lia wore cream silk and dark gold velvet trimmed in brown satin. Her sleeves shimmered with gold embroidery.

'Xania will not serve as your distraction while you decide on a husband.'

'*Mama!*'

Zola crunched my hand between hers: either a warning for me to stay calm, or because she was terrified.

'She's not a distraction,' Lia said. 'I'm hardly in the market for a mistress.'

I glared at them. 'I shouldn't have to say this, but I can *hear you both* and speak for myself!'

Lia looked briefly shamed. Mama pressed her lips together.

'Your Majesty surely understands our hesitation,' Lord Martain said, trying to play peacekeeper.

'Of course,' Lia said. 'Being a Queen's favourite doesn't guarantee safety.'

'We are Fifth Step,' Lord Martain said sharply, 'not naive. Being closer to the throne could bring both danger and advantage to our family–'

'–but Xania's well-being is our primary concern,' Mama finished.

It was impossible to ignore what she implied – she'd be damned if Lia treated me carelessly. I shouldn't have worried about acting like a besotted girl. Mama had always been able to see through me.

'Do you truly believe me so callous?' Lia asked. 'For all his faults, my uncle once loved my aunt. My mother still mourns my father. Even monarchs can love beyond politics and diplomacy.'

'No one is denying your ability to love, Your Majesty,' Mama said. 'We're trying to understand what you gain by loving my daughter.'

Lia looked at me apologetically, then said, 'Forgive my bluntness: you and your daughters are Fifth Step by marriage, and you wield little political influence. On the whole, I gain little.'

I couldn't hide my crestfallen expression.

'But Xania is beautiful and intelligent,' Lia continued. 'She makes me believe I can improve Edar and the future of my people.'

Everyone looked at me. My face turned hot.

'And if anyone tries to harm her,' Lia added, 'or use her against me, I will destroy them.'

Was this the kind of love girls dreamed of, emotions so strong that someone would kill for them?

Mama looked unsettled, if you knew her well, but kept her composure. 'It will do. For now.'

'Good.' Lia stood. 'Hopefully our next meeting will be more pleasant.'

ϙ ϙ ϙ

Matthias had left Lady Patrinne to me. Which is how I found myself standing outside her door, braced to knock, feeling like I stood on a frozen lake about to crack.

I was Lia's Whispers. And she was more than just my Queen.

I knocked on the door.

It opened. Patrinne grimaced at me, then stood back for me to enter. 'Miss Bayonn. A pleasure, as always.'

When the door closed, I said, 'Wonderful lies, as always.'

She smiled. 'I hope you were careful coming here.'

We sat. She didn't summon a servant for refreshment, didn't offer me anything, but I didn't expect it. This was not a social visit. I was following a Queen's doomed orders, pretending that I knew where – and whom – a murder's blood trail led to.

'So,' Patrinne said. 'Matthias visited prominent members of the Steps and Parliament today. The Queen is determined to fulfil promises made by her uncle before his death. Promises she didn't particularly care about before now. Curious.'

I stayed silent.

'And what have you, little spider-in-training, come to offer me?'

'I need information.'

She laughed. 'Of course you do.'

'Why has Lord Hazell become so interested in the Opposition?'

Patrinne's expression sharpened. 'You think he's behind Vigrante's death?'

'No one knows anything, yet.'

She drummed her fingers against the table. 'There were overtures of friendship made to others. There wasn't a pattern to his choices. I assumed he was deflecting from Vigrante.'

'So did I.'

'I'll look into it.' Her eyes narrowed. 'Terize doesn't mention you much anymore.'

'We're not together much outside of the Treasury.' It wasn't Terize's fault. Lia and I had agreed that I would pull back from the duties of her ladies and spend more time in the Treasury and as Whispers. Vigrante's death was the opening move of a chess game I didn't understand, and I suspected the Farezi spymaster was my opponent.

'You're not upholding your part of the agreement.'

'The foreign royalty speak to her.' This was technically true. They spoke to Terize, as they did to all the ladies, but they didn't like her. Her lack of confidence was off-putting, and she couldn't hide her nerves around them. Rassa hardly acknowledged her existence.

'I don't suppose you know who Vigrante's successor will be?' I asked with little hope.

'Only Vigrante's ministers know, and they're not telling.'

I sighed, then stood. 'I must go. A pleasure, as always.' Another lie: this visit had been worthless. I wasn't sure what I'd expected from it.

Patrinne stood. 'A piece of advice, Miss Bayonn.' She hesitated. 'Be careful of Rassa and the Farezi. I've heard he's... noticed you.'

As warnings went, it was too little, too late.

'Rassa has made his opinion of me perfectly clear. I'm only near him when absolutely necessary.'

'Even so.' Patrinne fussed with her sleeves. 'I've heard troubling things from my Farezi relatives. All oblique in their letters, of course. Their King no longer hides his erratic nature. The Queen is maintaining control and appearances, but Rassa's behaviour hasn't helped.'

Like stealing from foreign ladies and ruining their reputations.

'And you're not only close to the Queen, but immune to his charms.'

'I'm not the only one immune.' I curtseyed, trying to soften my words, and strode to the doors.

As I was about to open them, she added, 'Hazell enjoys Rassa's company a great deal lately.'

I froze.

'I'll find out what I can,' Patrinne said. 'Stay cautious, Miss Bayonn.'

CHAPTER THIRTY-FIVE

LIA

'Her Majesty, the Queen!'

As the doors to the throne room were flung open, the crowd curtseyed and bowed.

The Government comprised of over sixty members, with forty in Opposition, voted by the Steps and merchant classes. The Head of Government appointed twelve as ministers, with corresponding Opposition shadows. When choosing a successor, the ministers usually picked from amongst themselves.

A ripple spread throughout the room. The Court parted for the approaching ministers –

And Admiral Diana of Casa High.

It felt like a cruel joke.

Diana stopped before the throne. Back straight, hands clasped, she waited for me to speak first. Calm and proper from her hair to the tips of her boots, as if she had never asked permission to steal from our neighbours.

I took deep, even breaths against the panic curdling in my

stomach. Diana had held entirely opposite views to Vigrante. Something had changed on the political chessboard for her to become the new Government leader.

Matthias hadn't approached her yesterday. I'd assumed I already had her support.

Vigrante's second-in-command stepped forward.

'Your Majesty,' she said, 'in light of Lord Vigrante's unfortunate... demise, we have followed Parliament tradition and elected a new Head of Government.' She took a step back and gestured at Diana. 'We present Admiral Diana of Casa High, chosen by unanimous vote.'

Sticky political Court webs clung to me.

Calm. Calm. The crown weighed on my head, a reminder that I was the ultimate authority.

Diana curtseyed.

'Admiral,' I said, after an appropriate pause, 'rise.' She straightened. 'Congratulations on your well-deserved appointment.' *Why did they choose you? What can you, who scorned politics for the sea, accomplish that others can't?*

'Your Majesty honours me.'

Pretty words. Her eyes warned not to trust their beauty.

The ministers stood behind her like wolves waiting for their alpha to rip out my throat. The Court watched like carrion birds hoping for the entrails.

The silence lengthened, bordering on discomfort, until I rose. I held out my right hand, presenting my ring to her.

My grandfather had refused to stop the tradition, despite several Parliamentary attempts. My uncle had also refused, though Vigrante had surely tried persuasion. My father wouldn't have changed this, and so neither would I.

The ring reminded everyone that I served Edar. Each new Head of Government kissed it, acknowledging the reigning monarch and promising we'd work together for Edar's prosperity.

That was the idea, anyway. Reality didn't often resemble it.

Diana's smile brightened her sharp features. She kissed the ring, a brush of lips gone in a moment.

Xania came into sharp relief in the crowd, looking tense beside her family.

'Your Majesty,' Diana said, 'I urge you to forget any differences between you and Lord Vigrante. I am his successor only by vote.'

Careful, pleasing words.

Her expression said: *You're no longer able to refuse me so easily.*

'Such an agreement pleases us,' I said, since I couldn't tell her to kindly drop dead. She'd celebrate today with her wife, family, and friends. At sundown, we'd meet to discuss our political views and how to work towards common goals. Another lofty ideal that wouldn't match reality.

Back in the antechamber, I let out a long breath, the doors to the throne room shut and secured. Vigrante couldn't have planned this better himself. He was probably watching me, in death, laughing to the point of tears.

ဝ ဝ ဝ

Diana arrived on time for our evening meeting.

'Welcome, welcome,' I said.

Diana bowed. She wore her decorative uniform: dark trousers and boots with a white shirt and blue waistcoat. A blue leather coat completed the ensemble, replete with her rank and achievements. 'Your Majesty is too kind.'

'Don't be foolish, Admiral, this is tradition.' I kept my voice light as I picked up the coffee pot. 'I didn't think politics were to your liking.'

'They're not, but this is necessary.'

'Containing the chaos after Vigrante's death?'

'*Containing* you before you destroy Edar.'

I thumped the coffeepot onto the table.

She returned my stare defiantly.

'Someone has babbled nonsense at you,' I said. 'And you've done worse – you listened. I thought we understood each other.'

Her mouth quirked. She didn't reveal the faintest hint of nerves. 'There's no nonsense, only truth you won't believe.'

This was more than refusing to let her steal grain. 'Please, tell me what I'll refuse to believe.' I picked up the coffeepot again, determined to play out this scene as I'd intended, and poured.

Diana dropped sugar lumps into her cup – *plink plink plink* – until it was barely drinkable. 'We had to wait,' she said, 'for the King to die. We were convinced you'd bring change. You often pressed him for new legislation, persistent but polite so he wouldn't consider you a threat.'

'He didn't take any notice.'

'*We* noticed.'

'We?'

'Those of us trying to do better than our predecessors. We don't mourn your uncle's reign. We don't treat the lower classes as things to manipulate for our benefit. You have similar goals. You emptied your stores to keep your estate fed, when your uncle didn't care that people would starve. You curbed your aunt's greed. You fought Vigrante's entitlement.' She smiled bitterly. 'The Master of Coin adores you – he'd marry you if he didn't love his husband.'

'Good to know,' I said, trying for humour and braced for the *but*.

'Now. Well.' Diana's expression hardened. 'We're no longer fooled. You settled into royal comfort as easily as your uncle did, more concerned about the marriage dance than Vigrante. When I offered a solution to this year's harvests, you preferred keeping up appearances–'

'I refused because I'd already negotiated through *legal* avenues,' I said sharply.

Diana continued as if I hadn't spoken. 'When bringing change grew too difficult, you stopped. Faced with Vigrante's death, you reacted like him, despite claiming to hate his methods. It's worse because you wanted to be *better*. You wanted to do more.'

She didn't know the harvests had failed worse than last year's, or she'd have already insisted on doing things her way, whether I approved or not. With this self-righteous lecture, I could hardly broach the subject. If the Eshvon caravans didn't arrive soon, the price of bread would soar by winter.

I'd been ready to admit I was wrong. But now I trusted her almost as little as Vigrante.

I wanted to throw the coffeepot in Diana's face. She'd refused to participate in politics for so long, while I'd spent months fighting Vigrante with the little Opposition support offered me. I'd forced him to pay a death price to the Riavaan family, even if I hadn't publicly punished him.

After rising through the ranks, Diana had commanded the navy for almost a decade. Her predecessor had improved the competent, yet largely apathetic force, but Diana had turned it into a significant threat.

I shouldn't have ignored her because now I *couldn't*.

But, like I had before I took the throne, she thought politicians could be easily convinced to usher in reform. But they wouldn't be hammered or threatened into embracing change. It was a slow, painful process. The Government wasn't trained to obey like the Navy. When things turned uncertain or strained, there was no loyalty or trust.

'Patience,' I said, 'is a virtue.'

Diana returned my smile. 'So is my sword.'

'You assume I'll give up my family's legacy so easily?'

'You value your life. Keep on this path, and your line will end with you.'

I hadn't become Vigrante's puppet. I wouldn't be Diana's, either. Surely the Government had *one* politician who didn't expect the best or worst from me? One – just one – willing to work with me to help Edar?

'Unless memory fails me,' I said, 'you didn't attempt to overthrow my uncle.'

'We considered it, but you were too young to inherit the throne.'

'And my father was dead.'

'Your father, who loved Edar so much, he only returned when there was no doubt your uncle wouldn't have his own heir.'

She could belittle Uncle all she wanted, but mocking Father was too much. 'My mother would have been my regent until I came of age.'

'A lady more concerned with your clothes and marriage prospects than ruling.'

Yes, my mother, who'd taught me clothing was a different kind of armour, marriage another kind of weapon. My mother who, at this moment, was quietly learning everything she could about

Diana. She wouldn't have been the Queen I wanted to be, but it didn't make her useless. I knew better now.

Beyond the immediate fury of Diana dismissing both my parents, what she'd said before was more troubling. This shadowy group of insurgents, of whom she was my only proof, had considered toppling my uncle. I'd no doubt she was lying about my father: he'd have given Edar a solid foundation for me to continue with. His death was their biggest blow, they simply refused to admit it.

I would *not* be intimidated by her. It didn't matter that we wanted the same things for Edar, and Diana had no intention of keeping the nobles' privileges secure – they'd believe what they wanted. A careful word here and there, and she could turn them against me, so convinced of her righteousness that she'd alienate her true ally: me.

And the Navy would obey her over me, of course.

I almost laughed at the irony. For all her disdain for Vigrante, she used similar tactics. How foolish of me to think I could win Parliament to my side.

I stood. 'We will consider what you've said–'

Her eyes flashed, but she stood. 'You dare–'

'We both have Edar's best interests at heart,' I said, 'even if we disagree on methods. We need to work together. But I didn't back down against Vigrante. I won't for you, either.'

Diana clenched and unclenched her hands. 'Very well, Your

Majesty. But if I were you, I'd think hard about how you've come to this point.'

☖ ☖ ☖

'I couldn't have done worse if I'd run her through with a sword.'

Xania sighed. 'You know, if you want me to read these' – she waved the Aella novel in the air – 'going over what we already discussed isn't helpful.'

I pressed my cheek against her shoulder. 'I could tell you the plots and we could act them out.' I smiled, despite the fluttering worry in my stomach that hadn't left since meeting Diana. 'It'd be *much* quicker.'

'I'm not sure about *quicker*... This is what you really think about when you're elbow-deep in paperwork, isn't it?'

'You don't think about me?' I tried for mock-outrage, but Xania dug her fingers in my hair, laughing, and guided my mouth to hers. The kiss started slow, teasing, until I had to brace myself above her with trembling arms, our breathing harsh. We finally pulled away, gasping, and I slumped beside her.

'She's worse than Vigrante.' I pulled Xania closer, wrapping the blanket around us. 'He thought he could eventually persuade me into working with him. She doesn't.'

'Diana underestimates you.'

'Does she? She's been right so far. It's late autumn. I took the throne last spring, and what have I accomplished? I'm still at odds with Parliament, and I'm nowhere near marrying.'

Xania propped herself up on an elbow. 'If change was so easy, every monarch would live to see their grandchildren, and we wouldn't use diplomacy to outsmart each other. Wait until your first year is over, *then* start panicking.'

'Wise words.'

'One of us has to be sensible.'

We settled into silence as I traced lazy circles on her hip.

'I think there's a link between Hazell and Rassa,' she said.

'Of course. *Wonderful.*'

'It complicates things.'

'That's an understatement.'

'Patrinne's looking into it. I'll try and bribe Hazell's other servant. We need to know about all his visitors.'

Xania hadn't said anything about my disastrous attempt to court the Parliament and Step nobles, though I could practically see the *I told you so* lodged in Matthias's throat whenever he clapped eyes on me. Nothing could ease the shame coating the back of my throat.

'Are you meeting your mother tomorrow?' she asked.

'Yes. Let's hope the Court has interesting opinions on the Admiral of Casa High.'

'I'm meeting Lariux tomorrow. We should compare notes.'

I kissed her forehead, her lips, her neck. 'Matthias will bring the brandy.'

She attempted a laugh, trailing a hand down my cheek.

I kissed her palm, and intertwined our fingers. 'We either convince Diana to reconsider and work with me, or we destroy her.'

I'd always assumed, when I became Queen, that I'd have more options than manipulate or kill. But it always came back to them, no matter how I tried to change the path.

CHAPTER THIRTY-SIX

XANIA

'What sort of man clears his debts?'

Lauriux was all bright eyes, powerful gestures, and rhetorical questions. Never mind a merchant, he should have been an academic.

I drained my third cup of tea. 'An innocent man who fears his creditors?'

'A man with no debts either knows he's about to die, or he's preparing to flee the country.'

I poured fresh tea and dumped sugar into it, desperate to avoid an unintentional nap. Lia's bedroom suffered from winter like the rest of the palace. She was used to harsher weather, but more than happy to take advantage of my hatred of cold. It made for nights with less sleep, but I could hardly complain. 'Yes, well, Vigrante didn't so much clear his debts as manipulate them.'

'Perhaps Vigrante was preparing to flee,' Lariux said, 'but died before he could.'

'Why flee? He could handle his creditors.'

Lariux stuffed a cake into his mouth. Now that he was a soon-to-be baron, our working partnership had relaxed. He swallowed. 'Even his mistakes could come back to kill him.'

I ripped a cake to shreds with my fork. 'Your way with words is beautiful.'

'I was a poet in a former life.' He smiled, but didn't lose his serious expression.

I sighed. 'You're wearing your *I have bad news* face. Get it over with.'

This week had been all about *I have bad news*:

Matthias: '*I have bad news*, Vigrante's financial discrepancies are worse than we thought.'

Lia: '*I have bad news*, I must dance with Aubrey for Midwinter.'

My relatively new foreign spies: '*We have bad news*, we appear to be dead.'

Lariux handed me a leather folder. I unknotted the straps, trying to ignore the foreboding creeping up my back.

The folder was stuffed with receipts for clothing, furniture, and entertaining: the staples of a wealthy noble. I carefully sorted through them for the link that had to be there.

I finally found it in a third of the receipts: a different bank account.

'Many of the high Step families have several bank accounts,' I said. 'It's not illegal.' In this, I was Mama's daughter.

'Of course. Until I discovered that bank account' – Lariux

pointed to the receipts I'd separated out – 'previously belonged to the old King.'

I went still.

'Before his death, the King agreed that deserving nobles – Vigrante's allies, of course – should get financial incentives.'

'The Queen revoked it because of lack of Treasury funds.' I'd had to endure Lia's rants when Vigrante tried to weasel it by her again a few weeks ago.

'It appears Vigrante was... less than forthcoming about minor details,' Lariux said. 'Ownership of the account was transferred to him a month before the King died.'

That explained where Lia's redecorating and wardrobe budgets had gone.

'So the King didn't inform the Master of Coin of the account transfer?'

'No. The royal family have their own bank accounts, which are not part of the Treasury budgets, though the Master of Coin is aware of them. The Queen should have inherited it.'

I rested my chin on my fist. 'Lying through omission to Her Majesty isn't justifiable treason, or she'd have to condemn half the Court.'

'Of course.' But Lariux's eyes gleamed with smugness. 'Except all those businesses he purchased from don't actually exist.'

Shadow accounts. Vigrante had been sending royal money to Farezi under the pretence of purchasing items abroad. 'So no one would think twice at foreign account numbers.'

'Ah, your father would be pleased with you. I've gone as far as I can, but if the Master of Whispers were to investigate further, I'd bet the accounts are all Farezi.'

The receipts practically glowed with a new light: physical proof of the discrepancies Coin had uncovered, funnelled into an account he'd thought still belonged to the King. I'd bet my dowry when he compared the amounts, they'd match the 'mistakes'. And it was more proof of a link between Vigrante and Farezi.

'Thank you, Lariux,' I said. 'I'll give these to the Master of Whispers immediately.'

'Glad to be of service, Miss Bayonn.'

I smiled. 'Xania. I think we're beyond formality now, don't you?'

'If so...' He hesitated, and I paused from retying the leather folder. 'I'm grateful you suggested to the Master of Whispers that I help with investigating Vigrante's murder. And for Her Majesty raising me to the Steps, of course.'

'You're a good agent, Lariux. One of my best.'

'There's... a great deal of faith in you from powerful people.' Lariux's confidence had turned into cautious determination. 'And I also have the utmost faith in you.'

He knew I was more than a link in the spy chain. He probably suspected I *was* Whispers.

'I appreciate your faith. As, no doubt, does the Master of Whispers, and Her Majesty. Faith helps most in our line of work.'

A lie: caution helped us most.

Lariux smiled at my delicate sidestep. We stood, said our good-byes, and I rushed to Matthias.

Φ Φ Φ

Winter deepened, its freezing winds and frost-tipped fingers changing to layers of snow trodden into sleek treachery.

The investigation into Vigrante's death dragged and crumbled. We followed leads and hunches, but a line of enemies had trailed after Vigrante. Had the opportunity presented itself, too many in Court would have gladly killed him.

Lia sometimes treated his death as a personal insult. Both of us were steeped in bitterness that he had avoided justice, no matter his violent end.

News of the failed harvests finally leaked. The initial panic had simmered with reports that the Eshvon caravans were near our border with Farezi. We'd have just enough grain to avoid obscene price hikes.

Midwinter arrived too soon.

Aubrey would be Lia's first Midwinter dance, her second, and her third. He'd have the majority of them, hinting that he was her favoured choice before the official announcement at the end of Midwinter. Despite Diana's criticism, Lia needed to show the Court she was still focused on the future benefits of a strong marriage. I'd be in the crowd, watching, nowhere close to her.

But while I wasn't Lia's favoured choice in public, our families knew I was in private, so certain expectations had to be met. Lord Martain ignored my protests and crunched figures with Mama to see how much they could spend on new gowns for Zola and me.

The dark blue silk was too expensive. But the bodice embroidery sparkled like stars across an evening sky, the full skirt shading towards night. I stood before my family, who assessed me from head to toe.

'We may have gone too far,' Mama said. 'You could catch a suitor by the end of tonight.' Her unspoken *As you should* lingered in the air.

'You look beautiful,' Zola said, who flowed where I glittered, dressed in dawn blue.

'So do you.' I grasped her hands, hoping my smile wasn't too shaky. We all turned at the sound of knocking.

A servant entered with a small clasped box, and bowed. 'Compliments of Her Majesty. She begs Miss Bayonn to accept this gift in apology for an unavoidable wrong.' He opened the box with a flourish.

My knees wobbled.

The sapphires were almost an exact match for my dress. They were stunning rather than ostentatious, reasonable cuts set in silver. I could wear them in complement to my clothing, not as a setting to show them off.

I knew by their simplicity we could never afford them.

Mama's face was torn between astonishment and irritation. It was a coup, of course, for me to wear jewellery like this. But it also looked like Lia throwing pretty things at a problem.

'Please pass on our grateful thanks to Her Majesty for this gift.' Mama's words were slow, measured. 'Such an apology is unnecessary. The supposed wrong was of no one's making.'

The servant bowed. 'Her Majesty also requests Miss Bayonn join her beforehand to see the full effects of her gift.'

Mama and Zola leaped into action, helping me with the jewellery and leading me to Mama's looking glass.

The reflection in the mirror – *me* – looked like someone who could stand at Lia's side.

I touched the glass, trying to slow my breathing.

Mama's expression in the mirror was one I'd seen her throw at Lia before: *You don't even realise how lucky you are that my daughter adores you.* She squeezed my arms and we shared a smile.

'Make her regret she won't be near you all night,' she whispered in my ear.

ϙ ϙ ϙ

When I entered the antechamber, Lia had her back to me as servants settled the folds of her dress, so she didn't notice everyone focusing on me. Their expressions made me tense.

No one in Court, until Lia, had looked at me with admiration or desire. I wanted to extinguish it. I only wanted her. No one else.

Matthias's gaze was assessing, clinical, but he leaned in to whisper, 'Congratulations, Miss Bayonn. You're wearing her great-grandmother's jewels.' He winked.

Royal jewels. Worth fortune upon fortune after all these years. Now I'd be afraid all night of ruining them.

'Relax,' he said. 'They've been through *far* worse than a Midwinter Ball.'

Lia turned, her skirts swirling. Her eyes widened.

I resembled twilight with stars; Lia was moonlight and frozen winter. Her dress was thin white silk, matched to her skin, with tree branches embroidered in blue and black, stark and winter-bare, studded with tiny diamonds. The Midwinter crown, a twisted silver tiara dripping with crystal and diamonds – her grandfather's nod to extravagance – held her unbound hair in place.

She walked towards me. The embroidered branches clung to her arms and chest and hips.

Lia smiled, almost shyly. I remembered myself, and dropped into a curtsey. 'Your Majesty, you – you look astonishing.'

'Thank you, Miss Bayonn. The dressmaker will have an avalanche of work after tonight.' I stayed in the curtsey, my head down, too afraid to meet her gaze and betray myself to everyone around us.

She eased me up. Her mouth quirked in a conspiring smile. 'It's Midwinter. Even I had to get a new dress.'

Midwinter had been the First Empire's most important celebration. Their seasonal gods had derived from magical roots, lords and ladies of frost and snow, spring and rebirth, worshipped by the same people whose new rulers walked among them blindfolded. As Lia had worn the silk blindfold at her coronation, now she'd spend the evening as Lady Winter –

I considered my dress and jewels in a new light.

She beamed.

Lady Winter's companions, according to legend, were Twilight and Night. The retellings lacked specific details from being passed down generations, so the roles and titles were interchangeable between people, but their status as Lady Winter's companions never changed.

In my most wistful daydreams, I'd hoped to be Twilight or Night. But I'd reminded myself gossip would follow, even though Lia would hardly honour any of her ladies, or Isra, with the role. But now, despite it all, I *was* Twilight.

Aubrey was surely Night.

In some retellings, Lady Winter had desired them both.

'You planned this,' I said.

'Of course. Did you really think I'd ignore you on Midwinter?'

'The Court will whisper.'

'Trust me,' she said, and turned back to an impatient servant.

Matthias swooped in and politely dragged me towards the door. 'Let me escort you, Miss Bayonn, so we're both present for Her Majesty's entrance.' He didn't speak until the door closed after us. 'I wanted to tell you, but Lia insisted on silence.'

'Aubrey is Night,' I said.

'Yes.'

'Does he know about me?'

'Unlikely.'

'This will be a disaster.'

'Not necessarily.'

I wrenched my arm from his grasp. 'Easy for you to say!'

He reached for my elbow again, but reconsidered at my glare. *'Calm down.'*

'Tell me again to *calm down*–'

He shook his head and forced me to stop with an outstretched arm. 'No, enough. It can't begin like this. I'm not sure what Lia's planned, but I trust her. So do you.'

After a moment, I nodded.

'Good. Follow me. One last thing.' We turned into a small library that people would use later tonight to debate or argue away from the ballroom. I blinked in the low light. Furnished with fabrics that could be easily cleaned or replaced (it wasn't a debate unless glasses smashed), it didn't have niches or corners for more... intimate discussion.

A servant waited with two flat square boxes. Matthias took them, and waited until we were alone before opening the first.

Twilight's diadem lay on faded blue velvet, silver with a large sapphire flanked by small diamonds. Mama had described it from the Midwinter balls she'd attended with Lord Martain.

I stepped back. 'I can't wear this.'

'You can, and you will,' Matthias said. 'Her Majesty has decided.'

It felt lighter than I'd expected. Matthias carefully arranged my hair around it. From the second box, he pulled out a gauzy dark blue train embroidered with stars. He attached it to my shoulders. It trailed on the floor behind me.

'Beautiful,' he said.

'Impractical.'

'Nothing about Midwinter is practical.' He nudged me, smiling. 'You'll stun them all.'

'I'm not ranked high enough for this.'

'The Queen's besotted with you. I think you qualify.' He surprised me with a hug. 'You look beautiful.'

'I feel ill.'

'Well, you're not eating until after the opening dances.'

Lady Winter, flanked by Twilight and Night, opened the ball with traditional dances. My chest tightened.

'I don't know the dance, or what I'm supposed–'

'Lia will control everything. Just don't forget she's dancing with Aubrey afterwards.' He coaxed me out into the hall, and we slipped into the ballroom.

A wave of heat made me glad I wore thin silk. The crush of bodies was stifling. Matthias guided me towards a pillar to the right of the dais. My train only got stepped on twice, before people recognised it and surged back, whispering. Zola betrayed a distinct lack of surprise at my appearance.

'You *all* knew about this.'

'Of course. Mama would never put you in such dark fabric otherwise.'

'I thought the blue was... respectable.' Hindsight was ridiculous.

Zola patted my arm. 'You were otherwise preoccupied.'

I'd moped about not being with Lia during the ball, oblivious to everyone quietly planning around me. I possessed enough decency and shame to whisper, 'Thank you.'

Zola smiled. 'Don't embarrass Mama.'

Aubrey appeared at the opposite pillar, dressed in black velvet. I was starry twilight; he was endless night. He raised his eyebrows at me.

'I can't do this.' *I'm nothing compared to Aubrey. I'm nothing compared to them together.*

'Yes, you can,' Zola whispered, unusually firm. 'It's you she prefers, not Aubrey.'

No one had mentioned love, including Lia and myself. We

knew better.

'Her Majesty, the Queen!'

Gasps and murmurs swirled around Lia like her gown.

Matthias nudged me forward. Aubrey and I bowed and curt-seyed, Twilight and Night honouring Winter.

It's you she prefers, not Aubrey. I allowed myself a small smile. Lia glided down the steps and presented her hands for me to kiss.

Lady Winter controlled the dance, even with a ruling King. Lia's aunt had done this last year, as had her grandmother and great-grandmother, a tradition stretching back to the First Empire.

A servant eased the train from my shoulders. Lia and I faced each other. I tried to keep my breathing level, conscious of the sweat under my dress and the feel of Lia's hands.

At the opening strains of music, we moved in a circle. The dance was faster than usual, but the first one usually descended into improvisation, the calm, brutal chill turning into a savage winter gale.

I concentrated on the steps and rhythm. Heat radiated from her, flared from our joined hands as we spun away and back towards each other. When we came together for the embrace in the middle, she pressed a hand to the small of my back and inter-linked our fingers. I succumbed to the feel of her sleek-rough dress, her perfume, her breath against my neck when she leaned our heads together during a twirl.

It was too much. It wasn't enough.

Faces blurred around us when we spun for the finale. I hoped my expression was difficult to read, as I could hardly hide how I felt with Lia this close.

We stamped and spun for the last time, our skirts settling as we faced each other, palm to palm, both of us gasping. Lia's cheeks were flushed, her eyes bright.

I wanted to kiss her until she couldn't stand.

She stepped back.

My stomach dropped, before she brushed her lips across the back of my hand, the most soft and gentle kiss she could manage in public.

It was enough. It had to be.

ϙ ϙ ϙ

I ate. Or maybe I moved food around my plate in an acceptable pretence of eating. My good spirits had dwindled to nothing by the end of Lia and Aubrey's dance.

'They made a good show of desiring each other,' Zola said. 'A poor imitation of you and Lia.'

Which was the problem. Had we shown the Court a *pretence* of desiring each other, or had we revealed too much? Had we brushed silk or skin too tenderly, gazed at each other a moment too long?

People made it worse by actually speaking to me. While I was part of Lia's circle, as Fifth Step I was also easily ignored. But Twilight and Night were tokens of immense royal favour: Lia had informed the Court I was someone to be taken seriously, as was my family.

Zola might be engaged by next Midwinter.

So might I, but that was the least of my worries.

After the meal, we moved to the ballroom. I managed a dance with Matthias, who didn't know whether to hug or laugh at me.

Zola politely and ruthlessly turned down Ernest Blackwood for a dance.

Later, I noticed Matthias leaning against a pillar with a tall man from the Farezi party, one of the junior diplomats. His smile was razor-sharp, both a warning and invitation, but the man didn't seem to mind.

Matthias always kept his own secrets best.

'I'm leaving,' I told Zola. 'It's – it's too hard.' I wouldn't look at Lia. Better not to know who she was talking to, or laughing or dancing with.

'I'll go with you.'

'No. One of us should enjoy ourselves.'

My heels clicked in the empty halls, the giggles and sighs from smaller rooms fading as I headed towards the residential suites. I hesitated at my door, then ducked into the passages and went to the royal wing.

In Lia's rooms, I sat and watched the guttering fire. I finally rose and wiped off my facepaint, then tried to read. The words blurred into nonsense, and I tossed the book aside.

Whiskey didn't help, either, but the trembling in my hands eased. The clock chimed the longest hour. Maybe I should go back to my rooms. Lia would surely have to stay until the end –

The main doors to her suite opened, then closed quietly. Footsteps crossed the outer foyer, then the door opened.

I froze.

Lia's eyes flickered over me, then around the room. I couldn't look away from her mouth. Her gaze lingered on my throat.

Heat rolled through me.

She stepped forward. 'You left early.'

I should have said, *I'm sorry, I was tired.* Instead: 'I couldn't stand only having one dance with you, and not being able to stay close, or talk–'

'You could have,' she said, 'as Twilight–'

'– or *touch* you –'

She paused, then: 'Midwinter is for lovers.'

'Is it? I wouldn't know.'

Her footsteps were slow, deliberate.

She traced my eyebrows with a fingertip, trailed her knuckles down the side of my face. I caught her wrist when her hand reached my lips, and kissed her knuckles.

I regretted nothing at the sound that trembled from her.

She crushed her mouth to mine. There was nothing gentle about the kiss.

We broke apart.

'The dress is lovely,' Lia said, 'but I'm afraid it must simply come off.'

I shivered at the roughness in her voice. 'Not difficult.' She laughed, reached for the necklace clasp, and carefully removed her great-grandmother's jewels.

I kissed her, and she didn't laugh again for a long time.

CHAPTER THIRTY-SEVEN

LIA

I hadn't wanted to get up, but the servant had said Rassa wished to speak with me and wouldn't leave. 'He's inclined to keep his word, Your Majesty,' she'd said, irritated, so I'd kissed Xania goodbye and rose to dress.

Now I found myself walking in the gardens, tired and hungry, while Rassa remained silent.

'You dragged me out of bed,' I said. 'Speak.'

Rassa smirked. 'You look tired. Did you overindulge?'

I was suffering from lack of sleep, not wine. I should still have been with Xania in my warm bed.

'No.' My voice was sharper than intended, but my patience was in short supply. 'It's unseemly.'

'Your uncle didn't believe that.'

'You arranged an early walk to tell me what I already know?'

'No,' Rassa said. 'You regard Miss Bayonn highly.'

Fear turned to ice shards in my stomach. 'Of course. She can sensibly converse. I value such skills.'

'Cousin.' Rassa's condescending tone made me bristle. 'You've formed an attachment to her. No one could miss it last night.'

I hadn't been careful. I'd shown my desire, even though I'd known better. I had to be delicate with this. Careful.

I rolled my eyes. 'I imagine you're attached to *your* closest friends.'

'I suppose.' His smile matched his condescending tone. 'But we both know that's not the attachment I mean.'

The ice shards turned lethal in my stomach.

'You mean, do I desire her? Yes.' I laced my words with scorn. 'It doesn't particularly matter. Miss Bayonn can do many things, but she can't give me an heir.'

He laughed. 'True.'

'I'm not ashamed of it, nor her. But if *you* are ashamed for me, it bodes ill for my affection for *you*.'

He stopped, unable to hide his shock and disbelief. I wasn't acting according to plan. 'Cousin, I would *never* – I didn't mean –'

'I will marry,' I said, 'and have children. That won't change. But what I do in *private* is my own business. I wouldn't be the first.'

'What you do in private is your own business,' Rassa conceded, as we resumed walking. 'And there would be no illegitimacy to contend with. But, well... some in Court won't agree.'

I laughed. 'In Farezi, perhaps, Cousin. Not in Edar. What is open and consensual between adults isn't condemned.'

Unless it involved power and bloodlines. Then everything

turned difficult. If I weren't a Queen and Xania an eldest daughter, no one would care we were together.

But if I hadn't been me, I wouldn't have met Matthias and crossed paths with Xania. Everything was built on from decisions and consequences: my great-grandfather rising up against a weak ruler; my father marrying my mother; my father dying. My meeting Matthias and saving his life; my uncle and aunt having no children. Matthias helping Xania to avenge her father, and him introducing her to me.

Xania and I admitting our feelings.

My refusal to give her up.

So much, built on so little.

'Be careful how far you think you can push me,' I said. 'I've fought and pushed and reasoned my way this far. I won't stop because of your misguided concern for my reputation.'

His expression hardened; I'd misstepped. Yet he was polite, if distant, when he said, 'I wouldn't dream of that. My concern is out of love.'

There was something else in his coldness, something I wasn't interpreting clearly. But between this and his implication I was unfit to rule, I had to make the next move before he did.

It would have to be Aubrey. And I'd have to announce the engagement sooner rather than later.

CHAPTER THIRTY-EIGHT

XANIA

It was inevitable I'd turn to Papa after Lia told me she'd chosen Aubrey.

Soon after my birthday, I finally realised why his journals were boring: they were written in code, each entry carefully hiding the truth.

It started simple enough: Papa had slipped in lies about Zola and me that only someone who knew us well would recognise. *Zola liked grapes.* (She didn't: she broke out in blemishes after eating them, once almost fainting after accidentally drinking a pear and grape cordial.) *I helped him plant a new batch of spring vines.* (I'd almost set them on fire, mostly by accident.) I hovered over phrases, flicked pages back and forth, picked out other seemingly innocent sentences, none of them true.

The cyphers started basic: each lie was the translation key until a new one took over for the next batch of entries.

My dearest Xania, if you're reading this, then you are of age, I am dead, and your mother was right about my foolishness...

He used more elaborate codes further into the notebooks. The technical detail was staggering. In some sections he used two codes, occasionally three, forcing me to translate, then re-translate. Sometimes I had to skip entire sections to find their codes later, then go back to decipher them.

Papa and I had bonded over codes and puzzles, which made the betrayal worse when he'd mentored Matthias. But the notebooks' growing difficulty finally made me turn to Lia, who searched her libraries for books written by and about previous spymasters – including their cyphers, since Papa had probably borrowed from the best.

It made me feel closer to him than in years. But I couldn't understand how he knew everything in the entries: alliances, financial records far beyond his Treasury access, conspiracies, treachery.

'Are you certain you won't come with us?' Lia propped her chin on her palm.

I stirred my tea, jerked out of my thoughts. 'Pouting is unattractive.'

'We have more financials to sort through,' Matthias said, 'as well as her father's journals. And Coin has requested an interview.'

'Which she can't attend,' Lia said.

'*In person.* She can eavesdrop perfectly well,' Matthias said.

Lia probably wanted to spend as much time as possible at the

Midwinter markets with me today, since she was announcing her engagement tonight. But we both wanted more than we could get.

Lia sighed, as if wrestling with similar bleak thoughts. 'Oh, *very well*. Stay and be responsible.'

I rubbed my thumb over her knuckles, and kissed her cheek. 'I'll miss you.'

Matthias flicked slices of pear at us.

Lia dawdled over breakfast until she could no longer ignore Matthias's pointed looks. We kissed again, slowly, before she left.

I frowned at my notes, forced the image of her and Aubrey at the markets out of my head, and got to work.

My side of Matthias's desk was relatively tidy, with Papa's journals spread out beside neat piles of cyphers and translations. Matthias's side was controlled chaos, piles of tagged and colour-coded receipts bristling alongside his growing temper.

After he heaved another sigh, I gestured at my translating. 'You can do this instead, if you'd prefer.'

'No, thank you,' he said. 'I'd still be on the same notebook a year from now.' Code-breaking was the one area I excelled beyond him, whether because I had a better knack or because Papa and I had spent more time doing it for fun.

Ten minutes before Coin's arrival, I hesitated over a sentence: *Matthias is loyal to the Princess for life. He will be useful to her with the right training, which I've agreed to do.*

How had Papa known about Matthias's friendship with Lia? Who assigned Matthias to him for training? He'd stumbled across Papa one day in the winter rose gardens, completely by accident.

'Xania,' Matthias said, pulling me from my confusion. 'Clear away your work, Coin can't know you've been here.'

I tidied everything away, and carried my current notebook and a lamp into the passages. As I waited, I wrestled with the entry. Papa had described how to charm, the power of small talk and silence, the higher Steps' formal etiquette – everything he'd taught Matthias. Coin arrived when I was in the middle of a knotty paragraph; I only half-listened as I concentrated on it.

'I've been working with Whispers on Vigrante's financials,' Matthias told Coin. 'His agents have made progress: Vigrante funnelled royal money into Farezi accounts.'

'Whispers will be pleased to know, then, that two days ago, Rassa requested money from me on the basis of *family affection*.'

I froze, my pen hovering over my paper.

'Rassa is three generations removed from Edar, no matter the blood link,' Matthias said. 'We don't owe his overindulgence anything.'

'But if Her Majesty dies without an heir, he rules Edar.'

'She is well aware. Did you give him the money?'

'I asked for past financials first. I wasn't going to let him fritter it away.'

'Her Majesty won't be pleased.'

'She has more to worry about. Does that account look familiar?'

I ground my teeth at the sound of rustling paper, frustrated at the necessity that kept me in the shadows. I nearly laughed at my audacity. I was Whispers. My role *was* to eavesdrop in the shadows.

'I recognise this account,' Matthias said. 'It was in Vigrante's paperwork.'

'Indeed. An odd thing to have in common with Rassa.'

'Were there deposits or withdrawals?'

'Both.'

'Vigrante was giving Edaran money to Rassa,' Matthias said.

'Unfortunately.' From Coin's grim tone, he was taking this personally. 'With Vigrante dead, the deposits have stopped. I'm sure Rassa's parents would be dismayed at the extent of his mismanagement.'

'I can't understand what Rassa could offer Vigrante for him to do this.' Or, more importantly, Matthias wasn't willing to voice his suspicions to Coin.

'Power. Position. Money. People commit treason for less,' Coin said. 'Or else it was what Vigrante offered Rassa.'

'Edar? Without Rassa's parents or Lia finding out?'

Vigrante had probably assured Rassa he could rule Edar as a puppet-state if he helped topple Lia's reign. Perhaps he'd reached out to Lia after realising Rassa wouldn't be easily controlled – or maybe he'd even heard rumours of a spymaster in Rassa's entourage.

Damn Vigrante's ambition, and damn Lia's mother for keeping her from Court. If she hadn't, Lia might have been in a stronger position when she became Queen.

No point in dwelling on it now. Vigrante was dead and a traitor. Rassa was somehow involved in his treason, and we still weren't close to the truth.

'Do you recommend informing Her Majesty?' Matthias asked.

Coin sighed. I'd never thought I'd ever feel sorry for him, but by admitting this, Coin was putting his reputation and security structures into question. If he didn't, Lia would always wonder if the Treasury was slipping further away under his watch. This would be a lot for her to forgive.

'She's announcing her engagement tonight' – as if I needed reminding.

'– it's best she's told before then. She needs to know before I partly reject Rassa's request.'

'Partly?'

'It'll be suspicious if I completely reject it, based – in Rassa's opinion – on little evidence. So I'll give him less than he wants, on the basis he'll get more... eventually.'

'Clever,' Matthias admitted.

'I have my moments.'

When Coin left, I still counted to a hundred before slipping into the room. Matthias, sipping the dregs of the thick northern tea he drank when coffee no longer worked, held out the papers.

It was as bad as I'd feared: a messy financial tangle between Rassa and Vigrante. But something had changed between them after Rassa had angered Eshvon and promptly placed the blame at Vigrante's feet.

'Would Rassa really want to take Edar from Lia?' I asked.

'For his sake, I hope not. Failed usurpers don't spend their lives in prison.'

Someone ran down the hall towards Matthias's door. I moved towards the passages, but he said, 'I'll make up a reason for why you're here.'

Someone hammered at the door. A palace guard rushed in, wild-eyed. Nothing was supposed to destroy their trained calm. 'Baron Farhallow!'

Matthias was already out of his seat. 'What's happened?'

'A riot broke out in the market square–'

My stomach dropped. I should have been there. I was *supposed* to be there –

Matthias didn't wait for me before bolting past the guard, but I was already running after him.

CHAPTER THIRTY-NINE

LIA

Aubrey accompanied Mother and me to the markets, then joined Isra and Hasan when we reached the city proper, while Rassa walked with his own courtiers. Mother stayed with me. As people moved back from the guards, they recognised me. Whispers trailed in our wake.

I hadn't travelled through Arkaala since my coronation. Something else had always got in the way and there was never enough time. Many stared like I was an apparition, but others curtseyed and bowed. They smiled, and shouted greetings, and handed me children to coo over.

As we neared the market square, I realised that despite the curious onlookers and well-wishers, hostility burned on other faces.

The Eshvon caravans should have arrived before Midwinter, but I refused to panic yet. I knew some would resent me for hiding the news of the failed harvests, but I'd hoped logic and common sense would prevail. Foolish. I was the Queen: I could never make everyone happy.

Xania had warned me. Diana had warned me, but still pushed through emergency legislation for eating houses to help the soup kitchens. If the caravans didn't arrive, all food prices, not only bread, would rise. I'd spent so long battling Vigrante and the Court's expectations of me, and fighting Uncle's reputation, I'd never considered people would make *me* the target of their dissatisfaction.

Even thinking so made me as bad as Uncle and Vigrante. As I met angry, tired eyes, I didn't see dissatisfaction. I saw freezing homes, fluctuating food prices, nobles taking more and giving less. While I lived in a palace with enough to eat, I helped pass laws that didn't do enough because Parliament fought me on easy *and* difficult decisions.

Before, I'd emptied my food stores to keep my tenants alive during winter. Now eating the same meals as Court was *doing my bit to help*. I'd become besotted with love and my future, and what I *wanted* instead of what I *had to do*.

Diana was right.

I stepped into the square. The bustle, shouts, and cries faded into silence. My vision blurred with tears.

We stopped at the first stall: silver-work. I examined the jewellery with little enthusiasm. Buying gifts for Mother and Xania had lost its appeal.

'Do you want to leave?' Mother asked. 'We can, if you wish.'

'Doesn't everything always come back to what I want?'

She stared at me, confused, when Rassa suddenly demanded, 'Why are we walking through the city like peasants?'

His words, loud and irritated, sparked against the disquiet bubbling around us.

'Not the wisest thing to say outside the palace,' Aubrey remarked.

Rassa threw him a disgusted look. 'How can you demean yourself like this? Approaching merchants like the dregs of nobility?'

I turned to him. 'You agreed to this, Cousin.'

Everyone flinched.

'Your Majesty is too exalted for this farce,' he said.

'My father visited these markets, as did my grandfather and great-grandfather.' People shrank away from me. 'Farezi may have its own views, but we acknowledge those behind the necessities – and frivolities – we take for granted.'

A muffled cheer was swiftly hushed.

The words rasped against my throat, tasted like defeat. I truly believed them, but now they reminded me of failure.

The crowd drew closer, muttering and grumbling. I scrambled for the right words to calm the growing rage.

Before I spoke, someone threw a rock towards Rassa. It narrowly missed me, or perhaps had been intended for me all along. He ducked, swearing.

A guard rushed to protect me. A knife slammed against her

steel vambrace, bouncing harmlessly away –

– she slapped a hand to her neck, then dropped with a cry.

A moment of silence –

People started screaming.

My sluggish mind finally caught up: *Assassin. Riot.*

Protocol demanded the ruling monarch and their family be protected first; then any visiting royalty; then other nobles. More guards closed around Mother and me, ushering us out of the square. Mother helped drag me along.

'The guard!' I yelled. 'Is she all right? *Is she all right?*'

No one answered.

After becoming my Whispers, Xania had kept me informed of all the intercepted assassination attempts, though she tried to bury her upset under a business-like veneer. The assassins were mostly foreign, with thin links to nobility that fell apart under scrutiny. But some were Edaran, mostly frustrated amateurs who'd suffered under my uncle's regime.

I wasn't making changes quickly enough.

I wanted to weep, even as I inwardly cursed my foolishness.

The screams followed me up the hill and into the palace, echoing in my mind. My thoughts spun: *what if I do this or say that or decree this?* I was sweating, but my hands were cold in my gloves. I blinked and found myself in the entrance hall. Servants and nobles swarmed around me. Someone removed my cloak and gloves.

The cold seeped up my arms and into my chest. It hardened and sharpened, sank into my bones. How many others had been injured while I was dragged to safety?

'Your Majesty!'

Matthias and Xania ran towards me. Matthias met my gaze and ground to a halt. He barely flinched when Xania slammed into him from behind, almost toppling them over.

She frowned, looked at me: froze. Something close to fear filled her face.

The cold must have reached my eyes.

CHAPTER FORTY

XANIA

'I think,' Matthias said, 'Rassa may be a lesser worry, for now.'

Earlier, I would have said nothing was more important than the threat of Lia being overthrown and Edar plunged into civil war. But she stood stiff and silent as people rushed around her. She hadn't been like this even after Vigrante's murder.

'What do we do?' I asked.

'What she commands,' Matthias said, as Lia swept towards us.

'Follow me,' she said, 'both of you.'

She strode through the halls. We followed her into her office, and from there into the passages. No one spoke.

We entered an unfamiliar room. Lia sat on a couch covered in faded green silk. Matthias glanced at the nearest chairs; Lia's mouth turned down. We remained standing.

'Are you all right, Your Majesty?' I asked. 'You're not injured?'

'I'm fine. They didn't hurt me.'

'The riot?'

'The assassin.'

'*What?*' Matthias seemed to age a decade.

I sternly reminded myself this wasn't the time to succumb to knee-buckling relief.

'Rassa insulted the crowd. Someone threw a rock. The assassin took their chance and –' Lia's breath caught. 'A guard protected me, and I never found out –'

'The guards will panic that you're not where they left you,' Matthias said.

'Then they should have ordered me not to move.'

They also expected Lia to have common sense, and not disappear when the palace was in an uproar. Something had changed since she'd left, and it had little to do with the assassin.

It didn't make sense. She'd stayed calm when told of other failed assassination attempts, though they clearly upset her. There was no reason for Lia to be dismissive about this.

Her shoulders slumped. 'I can't blame my people.' Her haughty demeanor slipped away, revealing exhaustion and sadness. 'The fault lies with me.'

Matthias narrowed his eyes.

'I've made no real change since taking the throne.' This wasn't her usual frustration at the political wheel's slow turning, but bitterness so strong it alarmed me. 'I've spent months hitting my head against a wall and calling it progress. So much for being better than Uncle. So much for making everything *right*.'

'You've been Queen less than a year,' I said. 'Sweeping in widespread change isn't practical.'

Matthias winced, but I ignored him. There was no point being gentle when I needed pragmatism.

Lia's face tensed.

'It may not be practical, but it might have averted civil war,' she said, too quietly.

'One riot doesn't make a civil war,' my traitor mouth said.

Lia narrowed her eyes. 'No, but there's a *strong possibility*' – I hated her sarcasm – 'how I respond *will* mean civil war.'

Matthias stepped back. 'What are your intentions, Your Majesty?'

'*You* will find this assassin. And I...' Lia's anger cracked for a moment, making her sound more like herself. 'The Court will bay for blood, and I will satisfy them.'

No. No, she wouldn't.

'You're killing the riot leaders? You're punishing innocent people for an assassination attempt?'

'They weren't innocent – the assassin used the riot as a shield.'

'The assassin would still have acted!'

'I can't have the Court turn against me–'

'What about your *duty*?' I said.

Silence.

'Do you know how our neighbours regard us?' Lia asked. '*Quaint*. Backward.'

'As if they've much to be proud of,' I snapped. 'Not executing *anyone* would make you look more progressive than all of them.'

'Xania—' Matthias said, a warning, a plea, before Lia shouted over him.

'Yes, not executing riot leaders who threw rocks at *visiting royalty*. I'm certain the other royal families will understand perfectly.' Lia's face twisted in disdain. 'And if I do nothing, they'll squeeze us for every concession. They won't give us what we need until I give them what we can't afford.'

'As if our diplomats would let them!'

'They won't be in a position to bargain!'

We glared at each other.

'Farezi will make things... difficult if this assassin isn't found,' Lia said. 'Rassa wasn't hurt, but I must still be careful. No matter what I do, I will appear weak unless I sanction the executions.'

'Farezi will twist this to their advantage, regardless—' Matthias stopped, so abruptly that Lia and I stared at him. His face brightened. 'But even if he'd employed the best assassin, so much was still left to chance,' he said slowly.

'Who?' Lia demanded.

'Rassa.'

'You think he hired the assassin to *almost* kill him?' Even though I only knew about the Farezi Shadow, it made sense. Again, this had been sloppy, and it reeked more of Rassa than an experienced spymaster. I certainly wouldn't have orchestrated a public assassination attempt: too many things could go wrong.

Matthias glanced at me, then told Lia, 'Rassa has more of an invested interest in Edar than we realised.'

'Explain,' she said.

Her face darkened when Matthias told her about his meeting with Coin. 'So Rassa wants Edar for himself.'

'He's never shown ambition,' Matthias said.

'Publicly. He probably considers his inheritance stifling. Farezi is seeped with his ancestors' work, and his parents' legacy will be strong when he takes the throne. Edar is a fresh slate. Or this could be his father's plan. It's easier to rebuild an empire when your son rules the weaker neighbour.'

'We have our own history and traditions!' I burst out.

'Southern Edar's been influenced by Farezi for centuries. The foundation is already there.' Lia paused. 'The north would resist. I hope.'

'As if you wouldn't help them!'

She smiled wryly. 'I'd be dead.'

Of course. You didn't let the previous monarch live.

Lia touched my arm. 'I won't let him kill me. I'll grind him to a bloody pulp first.' I managed a brief smile. 'He's trying to create a scandal so large, I'll either have to abdicate or Parliament will turn against me.'

'How will you stop him?'

'Delicately,' Matthias said.

Lia nodded. 'I can't accuse him of hiring the assassin, and sharing accounts with a dead man isn't enough.'

'I'll track down the assassin,' I said. 'You won't have to kill anyone involved in the riot.'

Their pitying looks were answer enough. I clenched my hands into fists. 'They're innocent people. Everyone outside the Steps will despise you!'

'Innocent people who wanted to hurt foreign royalty and me,' Lia said. 'I must make an example, whether I want to or not.' She thought for a moment. 'I could imply one of them was also connected to Vigrante's murder. It would satisfy the Court.'

This was the path Vigrante would have taken.

Matthias's expression and body language told me *not to react*. For a moment, I wanted to hurt Lia. I wanted to see her flinch and crumble from pain. Maybe it was the terrible part of loving someone. Perhaps I was the only one foolish enough to tell Lia what she needed to hear when she didn't want to.

I'd have to warn Lariux and his family to disappear. If Lia wanted someone blamed for Vigrante's murder, he'd be an easy target.

'I think you *want* to execute them all,' I said, and had the gratification – and fear – of watching her stiffen. 'I think you're desperate to prove yourself to your *royal cousins*.'

Lia's gaze remained steady. I was right. Whatever had happened earlier, it was to do with proving herself.

'Tell us what happened,' I said gently. 'Matthias and I will always help.'

Her expression shuttered again. 'You don't already know? That's shocking. You act like you know more than me about being Queen.'

'Fine.' I strode to the passage entrance. 'I'll find the assassin. I'm still your Whispers and *follow orders*. But you might prefer to find a new one. I apparently lack the stomach for this, after all.'

'Remember your father,' Lia said when I stepped into the passage. 'Remember our agreement. If you walk away, I'm under no obligation to uphold it.'

Remember the executioner's axe.

I looked over my shoulder. 'My father was murdered. He was a good man.'

Matthias is loyal to the Princess for life. He will be useful to her with the right training, which I've agreed to do.

'I think he'd agree with me, Your Majesty,' I said, 'not you.'

It felt like a lie. I no longer thought he was a good man.

I walked away before she could answer.

ΦΦΦ

My candles were half-gone. The spymaster was late.

Two days ago, after walking out on Lia, I'd drafted a letter to the Farezi Shadow. I'd spent so long focused on uncovering their identity, I hadn't considered another way to do it: by asking for their help.

A tall, pale man with dark hair was part of a small group in Rassa's entourage that acted more like guards than courtiers. Aloof and hostile, the other Farezi nobles disliked and feared them. He could have been too obvious for a spymaster, but I didn't have the luxury of time or caution anymore. The letter was written in a moderately complex code. If he didn't meet with me, I would have to contain him *and* the letter. If he did...

The note had passed through several agents and palace staff, finally delivered by a Farezi servant. While awaiting a response, I stayed busy with the avalanche of conflicting reports, conjecture, and panic from my other agents in the wake of the assassination attempt. It also kept me away from Lia. Not that she had much time for me – she'd spent the last two days in crisis talks with the Farezi.

In the aftermath of his near-death, Rassa was pushing for all possible retribution. The last meeting between him and Lia had apparently ended in a shouting match.

A tapped pattern echoed from the wall. I stood and released the catch.

Around the Farezi, the man moved casually, unhurried, like other courtiers. Now he entered my office like a hired killer, stealth and sharpness and cunning. In a crowd, I'd avoid him. My muscles tensed, trying to convince me to bolt.

'Hello,' I said.

His eyes were black. He seemed amused. 'I thought it was the secretary.'

'Most people do.' I gestured him towards my desk. I'd cleared away everything, hiding my stacks of paper and Papa's final half-translated notebook.

'Your code was excellent,' he said.

'Thank you,' I said. 'How do you wish me to address you?'

I'd expected *Shadow*, but he said, 'Truth will suffice. I will use Whispers. Why make anything easier for the ears in the walls?'

My skin crawled. Matthias and I still checked for people in the passages. 'Thank you for agreeing to my request.'

He smiled without showing teeth. I poured the first glass of wine smoothly, but my hand shook during the second. He waited for me to drink first.

I tilted my head. 'So you're the reason someone ruined one of my favourite dresses with a knife.'

He paused, his lips pressed around the glass rim.

'The man knew how to enter and negotiate the passages. And you got here with little difficulty.' My office could only be reached through the passages. It would have taken him longer to get here, since I'd just reset all the route codes, but it proved he knew about them.

Vigrante had probably told Rassa. I didn't know who to be more furious at: Vigrante, or Lia's uncle for giving him the knowledge in the first place. Hypocritical, since Matthias had told me about the passages without Lia's permission.

Truth finally sipped his wine. 'That was unfortunate.'

'The assassination attempt in the market square,' I said. 'Was that your work?'

'No. My concerns were ignored.' A hint of buried rage in his voice.

'Do you know the assassin's identity?'

'No.' At my raised eyebrows, Truth said, 'It would raise suspicions if I enquired. It is not professional.' His own raised eyebrows implied I should have already known that.

I hesitated. Asking this was a risk, but I had my duty and had paid for his, not that his bought loyalty would go far. 'Can you find out?'

He held his glass near the candles, admiring the wine. It reflected like blood over his pale face. 'You are under orders?'

'My Queen wishes to make an example.'

'You understand my position.'

'I believe my Queen is in danger from your employer. If I'm correct, I want your word that you'll help us with all the knowledge and means at your disposal.'

He went silent, long enough that my pounding heartbeat hurt.

'I require a new contract,' he finally said.

We hashed out new terms, complete with new payments. If we went up against Rassa, I wanted Truth on my side, even only for as long as it was convenient for him.

He eyed me thoughtfully. 'You're an unusual choice. Low-ranked.'

'You radiate violence. I suppose you're not usually seen in public.'

He laughed into his glass. 'Why do you want your Queen to spare the rioters?'

I blinked at the subject change. 'Even a noble can fight against a waste of innocent life.'

'Of course,' Truth said. 'It's merely odd a Whispers would fight to save those who threatened her Queen.'

'Meaning?'

'It's not the commoners you're truly concerned about.'

'Oh?'

'You want to save your Queen from who she threatens to become.'

Silence.

'This meeting is finished,' I finally said.

He stood. The candles were guttering. 'You should take more care. You are also watched.' He left without a backward glance.

I couldn't shake the feeling I'd just drunk wine with Vigrante's killer.

I pulled out Papa's notebook and picked up a pen, trying to ignore my shaking hand.

On my fourth attempt, I broke the cypher by using the number of strikes through certain words. The truth spilled from my pen, blotting what I'd always believed about Papa.

The Duchess finally admitted what she's hinted at for so long. She has a job prospect for me: the King's Master of Whispers. She doesn't trust him, or Vigrante, and wishes to have someone loyal to her in the position, for the sake of the Princess. She believes I'm suited to it.

I didn't realise I was crying until my tears smeared the ink.

Papa had once been the Master of Whispers. Now, the cause of his death was all too clear. No wonder I hadn't been able to find any clear evidence of his murder. As Whispers, he'd ensured there was nothing to find.

And Lia's mother had recommended him to the position.

When I stopped crying, the candles were almost out. I walked back to my room through the passages with a fresh light, not so foolish as to ignore Truth's warning.

⚘ ⚘ ⚘

The next morning, I couldn't face eating with Lia or Matthias. I dressed, then begged for coffee and pastries in the kitchens. After gulping them down, I pulled on a thick coat, scarf, and gloves, and trudged outside.

There was no wind, but the chill bit through my clothing. I hurried to the winter rose gardens, brushed snow from my favourite bench, and sat with a book I'd no intention of reading. I stared at it, unwilling to go back inside.

I'd slept, somehow, waking before dawn. My mind immediately clogged with everything I wanted to ignore: Lia, Hazell, Rassa, the riots. Truth. It was all too much, screaming for attention, and I was so *tired*. There was never enough time.

And Papa. Papa. Had Mama known he was Whispers? Had she suspected? I wanted to treat this like a betrayal, twist my shock into indignation, but I was doing the exact same thing to Mama and Zola. I'd made the same choice.

I pressed my hands against my mouth. A sob climbed up my throat. Everything I'd worked for, everything I'd wanted, felt like it was slipping through my fingers.

Footsteps crunched in the snow.

I froze, and dropped my hands onto my lap.

Lord Hazell broke a path through the snow. He didn't speak or look at me, just dropped onto the bench beside mine. He stretched out his legs, folded his arms over his padded coat, still silent.

My heart raced.

Did he know about my suspicions? Had Patrinne betrayed me?

The quiet deepened around us, occasionally interrupted by a *plop* of falling snow. Every breath I took, painful from the cold, seemed unnaturally loud.

At last, when I was ready to leap up and go back inside, Hazell brushed at his trousers and stood. 'Good morning, Miss Bayonn,' he said, and returned indoors through his path of broken snow.

His footsteps squeaked on snow, then tapped on a cleared path. A door opened and closed. I sucked in a trembling, harsh breath, then bolted from my bench and back indoors.

I chose another entrance that led to the same large corridor, yanked off my outdoor layers and flung them into an alcove. Hazell turned a corner, just ahead of me, and I hurried after him.

There were enough people around for me to stay close without drawing unwanted attention. Every time Hazell stopped for conversation or a quick greeting, I become enamoured of the nearest painting. I followed him through corridors, hallways, and around corners. Stairs were the trickiest, so he wouldn't notice me in the turn.

Another corner, and he disappeared through a set of doors. I rushed forward to catch a glimpse, unable to follow in case he saw me in the doorway –

He strode towards a dining table where Terize waited for him, smiling.

ቀ ቀ ቀ

Three days later, I crept through the passages to Lia's rooms. I tapped the pattern and waited for permission to enter.

She was surrounded by books at her desk – red histories and green law tomes. She put down her pen. 'Hello.'

'Good evening, Your Majesty.' I held out a plain leather packet.

'The information you requested.'

She flicked it open. As she read, she gestured for me to sit in the opposite chair, and didn't offer me a drink.

Truth had been circumspect and thorough. There was little chance of the assassin realising we knew his identity and fleeing.

'This is impressive,' Lia finally said.

'I used the best at my disposal. Your safety is my utmost concern.'

She smiled. 'And Rassa's safety?'

I'd slide a knife through his ribs. 'Of slightly lesser concern.'

'You've become diplomatic.'

'I have *some* diplomacy,' I said, shoving away the memory of brandishing a knife at Matthias.

Lia stiffened. 'Of course.'

How could we have been so close and now hurt each other so easily? Returning to safer topics, I said, 'If you dispatch guards now, the assassin will be captured soon.'

'Yes.' Lia hid behind her cool, distant persona – how she'd acted when we first met. 'I'll inform Rassa when we have a confession. He can witness the death. I won't let him make it a public affair.'

I hesitated. 'And the rioters?'

'The ringleaders will be executed in two days.'

It was beyond foolish to try and reason with her, but – 'I wish you'd reconsider. Please.'

'I'm not having the same argument.' She pressed her hands

against her face. 'I can't give Farezi the slightest means to threaten me.'

'Rassa's bluffing.'

'He's Farezi's heir, regardless of what happens to Edar. Perhaps he simply wants to remind me he has more power.' Lia's mouth curled in a snarl. 'It'll be easier to get what he wants if I'm cowed.'

'If you condemn these people, you're doing exactly what he wants.'

She bowed her head. 'I've no choice. Rassa must believe I'm so engrossed in duty and dignity that I can't see his net closing around me. He'll want *an example made.*'

I glanced at the law and history books, trying not to feel hurt when she closed them. Before, she would have told me her plans. How had everything crumbled so quickly between us?

I still had to try and find a way for her to reassert her authority without killing innocent people.

'I still maintain there's a link between Hazell and Rassa, and that Hazell was involved in Vigrante's murder.' Seeing him with Terize had unsettled me, but I couldn't fit her into the pattern I was struggling to make sense of.

Lia's eyebrows shot up.

'We need a resolution to Vigrante's death,' I said. 'Hazell's guilt and death will overshadow the riot and its consequences. You'll get what you need to keep Farezi at bay, and no one connected to the riot needs to be executed.'

Lia's silence stretched. Too late, I remembered she wielded quiet like a weapon.

'Where is your proof?' she finally asked. 'I can't condemn a courtier to death without it.'

'Your word should be enough! But I can find proof. I'll create it myself, if necessary. The Court will be relieved that the threat of murder is gone, and–'

'And you'll get what you want,' Lia said coldly. 'No riot executions. Vigrante's death was denied to you, but this way you can still take him down through someone else.'

How could she not see? Hazell and Rassa were far more important than Vigrante now, and yet *she would not see*. And I couldn't tell her about Truth, or Papa being her Uncle's Whispers. Things were so strained between us, I wasn't sure how she'd react, or if she'd turn her fury on me.

She wasn't acting like the person I'd fallen for.

'You are so quick to condemn my mistakes,' Lia said, blazing with anger, as if she could sense my thoughts. 'Neither you nor Matthias will forgive me for how I acted after Vigrante's death – yet I must accuse Hazell of murder without proof? The Court may rejoice, but eventually they'll wonder who else I'll accuse to maintain control. They will turn on me.'

My patience broke, even though I felt close to tears. 'I need to keep you safe, and stop you from condemning innocent people.'

'By condemning another man?'

'He's not innocent!'

My voice snapped like a whip. We stared at each other in stunned silence.

I'd worried about keeping Lia alive since becoming her Whispers. It lingered at the edge of every waking moment. Falling for her, admitting my feelings, had resulted in nights spent awake, staring at the ceiling, listing all the different ways she could die and if I could stop them.

My feelings seemed foolish now. I cared for Lia, I didn't doubt that, but I wasn't sure I could love who she was turning into. Maybe it was easier to avenge murder when no one looked you in the eye as a consequence of your actions.

'Do you think my uncle would have let you live if he discovered you plotting against Vigrante?' Lia's voice was dangerously soft, her eyes locked on mine. 'Offered you trust and a bargain? He certainly would have blackmailed you to keep you in line.'

I shouldn't have been surprised she threw this back in my face. She had always been so certain her path was better than her uncle's and Vigrante's. Now, nothing was certain.

Except that Hazell wasn't innocent.

'There has to be something else you can do,' I said. 'What – what if I... sent someone –' Truth would do it, if I paid him enough.

Her anger drained away. 'I have no proof of treason between Rassa and Hazell,' she said, too gently. 'Only speculation. If I kill

Hazell, the Court will turn on me. If I kill Rassa instead of the riot leaders, Farezi will crush us.'

'This will destroy you.' My voice finally cracked.

Her breath caught, but she said, 'I'll do it to save Edar.'

Tears slid down my face. 'I don't think I can love the person that makes you.' I wasn't sure she could love the person I'd just revealed myself to be.

The silence lasted too long. Lia's expression had cracked with stunned anguish. She pressed a hand to her mouth.

This wasn't how it went in Zola's novels. Love was always supposed to win.

'Very well.' Lia blinked furiously, as if trying to hold back tears.

The stab of pain in my chest made me believe, for a moment, my heart could actually break. Grieving for Papa had been far worse, but this still felt like I was being ripped to shreds inside.

I drew out several translated pages from my pocket. Papa's entries, explaining how he'd caught the attention of Lia's mother. How she'd eventually recommended him as the King's new Whispers after his predecessor had died from old age. Papa had done it for the challenge, and taken the first step onto the shadowy path that would eventually kill him.

I dropped the papers on Lia's desk, then backed towards the doors. My hand closed around one of the handles when she lunged from her chair.

Her mouth crushed against mine. We gasped and wept into

the kiss.

I pulled back and shoved the door open. Before Lia could speak, I hurtled through the doors and slammed them closed.

I braced myself for a moment, swallowed a sob, then hurried through the halls, ignoring any curious onlookers.

Inside my bedroom, I released the cry swelling in me since I'd run from Lia.

After a moment, there was a faint knock on my connecting door. I closed my eyes, ready to wait it out, then opened the door.

Zola caught me as my legs failed, letting me drag her to the carpet. My pain and worry and hatred poured from me in choked tears. She held and rocked me, as I finally let out everything I'd buried deep since Lia had returned from the markets.

CHAPTER FORTY-ONE

LIA

The day of the executions dawned clear and bitterly cold. I wore blue hemmed with violet. Blue for justice. Purple, the colour of royal grief; the closest I could hint, with Rassa present, that I regretted this.

The executions took place in the market square where everything had started. The stalls had been cleared out, in exchange for a compensation fee none of the owners would accept. The dais had been a rush job.

I wished Xania were with me.

I understood what my cruelty had done – what *I'd* done – when I let her run from me. But I still missed her, and her frankness that was different to Matthias's.

She was right about the rioters. Executing them was a short-term solution. But I had no other option. Anything except the rioters' death would lead to hostility with Farezi and devastation for Edar.

If a handful of riot leaders had to die so thousands would live, so be it. I'd deal with the repercussions.

The higher Steps followed me to the square. I walked alone, the Master of Justice three steps behind me. My mother, Matthias, and Rassa trailed after us.

I stood on the dais with the Master of Justice. The executioner waited, masked and silent. The nobles arranged themselves behind the dais. The front was for everyone else.

The crowd regarded me warily. Outside the Court, this wasn't a popular decision, as Xania had predicted. But they'd react worse to Farezi threatening war, or so I consoled myself.

Justice spoke first: a list of names, the charges against them, and a ridiculous reminder of our laws and why this execution was for everyone's own good.

Only Farezi gained anything from this. When the assassin confessed that I was his intended target, not Rassa, it had been too late to stop what had been set in motion. I couldn't stop executions for a riot that had put me in danger, no matter that the instigators had responded to genuine insult. Rassa would ensure his parents heard about it.

And despite my fury at being backed into a corner, the thought of how close I'd again come to death spread ice up my spine and kept my back straight.

Justice finished his speech. After a moment of uneasy silence, I spoke. Empty, pretty words, carefully crafted, appealing for reason and respect for our laws, explaining the balance between my duty and the law.

I was being manipulated, and I despised it.

As my words dissolved in the icy air, I wanted to go back to Uncle's death last spring and start all over again.

The guard who protected me from the assassin had died last night.

I wanted Xania beside me.

ᛮ ᛮ ᛮ

I took another gulp of cordial, unable to look away from the envelope. Matthias had given it to me when we'd returned from the executions. A tiny, elaborate *W* on the outside corner showed Xania had already read the contents. I tried not to feel hurt that she hadn't come herself. The distance between us now seemed insurmountable. She was still in the centre of the web, but now Matthias reported to me on her behalf.

The distinction was clear: Xania was still technically my Whispers, since rebuilding the network around someone else would take months, but everything else between us was finished.

I stared at the envelope as the lamps burned. Matthias left for the evening at my urging. Outside, the night drew in. I finally ripped it open.

The Eshvon caravans, with our desperately needed grain, had been attacked at our border with Farezi. The merchants were dead, everything burned. A potentially disastrous winter was now assured. Farezi was our only chance for emergency grain so people wouldn't starve.

Rassa had surely orchestrated this.

Diana had been right. I'd been foolish to refuse her, so certain in myself. For all Uncle hadn't cared and let others do his duty, I'd made worse mistakes by caring.

I dropped the reports and picked up the notes I'd written in code. The words blurred from exhaustion, but I moved steadily through the pages, searching for any loophole. This was more important than any law I'd pushed through, every snare I'd hidden for Vigrante. If Rassa outmanoeuvred me, I had to depend on Othayria and Eshvon containing him with international law. There couldn't be a single mistake, or I wouldn't survive this.

Someone knocked, and I hid the papers under a pile of reports. A guard entered, opened her mouth – and scowled when Rassa breezed in.

'Cousin.' He dropped into a seat and smiled.

Deep breath through the nose. No outward anger at Rassa's disrespect.

'Thank you,' I told the guard, who left, still scowling. I hid the papers deeper under the guise of tidying. Rassa glanced at the glasses by the decanter, but I ignored him. He could get his own damn drink.

I sipped my cordial as the tension rose between us.

He cracked first. 'You're up late, Cousin.'

'What's on your mind, Rassa?' I used the clipped tones of one who was tired, yet still working. He had to think I was annoyed at being interrupted, not that I knew he wasn't trustworthy. Not that I was furious because I'd have to ask him for help, regardless.

He traced the whorls on my desk. 'I'm grateful for your speed in capturing the assassin and making an example of the rioters.'

'You don't appear to be grateful.' I wanted to chop off his hand and see how he felt about that *example*.

'Oh, no, please—' Rassa began.

'What do you expect? Their heads on a silver platter?'

Rassa looked like I'd sprouted claws and swiped at him. 'No, no! I simply... feel you should be taking diplomatic relations between our countries more... seriously. In light of recent events.'

'And if I should not?'

Rassa stroked his chin. 'My parents could react to my unhappiness with... drastic measures.'

'Drastic measures' could range from grain penalties to a declaration of war.

'I see.'

I met Rassa's gaze with the intention of a brittle smile. From the change in his expression, I didn't come close. His knuckles tightened on the armrests. He rose halfway out of his seat, before catching himself and sitting again.

'That will be all, Rassa.' He tightened his lips, then stood. He flung his arms out in an elaborate bow from our grandparents' time, when monarchs could behead people where they stood for displeasing them.

He paused by the decanter, downed some cordial, and saluted me with the empty glass before leaving.

If only I could behead people where they stood for displeasing me. Life would be much, *much* easier.

CHAPTER FORTY-TWO

XANIA

The executions did exactly what I'd thought they wouldn't: they made Lia popular with the Court.

I couldn't forget the first death, the ruddy-faced merchant who'd trembled and told his family he loved them, or how blood had scented the air when the axe went down. Yet the Court felt chopping people's heads off was decisive action expected from a capable Queen. Someone – perhaps Matthias – had spread rumours that one of the executed men had been connected, somehow, to Vigrante's death. It was flimsy speculation, but the relieved Court seized it as proof that the threat of murder was gone.

I was still angry, but I spent my time with Zola, and occasionally Astrii. I avoided Terize, claiming overwork at her baffled upset.

But as Court support for Lia grew, so did public anger. Now that Lia had nobles to support her reforms, her people were turning against her.

When I mentioned this to Matthias, he replied, 'Politics isn't fair.'

Lia had called a sudden meeting for the higher Steps and foreign parties. Zola and I were members of the royal ladies for this occasion.

I'd dressed carefully from obligation, not expectation. We hadn't spent time together privately since after the riot. I missed Lia's laughter, her perfume, her overacting as she read to me. I missed dozing in her bed. I missed waking up beside her, warm and content.

With too much time on my hands, I obsessed over the connections between Hazell and Rassa, and the Duchess's role in Papa becoming Whispers. Lia and I hadn't spoken about the connection between our parents. We needed to, but for now I wanted to avoid the inevitable argument.

I sat in a corner with Zola. She'd already asked if I knew why Lia had called the meeting, her disappointment obvious when I shook my head. She'd taken the estrangement hard.

The Seventh and Sixth Steps had dressed to impress: lace and embroidery clung to velvet and silks; jewels gleamed against skin and hair. From their excited whispers, everyone expected an engagement announcement.

Zola nudged me. 'Don't scowl.'

I had plenty to scowl about, but I changed my expression into general lack of interest. Once this was over, I could hide and mope.

A flash of red, like blood before it dried, caught my eye. Aubrey stood near the empty throne, talking with a small crowd of Othayrians. He noticed me, but I looked away.

Silence descended when Lia appeared on the dais. We dropped into curtseys and bows.

She wore layers of cream silk webbed with blue lace. Her collar and sleeves were blue velvet; the embroidery and sapphires caught the light. She was beautiful, but the effect was stern, a reminder that she ruled us.

'Daughters and Sons of Farezi, Othayria, and Eshvon,' Lia said, 'please step forward.'

They approached the dais. Othayria and Eshvon stayed close, but the Farezi party kept themselves separate, in either pride or a pointed reference to Rassa and Lia's blood tie.

'We thank you for coming here,' Lia said, 'with the intention of strengthening our countries through marriage and renewed trade.'

Aubrey's smile wasn't smug or triumphant, merely relieved. He could finally do his duty.

'However, we must regretfully request that you leave Edar,' Lia said. 'Immediately.'

Aubrey frowned.

Lia looked directly at him. '*All* of you are to leave.'

Zola dug her nails into my arm. 'What is she doing?'

Matthias stood frozen near the dais.

Lia had rejected all the suitors. And she was kicking them out in late winter.

'I expect you through the border by sundown tomorrow,' Lia said.

Aubrey's face fell. Angry whispers and muttering swarmed around us.

'That is all,' Lia said, cold and proud.

The room exploded into noise.

Lia turned back towards the antechamber.

'Your Majesty!' Isra called out.

Lia paused, then turned.

'What about your decision on your future marriage?' Isra asked, tense and defiant. 'Since that was why we came here.'

'I must regretfully decline all offers of marriage,' Lia said, 'for there is another.'

For there is another.

She didn't look at me.

Aubrey whirled, as if searching the crowd.

I didn't look at him. I didn't look at anyone. I stared at the wall behind Lia.

There is another. There is another.

Zola didn't say or do anything that would give us away. Better to stay still, keep quiet, and wait for it all to pass.

Lia turned again to leave.

'You can't do this!'

She swept back around in a swirl of skirts. The accent had been Farezi, but Rassa's party stayed close together, refusing to reveal the speaker.

Lia descended the dais slowly. The Court, along with the Othayrian and Eshvon parties, moved back, abandoning the Farezi to her wrath. Rassa stood before his people like a shield.

'Reveal her,' Lia ordered him.

'I won't give up any of my people,' Rassa snapped.

'But it's acceptable for me to *execute* mine for your satisfaction?'

Gasps rang out.

Rassa grimaced.

'Reveal her,' Lia said.

He turned at hissed voices and scuffling. A girl with light brown skin and gleaming hair, around our age, burst from the knot of Farezi. She faced Lia, her head high.

Lia eyed her thoughtfully.

'You can't do this,' the girl repeated, quieter this time but no less certain.

She had to be in love with Rassa. Only love would make someone face down an enraged Queen.

Lia gripped the girl's chin – Rassa sputtered – and stared into her eyes. 'I am the Queen,' Lia said, soft enough that I shivered. 'Of course I can.'

She released the girl, and slowly looked around. 'Does anyone else wish to question my judgment?'

No one spoke.

'I thought not.' Lia swept back up the dais and left the room.

'You have to go to her,' Zola whispered.

I shook my head. Lia had just caused a diplomatic incident. I had to be careful.

'Matthias—' Zola said.

I looked up just before he hauled me to my feet.

'Wait,' Zola said, 'what are you—'

Matthias pulled me away before she could finish. I barely managed an astonished glance over my shoulder before we disappeared through a side door.

I expected us to zigzag through a few halls before ducking into the passages, but Matthias kept to the busy routes, leading me past groups of huddled courtiers. Two corridors away, I realised he was taking me to the royal portrait gallery. I didn't spend much time there: I didn't like being surrounded by Lia's exalted ancestry.

It felt like the portraits were watching me, like when I'd first sneaked into the royal wing. I kept my head down until Matthias stopped and relaxed his grip. 'Look.'

We stood before Lia's great-grandfather. The only one painted in full battle armour, his sword seemed almost as tall as me. Lia's hair was a few shades darker, their eyes similar under a certain light, but they otherwise didn't share much resemblance, except –

'Oh,' I said.

They said the truth of a person was in their eyes. From the steely gaze of Lia's great-grandfather, I could believe he'd raised armies. I could believe he'd fought and killed in battle. And I could believe he'd held the Aurien King's head aloft, roaring in triumph.

Lia had faced the Farezi lady with the same steely gaze.

'She didn't tell you what she planned.'

'No,' Matthias said, quietly furious.

'We have to talk to her.'

'I tried to see her this morning. I was refused,' he said.

I frowned. 'She's planning something she knows we won't support.'

'Most likely.'

'We have to stop her!'

'She won't see us,' Matthias said, 'and will have closed the passages to us.'

'She needs our help.'

'She needs our help when she decides it.' Matthias looked sympathetic, which was marginally better than pity.

I wanted Lia beside me, not him. I wanted her to need me again.

CHAPTER FORTY-THREE

LIA

I changed out of the beautiful, ridiculous gown. A measure of brandy couldn't stop my pacing. Everything was falling apart: my duty, my hopes, my dreams.

I had to tell Xania. Rassa would act immediately, now that I'd given him a time limit.

My pen trembled over the paper as I struggled with the code. If Rassa forced me to abdicate, international law stated I would still be Queen for another three days. It wasn't enough, but I didn't know what else to do. Xania and Matthias would have Aubrey and Isra on side, representatives of foreign crowns who might curb Rassa long enough to –

To what?

Reverse my panicked decision? Reinstate me as Queen?

Offer me a place to survive my exile?

Rassa wouldn't let me live, no matter what he told others.

My dearest Xania, I wrote in shaky letters, *if you're reading this, then Rassa has...*

Has what?

I didn't know what else to do. But Xania and Matthias would never support my abdication.

Someone knocked on the door.

I dropped my pen. Ink splattered over the paper.

They would dethrone me politely, at least.

Three of Rassa's lawyers entered. They should have been frazzled, the tools of their trade trailing after them, but instead were formal and neat.

Rassa had changed into a fresh shirt and a jacket thickly embroidered in gold. His smile was almost as bright. 'An impressive display.'

'I'm glad you approve.'

He laughed. 'A pity you never follow through on your promises or threats.'

'Have you already forgotten that people are dead?'

All vitality drained from his face, leaving him cold and hard.

I could barely hide my weariness. 'Do you truly think no one will wonder at my neat abdication?'

'Of course they will. Your Court's extravagant and selfish, not foolish. Your statement will reassure the confused and the skeptics, and my supporters will ensure my ascension is smooth.' Rassa dropped into a chair, uninvited. 'You know what will happen if you fight me.'

My temples throbbed.

The Farezi diplomat had visited me earlier, clammy and desperate. He'd presented reports detailing the daily routines of my mother, Xania, and Matthias, with additional notes on times and places where they were *potentially vulnerable* to accidents, poison, a slit throat.

I'd read in silence, as the ambassador wrung his hands.

'These people are the dearest to me still living,' I finally said.

'Then you must stop him.' The ambassador took a shuddering breath. 'I will help you any way I can, but I also wish to apply for asylum.'

By helping me in defiance of his prince, it was a reasonable request. We'd also have to get his family out of Farezi.

Except I wouldn't have any power if I did what was necessary to save my loved ones.

'You would be better served by asking Othayria and Eshvon,' I said gently. 'I will assist you wherever necessary, should they prove reluctant.'

He'd nodded, crestfallen and afraid.

I clenched my jaw at Rassa. 'You're a fool to give up Farezi to your sister. Edar is smaller, poorer: a costume counterfeit to Farezi's jewel.'

'Edar has potential, and you'll throw it away like your ancestors did,' Rassa said. 'You'll never accomplish anything by reasoning with a Parliament. Change happens through threats and force. Your great-grandfather knew that, and he gained a crown and a throne. But his son failed, your uncle was useless, and your father died young.' Rassa smirked. 'And his daughter will throw it all away for a Third Step nobody.'

He knew about my feelings for Xania, but not that she was my Whispers. I couldn't be certain her network was still secure. From certain phrases and excerpts in the ambassador's reports, not all the sources were Farezi. Some of my own Court had committed treason for whatever Rassa had promised them.

I remembered the Government names Vigrante had hinted at. Was that why he'd reached out to me? Had he realised Rassa was stealing his own support, not so easily manipulated as he'd assumed?

Damn Vigrante. Even to the end, he'd played his cards too close.

I trusted Xania. But not my Court.

'You've nothing to bargain with,' Rassa said. 'I won't marry you, and I certainly won't have a child with you.'

'But you're perfectly happy to rule my country!' The pain spread from my temples across my forehead and down my cheekbones.

'I can do much with it,' he said.

'Edar's up to its eyeballs in debt. Probably up to the hairline now, after months of entertaining and feeding you all.'

Rassa narrowed his eyes. 'That can be fixed.'

'How? Tax everyone? The nobles will demand it from their tenants, who can't pay more. The merchants will fight you every step of the way. The dissatisfaction I deal with now is nothing to what you'll face.'

'There are always ways to handle it,' Rassa said.

He had no idea how to rule. He spent his days drinking and entertaining. His parents gave him minimum responsibility, and he responded with more irresponsibility. A never-ending circle that wouldn't change until Rassa admitted he had to do better.

Instead, he'd gone behind their backs to take Edar.

I can't do this to my people. I can't leave them depending on Rassa. But Mother, Matthias, and Xania, all dead –

I couldn't think through the pain. Needles scraped along my face, trailing fire in their wake.

Mother had warned me that one day I'd face a decision as Queen that would pit my personal wishes against duty. If I was particularly unlucky, I'd face it repeatedly.

I hadn't expected it to be this.

'Have you discovered who killed Lord Vigrante?' Rassa smiled mockingly. 'Such a pity. I liked him.'

I'm sure you did.

'He knew so much about the palace and secrets.'

Secrets: Xania in the passages, bleeding and terrified. The assassin's Farezi accent. Not a decoy, after all.

'That's the problem with old buildings,' I said. 'So many secrets and *passages.*'

Rassa's smile faded. 'They'll be dead by sundown if you don't act.'

He was using my own deadline against me.

He'd follow through. They'd all die.

I had my plan, had to hope Xania and Matthias would realise what to do.

Pain pain pain. Waves of fire pounded in my head.

'I trust the paperwork is ready?'

A lawyer smacked down a stack of paper. I flicked through it. For someone who'd planned this for a while, Rassa had rushed the details. There were several small points of Edaran law his lawyers were likely familiar with, but he'd probably dismissed their requests to clarify and check, preferring speed over quality. It was his loss and my gain.

There was no mention of the law my plan hinged on.

Good. His carelessness would help me.

I picked up my pen. Casually pushed aside the note I'd been writing to Xania.

My ancestors had been a usurper, a warmonger, and a diplomat. My uncle had been a fool and a disappointment.

In a few pen strokes, I destroyed everything they'd done. Dripped the wax and sealed it.

I was the abdicator.

I'd faced the difficult decision and crumbled.

My vision blurred. I frowned at my shaking hand. The trembling wouldn't stop even when I concentrated.

It took three tries before I focused on Rassa. Despite the pain, his smile turned my spine to ice.

'The brandy,' I slurred. 'You drugged it.'

He leaned in and stroked my cheek. I jerked back. 'I know you too well, Cousin. *Of course* you'd drink before giving up your birthright for someone you could replace in a moment.'

I wouldn't give it up just for Xania. I'd do it for Mother, who'd raised me after Father's death. For Matthias, who'd devoted himself to me after I saved him from the river.

'The ones you're sacrificing yourself for wouldn't let you give up the throne,' Rassa said. 'They'd fight me, whether you wanted them to or not. So for my own sake – and their lives – you must be contained.'

The waves of pain crested, then crashed around me.

CHAPTER FORTY-FOUR

XANIA

Long before dawn, I finally gave up on sleep and worked on Papa's last journal.

Mama had probably hoped this would make me feel closer to him. Instead, I felt like everything I remembered was a carefully maintained facade. I wasn't sure if Mama had known he was Whispers. I didn't know if I could ever ask, too afraid of truths I no longer wanted to know.

I'd struggled with the final cypher for days. Nothing I'd previously used in this notebook worked. The latest frustration in a long line.

I paused at *I will die old and beloved*. Something small and painful dropped into my stomach.

I had the code on my second attempt. The truth flowed from my pen indecently fast:

Vigrante suspects me, somehow. He is too close to the King. The Duchess wishes me to have more sway, but the King will hear nothing against him.

Vigrante will probably try to kill me. If he succeeds, he'll undoubt-edly convince the King to make him the new Whispers. He'll be unstop-pable. Hopefully, I've trained Matthias enough to help the Princess survive until she inherits. My lady will protect our daughters.

Xania, my dearest, I'm sorry for choosing this. Do not seek to avenge me. There is nothing glorious in this path. If I die, it is because of my desire to prove myself. Let me stay dead.

My tears splotched the paper. I finally had the proof I needed. And despite Vigrante's death, I'd pursued a path Papa hadn't wanted for me. Lia had worried about becoming like her uncle, never living up to expectations. Consumed by revenge, I'd done the same.

Almost immediately, anger swallowed my guilt. How dare Papa lecture me about glory or vengeance? This had all happened because he'd *died*. And even if he hadn't wanted me to do any-thing, he'd clearly changed his mind during his slow death: he'd told Mama to give me his journals when I came of age. He'd hoped I would translate them. And for what else but vengeance? I scrubbed my eyes, blew my nose furiously with a handkerchief.

No wonder Lia hadn't discovered anything about her uncle's Whispers. Papa and his predecessor were both dead, and Vigrante would never have admitted his involvement.

I had to tell her right now.

I almost fell out of bed at the hammering on my door.

'Xania!'

I'd barely unlocked the door when Matthias stormed in. 'She's gone!'

'Who?'

'Lia!'

'*What?*'

Someone thumped on my connecting door. I rushed to unlock it.

Mama stomped in, eyeing Matthias with a promise of justified violence.

'Mama, stay where you are, please.' I caught hold of his arms. 'What's happened, Matthias? Where has she gone?'

'She abdicated.' The catch in his voice felt like a knife between my ribs.

'She can't,' I whispered. 'She wouldn't.'

'She did.' He dragged his fingers through his hair.

'Sit,' Mama ordered. '*All* of you.'

Zola, who'd slunk in after her, sat beside me. Matthias flung himself into a chair and ground his teeth.

He hadn't known. Matthias was closer to Lia than her own mother, and *he hadn't known*.

Mama disappeared and returned with a wild-eyed Lord Martain.

'Has Rassa called the Court together?' he asked Matthias.

'Servants have been dispatched. I ran here, but one will arrive shortly.'

'Then we must act surprised,' Lord Martain said. 'It pains me to say this, but is your friendship a liability now?'

I shot to my feet. 'This is ridiculous!'

'He's right, Xania,' Matthias said wearily. 'He has to protect you.'

'I can protect myself!'

'Xania!' Mama snapped, right before the polite knock.

Lord Martain hurried Matthias into their bedroom. Zola and I arranged ourselves with books and pamphlets, as if we did this in our nightclothes all the time. Mama answered the door.

Matthias slipped into the hall after the servant's departure. We scrambled to dress and joined the stream of people in the halls. There were no pointed whispers or speculative glances. We were only another Step family. My secrets were still safe.

In the throne room, Lord Martain kept Matthias in our line of sight. There was a noticeable gap around him. No matter how many nobles desired his competency and discretion, he had always been Lia's. Now the unfavourable light of her abdication reflected upon him.

The antechamber doors opened, and Rassa strode in. The Court exploded into surprised, uneasy noise.

Rassa wore a freshly pressed shirt and trousers, his boots buffed and oiled.

The Farezi royal colour was dark green.

His coat was Edaran blue, embroidered in silver and gold, similar to Lia's coronation dress.

Where is she?

I knew within moments that Lia hadn't written her 'statement'. None of it rang true, and this was reflected on other faces. Anyone who'd spoken to Lia, or heard her addressing Parliament or the Court, knew Rassa read out nothing but lies and twisted truths.

With each sentence, my heart sank further. Panic clawed inside me. Rassa would soothe everyone's doubts with smiles and laughter and promises. He'd be the opposite to Lia's frugality and common sense. He'd turn her into a distant memory, a troublesome monarch now gone, though eventually he wouldn't be able to ignore Edar's financial realities.

Why isn't Lia announcing her own abdication?

Is she dead?

Lia's 'statement' was difficult to stomach, but Rassa's speech was intolerable. Zola gripped my hand to the point of pain.

He finished and sat on the throne.

I wanted to scratch his eyes out.

An Arch-Bishop came out with the crown, followed by a bishop with the bell, the blade, and the fiery bowl. There was no pomp, no ceremony, no travelling amongst the people. A hurried coronation to avoid awkward questions or interruptions.

He'd planned this.

Zola glanced at me when he said the vows Lia had sworn

almost a year ago, as if she feared I would cry. There were no tears when the Arch-Bishop crowned him. Only hatred.

Vigrante didn't matter anymore. Neither did Hazell.

We had to find Lia.

We had to get Rassa off the throne.

The Court clapped and cheered when he rose, bloodied and crowned. What else could they do?

I jumped at the touch on my elbow. Matthias had sidled towards us, using the noise and shock as cover.

'We need to go to Lia's mother immediately.' He barely moved his lips. 'Aubrey and Isra are with her.'

I'd imagined finally coming face-to-face with the Duchess so many times, now knowing her link with Papa, but always with Lia for support. Now Lia was gone. 'We can't be seen leaving together.'

He nodded, and disappeared back into the crowd.

Zola tightened her grip on my hand. 'You can't go. Rassa is King now. You don't have standing anymore.'

'I have to know where she's gone.' I kept my voice low, but glared until Zola let me go.

'Be careful,' she said. 'Rassa will have little favour for Lia's allies.'

'That's my problem, not yours.' I smiled to take the sting out of my words, and plunged into the crowd.

I scribbled a short note and dispatched it with a harassed-looking servant, then went looking for Matthias.

He waited in an alcove not far from the throne room. We hurried through the halls, ignoring the frantic servants trying to make sense of their new pecking order.

The guard at the Duchess's doors ushered us inside.

The Duchess sat with Isra and Aubrey, a breakfast service scattered between them; a polite shield against the horror of her daughter's abdication and flight.

Of course, Lia could already be dead. But if I lingered too long on that, I'd sink to the floor and not get up again.

'A wonderful coronation,' Isra said, lifting her teacup in a mocking salute, 'wouldn't you agree?'

The fear and hurt and rage burst inside me, building since Rassa had walked out in Lia's colours. 'Rassa has *everything* now! He'll get Lia's estate, and he'll destroy everything she's done–'

'No, he won't,' the Duchess said. 'My brother-in-law drafted a clause into Lia's inheritance. If she dies – or abdicates – without marrying, the estate reverts to me, and *my* bloodline.'

We stared.

She smiled bitterly. 'He knew Lia would likely marry outside Edar. My brother-in-law hated our neighbours.' She glanced at Aubrey and Isra. 'No offence, naturally. He hated knowing the royal bloodline would be... *sullied*.' The Duchess rolled and spat the word.

Matthias paced. 'So no one knew Lia planned this?'

We all shook our heads.

The Duchess turned to me. 'Even you?'

I shook my head as my cheeks burned.

She flicked her fingers. 'Oh, don't be coy. You shared her bed. Of course she'd confide in you.'

Aubrey looked relieved to know the truth, once and for all, while Isra seemed grimly thoughtful, as if her suspicions were finally proven right.

'No,' I said, 'she didn't tell me. We hadn't spoken privately since before the executions.' When she broke my heart, and I stomped on hers. I suddenly remembered the stacks of red and green volumes. 'But she *was* planning something. She was researching history and law.'

Matthias dug his heels into the carpet. 'Law books? Did you notice anything in particular?'

'No. We weren't – it wasn't a pleasant conversation.'

Matthias frowned. 'She must have been researching current legislation.' He bounced in place, thinking.

'Abdication laws!' he and Isra shouted together.

A quick glance confirmed I was the only one willing to entertain them. 'Pardon?'

'Lia technically relinquished her rule the moment she signed the paperwork, and Rassa is legally King once crowned. But other countries don't honour abdications until three days later.'

'That makes no sense,' Aubrey said.

'It's to stop usurpers from invading other countries,' Isra said. 'For three days, they can't do anything in the previous ruler's name. If they do, they can be answered with full force – even war, if it escalates.'

'Lia willingly abdicated,' Aubrey said. 'So what if our families don't recognise Rassa for three days?'

'It means,' Matthias said gleefully, 'to Othayria and Eshvon, she's still legally the Queen! She still has power.'

'But she *abdicated*!' Isra said. 'She can't win back a throne she gave up. And even if she unwillingly abdicated, we don't have proof. It's her word against Rassa's, and the law is on his side.'

Matthias gnawed a knuckle in thought.

My brief euphoria deflated back into disappointment.

'Actually,' Matthias said, 'we do. The Farezi ambassador sought asylum in Edar. Lia rejected the request, since she clearly intended to abdicate, but wrote him an application to use for Othayria and Eshvon.'

Isra raised her eyebrows. 'Written evidence you *happened* to procure?'

Matthias beamed. 'I'm a talented secretary, Your Highness.'

Or he was still close to the tall Farezi diplomat from Midwinter.

The Duchess cleared her throat. 'You may dismiss this as a mother's fretting' – we stilled at the fear in her voice – 'but none of us knows where Lia is, nor do her personal household –'

My stomach suddenly cramped. How many, exactly, had Rassa bribed or threatened into his service? If there was a list, would the names match those Vigrante had wanted to ruin? Had he realised Rassa was stealing his own supporters? Would he have admitted his suspicions to Lia if he hadn't been murdered?

'And what if...' The Duchess's true years crept over her face. 'What if Rassa had her kidnapped? What if she's held captive to solidify his claim? What if –?' Her voice broke.

What if she's dead?

My body broke out in a cold sweat.

'He'd want her far away, if he wants to kill her.' Aubrey's words were hollow. 'It's in his best interests.'

'Most Edarans will expect to hear about her eventually,' Isra said, 'even if she never returns to Court. Rassa's reign would crumble if they thought he had her killed.'

'If she's killed in Farezi during the next three days, under international law he's killed Edar's Queen,' Aubrey said.

The Duchess turned sickly pale. I didn't feel well myself, but wasn't sure whether to try and comfort her.

Isra frowned. 'Even if he kills her in the next three days, she may never be found. Any witnesses or killers will also die. Rassa's smart enough to usurp the throne through stealth. He won't leave himself vulnerable to mistakes.'

'If he's unaware of the different abdication laws, he already has,' Matthias said. 'Otherwise, he'd keep Lia close. If he was sensible, he'd keep her hidden until the dust settled, then trot her out to show how wonderful he is.'

Perhaps Rassa wasn't supposed to take the throne like this. Perhaps his ambition had again outstripped his abilities, propelling him to act rashly.

'This being Rassa, sense isn't always involved,' Isra said.

'We're wasting time debating this!' I regretted the harsh words, but ploughed on before I could lose my nerve. 'We have to get Lia back, and it'll take longer than three days.'

'Of course,' Isra said. 'But Rassa breaking international law is the best way for Eshvon and Othayria to support you. And your Queen has already thrown our time, energy, and sincerity back in our faces. She hardly gave us a day to leave!'

'And yet you're still here,' Matthias said acidly.

'Lia was surely protecting Aubrey by rejecting him,' I said. 'Why would Lia's marriage curb Rassa's ambition? Aubrey could have suffered an *accident*. Lia could have died giving birth, along with the child. If the child survived... well, children die *so easily* from many things.'

I glared, secretly vindicated at their horror and revulsion. 'Rassa would have still found a way to the throne. Even if there were suspicions, he'd have dealt with them. Lia did her best to protect you. Now you can help us, or rely on Rassa's poisoned courtesy.'

'Of course you'd claim that,' Aubrey said. 'You shared Lia's bed.'

'She shut me out, regardless.'

'She declared her love for you,' he said. 'As much as she publicly could.'

'It doesn't matter now.' Of course it did, but I wouldn't admit it to him.

'If we could get back to the matter of my daughter's disappearance?' The Duchess's polite veneer splintered.

Matthias resumed pacing. 'Check with your agents if anyone saw anything,' he said to me. 'Do you suspect any have turned on you?'

I shook my head.

'Regardless, be cautious. If Rassa's ignorant of international law, he's slipped up somewhere else. We only need the barest hint of a trail. Your international network isn't fully secure, but there's nothing we can do about that now. If Rassa sent her abroad, we have links at our disposal.'

'I've lost the most agents in Farezi,' I pointed out. 'We shouldn't underestimate him.'

Matthias sighed. 'He'll have sent her to the middle of nowhere in Farezi. Stick with what he knows, no other countries involved.'

'What are you talking about?' Isra demanded.

The Duchess straightened in her seat. 'You're Fifth Step through remarriage, Miss Bayonn. What would you know about agents and spy networks?'

Aubrey's face bloomed with disbelief.

I glanced at Matthias.

'Lia's no longer Queen,' he said. 'We need your contacts to find her. There's no reason to hide this anymore.'

I took a deep breath. 'I was – I am – Lia's Master of Whispers.'

I'd finally spoken the secret so few knew, not even my family. The catalyst that had caused me to fall in love with Lia.

I knew it now. I didn't love her just because she was my Queen, or because she was beautiful, or because I shared her bed. I loved her because she'd faced corrupt nobles and frustrated people while still fighting to do what she considered right. Because she loved the north, and its people, and she loved her parents.

Because she loved books, and curling around me in bed. Dragging me for winter walks because it reminded her of home.

Because she loved me, and she loved Matthias, and she'd kept him close even when my presence changed their routines. Because she'd let me go, even though it broke her heart. Because she'd stopped me from making a decision I'd regret for vengeance.

I loved her.

I'd lost Papa. I wouldn't lose her as well.

And if I had to destroy Rassa to get her back, so be it.

The Duchess frowned, considering me.

Aubrey raised his eyebrows.

Isra laughed, as if waiting for a punchline, then sank into

shocked silence when none came.

'My daughter chose well,' the Duchess said. 'No one suspected you. I'd never have thought being Whispers and beloved would mesh well, but no one else, aside from family and close friends' – she nodded towards Matthias – 'would have ensured Lia's survival so well.'

The roles hadn't meshed well, but I wouldn't admit that.

'I suppose,' I said, 'I'm like my father, in that regard.'

The Duchess's nostrils flared, the only indication she knew what I was talking about. For a single moment, I was at a crossroads, caught between Lia and Papa.

'We need to find witnesses to Lia's departure,' I said, choosing my direction, 'or mistakes in covering up the trail–'

'*You have spies in Eshvon?*' Isra exploded.

'*Eshvon has spies here!*' Matthias shouted back.

I grabbed a thick leather-bound book and slammed it on the table. Silence fell. 'We need to find the trail before it goes cold.' I kept my voice low, refusing to give in to panic. 'I have an agent who can help.'

I went to the panel in the wall, and rapped a four-tone rhythm. A pause of three heartbeats, then it was repeated back. He hadn't wasted time coming here after getting my note. I flicked the hidden catch to reveal the passage entrance.

Truth stepped into the room, and swept his cold gaze over everyone.

Φ Φ Φ

Matthias turned to me, stricken. 'What have you done?'

I raised my chin. 'I didn't need your permission.'

'You have no idea of the danger you've put us in.'

Unlikely. It only took a moment in Truth's company to realise he was death. He delivered murder immediately, or quietly weeks later. Around him, people abruptly remembered how easily they could die.

Aubrey and Isra stood close together. The Duchess backed away, putting as much furniture and people as possible between her and Truth.

Truth rolled his ink-dark eyes towards me. 'Whispers, I said you were watched. You didn't heed me, and now your Queen is gone.'

I bristled. 'Everyone is watched.'

'Ah, but you – you – and you' – he pointed at the Duchess, Matthias, and me – 'were *particularly* watched. Your deaths were planned in loving detail. They would never be traced. Your Queen was forced to abdicate to keep you all alive.'

My chest tightened. It was my fault that Lia had abdicated. Everything happening to her now was because of me.

Matthias sputtered, but I cut my hand through the air. He

stared, as if I'd threatened him with a knife.

'I paid you so you'd help when Rassa acted against Lia,' I told Truth, 'not to berate me.'

He laughed. He made it sound sincere. 'I knew you had a backbone.'

'Has Rassa taken my Queen?'

'He drugged her. She signed the document before passing out.'

The Duchess's face drained of colour. She sank into the nearest chair. 'He's taken my child.'

'Where did he send her?'

'Farezi.' His gaze flickered towards Aubrey and Isra. I suppose I wouldn't want specific details revealed to other royalty, either. And knowing Truth's reputation, he'd probably sabotaged the Othayrian and Eshvon spy networks several times.

'So Rassa technically drugged the ruling Queen and kidnapped her,' Matthias said.

Truth nodded.

'It'll take longer than three days to find her,' Isra said. 'She'll no longer be Queen.'

Matthias laughed. 'As you said, it will help with international support. And when we get her back, how long will Rassa stay in power when faced with Lia, outraged and very much *alive*?'

'The law won't be on her side,' Isra said.

'She abdicated under duress. She never agreed to being drugged and kidnapped.'

'We'll have to keep at least one witness alive for their testimony,' I said. 'We don't know how damaged Lia's reputation will be when we find her. Rassa could convince the Court she wasn't making rational decisions. No one would believe anything she said.'

Truth looked terrifyingly pleased. 'The Whispers speaks sense.'

I sighed. 'My name is Xania. You may as well use it. We'll be spending a lot of time together.'

A *wait, you think you're coming?* look spread across Matthias's face – only for a moment, but long enough for him to turn sheepish at my glare.

'You'll have to be organised and swift,' Truth said. 'Rassa will react quickly once he realises you're gone.'

Aubrey glanced at the Duchess. 'Isra and I will stay as long as we can.' *And protect Lia's mother.* He went to her and bent his head, murmuring. He'd have made a good son-in-law.

No matter. That future was lost.

I had to find Lia. I wouldn't let Rassa take her future.

She'd given up her throne to protect us, even if it meant ignoring her duty. Monarchy meant choosing many over few. She'd failed the choice, and I loved her anyway.

She'd done it to protect us.

Now we would save her.

CHAPTER FORTY-FIVE

XANIA

We wasted little time. We'd depart before sunrise and head south.

Matthias and I gave the Duchess copies of Vigrante's treason with Rassa. He squirrelled away the originals.

I sent messages and dragged in agents for urgent meetings. I did everything to blow my cover except actually admit it – no agent could now still think I was only a cog in the Whispers' wheel. But once Matthias and I were gone, it wouldn't matter. Rassa would appoint his own spymaster. If he realised I was Lia's...

No. I wouldn't admit anything.

As I was on my way to pack, a servant in Rassa's colours stopped me. 'His Majesty requests an audience.'

I didn't want to face him.

'I'm Third Step by birth,' I said. 'I'm unworthy of the King's attention or time.'

'His Majesty has decided otherwise.'

I hoped I wasn't about to disappear myself. There wasn't time to warn Matthias.

We entered the royal wing. I found myself in a freshly-opened suite still smelling of dust and stagnation. The windows were wide open, despite the cold. Rassa held court around a large table.

His smile didn't reach his eyes.

I curtseyed, though not as deeply as I would to Lia.

You are not my King.

He narrowed his eyes, then flashed a grin. 'Gentleman, if you'll excuse us a moment.'

Amid suggestive laughter, I followed him into a small study. The shelves were empty, the paintings small.

He picked up a carafe of red wine. 'Sit.'

I waited for him to speak, but he drained his glass and watched me.

'Your Majesty,' I finally said, 'I'm at your service.'

I want to break this glass and carve your treason on your skin.

'No, you're at *her* service.'

'She was my Queen.'

'You were her *dalliance*. You entered a room, and she undressed you with her eyes.'

The memory of Lia's bed, the soft sheets and her softer skin, her drowsy reluctance to get up on cold mornings –

I had to stop underestimating him. He didn't know about the abdication laws, but he charmed and manipulated people as easily as breathing.

'Your father was a baron.'

'I come from... humble nobility, Your Majesty.'

'The only talents your father cultivated were gardening and a fascination for merchants.' *Deep breaths. He's trying to make you angry. He didn't know Papa at all.* 'My mother was briefly charmed by his winter roses.'

I forced a smile. 'Mama will be thrilled.'

'I also heard,' Rassa added, 'your father cultivated an unfortunate talent for curiosity.'

'He had many interests.'

'Mmm. Curiosity often leads to... *unfortunate endings.*'

I froze. 'My father died from a slow illness.'

Rassa smiled like I was a precocious child.

If Papa had discovered Vigrante's treason, he must also have discovered Rassa's ambitions.

Over the coming weeks, even months if Rassa truly wanted to be careful, Matthias and I would meet *unfortunate*, even *regrettable* accidents. The Duchess would offend Rassa so badly, he'd have no choice but to banish her from Court, and everyone in Lia's estate would be ill-equipped for winter.

There would be suspicion, of course, but no proof.

'Your mother would be devastated by another death in the family,' Rassa said. 'I've also heard rumours about your unfortunate history with knives.'

Apart from Papa's notebooks, I'd never find better proof that

Rassa had ordered his death. It had been sloppy, a trait I now linked with Rassa's impatience. Discovering the truth behind Papa's death had been possible when it was only Vigrante, but I couldn't go up against another royal line and survive. Vigrante had worked with Rassa and still met a horrifying end when his usefulness ran out: exactly what he'd done to Brenna.

If I was still the same person who'd met Matthias, before I became Lia's Whispers, I'd try to slit Rassa's throat. I'd die – quickly, slowly, or on a public scaffold – but I'd try to take him with me.

My hand twitched for the knife hidden in my skirts.

Rassa's smile faltered. His fear was intoxicating.

Except my family would never understand why I'd try to kill him. They alone would mourn my treasonous death.

And Lia needed me.

My hand went still. I looked Rassa in the eye, holding it until he turned uncomfortable.

'There's no need for concern, Your Majesty,' I said. 'I'm in no danger from illness or... curiosity.' I stood to curtsey, even though he was still seated. 'If you'll excuse me. My family is expecting me and will worry. And neither of us would want that, Your Majesty, would we?'

If I'd wanted to twist the knife another way, I could have hinted at Vigrante's financials, how things somehow *hadn't added up*. But it was safer to keep the few secrets left to me.

I left before he dismissed me. I strode by Rassa's men, baring my teeth when they leered.

I turned a corner, and another, and then slumped against a wall. My legs trembled. I sucked in breath after breath. I wasn't dead yet.

'Not so easy when you're no longer in favour, is it?'

I jerked my head up. Terize stood before me, her arms folded. Something didn't look right... her posture, that was it. Terize usually hunched her shoulders. But now she stood tall, her shoulders back, her expression almost haughty.

I frowned. 'Terize?'

Her dress was new, with richer fabric and better stitch-work than Patrinne would have allowed.

'Rassa was right about you,' she said. 'Those who rise swiftly fall even faster.'

Rassa? What did Rassa have to do with –

Hazell.

Terize.

The Treasury.

That had been the missing link.

'Oh,' I said.

Hazell's discussions with Alexandris had been a smoke-screen for his Treasury involvement. There had been financial links between Vigrante and Rassa, but none involving Hazell because he had overseen Rassa's finances in a different way. At some point,

Hazell had betrayed Vigrante for Rassa. And when Vigrante had realised his dwindling usefulness to Rassa, he'd turned to Lia for help.

Hazell had probably not killed Vigrante. But he'd certainly allowed it to happen.

All those financial discrepancies, including the one Terize had 'uncovered' and shown me to keep suspicion away from her, must have been overseen by Hazell. Coin never would have done it. So –

I met her gaze, pretending calm I didn't feel. 'Does Hazell claim to love you? Men like him, who follow Rassa – they're all like that. You're wonderful, you're beautiful – until there's some-one prettier, wealthier, more influential.'

Terize laughed. 'Hazell doesn't love me. But he's useful: he introduced me to Rassa. Marriage was my mother's plan, not mine.'

'And what do you want?' I'd been as silly as I'd believed Terize, falling for her poor self-confidence and awkward attempts at friendship.

Coin's cat had never liked her.

'I want freedom.' Her expression hardened. 'I want my own life, away from my stupid mother. I want my own choices.'

'What about the consequences of your choices?'

'I'm favoured by royalty now, not you. You should be more worried about the consequences of *yours*.'

'Rassa is worse than Hazell,' I said. 'How can you follow him knowing what he did to Vigrante – to *the Queen*? He'll discard you when his power is secure.'

'I'll be long gone,' Terize said. 'Whatever he does to my reputation here, it won't matter. My life will be my own.'

Mine was littered with secrets and lies, but I loved my family and Lia and Matthias. Terize despised her mother, and probably her extended family. What sort of empty life could she lead? If I hadn't met Matthias and Lia, would I have turned out like her?

'Please,' I said, 'help me. Whatever he's done to Lia–'

She stepped back. 'I look forward to seeing how hard you fall. A privilege, since you believed yourself better than me: poor, sad Terize, belittled by her viper of a mother. No one will help you.'

Here was the daughter Patrinne had wanted: cold, cunning, and ambitious. She'd been there all along.

Terize curtseyed, mockingly, and walked away.

I don't know how long I leaned against the wall, but I finally forced myself to move, one shaky step at a time. I turned a corner and doubled over, let out a soft moan. I'd allowed Rassa to live and protected Terize when all along she'd helped plot Lia's downfall.

Lia had failed when she chose us over her duty.

I'd failed Papa by not killing Rassa.

Love had ruined us, just as it had Brenna and Naruum.

I didn't cry.

Crying was for later.

I hammered on Patrinne's door, and nearly toppled through when it flew open. She grabbed me before I hit the carpet nose-first.

'I need your help.'

She released me. 'I don't know where the Queen is.'

She still called Lia the Queen. 'It doesn't matter. I do. I need a letter of introduction to your Farezi relatives.'

Patrinne almost choked on a breath. 'Why would I give you that?'

'I'm going to find Lia. I'll need help in Farezi and they live in the capital.'

'Isn't that why you have agents, little spider?' She laughed, perhaps at my distinct lack of surprise. 'I suspected. When you had nothing to offer, yet went straight to the matter of Hazell. Only the Whispers would still be concerned with the chessboard in the middle of a general panic. And you were *far* too well-informed for a thread in the Whispers' web.'

'It doesn't matter now,' I said. 'Lia is gone, and Rassa is King.'

Patrinne lowered herself into a chair. 'I warned you about him. Regardless, I'll be going to my relatives for an extended stay.'

I had one card left to play. 'Terize allied herself with Rassa and committed treason.'

Something flickered across Patrinne's face: perhaps fear, or heartbreak, or despair. Then it disappeared, and her expression hardened. 'I wondered. Her mask slipped occasionally, though she assumed I never noticed. I couldn't guess her full intentions.'

'Freedom,' I said. 'The chance to live her own life.'

'Then she's a fool,' Patrinne said flatly. 'Terize will never be free of Rassa.'

My skin crawled. Patrinne and Terize had never had an easy relationship, but I'd always assumed they loved each other, deep down. It only made me realise how much Mama loved me, and appreciate everything the Duchess had done to keep Lia safe.

'And my letter?' I asked.

Patrinne worked her jaw back and forth, then stood and went to a desk. 'I suppose if I refuse you' – she pulled out paper and readied her pen – 'then I'm complicit in my daughter's treason. You'll get your letter. And my relatives will have time to prepare for my visit.' She wrote quickly, scattered sand to dry the ink, and sealed it blankly.

She looked almost disgusted as she held it out. 'My relatives, I assure you, *will* help.'

She wasn't telling me something. But there wasn't enough time to figure it out. 'Thank you.'

'Don't thank me,' Patrinne said. 'I have no wish to suffer for my daughter's crimes. And I never wish to see you again.'

CHAPTER FORTY-SIX

XANIA

We'd travelled since before dawn to reach Zeffari, the largest southern port, in late afternoon. It was a bustling, loud slap in the face. Merchants sold their wares, servants hurried through the streets, publicans coaxed coin for liquid oblivion. For them, it didn't yet matter who now held the throne. Surrounded by so many foreign accents and languages, it struck me how little I'd seen of the world.

Halfway down the docks, we'd found a ship waiting for us with no official flag – a green-edged private one fluttered in the breeze – but it was too sleek and well-maintained to belong to an average merchant.

Abroad, we'd found Captain Seymour, one of Diana's sailors, and I'd realised Matthias had somehow convinced Diana to grant us passage on one of her ships. While King Rassa was hardly in Diana's interests, Seymour had worn no uniform and was temporarily relieved from duty. Diana's help only went so far. If Rassa's men caught up with us, officially she wasn't responsible. If all else failed, Seymour would probably claim Matthias and I had threatened her to gain passage. We'd have no escape from Rassa's tender mercy.

I'd also realised, suddenly, that ships and sailing didn't agree with my stomach.

The sky seemed larger at night. The darkness stretched in every direction, scattered with stars. I felt small and insignificant. And ill. I could keep water down now, but the thought of food made my stomach revolt. Since the night was warm, I'd followed Seymour's orders and slept on deck with some of the crew. The benefits of space and fresh air had been stressed. I'd also reach the side faster.

Matthias's brisk footsteps approached. He appeared at the edge of the lantern-light, trailing his blanket.

'Your sleeping quarters weren't dignified enough?'

'I kept waking everyone with my fretting,' he said. 'So I came to fret at you.'

'So considerate.' I moved over so he could lie beside me.

We stared at the sky in silence.

'We'll find her, won't we,' I said.

'I hope so.'

I wanted – needed – his empty assurance, like a child wanted to know everything would be all right. I reached for his hand. 'I miss her.'

'Me, too.'

'I keep remembering what I said to her before I... walked away. Over and over, like I expect it to end differently. I was so foolish–'

'I didn't think she'd abdicate,' Matthias interrupted wearily. 'We were both foolish.'

I also couldn't stop worrying about Farezi, which was three times larger than Edar, and our dependency on Patrinne's relatives and a fragile agent network. As rescues went, it wasn't the most achievable.

'I didn't tell you about Diana because there wasn't enough time,' he said abruptly. 'I wasn't sure who we could trust. We had to leave. And who was the last person Rassa would think we'd turn to for help?'

'Diana.'

'Exactly. If she was frustrated with Lia, Rassa is her worst nightmare. He'll try to have her replaced in weeks. She's too assertive and accomplished.'

'Diana's only helping us because we're the best of her bad options.'

'We need all the help we can get.'

We went silent, listening to the slap of water against the ship.

'I planned to tell you about Truth,' I said. 'I wanted to get more information first, but then...' *Lia disappeared.*

'I don't trust him,' Matthias said.

'Neither do I.'

More silence.

'What your father taught me to help Lia,' he said, slow and careful, as if unravelling an old secret, 'and keep me a step ahead of the Court – he wished he could teach you.'

'I needed a good marriage more.'

The other secret I'd kept from Matthias – *he will be useful to her with the right training* – swelled between us, worse than not telling him about Truth. But I didn't want to tell Matthias like this.

Even if Papa had wanted to teach me, he hadn't expected Matthias and I to cross paths. He hadn't hoped I would be taught one day. He'd preferred Zola and I to marry well. That bitterness cut deep, but being upset at a ghost was useless. And I'd already kept Truth from Matthias.

'I... I found something else in Papa's journals.' I pulled away from Matthias and cleared my throat. 'I didn't know how to tell you.'

He frowned. 'Oh?'

'The Duchess has always been assured of your loyalty. She wanted Papa to train you' – Matthias went still – 'so you'd be... useful to Lia.'

He didn't speak for several heartbeats. His face turned bleak and tight. The last time I'd seen him like this, he'd just heard about Papa's death.

He took a shaky breath. 'I see.'

'Matthias, that doesn't mean Papa didn't care for you, or–'

'It seems neither of us knew him as well as we thought.'

'You were important to Lia before Papa trained you,' I said. 'That never changed.'

Matthias pressed his fingers to his eyes, and took slow, deep breaths. 'Sometimes I wish he could tell us what to do.'

'It doesn't hurt as much anymore,' I said, 'but there are days when someone says or does something, and I still think: *I have to tell Papa.* I keep waiting for it to stop, but I don't think it will.'

He hugged me close.

'Why are you so loyal to Lia?' I asked. 'You never told me the full story of how you met. You could be so much more than a secretary.'

He scrubbed a hand over his face. 'When I was... must have been about ten, my family accepted a pity summer invitation to a northern estate. I spent a lot of time on my own. The other children ignored me. I tried to pretend it didn't hurt. One day I fell into a river, like the capable child I was. The water was still so cold. I could barely breathe, but kept trying to scream for help. All I could think was: *I'm not ready to die yet. I'm scared.*' There was a careful flippancy to Matthias's words, but I knew him well enough to catch the tremor in his voice. He still remembered every moment. He couldn't forget how close he'd come to dying in freezing water, all alone.

'Thankfully for my life expectancy, Lia had sneaked out and was further downstream.'

I pressed my hands against my mouth, not only because Matthias had almost died, but because Lia had sneaked out, still unaware of her importance in the line of succession. It matched the woman I loved instead of the Queen I served.

'She climbed out on these thick branches over the river. I almost managed to grab one that she held out for me. When I went under, she caught my jacket in the branch and dragged me close enough to the bank so she could wade in and get me. I woke up on the grass, vomiting water, with a sodden Lia beside me.'

Despite my best efforts, I burst out laughing.

Matthias smiled. 'She took me back home. Introduced me to her parents, endured their frantic yelling because she'd clearly been in a river, and said I was her new friend.'

'You'd no choice in the matter?'

'She saved my life. We've fought about this for years. She wants me to have my own life, away from her. But... if I'm not a Queen's favourite, someone she *literally* saved from drowning, who am I?'

'I told her to change the laws of succession and choose her own heir, even if they're not related to her.' I laughed bitterly. 'Part of me secretly hoped she'd ignore her duty, ignore everything, and be with me. As if I could be more important than Edar.'

'She gave up Edar for us,' Matthias said. 'And you committed treason to find her. I think you're more important.'

I raised my knees and buried my face against them. 'I love her.' I knew he could hear. 'If anyone tries to hurt her again, I'll rip their eyes out. Or try to. I failed Papa, and now Lia. I have to find her.'

Matthias rested his hand on my shoulder. '*We* have to find her.'

CHAPTER FORTY-SEVEN

XANIA

Seymour dropped us at the closest Farezi port three days later, wished us luck, and washed her hands of us – though not before bulking up our food rations. Since Matthias and I only knew Farezi's geography from maps, Truth led us inland.

Between cities, we kept to large towns where we wouldn't attract too much notice. Truth and I met our respective contacts, trying to find out anything about unmarked carriages or families abruptly returning from their estates. If Rassa had hidden Lia, he wouldn't do it in a royal estate.

'Though it would be just like him to choose the obvious path,' Matthias said.

As far as we could tell, Lia had been zigzagged through southern Farezi. Each town and city brought news of different families who'd unexpectedly returned to Court, all lower-ranked, who would have unquestioningly accepted Rassa's bribes. As we neared the capital, we mapped out a trail of residences like a tainted constellation.

Rassa had probably assumed we wouldn't discover the pattern, like he hadn't realised I was Whispers, and assumed I didn't love Lia enough to find her.

And he had probably assumed I wouldn't leave my family behind, either.

I hoped they were still safe.

As we passed through towns closer to Triala, the Farezi capital, gossip filtered through from Edar about Rassa's rule. He'd promoted many of his followers into prominent positions, giving them roles previously held by women. The Court women were bewildered and slowly rising to anger, but Rassa was King. His word was law, even if it was wrong.

Removing Diana from power, however, wasn't as simple as he'd expected. The rules that Lia's grandfather had created to keep Parliament and royalty in careful balance worked in her favour. Diana was fighting him with every resource and ally in her possession.

And as she fought for her power, the assassins finally caught up to us.

☖ ☖ ☖

'I wish I had better news,' the agent said. 'But the Court is closing ranks. Even when the King was at his worst, the nobles still gossiped.'

Matthias and I exchanged looks. This close to Triala, all my agents reported similar stories. The gossip was thin, or nonexistent. Everyone had suddenly turned cautious. If any more families had unexpectedly returned from the country, people remarked on it behind closed doors.

I'd reached the limits of my sources. Once we reached the city, it was time to ask Patrinne's relatives for help. Now we were entirely at Truth's mercy for what he decided to tell us.

'Thank you for your time and effort,' I said. 'On behalf of Whispers, thank you for your service.' With each meeting's conclusion, I'd severed ties. I'd hardly resume being Whispers when Matthias and I returned – if we did. Without Lia, only traitor executions awaited us.

The thought of never seeing my family again...

We left the loud eating-house for the street outside. Our breath clouded before us. The temperature had barely risen above frozen all day, and the paths sparkled with frost. I tucked my arm into Matthias's elbow, and we picked our way back towards the rooms we shared with Truth.

'She was my last hope for information,' I said.

'Truth will tell us what we need to know.' Matthias sounded more confident than I felt. 'If we don't find her, he'll have failed, and Truth takes personal pride in his reputation.'

I didn't reply, focused on the sudden prickling across the back of my shoulders and neck. I peered into a shop window as we passed, but nothing seemed unusual.

Were people ever going to stop following and trying to kill me? Just once?

I kept my voice low. 'Can you feel–'

'Keep walking,' Matthias said. 'Act normal.'

He guided me through more turns than I remembered taking earlier, just fast enough to put distance between the crowds and our follower. We ducked into a shop's delivery door, recessed into the wall so it blocked us from view. After three hundred heart-beats, we both sagged.

'Should we continue back?' I asked.

Matthias flexed his jaw, thinking. 'We don't have a choice. Neither of us knows the streets well enough. We'll probably get lost trying to shake them off, and we can't draw attention to ourselves.' He gritted his teeth. 'Let's just get back. Truth will be there: safety in numbers.'

We walked back to the boarding house, brisk enough to make good time. No more prickling across my shoulders and back, but I didn't trust myself. Matthias knocked on Truth's room, while I went straight into ours.

I let out a deep breath, and the window smashed.

A glimpse of black clothes and a pale face, before I dived across the room. I landed hard enough that I wheezed, hauling myself up to crawl until I backed against the wall. The door was to my right. Truth and Matthias were just down the hall, and Truth had an alarmingly acute sense of hearing. I pulled out my dagger. I just had to keep myself alive until they arrived.

I darted forward as the assassin turned towards me, shrieking to unnerve him as I whipped the dagger across the air. The man didn't hesitate, moving with me, and almost propelled me into a chair. I whipped it around and shoved it straight into him.

He grunted, then kicked it away.

Footsteps pounded down the hall outside.

The assassin closed in on me, and I swiped the blade across his torso. A hiss. A blur. My body moved before my mind caught up, so his fist only clipped my shoulder to send me spinning to the ground. I'd forgotten about his other hand.

Pain flared down my arm. The dagger slipped from my hand, and I snatched it up again, panting.

Matthias charged into the assassin from behind, smashing them both into the bed. Truth was right behind him. He crouched in front of me. 'Are you all right?'

'Just my shoulder,' I said. 'No blood.'

He nodded, briskly efficient, and turned to the swearing and scuffling on the bed. 'Pull him up!' he yelled at Matthias, and helped him haul the assassin up from the bed, dodging his fists.

'Hold him out,' Truth ordered, and Matthias held him at arms length. His hair tumbled across his face, ripped from its hair tie, and one of his eyes was closed as if about to swell.

Truth gripped the man on either side of his face, forcing

him still.

'Traitor,' the man said.

Truth smiled.

A snap, a sound I'd never forget, and the man sagged in Matthias's arms.

I let out a shaky breath.

'A lesson for you, Miss Bayonn,' Truth said. 'Not all death needs to involve bloodshed.'

My mouth opened and closed, several times, before I said, 'I-I'll remember that.'

Matthias took a breath breath through his nose. I practically felt him wrap a facade around himself, before he brightly asked Truth, 'Ready for disposal duty and three to a room?'

Truth sighed.

I ripped off the bed sheets to wrap the assassin in. We worked in silence. A third assassination attempt was too soon for us to become comfortable at cleaning up, but paranoia and several brushes with death did wonders for motivation.

Matthias and Truth disposed of the body.

'We'll reach Triala tomorrow,' I said when they returned. 'We must introduce ourselves to Patrinne's family immediately.'

'And meet our contacts,' Truth said. We didn't know the identities of each other's agents. Matthias was becoming convinced that Truth was leading us into a trap. I suspected Truth's contacts were high-ranked. If he'd wanted us dead, he'd had plenty of chances before reaching Triala.

Matthias and I glanced at each other.

'How much time do you need?'

'A few days,' Truth said.

I chewed my lip. 'We need safety, then. Patrinne's relatives could hide us. A chance to breathe, and not worry we'll be killed in our beds.'

'That's significant faith to put in people you've never met,' Matthias said.

'Patrinne said they'd help us. If I trust anything, it's her ability to save her own skin.'

Matthias sighed. 'All right. Fine.'

We had no other choices left.

$$\oplus \ \oplus \ \oplus$$

I'd expected Patrinne's relatives to be like her.

I was wrong.

Their eldest daughter, Selene, still lived with her parents. The other daughter had married and lived elsewhere in the city. Their household was quiet: they were unpopular at Court and spent most days at home, or in the parks and theatres. The situation gave Truth and me time to visit our networks in the city, free from the Court's eyes.

Matthias justifiably feared that they'd betray us, but I trusted

Patrinne's tattered pride. It took some convincing even to be admitted – she had given us one final obstacle in the blank seal – but they eventually opened the letter.

I'd expected them to be afraid, even worried, while reading it.

I was wrong.

They'd been angry, but not at us or Patrinne.

'Of course,' Selene's father had said. 'Spend as much time with us as you need.'

I'd never take bathing and clean clothes, even slightly ill-fitting ones, for granted again. That first night, I slept through dawn, something I hadn't managed in months. It made everything feel a little less hopeless, as if we still had a chance.

As Truth and I established meetings with our contacts, Selene was an unexpected help. Almost a decade older than me, she helped me navigate the city so I didn't have to depend on Truth or Matthias, and attempted to cheer me up when I teetered on despair.

One day, after I'd returned from another fruitless meeting, she came to the fireside where I sat, staring into the flames. 'Here.' She held out a cup of spiced cider.

I cradled the warm cup and sipped. 'Thank you.'

She settled in the opposite chair. 'It's not going well, then?'

'Progress is slow,' I said. 'Truth is having better luck, but this is his country, his people.' Families had stopped returning to Court, hinting that Lia hadn't been moved from her current location, but the trail had gone cold. It was as if she'd truly disappeared on the road.

'Only love for your Queen would drive you to this,' Selene said, then went silent until nerves pricked my stomach.

How much did she know, or suspect? How much could I admit?

'I was… attached, some years back,' she finally continued. 'The woman I loved joined the Navy to prove her worth. She was prepared to meet all my family's demands.'

There had been no mention of her attachment before now, only her sister's. 'Are you still happy?'

Selene smiled ruefully. 'The Navy proved that my lady's other love was the sea. I grew tired of sharing her, and demanded she choose.'

'And she chose.'

'She did.'

'Do you regret it?'

'Sometimes. I had other marriage offers, but they weren't right.' Selene smiled. 'Perhaps I'll marry, perhaps I won't. I'm not lonely. Some enjoy having me in their bed.'

Apart from my family, I had no other support if I didn't find Lia. Books could provide only so much comfort. Not even my vengeance for Papa was sustainable these days. Fleeing had ensured I'd never recover my reputation, so marriage was doubtful.

'I love my Queen,' I said. 'And, yes, my love for her is beyond duty.'

Selene knocked our cups together, and drained hers. 'Farezi is not respectful of women anymore. The number of women in our Navy has dwindled in the last decade. They're not banned, but there's subtle discouragement.'

'Why?'

Selene scowled. 'The Othayrian and Eshvon Queens haven't compromised well with us lately. Our King has made his feelings clear on their rule. Female sailors are mocked and endangered.'

'That's despicable.' Diana would never allow such behaviour. I paused, then asked, 'Why is your family helping us? You have no reason to. You'd have royal favour if you turned us in.'

Selene stared into the crackling fire. 'One of my uncles married into Eshvon. Two summers ago, his daughter and one of my other cousins swapped places to experience another Court. She fell into Rassa's company, despite our warnings. He swindled her, and humiliated her before she fled home. The families still hardly speak.'

The Eshvon noble, the catalyst for Isra coming to Edar, was distantly related to Patrinne. That was what she hadn't told me, unable to admit how deeply Terize's betrayal hurt, and how much she despised Rassa. There was always a high price for betraying family.

'So your family has personal investment in Rassa's do⸱ I said.

'Even if it's only a place to stay, we'll help you find your Queen,' Selene said. 'And we'll enjoy our darling prince's ruin.'

ȹ ȹ ȹ

The next morning, Truth informed us his latest drop had been successful. We now had a day, time, and meeting place. He'd tested the paper for any hints of a trap, but each marking and delicate flourish in the text passed his intricate examinations.

'Bathe,' he'd said. 'First impressions matter to this contact.'

We went to a respectable eating house in a merchant neighbourhood. Despite the clientele's polite quietness, Matthias and I stayed close.

For the first time since we'd left Edar, no one seemed perturbed by Truth.

He handed the barman something like a tab settlement. The barman flicked it open under the counter, then gestured for us to follow him to a plain door at the back. Matthias met my anxious look with a tense smile.

The hilt of my knife rested in my hand when I stepped through the door. I whirled. A woman moved, faster and stronger, better trained than the man in the passages. In moments, she sent my knife spinning and pressed me against the wall with hers at my throat. Matthias was similarly disarmed and punched in the head. He slumped in the grip of two others, furious despite the blow.

'Don't worry,' the woman said, before she knocked me out, 'we're not allowed to kill you.'

CHAPTER FORTY-EIGHT

XANIA

I woke to the smell of over-steeped tea.

'You should drink something,' Truth said.

The ache at the back of my head strengthened as he came into focus. Squashing the urge to spit at him – my mouth was too dry, anyway – I croaked, 'Tea.'

He held the cup to my mouth as I forced down lukewarm sips. 'How long?' I asked. Exhaustion pulled at me, enticed me towards sleep and oblivion, to give into weeks of worry, stress, and fear.

I gritted my teeth, though it made the pain worse. I had to find Lia, even if the idea of her still being alive felt increasingly hopeless. The longer Rassa ruled Edar, the less useful she was.

'Barely an hour,' Truth said. 'Can you walk, or do you need help?' His gentleness and consideration only made me more wary.

'I can walk,' I said, though the room lurched when I stood. I closed my eyes, waiting for it to subside. When everything was still again, I gestured mockingly at Truth. 'Lead on.'

'I apologise for the deception,' he said. 'I dislike such actions, but my employer insisted you couldn't know any locations in the network.'

I didn't reply.

I followed Truth through a compact maze, the hallways painted brown with unfinished wood. There were no windows to hint where we were. We finally stopped at a brown door, same as all the others. Truth knocked: three staccato raps.

It opened a crack, revealing a pair of bright blue eyes and a scowl. After an exchange of rapid Farezinne, we were ushered in.

A woman sat facing us. Her hair was pulled into a loose bun at the nape of her neck. She'd edged her eyes with kohl, and her pale skin was smooth and clear. Her expression made me feel, as with Mama, that I'd inexplicably done something wrong.

She wore a long dark red jacket, and trousers tucked into leather boots stamped with gold vines. Her jewellery was subtle, compared to what I'd seen of other Farezi women: only a single ring, necklace, and earrings. Her clothing reminded me of Lia's: their simple elegance showing their lavish cost.

Her thickly-lashed eyes were familiar.

I lingered on her ring, stamped with a lily: the Farezi royal seal.

Matthias arrived through a different door, tired and shaken. Relief flooded his face when he saw me.

Truth bowed. 'Baron Farhallow, Miss Bayonn, may I present my employer: Her Majesty, Queen Arisane of Farezi.'

Rassa's mother smiled at us, cold and stern. 'I believe you need my assistance.'

$$\oplus \ \oplus \ \oplus$$

I dropped into a shaky curtsey, then turned on Truth. 'But you're Rassa's spy!'

'I'm employed by Farezi royalty. You came to your own conclusions.'

'He followed our orders,' Queen Arisane said coolly. The royal *we* quelled me to silence. 'The less knowledge you had, the better your chances of survival.'

Lia had always spoken respectfully and fondly of Rassa's mother, a lady who suffered neither fools nor nonsense. I was officially out of my depth, hiding my terror with indignant anger, and I didn't know how to handle it.

Queen Arisane eyed me like Mama did when I was gripped by a childish temper. 'Sit. We have much to discuss.' The servant produced food and drink, while we sat around a table. The food was decent inn fare, but my mouth watered just from the smells.

Matthias and I hesitated. The Queen glanced at Truth, who ate from our plates first.

'If you'll pardon my saying so, Your Majesty,' Matthias said, 'it's unusual for a Queen to be in such... plain surroundings.'

'Several branches of my line were extinguished through rebellion,' Arisane said. 'We're raised to appreciate our wealth and lives for how quickly they can be taken from us. Lia was raised with similar ideals.' She pressed her lips together. 'Rassa could learn much from an old-fashioned rebellion.'

I stared, openmouthed, at a Queen holding her son in such contempt. If Lia had kidnapped Rassa, Arisane might have congratulated her.

Even more interesting was how she and Truth regarded each other. She leaned towards him as he spoke. She showed no wariness or uneasiness; his demeanor was of courteous respect.

I drained my water for courage. 'When did Truth become your Shadow?'

Matthias bit down on his fork. Truth smiled and cut a slice of pork.

Arisane patted her mouth with a napkin. 'Perceptive, as you said.'

'I can't stop you from underestimating her, Your Majesty,' Truth said. 'I wouldn't have done this if I didn't respect them.' He paused. 'Farhallow is vexing, however.'

Matthias grinned as if Truth had complimented him. Perhaps it was a man thing.

'The Farezi Court,' Arisane said, 'requires both monarchs to have their own Shadows. They usually work together, but also focus on concerns specific to each monarch. Imagine my upset upon learning my previous Shadow, in my employ for well over a decade, had devoted himself to my eldest son's concerns.'

Rassa had *stolen* his mother's spymaster, even though heirs weren't entitled to them. I couldn't decide whether to be impressed or appalled.

'Truth took over the position before Lia's uncle died,' the Queen said. 'When we discovered a new Edaran agent in Court, Truth decided to investigate. Don't be angry: he wasn't able to discover your identity.'

My agent who'd had to flee. My stomach tightened. I didn't know if she'd survived. 'Are they alive?'

'She reached the border,' Truth said sourly.

I let out a relieved sigh.

At the end of the meal, Arisane snapped her fingers. The servant rolled out a map.

She tapped a point near the centre. 'You're deep in Farezi now. If our information is correct, Rassa has sequestered Lia here.' She pointed at a new spot further down in the south-east.

'I was right,' Matthias said, stunned.

Rassa had hidden Lia in Goldenmarch: the Farezi heir's estate. It was deep in forest country, popular for hunting and inevitable poaching. As Matthias had predicted, Rassa had chosen the obvious path.

'Damn him.' I wanted to take a knife to Rassa until he couldn't breathe anymore. It would only be a fraction of the pain he'd caused us, never mind Lia.

'It's about a day's ride from here,' Queen Arisane said. 'The proper provisions will be provided, naturally.'

'While your help and resources are appreciated...' Matthias hesitated. 'You're blatantly working against your son. It's – unexpected.'

'We tried to curb our son's ambition.' Arisane's nostrils flared. 'Our lord husband aspires for Farezi to regain its Empire. Rassa shares his ambitions, despite my efforts. He hasn't been as subtle in his maneuverings as he imagined.'

She knew about Vigrante, and the money and the treason. She knew – or at least had suspected – that Rassa had intended to usurp Lia's throne. She knew, and had sent Truth to Edar as her eyes and ears to discover the extent of her son's plotting, but had only acted after Rassa broke international law and she couldn't ignore his treachery anymore.

Lia wouldn't remember Arisane fondly after this.

'I thought I'd managed to raise Rassa well,' she continued, 'despite his father's indulgence. But we're blood-related to Edar, thin as it is. There is always a high price for betraying family.'

She had no idea how high the price would be when I got my hands on Rassa.

CHAPTER FORTY-NINE

XANIA

Lieutenant DuBois, one of Truth's spies, waited for us near Goldenmarch. She struggled to hide her trembling, but bowed flawlessly. On the Queen's orders, she would help us take Lia from Goldenmarch.

After inspecting the Queen's mark, she said, 'Captain Lafaure is waiting for you.'

We dismounted, tethered the horses, and followed DuBois quietly. Goldenmarch, along with magnificent forests and land, boasted a large orchard inside its north-western border. DuBois led us there. She scaled the wall easily, waiting as we hoisted ourselves over. Winter was reluctant to ease its grip: we crunched through frozen grass stained with lengthening dusk shadows.

'Those loyal to Rassa have been subdued,' she said. 'The Captain will bring you to her. No one will prevent you from leaving.'

Despite her assurances, Matthias didn't put the Queen's mark away.

As we approached the manor, solid and proud in the fading

light, DuBois paused. 'A warning, however. Rassa's people tried to kill the lady while we were on the road. They – they thought it would solidify his claim.'

Panic burst in my chest, clawed up my throat, echoed by the terror flooding Matthias's face.

'My captain killed the men responsible. Our orders were to keep her hidden, not attack or threaten her. Nothing has been attempted since—'

'I find it difficult to believe you'd allow a kidnapped Queen freedom of Goldenmarch,' Matthias said.

DuBois clenched her jaw. '*Abdicated* Queen. You... you...' Her defiance faltered. 'You may not like what you see.'

'*What did you do to her?*' I demanded at DuBois.

'They call it the White Silence.' DuBois's voice cracked. 'It came from the far north, where it snows almost year round. The prisoners are surrounded by white: white rooms, white clothes, and given pale simple foods. The windows are barred. They're allowed no darkness to sleep. No one speaks. No one touches them. They're left in white silence for weeks. It's supposed to break them for information. Mostly it just breaks them.'

I wouldn't cry. I had to be strong for Lia. *We* had to be strong for her.

Matthias turned pale. Lia had been gone almost two months. 'Can the damage be healed?'

'I don't know,' she said.

'Take us to her,' Matthias said. 'Immediately.'

Captain Lefaure didn't bother with introductions. He led us through the front doors and into the white horror Goldenmarch had been twisted into.

He stopped before a set of double doors and faced us.

'Her Majesty ordered the lady's chambers to be unlocked. It was... They were locked again for her own safety.'

Matthias and I exchanged anxious looks. The Captain turned and unlocked the doors.

The whimpers confused me. It sounded like an injured kitten, tiny, hoarse sounds, as if someone had screamed until they couldn't anymore.

My legs shook, but I forced myself into the room.

Judging by the musty air, the shutters hadn't been opened for some time. Sweat, blood, and fear – I wrinkled my nose, squinting against the bright light.

'Why haven't you opened the shutters?' Matthias asked.

'You don't want me to open them,' Lefaure said.

Everything was white except for a flash of brown –

Lia lay curled on the bed, her hair a mess of matted curls. Her shoulders shook as she wept, staring at nothing. Her bloody hands were cradled against her chest. Her face was lit up with livid scratches.

Matthias stared at the walls. Tears dripped down his face.

She'd tried to get out.

She'd clawed the shutters, and slammed her fists against the walls until they bled.

She'd screamed until her voice was gone.

She'd written on the walls with her bloodied fingers.

I am not my father.

I am not my father.

I am worthless.

No one will come for me.

I staggered towards the bed – one foot in front of the other, *stay upright* – and reached for her. My legs gave out.

I rested my hands against her tangled hair. 'Lia. Lia. We're here.'

I felt warmth against my cheeks, at odds with the cold spreading through me. Tears.

'Lia. My Queen. I'm here.'

Lucidity filled her eyes for a brief, wonderful moment. 'X... Xan... Xania...?'

I flinched at her rasping voice, and nodded. My tears fell faster. 'I'm here.'

She reached towards me, maybe to wipe my cheeks, but yelped when she moved her hand.

I wrapped my arms around her and pressed my face against her hair. 'You're safe. I love you. I'm here, I'm here.'

Matthias sank to his knees on Lia's other side. He held one of my hands against her and wrapped the other around me, shuddering with his own sobs.

Lia trembled against us. We'd spent two months searching for her – how long since anyone had touched her? In all that time, had anyone spoken kindly to her? Her screaming cries felt like swords against my skin, but we didn't let her go until her breaths turned slow and deep, like she'd realised she was finally safe.

CHAPTER FIFTY

XANIA

We allowed the rumours to race ahead – *the Queen was kidnapped, the Queen is alive, long live the Queen* – for the tide to slowly turn against Rassa. The Farezi ambassador was caught between Arisane and the thwarted King. As Rassa's ambitions faltered, it became clear that Arisane held the true power in Farezi.

When we reached Arkaala, I was ready to destroy him.

He leaned against the closed doors. His face was haggard, his eyes smudged with shadows. He went straight to the decanters. His hands trembled; whiskey sloshed onto the table. He gulped down a glass, turned towards the chairs –

And found me sitting in one.

He choked for breath.

'Hello, Rassa.' My voice could have frozen the air.

'Miss Bayonn. To what do I owe this unexpected visit?'

'I suppose I should be grateful you didn't kill my family.' I'd never, ever admit to him that I'd cried with relief.

'You're still a traitor,' he said. 'You *should* be grateful.' He glanced over his shoulder –

'You won't call the guards.' Rassa glared, and I added, 'Have you felt well lately?'

He paused, reconsidering every meal, every drink, every twinge and ache. 'What did you give me?'

I raised an eyebrow. 'I gave you nothing. I haven't been here. Do you know the first change Lia made when she became Queen?'

'Tell me what you did!'

'She told the kitchens that she expected the same meals as the Court. She considered it a waste of time and food to have separate dishes prepared for her. The kitchens were shocked, but pleased about less work. One of the first things you did was change it back. So many more ingredients, and time, and work... It's never wise to overwork your kitchens, Rassa. A slip of the wrist over an unguarded bowl...'

'You poisoned me.'

'I didn't. Unfortunately. But you still won't last the night. If you've any grievances to set right or apologies to make, now's the time. If you can walk.'

'I'm not dead yet, Bayonn,' he snapped, 'and your Queen isn't here to protect you.'

'I know where my Queen is,' I said. 'Do you know where yours is?'

He'd married the girl who'd faced Lia for him, despite his

438

parents' horror at the rushed match. She was besotted, and had missed her bleeding.

'Where is she? If you dare–'

'*I dare!*'

He studied me with new intensity, as if just realising I wasn't the same person from before.

'You had my father murdered. You kidnapped and tortured the woman I love. Why should your wife stay safe? Do you assume because I'm a woman, I'll be *kind*? If I had any kindness, Goldenmarch destroyed it.'

Papa was wrong. Vengeance was wonderful and terrible, easy and horrible.

Rassa straightened, trying to pull shreds of authority back around himself. 'You said I won't last the night, and dawn's several hours away. You and your family will all die before me.'

I approached him, my dagger pressed against my skirt folds. 'Circumstances have denied me the death you deserve.' I leaned forward, wound one of his curls around my finger, and whispered, 'I lied.'

I whipped the dagger up. Candlelight bounced off the blade against his skin. 'There's no poison in your veins. Any symptoms are the products of a guilty conscience.' I ground the tip into one of the armrests. 'You still won't last the night. You won't have enough time to kill me or my family. You won't even be able to call for the guards.'

The fingers of my other hand twitched. Rassa followed the movement. I kissed him. Twisted my wrist, pricked a needle against his neck. He flinched, opened his mouth, and the pill slipped from my tongue into his mouth.

I pulled back. Clamped my hand over his mouth. 'Surprise.' I twisted the empty needle back into the pen. Forced him to swallow the pill.

When it was done, he slid to his knees. Still staring at me with glassy eyes, he slumped onto his side.

I knelt. 'Your mother sends her regards. Your child will be raised well, since your wife isn't strong enough to rule. Queen Arisane will take care of that, too.'

He tried to take a proper breath, but shook too hard. I leaned close enough to kiss him again. 'If you didn't die, you'd never let us be. We'd always be afraid. I won't let Lia be afraid anymore.'

Rassa let out a stuttering gasp.

I dug my fingers into his hair until tears came to his eyes. 'This is for her. And my father.'

ϙ ϙ ϙ

Diana arrived hours after they would have found Rassa's body. I gestured for Matthias to stay with Lia as she slept and hurried downstairs.

She paced in the reception room.

I curtseyed. 'Admiral, welcome.'

'Rassa is dead,' she said. 'You must bring the Queen to the palace so the Court knows she's alive.'

My polite veneer shattered. 'Her Majesty can't be moved at present.'

'You don't have a choice,' Diana said. 'Otherwise, you'll have every noble faintly related through her mother's side, or with Aurien blood, declaring themselves the next monarch. The Queen *must* reassert her authority, or we face civil war.'

'Why did you supply us with the ship and Seymour?' I asked. 'You're ideally placed to take the throne now.'

Her right eye twitched. 'I'd rather be eaten by a sea monster. I don't want the throne. I didn't even want Vigrante's position, but I didn't trust anyone else.'

'If you're planning on stepping down from Government,' I said, 'it won't be for a while yet.'

Diana narrowed her eyes. 'There are rumours you're the Master of Whispers.'

'I'm only Fifth Step.'

'A Fifth Step woman who committed treason to find her Queen.'

'With the help of *your* captain and *your* ship.'

'So we're both traitors. Wonderful.' Her smile could have cut through skin. 'Several of Rassa's supporters have abruptly fled the palace.'

Hazell and Terize could run as fast as they liked. It wouldn't matter.

'I presume their journeys will be shorter than planned?'

Diana's smile turned into a vicious grin.

'And,' she said, feigning casualness, 'the Farezi Queen apparently orchestrated her own son's death.'

I wouldn't have nightmares about the poison taking Rassa. No, I'd be haunted by Arisane giving me the poison and coolly describing the effects. She'd promised Farezi would support Lia retaking the throne, and Matthias and myself would stay alive, if I killed Rassa under her orders, and not only for my vengeance.

I didn't know if I would ever tell Lia. Farezi would always have to be watched.

'Their Majesties in Farezi are probably more concerned with the consequences of their son's power play.'

Diana sighed. 'What do you need?'

We'd returned to Edar as fast as Lia's health allowed. Since she was still technically abdicated, and Matthias and myself were traitors, we'd reached Arkaala, got word to Lord Martain, and crept into his townhouse.

Lia had been ill and hysterical on our journey back. She constantly wept and screamed. A lit or darkened room made no difference. She couldn't banish Goldenmarch. I didn't know if she could recover, never mind take the throne again. But I had to do this for her.

'You're the Head of Government,' I said. 'And there's a power vacuum. Change the abdication laws so Lia can take the throne again. And change the succession laws so she can choose an heir, blood-related or not.'

Diana's expression turned calculating.

'You want her back? Change the laws so she can return without penalty. Give me until you have the laws changed. She'll come to the palace and meet the Court, even wave at people from the balcony.'

After several moments of silence, Diana finally nodded. 'I need to see her for myself.'

I hesitated. 'She's sleeping. And... you may not like what you see.'

Diana's face tightened. 'Show me.' As I turned, she added, 'I hope you made Rassa suffer.'

I swallowed. 'Not enough.'

CHAPTER FIFTY-ONE

LIA

Over a year ago, I thought I could change everything. Iron will and hope would carry me through every obstacle, every doubt in my path.

If I could go back, as the rider approached with news of my future, I'd weep for what would happen. And slap myself across the face.

I'd failed.

I'd abandoned my duty, my country, my people. For all my scorn against Uncle, in the end I was worse. He hadn't abdicated out of fear.

If I couldn't be a good Queen, what was I?

I flinched at the knock on my door, even though it was gentle, as all noises and movements around me now were. 'Enter.'

The door opened.

'Lia.'

I glanced away from the overcast, damp morning, as dreary as I felt, and gestured for Mother to sit. 'Lovely day, isn't it?'

'I don't care about the weather.' Father's death had aged her, and Uncle's had filled her with joy, but my disappearance had almost broken her. According to Xania, Mother had cried after seeing me, certain I'd die. In the two months since then, her face had tightened into sharp angles. Sadness followed her like a cloak.

I missed our old life.

My eyes burned. I spent my time constantly on the brink of tears.

'Lia.'

I was in Mother's arms, trembling, even as the tangled mess of fear and loathing inside me howled at the contact.

Rassa had not killed me. All my physical wounds had been self-inflicted. But the cracks showed. I'd jerk from sleep, screaming. It took hours at first to calm me. I could finally stomach mild broths and bread after months of small, tasteless meals.

I couldn't bear even having my hand held. My mind insisted no one could be trusted. Xania and Matthias stressed they loved me, but they had no reason to: I'd failed them. I waged war against their smiles, and tears, and reassurances that I was safe.

I couldn't abide their closeness, even as I wanted them to stay with me.

They wept at night, together and alone, when they thought I couldn't hear.

Now Rassa was dead, and Farezi was in disgrace.

'I don't know if I can do this,' I whispered.

'Of course you can,' Mother said. 'You're my daughter.'

Over a year ago, I'd scorned her, and her desire for beautiful things, her views on politics and Court. Yet she'd protected my name and reputation while I was gone, maintained support for me against Rassa's cajoling and promises. She'd trickled her own rumours through Court: Rassa couldn't be trusted; I'd abdicated out of love and fear for my family.

'And Father? What would he think?'

'It no longer matters,' Mother said. 'We can pretend to know what he would have wanted, how he'd have acted. But we'll never know. He loved you, I know that.'

Mother had spun everything I hated about my abdication – my fear, my weakness – into virtues. Rassa was now a ruthless, immoral noble whose ambition had outstripped his reach. People should have hated that I'd acted on emotion, ruled by feelings instead of duty – instead, they revelled in it. I was royal, but also exactly the same as them.

Xania, once rejected by the Court, was revered for committing treason for love. Nobles once more courted Matthias for employment because of his loyalty and devotion. They laughed about it in private, bitter and exhausted.

People wanted stability. They remembered I'd made progress before Rassa had usurped me. I was surrounded by people who loved me enough to commit treason.

Today, I would face Parliament for the first time since returning to Arkaala. Diana had changed the ascension and succession laws, but I had to present myself and prove I was fit to rule again. Edar had been mired in uncertainty since my return. I was making decisions, but they had to go through several people first.

Another knock. Xania peered around the door. 'Ready?'

I stood, plucked at my clothing in Edaran blue and silver. 'Not really. But I'll never be.'

'I have faith in you.'

'We all do,' Mother said. I hugged her. She froze, as if waiting for me to pull away, then wrapped her arms around me. For a moment, I was a child again, and Father was dead, and she was the only one who understood my grief.

'I love you.'

'So do I,' she said. 'Always.'

I faced Xania, whose smile dimmed a little.

She sat with me every evening, reading or telling me about her day. Her words often faltered into silence. I didn't know what to say. Some days her presence overwhelmed me. I remembered kissing her, lying beside her, laughing into her skin. It felt impossible now, an unreachable past because of my terror at the kindest touch.

I still wanted that life, somehow. I still wanted her.

I wasn't sure if she needed someone like me now.

But she'd stayed through the screaming and fear. Her family had begged her not to; Mother and Matthias talked about it, when they thought I was asleep. But every morning Xania arrived with the maid, as consistent as dawn.

I curled my arm through hers, stifling the urge to shudder or flinch. I was the Queen. I would not let Goldenmarch define me forever. 'Lead on, Miss Bayonn.'

Xania's smile lit up her face. 'As you wish, Your Majesty.'

CHAPTER FIFTY-TWO

XANIA

Now that Lia was back, and slowly recovering, no one knew what to do with me.

I was a pardoned traitor who kept the Queen from succumbing to anxious fears. I was Fifth Step, yet had the Crown's respect. I rejoined the Treasury, but the desks around mine stayed empty. Terize was gone, and only Coin's cat treated me the same.

Finally, after three months, Diana summoned me.

Mama didn't want me to go. She still couldn't forgive me for leaving without a word. For two months, she hadn't known if I was dead or alive. I couldn't blame her for how she felt, but I'd also do it again.

Before I left, Lord Martain and Zola wished me luck.

Diana's office was dark wood and large windows. Shelves and drawers filled most of the space, reminding me a little of the Treasury. A huge map of Edar and our neighbours hung on a wall. There was no trace of Vigrante anywhere.

Diana waited with the Duchess and Coin. They'd turned into

a triumvirate of power while Matthias and I were in Farezi, and now they supported Lia as she readjusted to ruling again.

'Miss Bayonn,' Diana said.

I kept my back straight, and refused to look away. 'Admiral,' I said, glancing at them in turn. 'Duchess, Master Coin.'

'Thank you for meeting with us,' Diana said.

As if I'd had a choice.

'We have a problem,' she said. 'You.'

'I don't understand.'

The Duchess leaned forward, pinning me with her gaze. 'You are important to the Queen. Indeed, you're the reason she's here at all. You're a hero, in the grand scheme of things. But you're Fifth Step.'

I'd heard some of the gossip as I walked by. It was remarkably similar to what people had said when Mama remarried. *Grasping for power, making herself indispensable to the royal family. Thinks much too highly of herself.* The Sixth and Seventh Steps had little imagination.

'So you need to reward me,' I said. 'Everything must be neat and proper, and my reputation a little less tattered.'

'It sounds worse than it actually is,' Diana said.

The Duchess grimaced. 'I will never be able to repay you for finding Lia. That debt will never be settled.'

Coin looked uncomfortably angry, a strange combination that didn't suit him.

'Well,' I said, 'I have a suggestion.'

Amusement flickered around Diana's mouth. 'Oh?'

'Yes. Elevate me to Seventh Step.'

I didn't know if Lia and I could have a future together. Goldenmarch had marked her in ways I would never understand. But with a higher rank, I could stay close to her. And, frankly, after everything that had happened, it was the least they could do.

Diana frowned and turned to Coin. 'Is there a precedent?'

His mouth twitched. 'No, Admiral. But there was also no precedent when you changed the abdication and inheritance laws.'

I could have hugged him, if he wouldn't have reacted like a block of wood.

Diana continued frowning. 'The Court won't accept this.'

I wanted to reply, *And where was the Court when Rassa sent Lia to Farezi?* From the way Diana eyed me, my face reflected my thoughts.

'I also want my family elevated.'

Diana lost control of her expression. Coin seemed incredibly proud, as if I'd solved a convoluted financial discrepancy and joked about it.

'Very well,' the Duchess said.

'Duchess—' Diana began.

'*Very well*,' the Duchess repeated, an edge in her voice. 'She saved my daughter, and Lia loves her.'

My heart twisted. But I kept my face calm.

'The Crown must reward her, and if she wishes to join the Seventh Step, we won't refuse her. It needs new blood.' The Duchess was a force to be reckoned with now. Diana and Coin would eventually agree with her.

Diana still looked unhappy, but said, 'Very well. I'll speak to the Queen, and then to Court and Parliament. The paperwork–'

'I'll be the witness,' Coin interrupted. I glanced at him, startled, and he smiled.

I was the daughter of Baron Bayonn and Lady Harynne, stepdaughter of Lord Martain. I was born Third Step, now Fifth Step, and soon to be Seventh Step. I loved my father, mourned him, and had avenged him. I'd fallen for a Queen, and committed treason to find her when she was lost.

I was Xania Bayonn.

And I would live.

XANIA

Lia found me sprawled on the couch by the corner windows in our shared study, staring at my paperwork and considering the wine decanter.

'Was it that intolerable?' She crossed the room in a swirl of skirts, smiling, and perched on the couch arm. She brushed her fingers against my cheek, then behind my neck.

'No, it was tolerable. Just about.' As tolerable as a Treasury meeting could be. Following Lia's return over five years ago, Coin had kept me in the Treasury because under no circumstances was the time and energy he'd put into me going to waste. Everyone, myself included, had been terrified that he was grooming me as his successor, but either Lia had confided in him or he'd seen where her intentions lay.

When she'd asked me to marry her a year ago, I was ready for the responsibility of overseeing the Treasury – and Coin.

He'd brought honey whiskey to our first meeting.

I placed a cushion on my lap. 'How was the new Othayrian

ambassador?'

'Better than the Eshvon one,' Lia said, 'but that's to be expected.' She settled her head on the cushion, her skirts and legs dangling over the side.

'We should have our mothers write to Juliaane. They could all commiserate on stubborn daughters.'

'I don't think Juliaane is ready to commiserate yet.' When Isra was summoned home, and had just as politely refused to go, we'd offered her a proposition: to become the new Whispers. She couldn't return home, whatever her reasons, and the decision was made easier by Aubrey also deciding to stay. Isra was suited to it, but it had meant cutting ties with Eshvon. Juliaane was still making her feelings on the matter quite clear.

Isra and Truth *delighted* each other.

I gently twisted Lia's hair into curls around my fingers, breathing in the scent of her perfume, delicate and sweet. The spring sunlight caught against her eyelashes and mouth. It made the gold in her dark brown hair gleam, and sparked against the silver strands: a permanent reminder of Goldenmarch. Her grey eyes were calm. As she brushed her thumb over my knuckles, our silence deepened, only broken by birdsong through the open windows. After Rassa's death, I couldn't even hope that we'd have moments like this. If *she* could ever find peace within herself.

It took months before Lia could sleep without nightmares. Months before she didn't flinch when someone brushed against her. I'd read to her every night, sitting first in a chair and then on the bed when she allowed it, lulling her with books against our grim reality. We slowly relearned our friendship as Lia relearned herself.

One night, almost a year after she'd been taken, I'd closed my book and worked myself up to goodnight. Lia had stared at my hand, then slowly, painfully cautious, kissed it: the first sign of physical affection she'd shown me since before her abdication.

I'd returned to my room, connected to hers, and sobbed into a pillow. Not for what I'd lost, but for what we'd regained.

The second summer after her return, Lia travelled north with Matthias and me. I saw where they'd wandered as children, their secret places and memories. She showed me where she'd stood, surrounded by dead sheep, when the rider arrived with news of her uncle's impending death.

Something had changed, then, flickering between us when she took my hand. We stared at each other, then looked away. I remembered how we'd circled each other years before, reluctant to admit our feelings.

She took me to her bed late that summer. It wasn't the same; we wore our history too heavily. We built something different, my fingers on her skin, delicately worshipping, her rediscovering the soft cries she could pull from me in the darkness.

I stroked a fingertip against her mouth; she kissed it. Her eyes closed as my fingertip trailed down her neck. Her pulse fluttered under my touch. As loath as I was to break the comfortable silence, the information on my desk wouldn't disappear. 'The Farezi Queen has written,' I said, soft and careful. 'Her ambassador is returning next week. She has agreed to the new terms.'

After Rassa's death, his grieving, pregnant wife had relinquished the Edaran throne. Queen Arisane and her husband had abdicated in Farezi, ostensibly to help their daughter-in-law, but actually due to international criticism. If they couldn't stop their usurper son, how were they fit to rule? Their daughter had become Queen.

And though Lia's reign had steadied, there was still the matter of an heir. It took a year of cautious groundwork before she'd suggested that she formally adopt Emri, Rassa's daughter, as her heir.

There had been uproar at a Farezi Princess eventually ruling, especially one related to a usurper. Lia had acknowledged the outrage, but pointed out that Emri was still distantly related to her. A woman with Edaran blood would still take the throne: the smoothest possible transition, a way to move beyond Rassa's treachery and strengthen ties with Farezi.

It took time, more than Lia wanted, but she won over her advisors, her Court, and her people. Emri had not yet set foot on Edaran soil, but most were ready to welcome her. It was a start.

For Farezi, it would take a child with a legitimate claim out of the succession, and away from a family with complicated feelings about her place in their history. Neither of us felt particularly ready for a child – would we ever be? – but we'd face it together. Both of us knew, all too well, that Emri didn't deserve to be judged by the actions and memory of her father. And she deserved to be loved.

When I felt Lia had brooded long enough, I poked her in the shoulder. 'Come on. They've prepared lunch for us outside. We should go for a walk afterward, since this' – I waved at the piles of paper on our respective desks – 'awaits us.'

She sat up and kissed me, a soft press of lips. When we pulled apart, she rose and sank into a deep curtesy, then offered me her arm. 'My Queen.'

They'd crowned me in my own right. I ruled with her, First of My Name.

'My lady.' I beamed and tucked my hand into the crook of her elbow. 'All will be well,' I added, for myself as much as her.

She loved me as I loved her, fierce as a bloodied blade.

ACKNOWLEDGEMENTS

While writing a book is often a solitary process, publishing a novel is not. There are many people who helped *Queen of Coin and Whispers* go from initial idea to drafts to novel:

My editor, Helen Carr, understood this book, and what I was trying to do with it, on levels I could only hope someone else would. Thank you for making edits fun and enjoyable, and always being patient when I answered character or worldbuilding queries with several paragraphs instead of a few sentences.

Thank you to everyone at The O'Brien Press for embracing this book. In particular, Michael and Ivan O'Brien; Brenda, Elena, and Aoife in Sales; Ruth and Tríona in Publicity; Bex and Emma in Production and Design (I will never get over the stunning cover); and Kunak in Rights. Thank you all for getting behind Lia and Xania.

My agent, Eric Smith, for being in my corner and loving this book early. Your initial email came at a hard time and convinced me to keep going.

For their unwavering support and belief that this book would get published: David R. Slayton, Elizabeth Freed (who read many drafts), and David Myer. Thanks also to the rest of the

Speculators for chats and commiseration: Alex, Rena, Kat, Axie, Amanda, Anitra, Erin, and Nikki.

The Marybeths: Courtney, Ellen, and Kathryne. You also read many drafts, and were there from the beginning when this book started going out into the world.

Thank you to Katherine Locke for your support through drafts and rewrites, querying, and the publication process, and for loving this book when I felt shaky about it.

Thanks to Renee Nyen, Ruth Long, Alex Harrow, Anitra van Prooyen, and Suzanne Hocking for feedback on various drafts, and to Corinne Duyvis for that all-important yes when I mentioned my idea for a queer Queen and spymaster book.

Thank you to Team Rocks and the UK/Ireland 2020 Group for support and friendship during the publication process.

To the booksellers and bloggers who supported *Queen of Coin and Whispers* early on: you are all so important for getting books into people's hands. Thanks especially to Martin, Mary, Gabbie, and Alan for being there when it all started happening.

Thank you to my family for buying so many books when I was a kid, though you had no idea where it would lead.

And thanks to the Harcourt and Dawson Street Starbucks, and the kitchen tables in Dubray Grafton Street and Dún Laoghaire. I spent way more time with you than anyone else during this process, and I always swore I'd put you in the acknowledgements.